© 2012 Swan of Ascent Media

The Julian Ark: A Madison Dawn Adventure
ISBN: 978-0615703503

10 9 8 7 6 5 4 3 2 1

Cover design by Kaycee Wilson

Visit the author's website at: www.davidjswanson.com

This book is a work of fiction. Any similarities to real people, living or dead, is purely coincidental. With the exception of historical figures, all characters and events in this work are figments of the author's imagination.

Printed in the USA

for my wife

my lifelong adventuring partner

CONTENTS

PROLOGUE

April 4, 1453 - Constantinople

Emperor Constantine XI looked out the window of his palace staring in abject wonder at the fleet amassed against him. The shadows grew long leading from the tower across the sprawling city of Constantinople below him. It would be night soon, and the vast army this flotilla disgorged onto Roman soil would soon encircle the great capitol city.

It was Constantine who brought us here. A new home for our empire. New Rome, Constantine called it: A new beginning for a dominant empire. That was over 1100 years ago. In 1100 years, the God of this empire, the Christian God had never turned his face from the Romans.

The emperor stood transfixed at his window, thinking through the reigns of Roman emperors after Constantine I, leading this Eastern Roman Empire to world dominance.

What has this empire become? This pittance of an empire. Where has our God gone?

Was it the schism? The great break between the Orthodox and those infernal Catholics? Where did our power go? *What could I have done?*

"Orders, sir?" asked a general standing nearby. The Emperor had momentarily forgotten that he stood inside his council chambers, with the best military minds in Constantinople.

"What orders need I give you? This is the best defended city in Europe. Those Muslims have landed on their gravesite. We have prepared this city's defense for the past year. The Theodosian Walls have held invaders at bay for centuries. They have never been in better shape thanks to the efforts of my brother. We will resist these invaders. Now is the time for every man to stand firm and fight."

"And what news from our allies in Europe?" asked the General. "When can we expect their arrival?"

"I have heard no reply from my messengers. I can only assume that they are readying their armies and will be here with all haste. We must hold out until they arrive."

"But sir, the envoy from the Sultan," said Popolous, his senior advisor. "He offered us peace, did he not?"

"I sent the envoy away. He's lucky he still has his head."

"You rejected his terms?" Popolous could not hide his wide-eyed disbelief.

"I did. The bloodthirsty sultan wanted this city. I offered to pay him an increased tribute, but would under no circumstances turn this great city over to his destruction."

"You have brought war to us."

"War was brought to us, Popolous."

"Then you have brought our doom."

"Enough! General, ready the men. Leave me. All of you. The time for council is over. Make peace with God and pray for our deliverance. For tomorrow, we fight."

The council left, including the waiting ladies. Only two of his personal guardsmen remained.

Constantine returned his gaze to the sea. The harbor was protected by the simplest of defenses: a large chain draped across the mouth of the harbor. Just beyond that chain, the floating menace waited. The blockade of his harbor meant no help could sail to his aid. The aggressors would soon be at the walls of this city, shouting in languages he did not understand. The heathens, the ones who prayed to Allah, the Ottoman Turks, had come. *Where is our God?*

In the quiet of the chamber, he offered a simple prayer asking that the Roman Empire would not die with him. He did not ask that God spare his own life.

A knock came at the door. The emperor nodded to one of the guardsmen who opened the door.

"Uncle!" said a cheery girl of no more than thirteen years old. "I mean, greetings Emperor."

"Zoe. What are you doing here? You should be in the Morea. Why are you here?" Constantine gave the little girl a terrifying scowl.

"But uncle, you sent for me."

"I did? Oh, so I did. Yes, I remember."

"Yes?"

"You must leave at once.'"

"But, I've just arrived. I'm weary from my journey. I haven't eaten since midday."

"It's too dangerous here. By morning this city will be under siege."

"But this is the best defended city in Europe. Everyone knows it. And we have the walls. Where else would I be safe if not here?"

"Zoe, dear. We barely have half the men to properly defend the walls. We will not hold out for long."

"What about the armies coming from the east? Our European friends?"

"I have no idea if our allies are coming. I fear they have forsaken us as a relic of the past."

"You're scaring me."

"Our moment is dire, Zoe. Our once great empire has shriveled up like an old man's… like a raisin. It is no longer the virile empire it once was."

"God will save us. You must have faith."

Constantine looked at his niece and gave her a patronizing smile. Her confidence was cute, but it did not bring him comfort.

"I need you to do something for me."

"Anything, Uncle."

"Who escorted you here?"

"Just Lucas and four of his squires. We came with all haste."

"This is good. This is what you must do. You must return to the Morea and take with you the Julian Ark."

Zoe's eyes glistened and she froze in place.

"Are you hearing me?"

"The Julian Ark? I cannot take that. It is for you to give to the next emperor and that is all. Do you remember as a little girl my pleading and cajoling, yet you would never let me even see it. Now you want to give it to me?"

"Zoe, I have no alternative. The ark contains our legacy, from Julius Caesar himself to Caligula, Hadrian, Constantine the Great and right up to your Uncle John. The next emperor of Rome will need it to establish his right to rule. You must take it with you."

Constantine XI went to his private bedchambers. After a few moments of struggle and clatter, he returned carrying a small bundle wrapped in muslin. He set the bundle on the desk and removed the muslin revealing a bronze box no broader than his shoulders and no deeper than the span of his hand. The dull glare of the plain box did not allude to its importance.

"This box travelled here from Rome amidst an army of 100,000 soldiers," said Zoe with a faltering voice. "How am I to protect it with just my five riders?"

"Secrecy will be your protection. Tell no one that you have this, not even Lucas. Keep it close to you at all times. When the time is right, you will reveal its contents. Marry a king or prince who is able to start a new empire- not new, rather, the next chapter of our Empire. You must find a *third* Rome, Zoe."

"How- Where-?"

"God will reveal his plan for you in time. You don't have to figure it out now. What you must do is to depart at once. The siege may be closing as we speak."

"I don't know if I can."

"You can do this, Zoe. You must do this. I am Constantine XI Palaiologos in Christ, Emperor and Autocrat of the Romans, and I don't intend to be the last. Now, fly!"

October 2007

I

AN EXPLOSION OF MIST AND LATHER

"An inconvenience is an adventure wrongly considered. "
G. K. Chesterton

Madison Dawn's day started off, as most bad days often do, by waking up in a stark panic. Why was it already light outside? She certainly had not woken up to the sound of her alarm. She interrogated the alarm clock, demanding how it could sit there, saying nothing, while the workday crept ever closer to the slumbering and slightly hung-over Madison. It glared back at her in plastic insolence: *7:24.* She scampered through her morning routine. She had seven desperate minutes until she absolutely *had* to be out the door and on her way (assuming she got all green lights, of course).

She showered in an explosion of mist and lather, threw her hair into a ponytail, and jumped into the first clean outfit she came across, not taking the time to put on her shoes or brush her teeth. *Don't do anything that can be done in the car.* She grabbed her make-up case, a pair of brown flats, her attaché case, a toothbrush and toothpaste, her purse, and her cell phone off of the charger, and in a flurry of wet hair, unkempt clothing, and an armload of necessities she burst through her apartment door twelve frenetic minutes after waking up.

She scampered down the front steps of her apartment, dancing on the balls of her bare feet, as the soft light of dawn brought slight definition to the details of her neighborhood. She slid into the driver's seat and tossed her things into the passenger seat of her sedan. She thrust her key into the ignition, waited for the engine to come to life, and then popped it into reverse.

If she had taken a few moments before dashing off to work, she would have noticed that not all was as it should have been in her sleepy corner of the world. On any other morning, she may have noticed the cable service van parked in the street and thought it odd that it might be on a service call this early in the morning. If she had been concentrating more on her driving than putting on her make-up, she would have noticed the silver Chrysler 300 that lurked behind her, careful to keep its distance, but close enough to make the same turns as her despite her complete disregard for using her turn signal. On a less chaotic morning she might have noticed the ownerless leather case in the back seat of her car.

Yet such is the case in life that one is often thrust into an adventure while consumed with the overwhelming minutia of everyday life. Madison's adventure started well before she was aware that she was having anything other than just a lousy Monday. Thus, she was taken completely by surprise when, dressed as she was, hair in a distinctly un-sexy ponytail, make-up half applied, shoes floating around the interior of her car, an unfamiliar electronic ringing noise disturbed her morning frenzy.

Perrrrrrrriiiiinnngggg- BEEP – Beep.

Perrrrrrrriiiiinnngggg- BEEP – Beep.

"What on earth is that?" The Perring-Beep-Beep sounded nothing like Journey's "Don't Stop Believing", her ringtone of the week.

The ringing came from above her head. She reached up, flipped the visor down and let out a yelp as an unfamiliar cell phone clattered off of the steering wheel and landed in her lap. She stared at the ringing device trying to make sense of it for just a second too long. In that extra second her car slammed into the pick-up truck stopped at the red light ahead.

The crumpling steel, the shattering glass, the explosions of the airbags, and the screeching of the tires drove every peaceful thought and every menial detail from her mind. She had seen countless car wrecks on TV and in movies. She had even been in a few fender benders. Nothing could have prepared her for the deafening impact.

The car spun wildly to the curb and flattened a vintage scooter. Metal tore along asphalt as its last unassisted journey ended atop a bike rack in front of a hardware store. Her ears rang with an oppressive hum joined by her own muted moan.

After a few moments, she sensed someone wrestling with her seatbelt and trying to free her from the twisted metal box. She assumed they were there to rescue her but, between the blurriness in her eyes and being preoccupied with making sure she had feeling to all of her extremities, she was unable to properly identify her rescuer.

Through the numbing fog, she realized that two men were rifling through what was left of her car.

"Stupid. I told you she was useless," said a gruff Latino voice.

"Did you take care of that truck driver?" said a slightly higher voice that seemed to carry more authority with less Mexican twang.

"Yeah, he's down."

"Alright. Help me find it before the cops get here," said the higher voiced man.

"I don't think it's here. Maybe she doesn't have it."

"Well, check the trunk."

With great effort, she pried open her eyes and stared at the man leaning in the window, not four inches from her face. A man with a black mustache, yellow-brown skin, and narrow brown eyes stared back.

"Ay, Maria! She's awake!" He reached into his pocket for what Madison presumed was a weapon.

A persistent sharp pain set into her head and she couldn't see through her right eye. She wiped a thick coat of her blood away and could make out a shattered windshield and broken plastic. Her strength left her as panic set in. Then she heard a third set of footsteps approach her car.

"Carlos. Ricky. I should have known he'd send bottom-feeders like you," said the third man.

"Stay out of this, hombre. Or I cut you," said one of the men.

For a few seconds, Madison heard nothing, followed by the unmistakable sounds of men scuffling. She listened to the smack of fist striking face, a stomach-turning crack of bone being shattered followed by a pitiful yelp. Two thuds signaled the end of the brief melee.

The newcomer, breathing hard, approached the car, poked his head in her window and without the least trace of mirth or patience demanded "Alright, where is it?"

His face was long and thin with short, disheveled hair, brilliant blue eyes and five days' worth of irregular stubble. The expression the man wore was intense, hard and not altogether likeable.

"Where is what?" asked Madison. "I don't... I was in an accident. I can't even move." A dull but constant pain developed in her right shoulder as the adrenaline began to wear off.

The man climbed over the car, kicked in the passenger window and climbed into the passenger seat.

"We don't have time for this. I need to know where the case is. They'll be here any moment." After several seconds of Madison's stunned silence, he grunted and turned his attention to the interior of her car. The man twisted around and sifted through the pile of papers, make-up bags, loose CDs and broken glass that littered the front and rear seat of the car. With a sigh of surprise, he lifted a brown leather case from behind Madison's seat and brought it onto his lap.

"And you said you didn't know what I was talking about," he said. "What the hell do you call this?"

Madison, not understanding why this man was shouting at her, began to cry. The man's demeanor softened.

"Come on, we gotta move," His muscular hands gripped her arm. Madison cried out as pain shot through her right shoulder. "I guess we're not going out the window." He leaned back in his seat and with several violent, powerful strokes, he kicked out the windshield. In one smooth motion, he unbuckled her seatbelt and lifted her through the opening he had just created. She tried to stifle her cries as he dragged her onto the hood of the wrecked car.

"Looks dislocated," said the man with all the concern one might show when remarking on an imminent light rain shower.

Madison looked outside the car and for the first time was able to take in the scene. Her car rested at an odd angle, having nearly flattened a bike rack. Shattered glass along with red, green, and black fluids littered the street. The pick-up truck rested in a heap in the middle of the intersection, its driver slumped over the wheel. A few cars crept by the accident but did not stop. They gawked at the scene as if it were a movie set before speeding off to their own important daily tasks. Several bystanders were on their cell phones, possibly calling 911, but no one came to help. A myriad of police and fire truck sirens wailed in the distance.

Madison noticed a white van parked down the street while a silver Chrysler 300 stood with engine running fifty yards up the street. Not ten feet from her car lay two motionless bodies.

"Are they dead?" she asked, wanting to look away but finding it nearly impossible.

Ignoring her question, he asked "Can you walk?"

She wanted to give him a sarcastic don't-treat-me-like-a-victim look, but instead swayed in an unsteady wobble and fell into him. She left a sticky imprint of her bloody face on his shirt and let out a dull groan. The man reached back into the car, grabbed her cell phone and shoes and then took her in his arms. He lifted her from the car.

"I don't think I'm supposed to leave the scene of an accident," she said through slurred speech.

"We need to get you fixed up first." Still in a fog, Madison clung to him with her left arm, letting her right arm hang limply since it tended to alight with sharp flames of pain every time he jostled her.

Madison and the strange man, who had either saved or endangered her life, got into the car.

"Where are we going?" She felt the strength leaving her, the adrenaline fading at last. "I've lost… blood…. What's your name anyway?"

Madison never heard the answer. She succumbed to the cloud that had enveloped her head and lost consciousness. She slumped against the car door as the sedan sped northward out of the city.

II

THE LITTLE INGRATE

"From the cradle to the coffin, underwear comes first. "
Bertolt Brecht

Out of the fog and weightlessness of sleep Madison became aware of an incessant ticking. She passed so slowly from the sleep state to that state just before waking that she had time to hear, detect, and become annoyed with the constant ticking. Her brain sorted through all the possibilities of what the noise could be and surmised the reasons why no one seemed to be doing anything about the annoyance. A brief, though stressful, image of her standing over a bomb where she was the only one who could disarm it entered her foggy mind. She then brought herself to the realization that she was lying down on her back with her eyes closed and that perhaps, with a little effort, she could open her eyes and find the source of the mysterious ticking noise.

She opened her eyes. She was lying down (which she already knew) but it was good to confirm that the ceiling lay just in front of her, or rather, now that she knew her orientation, above her. Her eyes darted from the ceiling to the walls of the room while confusion set in. This was not her room. *Where am I?*

Madison lay in a twin bed that sagged and squeaked whenever she made the slightest movement. Next to her, a frosted window let the cool air of the fall day pass into the room despite its appearance of being closed. Next to the bed was an overturned cardboard box that functioned as a nightstand upon which rested a small lamp, a box of tissues, and a small plastic wind-up clock. She stared at the clock for a moment as its annoying tick-tick-tick filled the quiet room. The clock read 6:18, although she had no idea if that was morning or evening.

The room was merely a space in the corner of the floor marked off with two free standing Japanese room dividers. Somehow, the room was spacious yet seemed cluttered. To her left she saw a wooden rocking chair and on the floor there was a portable stereo with several hundred CDs scattered around it in disorganized stacks. A wooden spool served as a table with a single metal folding chair sitting next to it. The floor was covered with an irregularly shaped throw rug that looked more like it had been cut from wall-to-wall carpeting than something purposeful and decorative. Resting against the room divider was a sizeable canvas bag with a large red cross emblazoned on it.

Madison tried to sit up, only to realize her right shoulder was heavily bandaged. Her entire right arm was bound to her torso with her forearm running across her stomach. She felt a pressure on her head as well, and careful probing with her left hand revealed that her head was also heavily bandaged.

Madison, what have you gotten yourself into now?

The last two months were perhaps the most stressful period of her life. She recalled that moment seven weeks ago when she'd announced to her family that she was leaving their suburban life along Lake Erie and was moving to Wichita, a thousand miles from home. It came as a shock to everyone. Her mother cried. Her sister couldn't understand. She lied and said it was because she was pursuing her dream, whatever that meant. Since then, she'd been on her own. She took a job as a secretary because the money was good; well, better than that waitressing job in the short orange shorts, and much better than any job she could find with her music degree. Since then, she'd just tried to keep afloat in a new city without any friends. And now, yet again, *life* had happened to her.

She sighed and stared at the ceiling. A new memory came to her, although this one arrived un-conjured. An imagined snow globe, sparkling with glitter, hovered in the air above her head. She saw it spinning slowly, the mushroom domes of the Kremlin entrapped in floating glitter. She recognized it immediately from a story her mother used to tell her when she was young. It was a recurring fairytale that her mom would turn to when Madison demanded a bedtime story.

It was the tale of a princess of a forgotten kingdom. The kingdom was attacked by their sworn enemy, an enemy Madison couldn't remember now. When her mom told the story they were always hated and evil and bent on destroying the kingdom. The princess was visited by a powerful wizard who, in trying to protect the kingdom from its imminent demise, used a spell to shrink the castle and fit it into a spellbound snow globe. The princess then lived a life of seclusion, hiding out in abandoned buildings and taking menial jobs to get by. In hiding, she kept her kingdom safe inside the magic snow globe until she could restore the lost kingdom to its former glory.

Madison didn't know why her groggy and clouded mind had chosen to refresh this particular childhood memory. Perhaps it was the feeling that everything she had known was falling apart around her. Perhaps it was feeling trapped in this room, not knowing to whom to turn. Perhaps she simply had a concussion.

She turned her head to survey the rest of the room. Hanging on the wall was an ornately framed painting that Madison recognized but couldn't place. It occurred to her that this painting had been in the news lately, though she couldn't remember why. On the floor against the wall under the painting rested several pieces of pottery, an ebony statue that looked strikingly Egyptian, and several bundles wrapped up in tan canvas.

Madison rested her head back on the pillow and tried to make sense of everything. She tried to think of how she'd gotten there, why she wasn't at home, what day it was, and what it would take to physically get out of bed. While she tried to piece together her immediate past, four thoughts materialized in her head almost simultaneously.

I hurt.

I'm starving.

My mouth feels gross.

What's that noise?

It was the noise that drew her attention, for it sounded much like someone hitting an aluminum bleacher seat with a rubber mallet: a thud followed by prolonged ringing. The thuds and the ringing approached the window near her bed.

The thuds stopped and a blurred impression of a man appeared in the frosted window pane. The window swung open and a man with a thin face, disheveled hair, brilliant blue eyes and an irregular beard stepped in from the fire escape. Madison scowled at the man trying to remember why he looked so familiar.

Why am I having such trouble putting the pieces together?

The man's raised eyebrows were his only show of emotion.

"Good, you're awake. Another half day of this and I was going to have to take more drastic measures." The man was dressed in a beige button down long-sleeved shirt well worn jeans. He sported a pair of worn hiking boots and carried two paper bags in his hands. One bag was clearly marked as being from a local coffee shop. The larger bag was unmarked.

"Hungry?" he asked.

Madison recognized the man from the accident the day before... or was it several days ago? *How long have I been unconscious?* She eyed him suspiciously, forgetting the question was even asked.

"What are you going to do with me?" she asked with a faltering voice.

He gave her a puzzled look as he removed two paper cups of coffee from the smaller bag along with two muffins, and set them on the wooden spool table.

"Do with you?" he repeated, mildly amused. He settled into the folding chair. "I'm going to find out what you know and see if you can't be useful to me."

"So... then, am I your prisoner?" She slid further under the covers, like a child who is sure her blankets will protect her. The bed squeaked at this slight movement.

"Prisoner? Of course," he chuckled. "That's why you've been watched by the armed guard over there and you're chained to the bed." He motioned to the divider behind him. Madison looked but saw no one. She was pretty sure there was no one behind the divider, and while she couldn't be certain, she didn't think she was chained to anything.

"You're being sarcastic, aren't you?"

"You think? Here, put these on," he said. He took a bite of his muffin and tossed her the unmarked paper bag. It landed next to her with a crinkly thump.

Madison pulled herself up with her mobile left arm. It wasn't until she sensed the sheets of the bed slide against her skin that she realized that the only thing she was wearing was the matching black satin bra and panties that she had so hurriedly put on the morning of the accident.

She let out a yelp, and quickly slid back down under the covers. She glared at him.

"You undressed me!" she said, her voice strengthened by shock and embarrassment. Madison pulled the sheets up to her chin so just her face was visible. "How dare you... undress me!"

"No. I dressed you. Your head was bleeding pretty badly and that shoulder wasn't going to reset itself. I dressed your wounds." The man was taken aback by this outburst.

"Where are my clothes?"

"Burned. They were cut up and covered in blood. You were never going to wear them again. Besides, I had to cut them off to get to your wounds," he answered.

"You cut off my clothes? While I was unconscious? What kind of a pervert are you?" She felt her strength returning to her with each thought of being violated by this stranger.

The man rose, his demeanor sour.

"I am a medical professional, you little ingrate. I saved your damn life. And just so we're clear; no. I didn't exactly get off on it. Unconscious broads bleeding all over my car aren't exactly my type, okay? Now put on those clothes if I embarrass you so much."

Grabbing his coffee on the way, he stormed out of the room and stood on the other side of the divider.

If what he said was true, then she had acted rudely to someone who had saved her life once, if not twice. If it wasn't true, well then, the fact remained that he was a powerful man who had beaten two men into a bloody heap in a matter of seconds and she was a woman with just one good arm, laying in bed in her underwear, in a building she didn't know, quite possibly in a city far from home. It was best not to upset the man.

"So are you a doctor, then?" she asked, trying to atone for her impertinence.

"I'm a medic," he said. "EMT. Well, I was..." his voice trailed off, implying a story not told. "But it was a good thing I was there. Your cuts were deep. You lost a lot of blood."

The accident came back to her more clearly. The collision. The two men. They were looking for something. The brawl. The broken glass. The silver sedan. The cell phone ringing. The strange cell phone that caused the accident-

"Was that you on the phone?" she asked.

"What phone?"

"The phone in my car."

"Is that why you drove into that truck without so much as a swerve or a brake? No. It wasn't me," he said, sipping his coffee.

Content that he was going to stay on the other side of the divider until she dressed, she sat up and pulled the bag to her. Inside she found a fuzzy pink sweater, a white cotton T-shirt, a sampler case of off-brand make-up, a pair of soft, pre-washed blue jeans, a package of three pairs of white cotton socks, and, to her surprise, a smaller bag from Victoria's Secret. This bag contained a purple satin bra with matching panties. She laughed inwardly at the thought processes that would have to go on inside a man's head in order to walk into such a boutique to select these items for a complete stranger. The make-up assortment was obviously an attempt to find something that might work without any knowledge of what a woman actually needs in cosmetics. What impressed her was that all of the clothes appeared to be her size including the bra. It was a little large, but she appreciated the compliment.

"It looks like they'll all fit just fine," she said, trying to show appreciation.

"I had your old clothes, so I just cut the tags out and took them to the mall with me," he said.

"Why did you go to Victoria's Secret?"

"Where else do women buy underwear?" he said simply. It was apparent that the purchase of the underwear was possibly the most awkward task he'd tackled in quite a while.

Of course, where else indeed? She chuckled to herself.

Madison sat up and attempted to remove the bandage that held her arm immobile. She turned and twisted but could not find the loose end of the bandage. There was no way she could change in this condition. Sighing, she sat still, brooding for a few seconds and then asked, "Can you help me take this bandage off my arm? I can't get dressed when I'm half mummy."

The man said nothing, but walked back into the room, put down his coffee and knelt at the side of her bed. As he reached behind her to loosen the bandage, she noticed that, while it appeared he lived his life much like a homeless man or vagrant, he smelled clean and fresh. His hair was even slightly damp, implying that somewhere recently he had showered. She looked at him through narrowed eyes, trying to figure out exactly with whom she was dealing.

"I'm Madison, by the way." She held out her left hand in an awkward attempt at a formal greeting. The man backed away from her. He looked her in the eyes and smiled at her.

"James." They shook left-handed and then he went back to work removing the bandage.

He passed the bandage around her body a few more times and Madison felt her right arm loosen up and become free. She clasped the bandage to her chest, as each wrap around her was slowly exposing her skin.

"Okay! Got it. I can get it from here," she said. "Now, shoo." James rose and went back behind the screen without comment or protest. "I'm going to get dressed and when I'm done, you're going to tell me what the hell is going on."

⋇⋇⋇

Madison felt more like herself in the new clothes James had brought her. Her shoulder felt a bit sore, but it seemed like it would be all right. She marveled at James' skill at setting her dislocated shoulder while she was unconscious. The clothes did, in fact, fit just fine. The pink sweater was warm and comfortable, although a little tighter than she would have preferred.

While dressing, James reassured her that she was still in Wichita, and was on the top floor of an old brick warehouse that had long since been converted to trendy, metro lofts. The developer had converted each floor, one by one, intending to make the top floor the penthouse suite for their most well-heeled clients. The developer went bankrupt before the project was completed and the new property owner was content to operate the apartments on the bottom four floors of the five story brick building. The top floor remained a large open, uncared-for shell that was largely forgotten by the building's tenants.

It wasn't until she asked James when she could go back to her apartment that his gaze dropped and he tossed her a copy of the Wichita Eagle.

"Here's yesterday's paper," he said.

"So, today's Thursday," she remarked, noting that it was Wednesday's paper. "I was out for three days, then." Her voice trailed off at the thought of the implications of losing three whole days out of her life.

Madison opened the newspaper and spread it out on the wooden spool table in front of her. She sat in dumbfounded silence, unable to grasp what she was seeing. A large picture occupied most of the space above the fold. She shook her head.

"That's my apartment," she said.

At least it looked like her apartment complex, but it was hard to tell. Flames filled the windows on the bottom two floors and smoke obscured the majority of the view. A large headline proclaimed the disaster:

ARSON SUSPECTED IN WESTSIDE FIRE

Madison read through the article which confirmed that the burning building frozen in time on the front page was the building she had called home these past few months. She scoured the articles hoping to find the answer to a question she had yet to formulate. She had wrecked her car, been confronted by two men she didn't know, saved by another man she didn't know, and then had her home burnt to the ground. She knew the answer wouldn't be on the front page of the Eagle but still she had to know *why*.

"Sorry about your home," said James as he finished his chocolate chip muffin. "But honestly, I'm not surprised."

"Oh, most of my stuff was still in storage," she said in a distracted voice. "My apartment was, well, not much more decorated than this place; sans the priceless painting and Egyptian statues, of course." She meant it lightly, but she noticed that James stiffened when she mentioned these items. "But still, that was my home-. Wait. What do you mean you're not surprised?"

"Just that this is what they do to people. Now maybe you can tell me how you got involved in all of this." He sat down on the edge of the bed and looked her in the eyes. He didn't have the hard-eyed look of an interrogator, but the gentle, prodding expression of a close friend sitting down for a friendly chat. At least, that was the way he wanted to appear.

"All of this? What's all this? I don't know what *this* is. I was on my way to work-" she paused, the realization suddenly hitting her. She turned to James, wide eyed. "Oh God! Work! I've missed four days of work. They are so going to fire me. I need to call them," and she instinctively looked for her purse which typically contained her cell phone.

"Hold on," he said calmly touching her arm. "You've been through a lot right now. You don't need to call anyone. You need to tell me how you got involved."

"I told you, I don't know how I got involved!" she shouted, getting to her feet, her stress level rising uncontrollably. "I was driving to work and that damn cell phone started ringing. It fell into my lap and the next thing I know I'm laying there with blood in my eyes and men were searching my car. Now my place is burnt to ashes and you're telling me you're not *surprised*. How am I supposed to know how I got involved?" she yelled. She suddenly felt queasy and a little unsteady. The shouting raised her blood pressure and now her head, still wrapped in a blood-stained bandage, throbbed in pain.

She staggered backwards and collapsed onto the bed with a squeaky crash. Madison put her elbows on her knees, her head in her hands, and quietly began to cry. Usually when Madison cried around men, they suddenly found their soft spot and apologized to her. It was a well practiced technique that she used frequently. James' reaction, however, was a little different.

"Don't give me that crap, Madison!" James said. Now it felt like an interrogation. "I find your wrecked car with Giovanni's men crawling all over it. Inside, I find something that clearly doesn't belong to you. Now, why are you working for Giovanni? Why are you running his errands?" He bent over, his face inches from hers. "How did you get involved?"

"I don't know! I told you, I don't know!" Her vision began failing as the throbbing in her head reached a new painful high. She fell back on the bed covering her head with her arms, gasping for breath between sobs.

For a few silent moments, she laid on the bed. James sat quietly on the bed next to her, examining the ruffled mass of hair and arms that covered her head. With a sigh, James relented. He gently put his hand on her stomach.

"Okay, okay. I'm sorry. I believe you," he said softly. "I had to find out if you were for real."

Madison pulled herself up and looked at him with puffy eyes; an expression of intense dissatisfaction on her face.

"You had to— find out?" she asked.

"Yeah, I-" he started, but his sentence was cut short as Madison slapped him across the face leaving a red handprint on his stubble-ridden cheek.

"You bastard," Madison hissed. "Don't you ever talk to me like that again," she said, quiet anger unsteadying her voice. "I will not be treated like that."

James said nothing. He got to his feet and retrieved a leather case from a trunk in a corner of the room. He set it down on the wooden spool and settled into the wooden rocking chair.

"Do you recognize this?" he asked.

"No."

"You should. I found it in your car when I pulled you out. That's what they were looking for. That's what Ricky and Carlos were sent to retrieve and that's probably what they went looking for when they went to your house the next day. That, my dear, is why your life has been irreversibly altered. So, why was it in your car?"

"I swear I didn't even know that it was in my car. What's inside?" she asked.

"Open it."

The bed made an embarrassing squeak ruining slightly the atmosphere of suspense and intrigue. She grabbed the leather case. The case had latches on it, but she was surprised to find that the case was unlocked.

"You've opened this already," she said.

"It took me three hours to get that open. Those are not ordinary attaché case locks. Someone went to great trouble to keep that case secure. Then for some reason they just stuck it in your car without you even knowing." His voice trailed off, leaving the possible explanations to a later conversation.

What Madison found inside when she opened the case was remarkable only in its plainness; a folder containing some sort of spreadsheet with columns of unlabeled numbers, assorted pens and pencils, and a blank spiral bound notebook. Madison studied the case until something struck her as odd. The interior of the case seemed shallower than the outside of the case would suggest.

She ran her hand along the bottom of the case and felt it yield to her touch. This case had a false bottom. Prodding, she eventually found a little piece of thread that, when pulled, released a pin that freed the false bottom. With great care, Madison removed the felt covered piece to reveal a thin sheet of porous grey foam. She peeled the foam back and gasped at what she saw.

Lying in the bottom of the case was a dark red jewel, an inch wide and two inches tall, cut in the shape of an arrowhead. For a few seconds, Madison stopped breathing.

"Now, how do you suppose you got that?" asked James.

Madison picked up the weighty gem and held it between her thumb and forefinger. The light danced inside of it and shone brilliantly as she held it up to the window.

"It's beautiful," she said. "It must be worth a fortune." She spoke in a whisper, careful not to disturb the simply beauty of the bauble.

"Yes, it is, though not simply because it's a cut ruby, but because of what it opens," he said with a wild look in his eye. The appearance of the jewel had brought out a passion in James that showed through his rough exterior.

"Because of what it opens?" repeated Madison, not understanding. "What is this?"

"It's a key," said James. "And there are a great number of people looking for it."

III

THE MUSEUM OF LOST ANTIQUITIES

*"Everyone who's ever taken a shower has an idea.
It's the person who gets out of the shower, dries off
and does something about it who makes a difference."*
Nolan Bushnell

"So, that's where you live?" asked Madison.

Madison and James walked down a busy street later that morning. Delivery trucks and taxis moved through the narrow streets as pedestrians, unified by the singular purpose of hurry, filled the sidewalks. Madison and James were the only ones who were strolling.

"I guess you could say that," said James, while he skipped over a pothole in the sidewalk. "I really just sleep there. If I'm up, I'm out in the city. The past few days are the most waking moments I've spent there since I moved in."

"How long have you lived there?" Madison asked. She privately mulled over the thought of someone living their entire waking life out in public.

"About a month. I move around a lot. You can thank my job for that. Ah, here we are." James rounded a corner and stood before an old wooden door that was propped open to bring cool air inside the building. Above the door was an unassuming sign that read *Young Men's Christian Association* with the year *1925* painted below it.

"This is where you shower?" she asked. Madison thought about her own life and her morning routine. A 10 minute walk and five flights of stairs from bed to the shower every morning was about as inconceivable to her as eating a plate of burritos every morning for breakfast; it could be done, but why would you?

"Yep. For a small monthly fee I get recreation, relaxation, exercise, and all the hot water I care to use. Best of all, they don't do background checks for membership," he said with a sideways smile.

"Is that important?" she asked.

He gave her a look that told her she'd asked a ridiculous question. Holding out his right hand he ushered her into the YMCA and to the front desk. He signed a form, showed his card, and marked an "x" in the column labeled "Guest".

"Well, showers are down the hall on the left," he said. "Here's a bag of shampoo and stuff. Hopefully you find something you like. Towels are inside. Come find me in the resource room when you're done." He walked off leaving her to the shower she had insisted upon not an hour earlier.

The ruby arrowhead had certainly made an impression on her. After looking at it for what felt like hours, she self-consciously insisted that he put it somewhere safe. He then put it into a small velvet bag and strung the bag around his neck; hiding it beneath his shirt.

Her head was hurting, but she desperately wanted to take the bandage off and wash her hair. She just felt too grungy. Besides, she did her best thinking in the shower and she was still processing all this new information. The Giovanni family. The Key. Why was she involved? Who is James? Can she trust him? Has she been kidnapped or rescued? She insisted on finding a place to freshen up and he had led her to the local YMCA.

Once in the ladies locker room, Madison removed the bandage, taking care not to disturb the cuts and bruises concealed beneath it. The blood had run through her hair and dried, leaving a crusty, dark brown glue that stuck the hair just above her eyes to her forehead. She undressed and started the water.

Drawing back the curtain, she stepped into the shower like a spirit passing from one world to the next. The former world was cold and dry and harsh. But once inside the curtain, she was in a cozy world of warmth running down her body, making her skin tingle and swell. The comforting sound of the running water drowned out the sounds of the city and left her in a womb-like bubble of respite. The images of the day, until then bouncing wildly around her mind, slowed and gently fell into some semblance of order. It was time to think through her predicament.

She was in trouble. Somehow, she had gotten involved by carrying a large jewel, a key, as James called it. The people on the phone had probably intended to call her with directions of what to do. Why would they think she would do what they wanted? Did they have something on her, some kind of blackmail? Was she some type of unwilling courier? Then she ruined it all when she wrecked her car. Those men? Giovanni's men? Were they the people who were supposed to receive the case? Were they about to intercept her delivery? Why was James there? And who is James?

James. She reflected that, while they were polite, they had both been careful not to exchange last names. James. Madison. They could be made-up names for all either of them knew. James seemed like a decent guy, but was he a criminal? Why did he live like someone so... out of the public eye? "Off the grid", as they say on TV? Who was he afraid of? The police? Someone else? What exactly did he do for a living?

There, in the shower, Madison made some important decisions. She decided that she would not allow herself to fully trust James; at least, not until he *proved* he was trustworthy. This certainly didn't feel like a kidnapping. She could have run off as she walked down to the restroom. No. She would trust her instincts on this. Yet, she must protect herself and that meant that she would not be lulled into blindly submitting to everything he suggested.

Next, she decided that she must contact someone in her life. Whether it was work, or her family back in Cleveland, someone would certainly be missing her and wondering if she was okay. She thought about her mother and how she would worry about her. She usually called two or three times a week. Surely her mother would be concerned at not having her Maddie call just to check in. She couldn't go home; her apartment had been burned to the ground. Yet home wasn't a location to her. Home was her family, her friends, the people in her life. If she could contact them, then she would know she'd have a home when this was all over.

Finally, she needed to find out about this ruby arrowhead. If it was stolen, it deserved to be turned in to the police. If it was some business transaction gone wrong, well then, the rightful owner deserved it. Key or not, it was a valuable stone and it certainly didn't belong to her or James.

Madison mechanically washed her hair, while her brain mulled these thoughts over. She shut off the water, dried off, and changed back into the clothes James had given to her. She walked to the sink and, for the first time in four days, looked in a mirror.

The first thing she noticed was that she looked tired, which she thought was ironic considering she had been asleep for the last 72 hours. Her eyes were puffy with faint black marks just underneath. Her cheeks looked whiter than normal. The next thing she noticed was a complete absence of cuts or bruises on her face. She had expected a mangled mess of her former self to show up in the mirror. There had been so much blood; she wondered how she could have escaped the accident with so little damage. Carefully she pulled her wet hair back away from her face and saw a four inch laceration at her hairline held closed by neatly tied sutures. The wound was surrounded by a bruise, just to the right of her right eyebrow. Madison touched it gently and smiled at James' handiwork. The wound looked clean and would probably not scar.

She applied her make-up, toweled her hair dry, took a seat on the couch in the ladies restroom and pulled her cell phone out of her jeans. It showed nine missed calls. Two were from work, the rest were from her mother. She selected "Mom" from her phone's address book and a few seconds later, the phone rang.

"Madison! Why haven't you called? I haven't been able to sleep. We're so worried about you. Darling, where are you?" asked Tara Monroe in a breathless torrent of motherly worry.

"I'm okay, Mom. I'm fine."

"The police have called. Everyone is looking for you. I was even about to head out there to search for you, if you weren't so far away..."

There it was. Madison's mother never seemed to miss an opportunity to bring up her contentious decision to move to Kansas. However, this time the criticism seemed warranted considering the situation.

"I'm safe, Mom," she said. She nearly added *I think* but thought better of it. "I'm with someone who's helping me out."

"Who?"

"Mom, I don't have time to explain, but I'm okay. I just wanted you to know that I'm fine."

"Your father thought about coming home from his trip to Europe to help look for you."

Madison clenched her teeth at the mention of her father.

"You can tell Dad that I'm fine and there's no reason to stop whatever important business he's doing. I'm sure there's a deal to be made that's more important than looking for me."

"Madison? Wha-" said Tara. "Your father loves you."

"I gotta go, Mom. I'll call you when I know more."

"But Madison-"

Madison hung up the phone and let out a low grunt of frustration. She ran both hands through her hair and took several deep breaths to compose herself. She slid her phone into her back pocket, gathered her things, and left the women's locker room.

The Resource Room at the YMCA was a little room in the corner of the facility with two bookshelves, mostly filled with incomplete encyclopedias, National Geographic magazines, a collection of classic novels and Reader's Digest condensed books. In the center of the room was a table with three outdated computers sitting on it with a chair at each computer. The resource room was the brainchild of some well-intentioned employee back in the early 2000s to provide internet access to their members. The room had not been updated since that first investment and now the dirty, off-white computers with 17" monitors connected slowly through the phone lines to the internet.

At one of the computers sat James with a worried look on his face. He stared at the screen scrutinizing a webpage Madison couldn't quite make out. She entered the room and James immediately looked up and said "We've gotta go."

"What? Why?" she asked alarmed at the sudden drama.

"Look."

Leaning over James, she looked at the webpage. It was the news department from the local NBC affiliate. She stared at the lead story, and there, on the screen, was her driver's license photo. Next to her picture was an article with the headline:

AREA WOMAN ABDUCTED AFTER TRAFFIC ACCIDENT

She read the text next to the picture.

```
    Police are looking for Madison Dawn,
24, after her car was found wrecked
downtown early Monday morning. Witnesses
described seeing a man in a silver
sedan pull her from the car and
forcibly take her from the scene. Police
say that Dawn is a recent arrival to
the area working as an administrative
assistant at a local tech firm and has
no previous arrest record. Anyone with
information as to her whereabouts
should contact police immediately.
```

"Why did they use that picture?" Madison lamented. "Of all the pictures-"

"It doesn't matter," said James quietly but with an intense energy. "What matters is that your picture is out there. You'll be on the news tonight and everyone will be looking for you. We've got to get out of the city. We've got to get out of *here*." He rose, shutting the computer off with a jab of his thumb.

They scurried onto the sidewalk, Madison struggling to keep up. She had so many questions and she was frustrated that once again she was following him blindly without knowing what the plan was, or even where they were going.

"James, wait." Then, in the middle of the sidewalk without regard for the other pedestrians attempting to move around her, she stopped walking and folded her arms. James was several steps away before he realized that she wasn't following him.

"What are you doing? Let's go" he said, turning around. He grabbed her arm, but she resisted.

"We're not doing this anymore, James," she said. "If we're going somewhere, you're telling me where we're going. I don't know anything about you. Maybe you abducted me and I just don't remember it because of the accident. Give me one reason why I shouldn't call the police right now and turn you in."

She was bluffing. While she didn't know how much to trust him, her intuition assured her that James had not abducted her. Nevertheless, he needed to know that he must earn her trust and that she was capable of thinking and acting for herself.

"We'll discuss this later. Let's go." She didn't move. Frustrated, James reluctantly gave in.

"How could you question if I abducted you? I stitched your head together. I bought you clothes and shampoo and make-up. I took you into my loft. You are the only person in the world that knows where I live."

"I don't know why that's important. You don't tell me anything."

An irritated stranger who was forced to step into the street due to the traffic problem this conversation had created elbowed his way through with a curt "Outta the way.".

"Alright, fine." James threw up his arms and then rubbed his eyes. "We're going to where I work. It's ten blocks away. We'll be safe there. Once we're there, I'll fill you in on the details. But for now, if someone recognizes you, everything falls apart. Do you understand? The same people that burned down your apartment will know where you are and they'll come after you. The police can't protect you, do you understand?"

"Why not? I have nothing to hide from the police," she said, spreading her arms out, palms up.

"The police are no friends of ours-" he stopped himself short and rubbed his temples as he emitted a frustrated sigh.

"Where are we going? I need something more."

"The Museum of Lost Antiquities. Now let's go," he said as he took her by the hand. Relenting, she walked with him, keeping up with his brisk pace.

≈✦≈

The Museum of Lost Antiquities resided in the old County Courthouse downtown. Its many wings and spacious lawn provided a stark contrast to the cube-like office buildings that had sprouted up around it in the 20th Century. The cut stone façade and striking bell tower offered a welcome aesthetic relief to the unremarkable buildings populating the downtown area.

The county had built a modern Courthouse in the mid 1980s farther uptown. The old courthouse, a stoic stone building listed on the National Registry of Historic Places, then sat empty and abandoned for 10 years before billionaire tycoon Gordon Hardbottle funded the creation of the museum. As Gordon Hardbottle stated in the museum's inaugural speech,

"We must always remember the past, for without it, we lose our identity."

It was nearly lunchtime before James and Madison reached the museum after snaking through side streets. It was a busy day with no less than seven different elementary classes coming to visit. James led Madison to a small service door on the side of the building rather than entering through the child-infested main entrance.

The service entrance led to a large storage room that also served as the loading dock for large deliveries. Aside from several pallets of wooden boxes that sat near the closed overhead door, several rows of tall storage shelves, and an unused hand truck, the storage room was startlingly sparse. Their steps echoed as they walked across the vacant room. Madison noticed that James had relaxed considerably since they had entered the museum grounds. She hoped that meant they were safe for a while.

"So are you a curator, or something?" Madison asked. They left the warehouse and now were walking through a hallway that led directly to a set of offices on the other side of the building.

"Huh?"

"You said that you worked here. Or are you a security guard or something?" Now that James had relaxed, she felt it was time he explained things to her.

"No. I work for the museum, but, uh… I guess you could call it freelance work." James stopped at a solid oak door and knocked. Without waiting for a reply he turned the door handle and entered the room.

A stout wooden desk, dark with the weathering of time, occupied the middle of the office. The room was tastefully decorated with reproductions of two of Monet's most famous works and a few unidentifiable trinkets on a bookcase in the corner. A plastic fern sat in another corner in desperate need of dusting. Two empty leather chairs faced the near side of the desk. On the desk was a copy of the morning paper, a magazine featuring sailboats on its cover and a large ebony cube engraved with some form of hieroglyphics.

An elderly man with bright white hair sat huddled over the cube, peering at it through a lighted magnifying glass that was mounted to the table on a metal articulating arm. Behind the man was another desk and a computer screen displaying the Google homepage beneath a poorly played game of Minesweeper. The man examined the cube and did not look up when the two of them entered.

"James, if I had a dollar for every phone call I had to make on your behalf this week, I could retire to my boat and leave this whole God-forsaken business. Instead I've got a splitting headache, I think I'm working on my third ulcer, and I'm honestly thinking of giving up this job and taking up something honorable like delivering mail or washing cars," said the man. He wore low riding spectacles, a grey vest over a white button down shirt and an impossibly large gold watch. "How much do you think postal workers make?" he said, and with that he looked up, acknowledging them for the first time. "Oh, wonderful, you brought the little headache with you," he said.

"Oh." Madison said.

"Easy, Devin, easy," said James. "Devin, this is Madison Dawn. Madison, Devin Aladore, curator and director of the museum." They took a seat. Madison decided that she wasn't fond of this petty little man.

"I know who you are Miss Dawn," said Devin. "Your picture is all over the bloody news. I can't believe you brought her here, James. You've jeopardized the entire museum."

"I didn't expect her face to be plastered all over town. As soon as I found out, we came here to figure out what to do next."

"You didn't expect it?" said Devin. "James, people aren't like artifacts. You can't just take them and hope no one notices. People notice when their friends go missing, especially particularly attractive ones."

Madison smiled somewhat at the compliment, but didn't like being talked about as if she weren't in the room.

"What exactly do you do, James?" asked Madison with narrowed eyes.

"I do what Devin tells me to. I investigate, I research, I… acquire… items lost to history," James explained in an evasive way.

"So you're a treasure hunter."

"He's an artifact recovery specialist, and he is in our employ," said Devin. "Not just this museum, but museums throughout the country owe a great debt to James here for his artifact recovering services."

"So you're like Indiana Jones?" Madison grinned and her eyes lit up at the prospect.

"Who?" asked James.

"Who? Who is Indiana Jones?" Madison couldn't believe the question had been asked.

"You'll have to forgive him Miss Dawn. When you grow up far from western civilization, pop culture references often slip through unappreciated." Devin turned his face and lowered his chin, indicating that a more serious matter was at hand.

"Where have you been for the past three days, James?" asked Devin, leaning forward and putting his elbows on the desk. "I've been trying to get a hold of you."

"I was at home. Madison was hurt pretty badly and I wanted to make sure she was alright. I thought it best to lay low for a while, anyway."

"You took her home? My God. James, that loft is one of our most closely guarded secrets." Devin was astounded. "Do you know how long we worked to set that? And why didn't you answer your cell phone?"

"Oh. I guess I forgot to turn it on. You know I hate those things."

"You forgot to turn it on." Devin sat back in the chair, removed his glasses and rubbed his temples. "Damnation, James, you'll be the death of me."

"Maybe this will help. Madison was carrying this in the back of her car," said James. He removed the leather pouch from around his neck and opened it, dumping the ruby arrowhead onto the sailing magazine. "But now, it's ours."

The elderly man froze, completely fixated on the red stone sitting before him. He didn't blink. He didn't breathe. Madison wondered if the mere appearance of the sparkling ruby arrowhead had killed him off. She smirked at the thought.

After several painfully quiet moments, life reappeared in the elderly man's eyes. He blinked several times and a broad grin came to his face.

"It's ours," he repeated in a jubilant whisper. Carefully, he picked up the stone and held it under his magnifying glass. "The Key of Caligula's Bath."

Several moments passed as he turned the stone over in his hands. He examined every cut facet as if looking for some imperceptible flaw. Devin sat back in his chair, turning the stone over in his hands, and gave Madison a satisfied stare, his previously hostile attitude erased from memory.

"Why did you have this in your possession, I should wonder. You don't look like the sort of person that would own something as nice as this." Even when being demure, Devin found a way to offend.

"It's not mine," said Madison. "I didn't know it was there. We think they wanted me to deliver it somewhere for them."

"Oh, I know it's not yours." Devin smiled. "And I know Giovanni's men wanted you to deliver it. They were following you when you decided to get yourself involved and wreck your car. The question is why did they select *you* to deliver the Key? And to whom were you delivering it?"

James spoke up. "Honestly, Devin, I think it's likely she was selected at random. I just don't see any connection. I think they thought she was weak-minded enough to do what they wanted and would do it without asking too many questions."

"Hey!" Madison objected. Her protest fell on deaf ears.

"Hmmmm. I don't think so," murmured Devin. "I think they needed her. There was a reason they chose her, specifically."

"Why?" said James and Madison in unison.

"I don't know. But there's a reason…" his voice trailed off in thought.

A few moments passed while James and Madison let Devin think in peace. Finally, when it was obvious that he wasn't going to miraculously think of the reason, Madison got curious.

"So, what is this thing anyway? A key? A key to what?" Madison reached across the desk to handle the arrowhead, but Devin snatched it up.

"Ah, Miss Dawn, that is a fantastic question," he said with measured condescension. "And normally, I would tell you that it's none of your business. It is museum business. But in this case, there may be value in you knowing. Perhaps by telling you what we're up against, we will find out why Giovanni wanted you involved. But I must warn you once you're in, you're in. There's no giving up and going home. No calling your family or checking in with friends. If you want to be a part of this, you're here until the end." He sat back with an ominous expression.

"I don't understand. In what? The end of what?" Madison asked.

"This!" Devin said in a particularly demonstrative though unhelpful way. "We have the key. Giovanni is after it. He's not going to give up. There are only three possibilities here. We use the key for its designed purpose, we hide the key somewhere safe, or we lose the key to those thugs. There is no other resolution, and I'll not have someone with vital information about our involvement walking away from here and out of our protection to be taken by the Giovannis. And believe me, young lady, Giovanni will find you and you will tell them everything that you know, either voluntarily or involuntarily. Do you understand, Miss Dawn?"

Madison sat quietly, thinking over the things Devin said. She thought back to her totaled car, her burnt out apartment, and her lost job. What else did she have to lose? Then she thought of her mother and the inevitable silence she would have to endure. She remembered her mother's voice and the worry she heard in it when they'd last talked. This would be hard on her family. She took her phone from her pocket and rolled it around in her hand.

"Your silence is the only way to protect your family, Miss Dawn," said Devin, sensing what she was thinking. Madison looked into Devin's eyes, saw trust and earnestness, and then handed him her phone.

"Alright. I'm in," she said. Then with a sideways glance she said "Maybe it'll be fun."

"Fun?" Devin nearly choked on the word. James winced on her behalf. "Miss Dawn, this isn't about having fun. This is history. This is about doing something that no one has ever done. This is about prestige and being first and uncovering mysteries, but it's also about hard work and miserable conditions and sacrifice. It's about danger. This is not about fun."

"Okay, okay. I was just trying to have a positive attitude about things," she said in as calm a voice as she could muster.

"Humph" said Devin. He got up, straightened his vest, and went to a nearby wall. Reaching up under a wooden sconce, he pulled down a world map that depicted the political layout of Europe and the Mediterranean from about 40AD. The Roman Empire dominated the map.

"How much do you know about the Roman Empire, Miss Dawn?" Devin asked. He was clearly in his element, and traces of his past as a college professor were evident. Madison recognized the impending lecture and felt herself immediately becoming sleepy.

"I took a world history course in high school," Madison admitted. "But I wouldn't say I remember a whole lot from it."

"Please, tell me you've heard of Caligula." Devin pleaded.

"Umm. Yes?" Madison offered. She'd heard the name, but couldn't recall anything about him.

"Caligula ruled the Roman empire for four years; from 37 to 41 AD. He came to power when Tiberius died, or was more likely, murdered."

"Wasn't Caligula the one that fiddled while Rome burned?" asked Madison, hoping to show some knowledge of the era.

"No, that was Nero; another of Rome's infamously evil rulers. No, Caligula was the son of Germanicus, a popular Emperor who was succeeded by Tiberius. Tiberius ended up putting nearly everyone in Caligula's family to death to retain power. But curiously, he spared Caligula the same fate. Caligula gained power after Tiberius' death or, more likely, murder, in 37 AD."

"Sounds like an epidemic, rulers being murdered."

"It's how things were done back then, unfortunately. Now, Caligula was known for expanding and building the Roman Empire, among his other less noble pursuits. He began work on aqua ducts, expanded trade- "

"And nearly spent the Roman Empire into bankruptcy," interrupted James. "He was as loony as a hyena on heroin and as morally bankrupt as he was ego-maniacal."

Madison turned to James. "Not one of your favorite rulers in history?"

"Let's just say that the more I learn about this sonufabitch, the more I wish we could erase his sorry face from the pages of history. Scum like this deserves to be forgotten." James folded his arms.

"Now, now, to be fair," said Devin, "much of what we know about Caligula was written by his enemies. We have no idea how accurate the accounts of his wanton murdering, incestuous lusting, and abuses of power are."

"Did he, or did he not, try to erect a statue of *himself* to be worshipped in the *temple in Jerusalem*?" asked James, stressing the last three words emphatically.

"That appears to be true," conceded Devin.

"And how many ancient historians referred to him as 'insane'?"

"All but one."

"I rest my case," James said, satisfied.

Madison said, "So, an all-around bad guy then."

"Indeed. But unfortunately, Caligula's personal history is rather irrelevant to our little quest," said Devin, regaining his teaching voice. "Now we come to the crux of the matter, as it were. Great leaders throughout history often create what archeologists now call 'Empire Markers'. Essentially, in some form or other, they bind their own wealth and legacy to their empire. If the empire falls, they fall, or, more often the case, their descendants fall. Call it motivation to see their lineage succeed.

"They take some portion of their wealth, or perhaps something of great sentimental value, and they secure it. Sometimes they bury it, the way a pirate might bury treasure, but more often than not, they lock their treasure away, and send it to one extreme end of their empire. Then they take the key, and send it to the other end of the empire. The thought being that if the empire were to fall, or even if the borders were to diminish, the next dynasty could not inherit that particular piece of wealth."

"So it's a form of seeking immortality?" Madison was suddenly interested at the thought of buried treasure and hidden keys.

"Isn't that what all great leaders want?" James answered. "They conquer the world and then realize it's only theirs for a short while. So they attempt to find ways to hang on to their glory long after they've passed on."

Madison considered this for a moment, for the first time in her life trying to understand the mentality of great world leaders.

"How many empire markers are there?" she finally asked, returning to the thought of hidden treasure.

"More than you would think," said Devin. "It was a common practice in nearly every major civilization since the Ancient Egyptians. The Ancient Greeks, the Romans, the medieval kings of England. Even Napoleon and Hitler are known to have left empire markers behind. The problem we have as archeologists is that usually either the key is lost or destroyed or the treasure itself is lost or destroyed."

"Or we find out how to open it without the key," added James.

"Right, but that doesn't always work. The wealth some rulers decide to conceal is often destroyed if you attempt to unlock it without the key. And oftentimes, it's not gold or jewels they bury, but secret information, historical records or the remains of loved ones. Those are invariably lost if you just go blasting away at every locked chamber we come across."

"So this arrowhead… is a key to…" Madison's voice trailed off, hoping Devin or James would fill in the blank.

"Caligula's Bath," said Devin excitedly. "As I said, in some cases, the empire marker was sent to one end of the empire, and the key to the other. But in this case, Caligula put the treasure right under his own nose. In the heart of Rome, he expanded the Imperial Palace and built an elaborate bath for himself. Legend says that, buried below the bath, below the furnaces that heated the water, he secretly constructed a chamber.

"That chamber contains the most valuable possessions of the emperor of one of the world's greatest superpowers."

The room fell silent. Their imaginations, restless at being restrained by so much exposition, were finally set free as they all stared starry-eyed at the giant red jewel.

IV

ON THE SPECTRUM OF RARENESS

"Life contains but two tragedies.
One is not to get your heart's desire;
the other is to get it."
George Bernard Shaw

James reclined in a comfortable lounge on the top floor of the museum and ran his hand thoughtfully over the cool leather armrest. The lounge was usually reserved for important museum donors or personal friends of Gordon Hardbottle and consisted of plush leather couches, beautiful walnut paneling, fine gold and emerald appointments, and a well-stocked bar. One-way mirrors formed one wall of the lounge, allowing the occupants to overlook the grandiose foyer of the museum, its T-Rex skeleton, elaborate Italian fountain, and working model of the solar system. The mirrored side prevented the well-heeled clients from being observed by the common visitor: the groundlings of the museum world.

The side of the lounge opposite the wall of one-way mirrors featured mahogany bookcases surrounding a pair of windows that looked out the front of the building. The sun was just beginning to set and the dim light that filled the room was a mere echo of the brilliance the sun had shown just an hour prior. The sky had turned a velvety purple as James and Madison waited in the lounge until the museum closed promptly at 6pm.

Devin, James, and Madison had agreed that it was best if James and Madison were not seen in the museum during regular business hours, and that they should avoid wandering the streets in the daytime. They retired to the lofty perch to await the end of the day.

Devin had been called away to tend to some other business and had left the two of them alone. James pondered their next move for so long that Madison had lain down on a plush leather couch and unintentionally drifted off to sleep.

At last, James, sure that he had seen things from every possible angle, broke himself from his trance and looked over at Madison as she lay there, eyes closed, breathing quietly. *She really is quite beautiful*, he thought. With a contemplative sigh, he admired her long, wavy blonde hair that cascaded down her soft cheeks. The milky light of dusk fell on her soft features, her full, red, kissable lips. Her sharp pointed nose was the only feature that broke the softness. James settled further into his chair and allowed himself to be content in that moment. For the first time since they met, he didn't think of her as a victim, a source of information, or a liability, but as someone to pursue; a beauty to be won. It was a rare thought for him.

"James Kynan!" said an excited voice, snapping James from his voyeuristic indulgence. "Holy crap, it's good to see you."

James looked beyond the couch to the door at the other side of the room. Standing in the doorway wearing a broad smile was a dark-haired man with an athletic build and a weather-beaten face. His half Italian, half Scandinavian heritage gave him a rugged though approachable appearance.

"What are you doing sitting here in the dark?" he asked. As the sun set, the room had indeed grown dark, though James honestly hadn't noticed. The man entered the room yet did not turn on the light.

"Brennan! I didn't know you were back." James hopped to his feet and gave Brennan a handshake that turned into a firm one-armed hug before ending with a solid slap on the back.

"Devin called me in. Said you were gonna need me," said Brennan flopping haphazardly down in a chair next to James. Brennan chomped a piece of gum and didn't seem to care how much noise he made. "So, Devin says you brought the chicky here. Where is she?"

"What, are you blind? On the couch," said James. "She's sleeping."

"I'm not sleeping," said Madison, sitting up. "I just dozed off for a second."

"Oh, sorry if I woke you up. I didn't see-" Brennan cut himself off. He stared slack-jawed through the murky light, his gum nearly tumbling out of his open mouth. An uncomfortable silence filled the room and Madison shifted uneasily on the couch. Finally, Brennan spoke.

"Um, James. Can I speak to you for a second? Outside?" He attempted to speak casually but his high arched eyebrows betrayed his thoughts.

"I know what you're going to say…."

Brennan nodded his head in the direction of the door anyway. They stepped out into the hallway, pausing just on the other side of the door to speak.

"James. You know I love you like a brother. But I have to ask… Is this going to be a problem?"

"It's fine, Brennan."

"Are you kidding me, James?" Brennan was animated, but not angry. "Just tell me you're going to be okay. Tell me you've put her behind you."

Now it was James who suddenly found intensity.

"I'm past her. I told you, I'm past her. I know Madison looks like her, but she's not her. So don't you worry about it, okay? I spent two years getting over that woman. I'm over it."

Brennan interrogated James' eyes looking for the truth. A few seconds later, he smiled and smacked James on the shoulder. "Well, alright. That's good. Glad to hear it."

The two re-entered in amiable spirits a few moments later. James flipped on the lights and Brennan asked Madison if he could get her anything to drink. She asked for a diet Pepsi that he promptly retrieved from the refrigerator in the bar.

"Oh man, James." Brennan crashed back into one of the chairs. He kicked a leg over one of the arm rests and smirked at his friend. "Man, have you stirred things up. I've never seen Giovanni so pissed. He's got every asset available looking for you. 'Course he suspects that you're here, but he doesn't *know*. I don't think he really believes you are dumb enough to come here, though."

"Well, we didn't have much choice," said James.

"You messed up Ricky and Carlos good, my friend. Carlos is still laid up. And they're pretty sure Ricky isn't going to talk right ever again. He's lucky he's not dead."

"Heh. He never talked right to begin with," said James. "But honestly, I had to put them down. I tried not to kill them though."

"What an excellent show of restraint, my violent friend," laughed Brennan. "Not killing someone. Hey chicky, how many people have you not killed today?"

"All of them," answered Madison, matter-of-factly. Brennan was about to respond, but froze as he tried to discern the logic behind her answer.

"Her name is Madison, Brennan. Madison Dawn, Brennan Nash," introduced James.

Instead of a handshake, they merely nodded at each other and said 'Hi'.

"Be careful, Brennan. She's smarter than you."

Brennan mocked an insulted look and then winked at Madison. His attitude was bold, even obnoxious, but Madison couldn't keep herself from liking this guy. Brennan returned to chomping his gum.

"So I have to ask. Who is this Giovanni? I keep hearing the name. Why is it that he seems like he's your archenemy?" asked Madison.

James and Brennan exchanged glances before Brennan spoke. "I guess you could say that the Giovannis fall on the opposite side of the antiquities code of ethics from us."

"What do you mean?" she asked.

"Well, let me put this hypothetically to you," said Brennan. "You're hiking along some dusty trail in the Sierra Nevada mountains, okay? You're all by yourself. Suddenly, out of the corner of your eye you see a quarter lying there on the trail. What do you do?" The simple and uninteresting question was clearly the set up for something more meaningful because Brennan could hardly contain his excitement for this exercise. James had been through this with Brennan before.

"I'd pick it up," she said simply, playing along.

"Do you keep the quarter?"

"Of course. I found it."

"Okay, now say that it wasn't just a quarter, but you found a rare $20 gold coin. If you had it appraised, it would be worth somewhere around $100. Do you still keep it?" asked Brennan, sounding more and more like a lawyer cross-examining a witness.

"I guess. I'd probably sell it, though. I don't collect coins."

"MmmHmm," said Brennan. "Now suppose you find a coin that is so rare that it's the only one like it ever discovered in the world. Moreover, the coin yields valuable clues about a lost civilization. Do you still keep it? It is, essentially, priceless." Brennan's eyes twinkled at this, the crux of his argument; the moment he trapped the witness into revealing her damning evidence.

"Maybe. I'd probably give it to a museum so it could be studied and so others could appreciate it. But honestly, I don't see the relevance here."

"What if you kept it?" asked Brennan.

"I don't think I'd feel right about that. I mean, I'm not a coin expert and I'm not an anthropologist. The coin should go to them, probably."

Brennan hopped up out of his chair, his trap sprung. "Aha! At some point, you've decided that this lost coin is no longer yours, but belonging to all of humanity, right? At some point on the spectrum of rareness, you acknowledge that you have some obligation to share it with the rest of us."

"Well, yeah, but it's still mine. I mean, I'm not a socialist or anything. I still acknowledge personal property." Madison answered on the defensive.

Now James spoke up. "Okay, so say you sell it to a museum. Do you hold an auction to get as much money as you can for it?"

"I don't really know, James," said Madison with a tired sigh. "What's your point?"

"My point is," said James "that there are two markets for antiquities. Museums all over the world are researching, seeking, discovering and displaying our history, the world's history, to anyone willing to come through their doors. They provide information to researchers and try to uncover the pages of our past.

"The other market is that of collectors. There are wealthy people, governments, and even corporations all over the world that love to collect rare things and show them off to their friends and only their friends. They have the resources to purchase anything they want and to keep it behind their gated driveways, their country club memberships, and their societal ties.

"Obviously, we work for the museum. Brennan and I work to find lost artifacts and bring them to the museum before someone else finds them and brings them to market.

"The Giovannis serve the collectors. They are looking for the same pieces of history we are, but they are doing so to sell to the highest bidder. Years ago, Giuseppe Giovanni found a few pieces of pottery at the ancient site of Ostia Antica near his Italian home. The pottery ended up being the personal washbasin of Caesar Augustus and was sold to a private collector for an amazing fortune. From then on, that family has been in the relic finding business. They expanded from Italy to Europe and now into the U.S. They have agents all over the world looking for artifacts to sell to these collectors. Their money buys them power with local governments and agents, effectively treasure hunting mercenaries, to help in their search. So yeah, I guess they're our archenemy, in the sense that they are our competition and every time we lose to them, a piece of history goes into a locked closet only to be appreciated by a select few." James sat back with a disgusted sneer.

"I see. So why the bad blood?" asked Madison. "It's just business, right? In business you have competitors all the time, it's not a matter of life or death."

James felt a swirl of emotions, thoughts and memories. Madison's words brought up a righteous anger in James and he fought to control his emotions. Wisely, he got up and went to the door.

"I'd better see what Devin is up to," he said and left the room.

The door clicked shut as James left. The manner in which he left told Madison that she had said something wrong, or possibly something hurtful. Brennan rose from his chair.

"You shouldn't talk about things you don't know, chicky," said Brennan quietly. "Trust me. It has been, and it is, a matter of life and death. I've found that if enough money is at stake, people are willing to kill for it. The Giovannis are no different. They've got enough money and power that if they want something, they can get it. Governments all over the world are paid to ignore their little transgressions, so the rule of law and the protections you think you have don't exist.

"You read the newspaper articles about your 'abduction', right?" he asked. Madison nodded. "Notice anything missing? You didn't read a single account of Ricky and Carlos, did you? They weren't there. Giovanni's reach extends to this town's government and its media. And it's like that wherever there are organizations actively competing against him for artifacts. So yeah, standing in their way, it's a matter of life and death. No one knows that better and more personally than James."

Madison considered apologizing but instead sat quietly. She hadn't meant to offend or hurt James, but obviously what she'd said had affected him. She looked at Brennan who returned to the bar to pour himself a drink.

"So, Brennan," Madison said in a lilting voice designed to lighten the mood. "How am I a problem?"

"Sorry?"

"I heard you through the door. If this is going to be a problem, I figure I should know about it." Madison got up and went over to him, leaning against the bar. She moved stiffly, courtesy of the soreness caused by the accident three days earlier.

Brennan splashed a healthy double shot of spiced rum over a few ice cubes, raised the glass to his lips, and looked at her.

"All right, sister. I'll be honest with you." He took a drink. "You don't know James, okay. You haven't seen him heartbroken and you haven't seen him wallowing in misery and self-pity. It's not a pretty sight. I hope I never see it again." Brennan moved closer to Madison, peering into her. She could smell the spices of the rum.

"My goodness, what happened?" asked Madison.

"This girl screwed with him. Messed him up good. If I ever see her again—" He clenched a fist. "He's since forgiven her, whatever that means, but this is a grudge I don't plan on letting go. That girl *destroyed* James. For a good two years he was worthless to us. He's finally making his way back, getting his life back together, getting his identity back. And then you show up."

"And then I show up," repeated Madison.

"I swear to God, doll face, if you hurt him, I will bring you down. Do you understand me? I won't let this happen again." All mirth had left Brennan and the flame in his eyes frightened her.

"Hurt him? The kind of pain you're talking about can only come from…." She paused. "Look, I hardly know him. How on earth can I hurt him?" She was feeling guilty but she didn't know why.

"Because he's already falling for you, sweetheart. I can see it in the way he looks at you."

Madison gasped as her mind became a battleground for a million warring thoughts. A first-strike platoon of thoughts demanded that she slap Brennan across his face for laying this burden on her. A brigade of thoughts insisted that she laugh and tell him that he's an idiot, while yet a persuasive regiment of thoughts proposed that she cry for a good twenty minutes. Those thoughts were ambushed by the small number of guerilla thoughts that took it as an extreme compliment and a giant standing army of thoughts demanded more information. The battle of emotions and thought came to a screaming zenith and culminated in an underwhelming yet honest response, spoken vaguely through the fog of war.

"What?"

The door to the lounge opened, terminating the discussion. James and Devin entered.

"Well, we'd better get started if you're to get on your way," said Devin.

"Where are we going?" asked Madison still reeling from the emotional conflict she'd managed to survive.

"Where else? The key doesn't do us any good hanging around here. You're going to Rome."

At last, Devin smiled.

V

LIVE FIRE

"Airplanes fly. Helicopters beat the air into submission."
Aviation Cliché

The brilliant morning sun crested the horizon and changed dawn to full day in a sparkling flash. The clear blue sky and cool autumn air meant that the sunrise was neither colorful nor subtle. A sedan pulled up to the rusty World War II era hangar and James, Madison, and Brennan got out.

They were at a rural general aviation airstrip just outside of town. Rows of hangars for small aircraft lined the taxiway. One early riser, a man in a homebuilt tail-dragger, was heard taxiing onto the runway, adding power and departing the airfield. The drone of his engine faded away, and the subsequent quiet returned the morning to its restful state.

Madison looked around, squinting into the low-hanging sun. She was up late the night before while the boys planned their course of action. She tried to be helpful when possible but eventually, feeling that she could just get caught up on the plan during the flight to Rome, she crashed on the couch leaving the final planning to them. She did not sleep well on the leather couch in the lounge at the museum, and the 4:30 am wake-up call had come as both a relief and a curse.

James unlocked the hangar door and slid open one of the imposing metal doors. Brennan pulled on the other door and Madison looked into the dark hangar at their next mode of transportation.

"You've gotta be kidding me," she said.

"Expecting something else?" asked James.

"I thought you said we were taking the museum jet." She gawked in disbelief at a single engine, four seat airplane with, of all things, the wing on the top. She was staring at a Cessna 182; a nicely equipped, general aviation airplane, suitable for four people, but a far cry from the luxurious Gulfstream jet she had pictured in her mind.

"No, I said the museum 'plane'. I never said 'jet'. You assumed jet," James said.

"How are we going to get to Rome in *that*? Will it even hold the three of us?"

"I don't think she was awake for that part, James," said Brennan. He unlocked the baggage door and began loading their gear into the back. Their gear, packed tightly in three canvas duffle bags, consisted of emergency rations, digging equipment and tools, their toiletries and a scarce few changes of clothes; the latter included due to Madison's insistence.

James climbed into the front seat and removed the checklist, a fuel drain cup, and a metallic dipstick from the cabin before stepping back out onto the hangar floor.

"She does tend to sleep a lot, doesn't she?" said Brennan hoisting the last of the three bags into the baggage compartment.

"Yes, but she's adorable when she sleeps." James was teasing. "with the exception of the snoring, of course."

"What? I don't snore."

"A little drool too."

"Stop it. I don't snore or drool."

"Really? Maybe you do and don't know," said James. "When was the last time you slept in the presence of someone else?"

"That is none of your business." Madison wondered how her love life, or lack thereof, had gotten into this conversation. She thought about defending her unlikely snoring by explaining how poorly a girl who is used to her supple queen bed sleeps on a cold leather couch. Instead, she returned the conversation to the practical.

"So why are we taking this thing?"

"We can't exactly drive to the airport and hop a flight to Rome, Madison. Giovanni's men will be expecting that. They're probably camped out at the airport right now. So we're just going to take the museum plane down south to Dallas. From there, we'll catch a flight to Rome. We can still get out of the country without them knowing. It just takes a little work."

Brennan and James removed the wheel chocks and pushed the little airplane out onto the tarmac. James completed his preflight check and the three of them climbed into the cramped aluminum aircraft; James and Brennan up front, with Madison tucked away in the back seat.

James flipped on the master switch and Madison could suddenly hear James and Brennan talking through her headset. The headset clamped on either side of her head, flattening her otherwise voluminous hair and slightly pinched her ears.

Madison could see James flipping switches and turning knobs, going methodically through his checklist, all the while Brennan was fiddling with some screen on the right. The whole process seemed rather random to Madison. From the few broken words she heard from Brennan, such as "waypoint", and "approach" she assumed he was programming their flight path into the aircraft's computers.

The last time Madison had been in a small plane was when she was eight years old. Her uncle had taken Madison and her younger sister up for their first experience with flight. The instrument panel looked a lot different then, though she couldn't say why. What she clearly remembered was getting sick halfway through the flight, throwing up all over the interior of the cockpit, and the flight ending prematurely amidst the screaming and crying of her younger sister. It was a time in her life she'd gladly forgotten.

"You know the last time I flew in a small plane, my lunch ended up decorating the entire airplane. Are you sure we can't find another way to the airport?"

"Clear!" shouted James just after popping open his window. Madison heard a brief whirr of the starter, the cough-cough-cough of the fuel injected engine turning over, and then a roar as the airplane shook with the engine finally coming to life. Madison's eyes narrowed as she sensed a distinctly unique smell; the unmistakable scent of leaded aviation gasoline. That smell brought her back to that day when she was eight and experienced flight for the first time. Brennan turned and handed Madison a motion sickness bag which ended the discussion about finding another way to the airport in Dallas.

James added power and they crept out to the taxiway and down to the end of the runway. They paused there, running the engine up for a few seconds as James completed his checklist.

Finally, Madison heard James' voice, confident and direct, over the headset.

"Riverside traffic, November 2342 Alpha taking runway niner, will make right traffic, departing to the south, Riverside traffic." His radio call was businesslike and monotone, yet relaxed and in control.

Taking the runway and putting the nose wheel on the centerline, James added power to the powerful Lycoming engine. The growl of the engine became an intense buzz and the aircraft lurched forward, rapidly building speed. Just as Madison was aware of the rush of air past the aluminum fuselage, James pulled the yoke back and the windscreen filled with an unbroken blue field. Madison felt the bottom of her stomach drop out and started to sweat as she saw the earth falling away from the small aircraft out the side window.

"You okay back there?" asked Brennan.

"Oh, she'll be fine. She's tough," said James.

Madison wondered when he acquired her permission to speak for her.

A thousand feet off the ground, James put the aircraft into a steep right turn and they turned on course, momentarily trapping the sun between the horizon and their left wing. They continued to climb, reaching for an altitude where James and Brennan could coax every available knot out of the little bird.

The soothing drone of the engine encouraged Madison to sit in silence and enjoy the scenery. However, the thoughts of where they were going and how they'd escape this mysterious Italian family compelled her to keep asking questions.

"So won't they be able to track us? I mean, by our flight plan?"

"No flight plan. Don't need one," said Brennan. "It's a common misconception amongst you people." By 'you people' Madison understood him to mean, the non-flying public. "But unless you're flying on instruments, or flying commercially, you don't need one."

"It's still possible to move around this country without the government knowing your every move," chimed in James, a note of bitterness and mistrust coloring his voice.

"How long's the flight?" asked Madison.

"A little over two hours if this tailwind holds," said James. Madison sat back in her seat, trying to get comfortable. She adjusted her seatbelt and smiled. The change in plans, the unknown, the early morning departure, the past week of hell she'd been through; none of it could detract from the simple truth that flying was fun.

Madison wondered if she could see other aircraft around her. She peered out her window but just saw endless farm fields and the occasional town. Craning her neck, she looked out the back window when something caught her eye.

At first, she thought it was just a large black bird silhouetted on the horizon by the blinding blue sky. In time, it was obvious that the bird was not only failing to fade away, but growing larger over time. She squinted and thought she could see some sort of flashing just above the black speck.

Madison said, "I think there's a helicopter behind us."

"Naw, not likely," said Brennan. "We're already through 6000 feet. Most helicopters stay pretty close to the ground. They're more efficient down there."

"Oh, okay. It's getting closer so I guess I'll be able to tell pretty soon."

"What?" asked James. He sounded alarmed.

"It's definitely a helicopter, guys," said Madison, still looking out the back window. Brennan twisted around, his eyes lighting up at the sudden approach of the aircraft.

"This is not good," said Brennan. The helicopter caught up to the still climbing aircraft at an alarming rate. At the last second, it slid to the right and came up beside the 182, just off the starboard wing. The massive blades of the helicopter whopped rhythmically as the vortex caused by the spinning rotor shook the Cessna violently. The helicopter, a speedy twin-engine Bell 429, had one unmistakable word painted on the side of the door.

SHERIFF

"What do the cops want?" asked Madison.
"It's not the cops!" shouted Brennan.

The door to the chopper slid open revealing a mounted mini-gun and a serious looking man in a helmet. There was no discussion, no radio call. Flashes erupted from the barrel of the mini-gun.

James pushed the nose of the airplane hard over and jerked the yoke left. Bullets tore through the fuselage and the right wing as bags, charts, pens and dirt flew to the top of the cabin. The wind roared past the airframe as the 182 rapidly picked up speed. Fuel trickled out of the right wing where the bullets had punctured the wing skin.

Madison fought against the g-forces to keep an eye on the helicopter. The 182 plunged for the earth, leaving the 429 high above them. The chopper may have caught their airplane in level flight, but the 182 could descend faster. The tactic worked, but only temporarily. The ground was fast approaching.

"What do we do, brother?" asked Brennan.

"Find me a TFR."

"Are you kidding me? We're out in the middle of farm fields. There's nothing like that out here." Brennan flipped through the screens on the Garmin G1000 panel. James slowed his descent, leveling out about a thousand feet above the ground.

"Okay, there's a TFR around a power plant about 80 miles away," said Brennan.

"80 miles? We'll be dead by then."

"There's nothing else- wait! There's a low level MOA 15 miles from here."

"Please tell me that it's hot," said James.

"What's an MOA?" asked Madison.

"It's a restricted area that the military use for live fire and training missions."

"Head 290. Yeah, it's active," said Brennan.

"Live fire? Like missiles and bombs? And we're heading *into* it- ugh?" Her last word slurred into a grunt as James put the aircraft into a tight right hand turn, the aluminum wing skin popping like oil cans under the g-load. The world spun for a second before clarifying as James brought the airplane out on course.

Madison turned in time to see the menacing helicopter filling her field of view. It had quickly closed the distance, helped by James' turn. Madison screamed as the helicopter swung around, exposing its mini-gun.

James shoved the aircraft into a tight left turn and pushed the nose down. The mini-gun opened fire tearing more holes in the right hand wing. He banked to the right, back on course, putting loads on the airframe the designers never intended. Madison's head swam in sensory overload.

With both aircraft in level flight at full power, the helicopter was faster but only slightly. Every time the helicopter turned to bring its gun to bear, it lost valuable airspeed. Even now, the helicopter had dropped behind significantly. The chase, taking place at 140 knots, was to be a slow developing one, like two large Spanish galleons at the mercy of the wind struggling to gain a firing position.

"There." Brennan pointed to a river bordered by thick trees and slightly rising terrain.

"I need to keep the chopper from getting alongside," said James putting the nose down further and banking to the right.

The little aluminum airplane swooped low over the river, dipping below the height of the trees. James shoved the throttle to full, pushing the airspeed indicator well into the yellow arc.

The angry chopper, nose to the earth, blades pounding furiously, tailed behind the Cessna, trying to close the distance as each minute brought the two aircraft, the hunter and the prey, closer together. James maneuvered the aircraft with skill and precision, following each bend of the river, staying close to the trees and diving below the occasional power lines.

Madison felt her body start to freeze up, the rush of information accosting her senses.

"We're in the MOA!" shouted Brennan, as if the chopper could hear him.

In fact, the chopper did react. The helicopter pulled up and turned to its right, seemingly giving up the chase. The side with the open door swung around and, as soon as the mini-gun was visible, Madison could see orange and yellow flashes leap from the muzzle.

Madison screamed and ducked behind the padding of the seat as bullets tore through the cabin. It was just a burst though, a parting shot, as the Bell 429 turned and fled.

The parting shot, however, did the most damage. Madison felt a slight vibration that became a violent shaking of the entire aircraft in just a few seconds.

"They got the prop. Help me shut the engine down." James' voice infused with comic vibrato. He turned the magneto switch off and started shutting down the fuel system. As he did this, the aircraft entered a gentle left turn while James turned the yoke until it was fully deflected to the right.

"Damn. I lost roll control," said James, flopping the yoke from side to side. "The ailerons are dead."

"I think I'm bleeding." It was Brennan. He was staring strangely at his hand, covered in blood.

"Stay with me Bren. We're going in. I've still got a little control with the rudder. I'm going to put it down in that field while I can still keep this thing wheels-side-down."

Madison's relief at the helicopter's departure was replaced by the fear of being in an airplane that was coming apart around her. She tightened her seat belt, wondering if there was anything she could do to help. Really, though, the only thing she was equipped to do was to hold on and pray.

The aircraft descended in a gentle glide as the engine sputtered to a stop. The vibration subsided leaving the eerie silence of an airplane gliding towards its inevitable reunion with the earth.

The wounded 182 tended to dip to the left, but was corrected when James pitched the nose up and gave a firm pulse of right rudder. When he did that, the aircraft would yaw smartly to the right, but the left wing would also come up. This nauseating cycle was repeated several times as he attempted to line the aircraft up with the plowed rows of corn in the fast approaching field.

"We've got to clear those trees, James," said Brennan. The field they were headed for was bordered by a line of trees running perpendicular to their path. If they cleared the trees, they'd probably have a bumpy, though safe, off-field landing.

The trees drew closer but, without power, there was little James could do.

"Just a little farther," said James. "Come on, baby."

"We're too low!"

The landing gear hit the trees and crashed through the branches. The aircraft lurched forward, throwing Madison hard against her seatbelt. The 182 slowed but did not flip, smashing the branches like twigs before a fire. James pulled hard against the yoke, flaring the aircraft just enough to avoid hitting the ground nose first. The aircraft stalled, smashed onto its landing gear shearing them off, and plowed a trough of its own through the cornfield in a deafening cacophony of crunching aluminum before finally coming to rest in a disheveled mess.

The quiet that followed the crash was palpable. The whine of the gyroscopes in the instrument panel was the only sound Madison could hear outside of her arrhythmic breathing and the drip of leaking fuel. Madison pushed a bag off of her, one of several that had been launched forward from the baggage compartment.

She let out a moan, more to hear her own voice than to describe any injuries she'd sustained. She was shaken but surprised to find that no part of her body was screaming in pain. Reaching forward she pushed on James' shoulder.

"Nice landing," she said in a sardonic murmur.

But James did not move. He was slumped forward, his weight resting against the shoulder harness. She looked over at Brennan. He too was motionless. His face was turned awkwardly towards her, a grotesque gash on his forehead covering his silent face in blood.

She struggled against her seatbelt, but it wouldn't release.

Madison froze. She couldn't get out. Panic set in. She sat there, pinned in her own aluminum tomb as the drip, drip, drip of leaking fuel ticked like a clock from somewhere behind her. She had to get out.

Minutes passed, seeming like hours, as she struggled with her seatbelt. She fought off despair at the thought of James and Brennan, the only two people in the world who could help her, being unconscious or even worse. Survival came to the forefront of her mind.

Finally, she heard something in the distance, faintly at first but getting louder by the second. She listened carefully, trying to discern the new noise. Her adrenaline spiked again. It was the unmistakable whop-whop-whop of an approaching helicopter.

The irrational panic of the helpless and hopeless leapt from her soul. Screaming for help, she thrashed against her seatbelt, bruising her thighs. She violently punched and shook the seat in front of her.

"Wake up! They're coming back!" she screamed. The sound of the helicopter grew louder. She looked behind her through the back window and there, cresting the trees they had just crashed through, was a large helicopter descending on her position.

But there was something different about this helicopter. It was bigger and beefier than the Sheriff's Bell 429. The helicopter descended and turned away from Madison as it brought itself into a hover. She could read six large plain letters painted in white on the side of the chopper.

US ARMY

VI

COLONEL HESSIAN

"Power is not alluring to pure minds."
Thomas Jefferson

The room was neither opulent nor sparse, neither comfortable nor harsh. The tidy room exuded military precision providing a durable and easily cleaned faux leather couch and chair. Adequate lighting was installed that was neither insufficient nor luxuriously wasteful. The furniture was arranged in neat squares designed to facilitate information transfer without emotional involvement. The room also lacked aesthetic touches of any kind, opting instead for paintings of military hardware and photos of past and current generals. The coffee table held neat, organized magazines informing their readers that the military required neat, organized recruits if the country were to remain free. Madison marveled at the coldness in the room, and remarked inwardly at the inevitable result when men were allowed to decorate without supervision.

Madison sat on the couch in an uncomfortably rigid posture, her back and neck having tightened up like suspension bridge cables since the crash. The metal cuffs chaining her wrists together reminded her that she was not a guest but a prisoner of the US Army.

An old wooden door with a frosted glass window swung open and in marched two men in uniform wearing MP arm bands with holstered pistols at their side. Military Police. They said nothing, but stood on either side of the open door, expressionless, as if there was nothing more to their existence than to walk into occupied rooms and look imposing. A calculated ten seconds later, another man walked in, an officer, moving in a precisely casual way and carrying a fresh manila folder. The man sported a silver eagle on his collar and a chip on his shoulder that manifested itself in an annoyed sneer and the occasional dissatisfied sigh.

"You can uncuff her," he said. One of the MPs moved swiftly to Madison and removed the handcuffs. Madison rubbed her wrists, trying to erase the memory of the pressing metal.

The officer sat in a sterile metal chair directly across from Madison and looked at her with an expression that said *I know who you are and, frankly, I'm not impressed*. It was a look of unquestioned ownership.

"Alright, Miss Green. I am Colonel Hessian. Why don't you start by telling me where the three of you were headed this morning?" He crossed his legs, looked disinterestedly at the corner of the room, and absently picked at his teeth his pinky finger.

Miss Green? Miss Green! Madison's cheeks flushed red as she realized that they were traveling under assumed names, but she didn't know the story. She'd been told that they would have documents made up, but she hadn't even looked at them before falling asleep the night before. There was supposed to be time on the plane to learn all of this. What was her name? Something Green. What was James'? Brennan's? What was their cover story? She had to think quickly.

"Where are my companions?"

The officer raised an eyebrow.

"Mr. Barlow is recovering nicely just down the hall. He's awake and alert. He'll have one hell of a headache for a while, though. Mr. Darby is a little more cut up, but should be alright."

Barlow and Darby. She assumed Mr. Barlow to be James, since Brennan had worse cuts on his face as well as the gunshot wound.

She closed her eyes and images from that morning filled her mind: The blood; The soldiers removing James' and Brennan's limp bodies from the airplane; The rough way they had extracted her from the twisted wreckage; The helicopter ride to the base; The quick check by the doctor and then the hours of silent waiting in this office wondering what was to become of her. She'd never felt so alone.

"One hell of a way to start a marriage, hurm?" said the Colonel with an annoying nasally lilt in his voice. "I guess you'll have to put the wedding off a few days, hurm?"

Madison looked at him. He was either careless or deviously setting a trap for her. There was little she could do but continue to piece together their cover story from what the officer said and to try to confirm as little as possible.

"Yes, we'd hoped for such a more restful honeymoon." Madison tried to look wistful, but couldn't hide her intense scrutiny of the Colonel Hessian's reaction.

"Well, Rome isn't a bad place to get married, if you like that kind of thing. But my question is: Why were you flying through our MOA?"

"I was in the back seat. Why don't you ask my fiancé? He was flying. All I know is that we were flying to a larger airport to catch a commercial flight."

"Well, Janice... can I call you Janice? It looks like your honeymoon has been put on hold for a while. You see, your fiancé did something exceedingly illegal here. And it's my job to see that all responsible parties are appropriately *punished*." As he said the last word he leaned forward, squinting with beady eyes.

"What do you mean?"

"Don't be coy. Your fiancé, is going to jail for a long, long time. Violating active military airspace. Reckless endangerment. Theft of an aircraft. And we haven't even scratched the surface of this little caper." He reached into his pocket and removed a small velvet bag. He dumped The Key of Caligula's Bath out onto the coffee table with a thunk.

"Now, I don't know for sure, but I bet that this little beauty belongs to neither you nor your fiancé." He said *fiancé* with a new level of disdain, rolling his eyes like a spoiled child describing his new homework assignment. "Now, why did Mr. Barlow have this around his neck? Transporting it for the black market? Buying something extravagant? Miss Green, do you know that it's illegal to transport gems across state lines worth more than $50,000 without a license, hurm? That amounts to conspiracy."

"I, I... " Madison could think of nothing to say. She was out of ideas.

The phone on the desk erupted like submarine klaxon. Colonel Hessian picked up the receiver. "Yes sir?" He was clearly talking to a superior.

"Yes sir. Of course, sir…. I do, sir. Yes, once they've recovered from their injuries we'll most assuredly have them on their way… Now, sir?... Absolutely. Yes sir." He hung up the phone and sneered at Madison who still crouched in the corner of the room. He straightened his uniform and brushed some imaginary lint from his lapel.

"It appears…" he said calmly, "that you and your associates have some influential friends. I have been ordered to escort you off of the base immediately and to provide you with transportation. You will take a staff car from the motor pool."

Colonel Hessian left the room and walked to the infirmary where James and Brennan were resting. Madison picked up the ruby arrowhead from the table and followed the Colonel out of the room. Entering the infirmary, Colonel Hessian flipped on the lights and ordered James and Brennan to rise. He explained that they were to leave the facility immediately. James and Brennan took a few moments to gather their bearings and collect their wits.

"Did you recover our gear from the plane crash?" asked James as he dressed. To Madison, James seemed a bit unsteady, but better to leave now than to stay in the realm of this maniac.

"Of course. It's in staging area Bravo. You'll take a staff car from the motor pool. When you reach your destination, call the number on the visor and I will have it returned here. I'll have Horowitz and Swain load your belongings into the vehicle."

"Thank you. Okay, here's the situation, Colonel Hessian," said James. "It's extremely important to us that no one knows we were here. Can you contact Devin Aladore at the Museum of Lost Antiquities and tell him that you have his airplane, or what's left of it? He'll know what to do to tidy things up."

"My superiors have already been contacted by your Mr. Aladore. He apparently is quite influential. As far as I'm concerned, you were never here.

"Alright, let's get out of here. Janice, Darby, let's go." James hobbled out of the room.

The car was loaded quickly, and a few minutes later they drove through the gate and off of the army base. James drove with Brennan wedged into the confined back seat. Madison stared out the passenger window, still and removed.

"He doesn't work for Giovanni too, does he?" she asked.

"No," said James. "Giovanni may be able to pay off small town governments and media outlets, but he doesn't have the power to buy off the military. That's why I knew his helicopter wouldn't follow us."

The setting sun turned the Oklahoma prairie to a melancholy purple and their trip to Dallas continued under cover of night.

"Well, James, your cover is certainly blown."

"Certainly."

"Do you have any idea how difficult it is to set up fake identities for international travel these days?"

"No, Devin, I don't."

"Of course not. You took a hell of a risk flying into the teeth of the military. We couldn't have gotten you out if they found out who you really are."

"It was the only choice I had. I knew Giovanni wouldn't have followed us in there."

"It's going to take me a few days. Can you lay low in Dallas for a while?"

"It's lost time."

"It's not a race anymore, James. Giovanni knows you have the key. And he'll be waiting for you when you get to Rome. If you get to Rome."

"Any progress on why they wanted the girl in the first place?"

"The girl?"

"Madison. Have you found out why Giovanni wanted her?"

"No. But you're on the path to finding out."

"Explain."

"Rome is Giovanni's backyard. When you get there, you can ask him."

"Call me back when things are set up."

"I will. James? Before you hang up…"

"Yes?"

"I got a call from Gordon."

"Gordon Hardbottle?"

"Yes. He's concerned about how messy this is becoming. Airplane crashes, kidnapping, the newspapers, melees in broad daylight, a fracas with the military. This isn't like you. You used to be so discrete."

"That was then."

"I told him I'd keep a close eye on you. Don't let this get out of hand, James. No more mess, okay?"

"Fine."

⁹⌒⋎⌐ᶻᶤ

It was two days before Devin sent them their new travel arrangements, cover story, and identities. James ditched the army's car at the airport and took a taxi to the Red Ranch Inn where they rented two rooms. The Red, as the taxi driver called it with a knowing laugh, was a crumbling motel in an industrial part of town that didn't ask questions, didn't take credit cards, and was genuinely surprised when they wanted to rent the rooms for the entire night. The rooms smelled like gym socks and the mattresses sagged like hammocks. The noise was entertaining at first, nauseating after a couple of hours.

The downtime was good for James, Brennan, and Madison. While James and Brennan had received medical care at the Army base, they needed time to let their bodies heal. Madison's legs bruised spectacularly where she had fought against her seatbelt. Her neck and back also stiffened. Brennan's gunshot wound was more of a grazing than a puncture, but the loss of blood he suffered left him weak. He slept most of the day as his body worked overtime to repair the damage. The gash on James' forehead was sutured shut, but the impact gave him a chronic headache that wouldn't be dispelled by sleep. The pain left him gruff and disagreeable.

Madison spent most of her time taking care of Brennan, sitting by his bed, bringing him food, and making sure he slept comfortably.

ᏝᏨᎿᏏᏏ

A short rap came at Madison's door.

"Yes?"

She heard James' voice through the door. "We got our package."

Fresh out of the shower, Madison finished putting on her make-up, drying her hair and dressing, and then went next door. James was sitting on his bed with a FedEx package on his lap. He had torn the end off and was sifting through its contents. Brennan sat upright on his bed, looking on in anticipation.

"Bren, you're up." She kissed him lightly on the cheek and sat on the bed next to him, looking at him attentively. "How are you feeling?"

"I'm alright. I feel like getting out of this crap-hole. James said you've been taking care of me. Thanks."

"Well, *someone* had to look after you," she said, eyeballing James. James missed the insult, looking over the papers: fake passports, fake drivers licenses, credit cards, and genuine cash. James picked up a book sitting next to him on the bed and tossed it at Madison.

"Here, Devin sent this for you."

Madison caught the book and looked at the cover.

CALIGULA: WHEN POWER CORRUPTS by Dr. Kali Johnns

"Oh joy, a book.". Madison enjoyed reading, but always fiction; always stories of fantasy, adventure, and magic. A historical biography about a long dead ruler excited her about as much as a calculus proof. But she had to admit, she didn't know much about the man and, after all, she was looking for Caligula's hidden keepsakes. Devin was looking out for her.

"Oh, you're going to love this." James laughed out loud reading a piece of paper. "It's our cover story." He laughed aloud. "Oh this is good. Mrs. Lawrence Vash."

Madison snatched the summary out of his hands.

"We're married?" Madison gasped in disbelief at the paper.

"Apparently Devin enjoys torturing me by having us travel as a couple. This time it's our five year anniversary." James smiled.

"And I guess I'm your chaperone, huh?" said Brennan. "Make sure you two don't take this cover a little too seriously."

"Don't worry," James and Madison said simultaneously. They glared at each other, each insulted by the other's response.

"Seriously, why can't we just be three photographers, or three scientists?" asked Madison.

"Actually, we're not three of anything. Brennan is traveling with us, but he's booked separately with his own cover story. Giovanni surely knows that the three of us are traveling together and will be looking for passengers booked to Rome in parties of three. There are far fewer parties of three than there are parties of two and one."

"Oh look, Bren," said Madison reading his cover story. "You're an aspiring novelist doing research for your book. That sounds interesting. Everyone loves a writer, even the pretty girls."

Brennan grinned. "Especially the pretty girls."

"What does this mean? Cabin 9217? Cabin?" Madison asked, looking at the travel arrangements.

"Flip the paper over."

"A cruise? We're going by boat?" Madison stood up at the realization. "It's going to take forever to get there," said Madison.

"A fourteen day transatlantic cruise, Miami, Florida to Rome, Italy," said James. "We catch a plane tonight for Miami. Embarkation is tomorrow noon."

Madison grabbed her new passport, driver's license, a credit card, a copy of the cover summary, and returned to her room in what her mother would have called a "huff". Yes, she was upset by the prospect of pretending to be James' doting wife for the next few weeks, but she was more concerned with hiding her immediate enthusiasm. She had never been on a cruise before; formal dinners, dancing, sunbathing. Madison grinned at the thought. She picked up the phone and called for a taxi. If she was going to be ready to leave tonight for a cruise tomorrow, she would need new clothes. There was shopping to be done.

VII

THE GLAMOUR

"At sea a fellow comes out.
Salt water is like wine, in that respect."
Herman Melville

Hi. I'm Valerie Vash. Lawrence and Valerie Vash. 206 Mulberry Terrace, Branson, Missouri. 417-555-1661. February 13, 1982. This is my husband. Lawrence. He works in floor tile.

Madison recited her information in her head, trying to memorize every detail. She had been caught in Colonel Hessian's office without knowing their back-story, and she was determined to be ready next time.

Hi, I'm Valerie Vash. Mrs. Valerie Vash. My husband Lawrence. 206 Mulberry Terrace, Branson, Missouri. 417-555-1661

"You're going through it again, aren't you?" asked James in a hushed tone as their taxi navigated the stop and go traffic on the way to the port.

"I just want to be ready" said Madison.

"You've been doing that all morning. Don't you know it by now?"

"I don't want to forget."

Madison looked at the foreign ring on her left hand. She couldn't help but play with it and spin it around her ring finger. The platinum-mounted one carat diamond looked strange to her. Stranger yet was the matching platinum band that James wore. She pondered the deceptive jewelry and the false yet tangible connection they shared.

"Oh, here is good," said James to the taxi driver.

The taxi scooted to the curb and delivered James and Madison at the drop-off for embarking passengers. As James and the driver retrieved the luggage from the trunk, Madison stood on the curb transfixed by the towering presence of the cruise ship *Glamour* docked at the pier. *The Glamour* looked like a skyscraper set on end but with the aura of a gargantuan opera house that moved simply through the beauty of its music. Endless streams of humanity pressed into the terminal to board the vessel; refugees from a life devoid of adventure.

"Oh, Lawrence, it's amazing," said Madison, careful to use his cover.

"Grab your things, dear," said James. Then he leaned in closely and muttered "and for God's sake, keep your eyes open."

A dozen buses every twenty minutes, scores of taxis and shuttle busses, and a flood of rental cars all converged on the pier providing a frenzy of activity as three thousand vacationers attempted to board the ship in a two-hour period. Madison and James deposited their checked luggage at the designated drop-off and entered the terminal via the end of a winding waiting line.

"Checking in?" said the chipper agent when they finally shuffled their way up to the counter.

"Yes, my wife and I," said James, handing the agent their passports and ticket books.

"Hi, I'm Valerie Vash," said Madison awkwardly. James squeezed her arm.

"Ah, yes, Mr. and Mrs. Vash, welcome aboard." Madison thought it was a funny thing to say as they were still ashore.

"And I see here that you're celebrating your fifth anniversary. Congratulations, you two. We have a bottle of champagne waiting for you in your stateroom to celebrate. And it looks like a friend of yours sent you a note. You'll find that in your stateroom as well."

"Probably Mom wishing us well," James said to Madison.

"Your luggage should be in your stateroom by 5pm. Dinner is at 6:30pm in the Platinum Lounge, casual dress tonight. Here are your room keycards. They're also the only way to purchase things aboard the ship. No money or credit cards are needed for the next two weeks." She said this as if she couldn't imagine anything more disconcerting than having to pull money from a wallet.

A young girl with lopsided braids at the counter next to them suddenly erupted into a tantrum, "I want it. Mommy! I want it! I want, I want, I want!"

The mother gave a keycard to the young child who immediately stuck it in her mouth. The mother looked at James and Madison with a sheepish smile and shrug of her shoulders.

"They're so cute at that age," said Madison. The agent at the counter smiled in agreement and then called for the next person in line.

"Ugh, children," said James in a low voice as they headed for the security gate.

"I know, right? Not all children, just when they're— like that," said Madison.

"When aren't they like that?"

The line shuffled through the security checkpoint. Cell phones off. Show their IDs again. Up the stairs. Stop for an obligatory picture in front of a fake backdrop of the ship. Meander past the handful of staff members handing out flyers for onboard products and services (all at extra expense, of course), across the gangway into one of the lowest decks of the ship, and into the buzzing lobby. James and Madison officially checked into the ship by getting their picture taken and their keycards swiped into the computers.

The orderly line dissolved into a frenzied chaos once aboard the ship. Madison wandered into the main lobby and was awestruck by the opulence. A wood dance floor surrounded by leather couches and chairs adjoined the pristine winding bar. The lobby danced with ten thousand colored lights and a grand piano that scented the air with the aroma of soft jazz. A bank of four glass elevators rose up towards the soaring skylight seven decks above them. The main lobby was the center of the ship and inspired dizziness in all who reveled in its majesty.

"What are you doing? Stay close to me. Don't wander off." said James in an irritated voice, shattering her wonder like glass.

"Is that how it's going to be? Two weeks of you barking at me, ordering me to stay close, stay paranoid, don't have any fun?"

The crowd swirled around them in a confused mass.

"No, it's just-"

"You're worried and stressed, I know. But, honey, we're celebrating our fifth anniversary." She didn't smile; she wasn't playing. Her message was clear: there was time to enjoy this.

"Alright. Tell you what. Let's go find out where our room is, and then, I'll explore the ship with you- wherever you want to go."

"You want me to lead?" asked Madison.

"Sure. Besides, it's important to know our environment. It'll be good to have some current reconnaissance of the ship. Deck layout, stairs and elevators, information gathering resources, sight lines, weak points, communications services, pertinent escape routes, et cetera." James nodded.

"and…" Madison's voice hung on a high note.

"And?"

"It'll be fun," she said.

James slumped his shoulders and nodded. He led her to the elevators and pressed the button for deck nine, Lido deck, six levels above them.

"Do you think Bren made it okay?" asked Madison when they had reached the Lido deck.

"He's never let me down before. Trust me, he's aboard. I'm sure we'll chance to run into him this evening and we will strike up an engaging and fascinating new friendship with the award-winning author."

The atmosphere of the Lido deck was a refreshing change from the confused Lobby. The Lido deck was the highest full deck on the ship and therefore housed the most pools and hot tubs, the most room for sunbathing, and several fully stocked bars. A handful of cabins were nestled together near the bow of the ship. Two cafeterias sprawled out across the aft end of the ship providing casual dining and expansive views of the horizon from a hundred feet off the water.

Amidships, a calypso band cheerfully played Caribbean tunes as passengers acquainted themselves with the ship's layout. Several experienced cruisers who had smartly packed their swimsuits in their carry-on luggage, enjoyed the various saltwater pools, while first-time cruisers jealously observed.

"Bahama Mama?" asked a perky waitress in a Slovenian accent. She was holding a tray of frozen drinks adorned with paper umbrellas.

"No-"

"Oh, yes please," said Madison as she took a frosty glass from the tray. "Lawrence, be a dear and take care of this?"

James reluctantly presented his card, and signed the bill while the steel drums plinked an energetic tune of staccato eighth notes.

"We should find the room. I'd like to see what that message is all about. Devin may have something for us."

"Can we eat first? If it was really urgent he would have called you on your phone." Madison sipped her beverage. "Come on. The last thing I ate was that stale bagel from the continental breakfast at the motel."

James and Madison headed aft along the ship and found a short Sicilian man serving burgers, hot dogs, and fries from a grill. Madison, looking for more options, continued past the grill and through a set of automatic sliding glass doors. Inside she found an extensive buffet serving a motley assortment of American, Italian, Mexican and Chinese cuisine. A winding line of comfortably clad, plump passengers grazed along the buffet. Madison and James got in line, filled a plate each, and sat down at a nearby table.

"Why don't we have any kids?" asked Madison between mouthfuls of enchilada.

"Why should we?" asked James.

"We've been married five years, yet no kids."

"Not every couple has kids," said James as he swallowed a bite of lasagna.

"But shouldn't we have them by now?"

"Maybe we don't want kids."

Madison's eyes narrowed as she processed a devious new idea.

"Maybe you're sterile."

"I'm not sterile."

"You might be."

"I'm not."

"Maybe you're a huge disappointment to me. Why can't you get me pregnant, Lawrence? What kind of husband are you? I want babies!"

Madison relished this particular brand of teasing. It was awkward and undeniably public; her specialty.

"Can we talk about something else?" James looked around and smiled sheepishly at those who had taken notice.

Madison cut another piece of enchilada and popped it into her mouth.

"You think you're funny, don't you?" said James.

"Maybe."

Madison swayed back and forth like a child enjoying her first bite of birthday cake. She gazed at James with twinkling eyes and hummed a tuneless refrain.

They finished their meal, leaving the trays of dirty dishes for the scurrying busboys, and headed forward to their room.

"Attention passengers," rang a voice over the loud speakers. "Welcome aboard, ladies and gentlemen. This is your cruise director Trevor speaking. Welcome aboard *The Glamour*. We are fifteen minutes from departure, which means we need all of you to go to your muster stations for the lifeboat drill. This is mandatory for all passengers. Please report to your muster stations at this time."

Madison and James were ushered along with 2900 other passengers back down to the Lobby Deck where they received remedial life jacket training, instructions on what to do in the case of an evacuation, and an introduction to the lifeboats and life rafts stationed on the vessel. Madison wondered if this joyless exercise was taken more seriously by passengers after the movie *Titanic* came out.

Madison noticed James carefully observing, not the crew member issuing instructions, but the mechanisms used to launch the lifeboats and other emergency equipment aboard the ship. Covered sixty-foot lifeboats, complete with motor, fuel and survival supplies, hung suspended from steel cranes along the waist of the ship. Racks of metal barrels containing inflatable life rafts lined the wall. Madison had no doubt that, after a few minutes, James knew exactly how to operate these devices. *Was James ever unprepared? Did he ever let down his guard?*

The drill ended, the people dispersed, the music returned, and James and Madison headed back to the Lido deck to find their cabin, this time making use of the carpeted stairs. As they climbed from deck to deck, they heard the unmistakable belch of the foghorn signal their imminent departure. Arriving on Lido deck, James led them forward along a narrow, though brightly lit, hallway to cabin 9217.

"One queen bed," said Madison standing in the doorway. She had pictured and expected two twins.

Madison moved past the cramped bathroom into the deep, yet narrow room and marveled at the paradoxical feeling of confined expansiveness. The bathroom, the sitting area and the vanity area all seemed like scaled down versions of what one would find in a middle class house. However, Madison had to concede that as small as the room was, it still contained those areas along with a full size queen bed, two nightstands, a television mounted on the wall, and a sliding glass door beyond the bed.

Moving past the foot of the bed, she slid the door open and stepped out onto the balcony. The shallow balcony afforded just enough room for two plastic chairs and a small glass table. Opaque dividers on either end endowed the balcony with a limited form of privacy.

"Ah, good. A safe," said James having opened a cabinet door. The safe was large enough for things like money, jewelry, and passports but not much else. Madison stepped back into the room to continue exploring what she would call home for the next two weeks.

"We've got a small refrigerator, too," said James.

He opened the door and took a quick inventory of the neatly arranged alcohol and cheeses; all selling for three and four times their actual value.

"Hello, my bubbly friend," said Madison finding the bottle of Champagne tucked away in the corner of the vanity along with a sealed envelope. "And here's the note."

"It's got to be Devin. I'd be worried if it was from anyone else," said James. He took the note from her, opened it and started reading. Madison could see his body tense as he read. She had the unnerving sensation that he'd stopped breathing.

"Dammit." He dropped the note, threw open the sliding glass door and lunged out onto the balcony. He stood erect for a moment before slumping against the railing.

Madison opened the note and read:

Mr. Lawrence Vash,

Your phone is compromised. Destroy it.

G- knows. Don't know how. Recommend you abandon plan. Ship not safe. Contact me ASAP. Stay alert. G- may have assets onboard.

DA   4 5

3

Shaking with fear, Madison followed James onto the balcony, looked over the railing, and watched the pier slide inexorably into the distance.

VIII

DR. AARON SWORD

"What does this mean, James?" Madison sat on the bed clutching the note as if it would relinquish more information simply by squeezing it.

James leaned against the vanity, lost in thought.

"It means we need to contact him," said James. "We keep cool. We don't blow our cover."

"James, he said there are assets onboard. The same assets that nearly killed me in that car wreck? James? Hey, where are you going?"

Madison chased James out the door, down the hallway and to the flights of stairs.

"I didn't want to do this yet. It'll look suspicious this early in the voyage, but we've got to get a message out." James scurried down the stairs, avoiding the elevators, easily ten steps ahead of Madison.

"Lawrence," said Madison in a commanding voice. James stopped, looked back at her and smiled.

"I'm sorry, dear. Where was my head?" He returned to her, took her by the arm and they continued down the stairs, moving elegantly while admiring the ship. They reached the Promenade deck and glided aft along the shop-lined thoroughfare. Madison felt the warmth of his arm resting comfortably on the small of her back as he escorted her through the ship. It seemed like it had been an age since she had walked in public as part of a couple. She knew this was an act— a farce— and she hated herself for enjoying it. She hated how much she longed for it.

Despite the casino, and the many shops and bars on this deck, there were few passengers on the Promenade deck.

"Argue with me," whispered James. Before Madison could ask him what he meant, he stormed off towards a sprawling bar in the middle of the ship. Aside from a couple of passengers purchasing their "all-you-can-drink" soda fountain cards, the bar and the adjacent casino were empty.

"Well that's not my job, Val," said James. He waited at the bar for the bartender to come to him.

"Well, it's not my job either, Lawrence." She had no idea what his plan was, but she played along.

"Can I help you, sir? Is there a problem?" asked the bartender.

"Yes. My genius wife didn't tell her parents to feed the dog. Is there any way to send email off this boat?"

"Hey, it's your dumb dog. You need to take care of it," said Madison in retort.

"Women. Am I right?" said James leaning against the bar. The bartender nodded in agreement.

"Yes sir, there's an internet café behind the Ivory Room one deck down. It's called Cyberspace," said the bartender. "It's not cheap. I think it's seventy-five cents a minute.

"Seventy-five cents a minute," roared James. "Do you see what you've cost us, dear? Highway robbery."

The bartender shook his head.

Madison and James walked along the waist of the ship, past the sushi bar, several night clubs, a pastry and coffee bar, to the aft stairwell, all the while holding their mock feud.

The internet café, Cyberspace, was a cramped long room sporting a single row of personal computers on one countertop, a shared ink-jet printer in the corner, four bar stools and nothing more. There was nothing that indicated it was a café of any kind. It should have just been called the *Closet of Computers.*

James signed on while Madison took a stool next to him. The automated prompts requested his keycard number, approval to charge their onboard account, acknowledgement of the $5.00 activation fee, acknowledgement of the usage agreement, acknowledgement of their privacy policy, and then showed a legal disclaimer.

At last, James was connected to the internet, signed up for a new email account through Yahoo and composed a new message.

```
    Still   onboard.  Haven't  contacted
author. Confirm there are agents aboard.
How many?  What should we do?
```

James asked, "See the number in the lower right hand corner of Devin's note?"

"'4 5 3'?. What's that mean?"

"It's how we'll communicate. The problem with most codes and ciphers is that they look like codes and ciphers. Gobs of symbols and nonsensical letter combinations. But if someone was to look at this email— and let's face it, Giovanni will— we need to make sure it doesn't look like a secret message."

"I'm assuming the address you're using is a secret account, not Devin's personal email."

"Exactly. Now, watch." James began typing words in between the words he had on the screen. He added three words before the word "still", so that now "still" was the fourth word in the message. He then added four words between the words "still" and "onboard" so that "onboard" was the fifth word after "still", and then put two words between "onboard" and "haven't" so that "haven't" was the third word after "onboard". Four, Five, Three. James continued adding words, and changing case and punctuation, until the message was lost in a completely different message:

```
    Hi.  Well, Valerie still can't stand
the  food  onboard.  And we haven't yet
even  been  contacted by your absolute
favorite  author.  Can  you  confirm
whether  or  not  there  are reservations
required?   We  are  convinced  travel
agents  are  just  lazy.  Aboard  the
Princess  line,  oh  how  we  loved  many
amenities that aren't what I would call
```

extravagant. Should or shouldn't we
plan to next do something else?

"See? It looks like a spoiled American couple whining about their cruise, with, I'll admit, some awkward grammar. But when Devin reads the fourth, then fifth, then third word, and so on, repeating the pattern, Devin will get our message."

James clicked *send* and logged off.

"It'll be a while before he gets his reply back to us. He's a bit slow when it comes to encoding his messages," said James.

"What do we do in the meantime?"

"How about dinner?"

✽✽✽

The dining room was a grand, two-deck affair, with a wide staircase in the center, dark red carpeting and intimate lighting. The dining room was at the extreme aft of the ship on the Lobby and Atlantic decks. Large tinted windows lined the back of the dining room revealing the milky wake of the ship bubbling in the twilight. The polished brass around the structural supports and windows, the fine white china, the smartly dressed wait staff, and the tuxedoed maitre d' brought a sense of sophistication and class to the otherwise fundamental task of feeding 800 people in an hour and a half.

One of the assistant head waiters indicated towards a booth in the corner with eight place settings. "Table 102, madam and sir." James and Madison slid into their assigned booth.

"You see him?" asked Madison.

"Not yet. He'll be here. Don't worry," said James.

A round man in a blue floral shirt, cargo shorts, and sandals approached the table and shouted over his shoulder, "Honey. Kids. Here's our table." He motioned to an even larger woman wearing over-sized sunglasses, and two stocky boys who were in the midst of a confrontation involving punching and twisting each others' nipples. The well-fed family bounced and jostled their way into James and Madison's booth.

"Hi. I'm Michael Anderson—oops, sorry about that," said the man, extending his gelatinous arm to shake hands while knocking over an empty wine glass. "And this is my wife Judy Anderson. This here is Grant, he's eleven, and his little brother is Charles. He's nine. Say 'hi' kids." The kids didn't.

James introduced himself and Madison. They exchanged pleasantries while the two boys entertained themselves by pounding on the edges of their spoon on the table and seeing how high they could flip them.

"This ya'll's first time cruisin'?" asked Judy.

"Yes. It's our first cruise," said Madison.

"Oh, well you two love-birds are just going to love it," said Judy in an enthusiastic voice that far exceeded what was required by decorum. James squirmed in his seat and tapped his fingers on the table.

"So what kind of work ya in, Lawrence?" asked Michael as he perused the menu.

"Floor tile. I'm in sales," said James. Madison was relieved they were not going to follow the *love-bird* thread of the conversation.

"Well, I'll be. Floor tile, no kidding," said Judy, both of her chins wobbling excitedly. "Just like you, Michael. You know, Michael works in floor tile too."

"What kind of tile, Lawrence? Granite? Ceramic? Self adhesive? You aren't one of those linoleum boys, are ya?"

James glared at Madison. It occurred to her that James was searching for the proper four letter expletive to mutter under his breath.

"No, no. No linoleum for me. I'm more in the ceramic tile line. Bathrooms, kitchens,…uh… kitchenettes."

"Yeah? So who's your distributor? Allied? Consolidated?" The man had come alive in this discussion about work.

"Oh, we have a number of distributors."

"How many pallets a month, ya do?"

Madison could see that James had no idea what a reasonable number of pallets per month would be. She decided to help him out.

"Now Lawrence, you promised me you wouldn't talk shop on our vacation. I tell you, with him it's always work, work, work. You know what I mean Judy?" Madison said with her best housewife impression.

"Oh, I hear you, doll. Once you get Michael going about tile, he'll talk your ear off. Okay, no shoptalk at the dinner table. But still, what a remarkable coincidence."

"Yes. Remarkable." James took a long drink of his water.

"Good evening and welcome to the Platinum Dining room." The head waiter, a distinctly Middle Eastern man who spoke with a curious lisp, arrived with small note pad and a congenial smile.

He took drink orders and explained the menu to the guests. There were a handful of selections for appetizers, entrees, and desserts.

"And of course, you may order as much as you care to eat."

"Thank God. So, I know you aren't American? Where you from?" asked Michael in a particularly indelicate way.

"Pakistan. I am hoping to-"

"Pakistan? You ain't a terrorist, are ya?" Michael laughed at his joke. The only other person laughing was his plump wife. She seemed to think everything he said was clever.

"I'll give you a few more minutes to decide." The waiter nodded and left the table.

If I have to eat dinner with the Anderson family every night, I may kill that man before we hit Rome, thought Madison.

A few minutes later the waiter returned, took their order and quietly left. He no longer smiled and spoke as little as possible.

Judy changed the subject. "How long you two love-birds been married?"

"We're actually celebrating our five-year anniversary this trip. Five years tomorrow." Madison looked at James.

James and Madison made small talk with the Anderson family, finding that they were from DeLand, Florida, a small town between Daytona Beach and Orlando, that they were on their sixth cruise in four years, and, above all, the thing they loved the most about cruising was the unlimited food.

"Shoot, I can barely feed the family for what it costs for one of these cruises," Michael exclaimed.

A minor commotion aroused the suspicions and concern of the dozens of people around them. James looked over Madison's shoulder and pointed with a flick of his chin. She turned around and saw the maitre d', a head waiter, and an assistant waiter approaching while carrying place settings and several glasses. A fourth person behind them, whom she couldn't see clearly, uttered threats and ultimatums that conveyed righteous indignation.

"If I'm to be put on this vessel, I demand to be treated respectfully. That waiter was rude beyond the pale," said the man.

The entourage stopped at James and Madison's table.

"Excuse me, sirs and madams," said the maitre d'. Typically we don't move people around, but this gentleman insisted on new accommodations. You have six at a table of eight. Would you mind if we added him to your table?" The question wasn't asking permission, but a polite way of informing the guests of what was to happen.

"Sure, I can't see the harm in it," said Judy, usurping her husband's right to object.

"Thank you. Sir, your table." The maitre d' motioned to the table, and the waiter and assistant set his plates, silverware, wine glass and water glass at the table and then left in a hurry.

A man in a light blue, three-piece suit and narrow wire-framed glasses sat down at the table and scoffed at the way in which his silverware had been callously placed on the table.

"Careless. All of them. Well, I do hope these accommodations are less offensive to me. Good evening, I'm Dr. Aaron Sword. The author."

❦

Madison cut into her roast duck, savoring her first fine-dining experience since before the car accident that started this whirlwind adventure a week earlier. In fact, it had been months since her last dinner out, a particularly forgettable date with an older gentleman whose name she couldn't remember.

James, who'd also ordered the duck, seemed to appreciate the soothing quiet that came over the Anderson family as they no longer spoke when food was before them. It was a little like watching vultures feast on the only lion carcass left in the Serengeti.

Brennan, on the other hand, completely disappeared into the role of Dr. Aaron Sword— pompous author-at-large. His personality dominated the table as he tore into his swordfish platter.

"I believe it was when I was in the Orient, doing research for my best-selling novel *Faces of Ginseng*," he paused a moment to allow the Anderson couple to nod dimly, "that I last had swordfish. Of course, in that part of the world, swordfish is prepared with a mix of local spices and banzai tree extract. This swordfish, mind you, might as well be battered, fried, and dunked in tartar sauce for all the care the chef has given it. It is a singular trait of the cruise ship chef to promise the finest dishes to a captive audience and then to disappoint so catastrophically. If you ask me, it's not unlike asking for water and being given a sponge of vinegar, not that I have much of a Messianic complex, mind you, ha ha."

Brennan chuckled to himself, adjusting his wire rimmed spectacles, and then continued before the Andersons could change the subject to something more interesting.

"I daresay, you've noticed the incongruous design of this room, no doubt." The others looked around meekly at the elegant lines of the dining room.

"Perhaps it is an inside joke amongst interior designers to mix carpeting that screams Louis XV with the clearly Victorian wallpaper. Perhaps they intended us to ponder the differences of 150 years or the cultural implications of the separation of the English Channel. But I doubt it. Now, I assure you that I am no Edith Wharton, but I did conduct considerable research for my novel *He Shot His Mouth Off*, of which you're no doubt familiar— where an aspiring young interior designer meets his demise in the form of a haphazardly discharged concrete anchor gun. The fact that he was also a braggart was merely a coincidence, I assure you. But one thing I did learn in that research was that continuity of design is paramount to successful interior decoration."

"I think it looks nice," said Judy Anderson, venturing a sheepish smile at Brennan.

Dr. Sword's fork clattered noisily on the plate as he sat back contemptuously in his chair.

"Of course you do. It is the simpletons of this world that allow the vile raping of the arts for the consumption of the masses on the basis that it 'looks nice'," said Brennan with a scowl.

Mrs. Anderson gasped. Madison suppressed a smile.

"Well, kids, what do you say we hit the arcade before bed? Sorry to interrupt your lecture, Dr. Sword, but we'd better be getting along." Michael Anderson's suggestion met mild resistance from the kids who protested with their desire for dessert. Faint promises were made about attending the ice cream bar, followed by vague salutations to their table mates, before the massive family of four waddled out of the dining room. Madison noticed the spiteful stare they gave the maitre d' as they left.

"Thank God," said James once they were out of ear shot.

"Bren, you were incredible! Sorry— Aaron. Did you make that all up as you went?" asked Madison.

"Shhhh. I've managed to draw a good deal of attention. But hey, my guess is that's the last you'll see of the Anderson family. I've got fifty bucks that says they'll be dining at the buffet for the remainder of the cruise."

"So, Dr. Sword, did you find your accommodations to your liking?" James asked.

"Oh, God. You wouldn't believe how screwed up things were. First, they almost didn't let me on the ship because I gave them the wrong birth date. For some reason I was thinking March instead of May. My mistake. Of course they were curious how someone could forget their own birthday. That's when I developed the pompous author character because it's much easier to believe that someone is mistaken if he presumes to know everything.

"They finally let me on board, but when I got to my room— which, by the way is on the lowest deck in the entire ship— there was already luggage in it, but it wasn't mine. Turns out they had me booked with another guy from Portugal. Nice enough guy, but it wouldn't work. I complained that I paid for a room for myself, and then they moved me to this interior closet of a room with two twin beds and three pillars stationed in the middle of the room. I still haven't seen my luggage, but hey, at least we're all safely aboard, right?"

"Not exactly." James slid Devin's note across the table. Brennan took the note and read it. He was quiet for a few moments.

"You contact him?" Bren glanced around the dining room.

"Email."

"What'd he say?"

"Haven't got a response yet. Look, we can't talk here. We're in room 9217. Meet us there after dinner. Make sure no one follows you."

"I'm ordering dessert first. There's some crème brulee calling my name," said Brennan.

"Okay. We'll go check the email account. See you at the room. Come along, darling."

"Goodbye, Dr. Sword." Madison took James' arm. She winked at Brennan as James escorted her out of the dining room.

❦

James logged in, signed in to his email account and found one unread message waiting for him. He clicked on the email:

SUBJECT: Happy Cruising

Your uncle said he is absolutely certain he knows which ship you are on. He went off to Europe to buy things to ship for Christmas. A leak onboard worries your mom in every way travel worries her.

The agency representatives called us while we dined to use your latest resume. He said your boss really doesn't seem to know you've even applied, which could make the whole ship sink quickly. Though, I've still found there is hope that last May was to be your best work.

Agents will not take everyone aboard, you know. Now there's either one or two remote possibilities that they'll want to join with the troupe at this uncertain time.

But, your hope that next week you
can stop auditioning is absolutely
foolhardy. If you think so much of
yourself, it'll be your downfall to
only audition to be seen when the one
job you really want or maybe the two
jobs are from agents you're not talking
to. Find them, call them.

Do this quickly before time runs out
and they no longer find anything
interesting in you.

Love,
Dad

"Geez, Devin. Could you be more awkward?" James clicked the
print icon, sending the message to the shared printer in the corner.

"I think it's pretty clever," said Madison.

James took a highlighter from his pocket and highlighted the
fourth, then fifth, then third word, repeating the pattern until the
message was decoded.

"What's it say?"

He handed her the message and logged off the computer.

SUBJECT: Happy Cruising

Your uncle said he is absolutely
certain he knows which ship you are on.
He went off to Europe to buy things to
ship for Christmas. A leak onboard
worries your mom in every way travel
worries her.

The agency representatives called us
while we dined to use your latest
resume. He said your boss really doesn't
seem to know you've even applied, which

could make the whole ship sink quickly. Though, I've still found there is hope that last May was to be your best work.

Agents will not take everyone aboard, you know. Now there's either one or two remote possibilities that they'll want to join with the troupe at this uncertain time.

But, your hope that next week you can stop auditioning is absolutely foolhardy. If you think so much of yourself, it'll be your downfall to only audition to be seen when the one job you really want or maybe the two jobs are from agents you're not talking to. Find them, call them.

Do this quickly before time runs out and they no longer find anything interesting in you.

Love,
Dad

"Let's head back to the room," said James.

❦

When they returned to their room, James and Madison discovered that their luggage had been delivered. After unpacking his things, James flipped on the TV in the stateroom and scrolled through the available channels. Several movie channels, a few news channels, and two cable-access-quality ship-produced channels were all that were offered.

"I guess you're not supposed to watch TV on a cruise," he said. Madison stood over an open drawer, unpacking the last of her clothes into the built-in dresser. She took the empty suitcases and shoved them under the bed.

"Oh, this is kind of cool," said James.

He had found a channel that consisted solely of a computer-generated map of the Atlantic Ocean with the ship's position, heading, and speed, along with the planned route and current sea conditions plotted on it. The state of Florida loomed large on the left side of the screen.

A rap at the door broke James from the spell that kept him transfixed on raw, real-time data.

"That'll be Bren," he said.

James opened the door and discovered his presumption to be wrong. Standing in the doorway wearing a smart grey frock and comfortable shoes, was a dark-haired woman looking up at him. The woman was a full foot and a half shorter than James, and her petite stature made her easy to confuse with a long-haired twelve year old boy.

"Hello, Mr. and Mrs. Vash. Welcome aboard. I am Lupe, your room stewardess. I will be taking care of your room for you," she said in a thick South American accent.

"Ah, I was wondering when you were going to stop by," said James. "So you're the person we call if we need anything, is that right?"

"Si. Just call 'attendant'," she said, referring to one of several pre-programmed buttons on the phone.

"Out of curiosity, Lupe, how often will you be in and out of our room?" James tried not to offend with the question, but it still sounded like he didn't trust her.

"Oh, usually two or three times a day. We clean room while you are having the breakfast, and, of course, turn down your bed during dinner. Then there are times when we drop off newsletters and things like that during the day." She wrung her hands. "You know how to work safe, no?"

"Yes, Lupe, we do. Thank you."

"You be needing anything else, tonight?" she asked.

"No. I think we're okay. Sweetheart, did you need anything from Lupe?" asked James.

"No. Thank you."

"Well, my room is at end of hall, so please call if you need something." Lupe smiled and walked down the hall to knock on the door of the room next door as James shut the door.

Madison flopped on the bed, picking up the newsletter that highlighted the evening's entertainment as well as the schedule for the following day.

"The *Welcome Aboard* show starts in half an hour, if you're interested," she said. "'Las Vegas style show' it says."

James looked at her as deep furrows appeared on his forehead.

"What?" She was somewhat surprised by his reaction.

"You know this isn't vacation right?"

"We have to maintain our cover."

"Yeah. We also have to keep from getting killed. You want something to do tonight? You can do some research." He tossed her the book Devin had sent her about Caligula.

"I'm not staying cooped up in this room for two weeks."

"Well, you're not going out and sunbathing all day, either. We leave the room for meals and that's it."

"You're insane. Since when did you think you were in charge of me?"

"Since you joined our expedition. Look, it wasn't my idea to go by ship to Europe."

"And it wasn't my idea to have people chase me and burn down my apartment so that I had nowhere to go but join your stupid *expedition*." She mocked the last word.

"Look, sister-" A knock came at the door. James, thankful for the interruption, looked out the peep-hole and saw Brennan, still in his three-piece suit standing patiently in the hall. James opened the door.

"Practicing your bickering, I hear. Convincing," said Brennan as he entered the room.

"The warden was just informing me that I was a prisoner in this room," said Madison moving from the bed to the couch. Brennan picked up the book lying next to Madison on the bed. He flipped through it tossed it aside and sat on the end of the sofa.

"James, you can't expect her to sit and read a book for two weeks. This is a cruise ship."

"It's for her own safety. This is what Devin sent back." James handed over the note with the highlighted words. Brennan read it several times, pausing occasionally to consider Devin's precise choice of words.

"'Leak in travel agency we use'," he quoted, "That's a little disconcerting. It sounds like our travel agent told Giovanni that we were going by ship, but didn't tell them which ship."

"Yeah, but how many ships are making Trans-Atlantic crossings right now? Not many. I bet Giovanni only had a handful of ships to track with his agents," said James.

"Well, maybe they couldn't get aboard on time. We only had one day notice," said Brennan.

"That's why he warns against agents coming on board at our next stop."

"Well that's Madeira, off the coast of Portugal," said Madison. "That's over a week away."

"That's true. If that's the case then we've got ten days of sanctuary," said James.

"Oh, I hope that's the case. It'd be so nice to be able to relax," said Madison thinking about spending hours on deck soaking in the warm sun, sitting in the bubbling pools, and sipping mixed drinks from the bar.

"'Find them before they find you'," Bren quoted from the note. "I wonder what that means. Could it be that they don't know who they're looking for. Or they will recognize you but don't know what room you're in." He sat on the couch next to Madison.

"I think it means that we have a job to do. Find the agents who are tracking us. Identify them before they can find us. They may be passengers or they may be crew members."

"They may not even be on board," said Madison.

"True. But we can't make that assumption," said James. "We keep our eyes open. We try to find out who's been asking questions, who's been following us, and so forth. We trap them into betraying their identity without betraying ourselves. The ruby arrowhead goes to Brennan's room. You have a safe there too, right Bren?"

"Yeah, all the rooms do."

Madison yawned, realizing how tired she was. Though it was still early, it had been a long day and the soft queen bed was calling to her.

"Sounds like a plan. I'm going to bed," said Madison. "It's getting late and I'm one tired girl. So besides the ruby arrowhead, you know what else is going to Brennan's room?"

"Your husband?" said James.

"Exactly. Good night, boys," said Madison escorting the two men towards the door.

"Actually, I thought it would be a good idea if I crashed in here for the night," said James. His shoulders came up and an air of uncertainty crept into his voice. "You know, to preserve our cover story. I'd sleep on the floor," he added almost defensively.

"I don't think so James. You can change clothes in here in the morning, and keep your stuff here. But the staff have gone to bed. There's no reason for you to actually spend the night here."

James started to protest, but quickly gave up the chase instead opting to say goodnight. Madison wished them sweet dreams and closed the door.

She undressed and put on a silk nightgown she'd purchased while in Dallas. She slipped between the sheets of the queen bed, falling asleep to the constant murmur of the engines and the gentle, soothing rhythm of the rocking of the ship.

IX

HAVOC AND DISORDER

"If you must break the law, do it to seize power:
in all other cases observe it."
Julius Caesar

Having slept with the drapes open, Madison was nudged awake as the early morning light gradually flooded her room. The first images she saw as she opened her eyes were the dancing reflections on the ceiling from the sun bouncing off of the tops of the waves. She awoke feeling rested, peaceful and above all, content. The rocking of the ship had given her some of the deepest sleep she'd experienced in her adult life.

Madison rose and slid open the glass door leading to the private balcony. The gentle hum of the ship's engine and the soothing sound of the wind rushing past her door awakened her senses. The cool ocean air spilled into the room and around her body. Her skin tingled, coming alive at the soft touch of the salty air. In that moment, she forgot the breathless pace of her life, the danger, and fear of the unknown these past few weeks had brought.

She enjoyed the moment and the precious time alone, then showered and readied herself for the day. When James finally knocked on the door, she was already nestled into one of the chairs on the balcony and had just finished the first chapter in *Caligula: When Power Corrupts;* the book Devin had given to her.

"I hope you slept well in that massive queen bed. It's twice the size of my little cot. Did you manage to enjoy yourself while I was gone?" James stepped into the room.

"Yes, it was nice to have some me-time."

"So, how's the book?"

"It's a little disturbing," she answered, returning to her chair on the balcony.

"What're you finding out?"

"Gaius Julius Caesar Augustus Germanicus. That was his real name. But somehow they got 'Caligula' out of that."

"It was a nickname he picked up as a child." James sat down in the other chair on the balcony. "It means 'little boots', specifically 'little soldier boots'."

"I guess I haven't gotten to that part yet. The book is really just giving the lay of the political landscape. It seems that all you had to do to be emperor back then was to kill off all the other heirs."

"That's not too far from the truth. Rome was a bit like the American old west back then: Might makes right. If you commanded the largest army and persuaded enough senators, you could rule the empire. That's how Julius Caesar set up the empire, and how the subsequent emperors were basically chosen." James put his feet up on the railing and slumped in his chair.

"Okay, so Julius Caesar was the first emperor, right?" Madison flipped through the pages looking for some sort of diagram. James had it all in his head.

"No. Caesar was essentially *Roman Dictator*. Ruler for life. He transformed the Roman Republic to the Roman Empire and started the first line of Emperors, but he was never emperor himself. His nephew, Caesar Augustus, more formally known as Gaius Octavius Thurinus, was the first emperor of the Roman Empire."

"Right, in 27 BC he was adopted," read Madison, "and became Gaius Julius Caesar Octavianus… geez, why do these people have so many names?"

"It's how they traced their lineage. That was critically important back then. Just call them what we call them now. It'll help keep things straight."

"Okay. So Julius Caesar, sets up the Roman Empire. His nephew and adopted son Caesar Augustus is the first Roman Emperor. That's the same Caesar Augustus as in the Bible right? At the time of Christ?"

"One and the same."

"So, then comes Caligula?" Madison knew that it didn't sound right and scowled at the book as she flipped through it.

"No, Caesar Augustus' step-son is Tiberius. Tiberius becomes the second Roman Emperor. Tiberius was known as one of Rome's greatest generals, but not an exceptionally good emperor. In fact, some claim he never really wanted to be emperor."

"Is that true?"

"I don't think so. Although it's disputed, I think once his own son died in 23 AD, he kind of went crazy and started killing people that would threaten his rule."

"A charming man, I'm sure. So he is succeeded by Caligula. But…" Madison looked up from her book, brow furrowed, "Caligula is his *grandson*. What happened to the guy in between?"

"Germanicus?"

"Yeah, him. Why didn't he become emperor?"

"That is a wonderful question. And I could go on discussing Roman politics for hours." James stood up, leaned against the railing and delicately pulled the book from Madison's hands. "But, I am absolutely starving. So I say, let's take a break and go get some breakfast."

"You mean you're going to let me out of my room?"

"Perhaps. Just this once. Shall we?"

✥

James and Madison walked aft along the ship, passing the first of the morning sunbathers, and entered the Red Tail café at the back of the ship. This morning the buffet was full of scrambled eggs, hash browns, sausage, bacon, waffles, a myriad of fresh fruit, assorted breads, jams, yogurts, cereals, and smoked salmon. There was also a separate line for those who wanted a fresh omelet made by a dedicated omelet chef. Madison shook her head at the sheer variety offered to her. She couldn't think of a single breakfast food that wasn't represented at the buffet.

James and Madison quickly went through the line and then, walking past a bar and one of the four salt-water pools, they took a table at the extreme aft of the ship with an inspiring view of the sea below. A wide milky swath of ocean churned and bubbled behind the ship.

Madison was surprised by James' change in demeanor as they were now out in public. He had seemed so relaxed and comfortable in the room that morning, but now that they were in public, he was constantly scanning those around him. He looked at others like he was looking through them, discerning their secrets and their unstated ambitions. James took a seat with his back to the ocean so he could watch everyone in the café.

Madison took a bite of a croissant. "It's funny, I keep having The Love Boat theme song playing in my head."

"Love boat?" he asked with raised eyebrows.

"Not, Love... I mean, you know. We're on a cruise ship. Actually, it was on before my time, but I've seen the reruns."

James looked at her as if she'd just read him the Magna Carta in Latin.

"♪The Loooove Boooat, promises something for everyone♪..." she sang. "You've never seen *The Love Boat*? Are you kidding me?"

"I've never heard of it," he said, taking a sip of coffee.

"Okay, seriously. What's your story? You've never heard of The Love Boat or Indiana Jones. What kind of childhood did you have?" Madison sat back in her chair like an inquisitor demanding a satisfactory explanation.

"One different from yours, I guess."

"You didn't grow up in the States, did you?" Madison detected a bit of evasion on James' part.

James took his napkin, wiped his mouth and then drained his coffee mug. He looked around one more time and then reluctantly began to speak.

"I didn't have your typical American upbringing. I didn't have Saturday morning cartoons, weekends at the mall and new clothes every fall. I grew up in a rough-shod hut with nothing but the forest, the villagers and my imagination to entertain me. I grew up in the Philippines."

"You don't look Filipino," said Madison.

"I'm not Fili-," James sighed, "My parents were missionaries," he said at last.

"You were a missionary kid? So you probably didn't get much network TV in the jungle, did you?" she said.

"Not exactly. I mean, I went to a boarding school for missionary kids in the city. We came back to the States for furloughs and stuff, so it's not like I was completely removed from civilization."

"So what did you do for fun as a kid? I assume you were outside for most of it."

"I spent most of my childhood exploring the secrets of the jungle. My friends and I, usually local Filipino boys, would go off for an entire week. We'd find old relics from the Spanish. Sometimes we'd find whole settlements that had been swallowed by the jungle."

"It sounds like you're still out playing."

"Some people grow up and others just grow older. I figured I'd stop this whole relic-finding business when I grew out of it. Hasn't happened yet. There's something that excites me; that makes me feel alive when I'm out in the field, discovering things that have been hidden for hundreds or thousands of years. It's like being the first person to open a lost history book, one that tells you who you are, where you came from, and what you're here for." James squinted towards the sun, now towering above the open ocean.

"Oh joy. Here come your buddies," James said. Madison looked up and saw the Andersons waddling towards them, each carrying two plates of breakfast foods.

Michael Anderson said "Well fancy this. Good morning, Mr. and Mrs. Varnish." His wife and two sons followed behind him.

"It's Vash," said James.

"Did y'all guys see the show last night? Good music, some fun jokes and the dancing girls... mmmm," said Michael Anderson sitting down at the table next to James and Madison.

"Oh, Michael, don't be a pig," said his chortling wife.

"I tell ya Larry, those girls don't wear nothin' but a little piece of dental floss under those itty-bitty skirts. Did ya notice?" The man crammed an entire pancake into his mouth.

"No. Valerie and I turned in early last night. We missed the show," said James.

"Oh, that's right, Michael. Of course the little lovebirds would rather spend time alone in their room than at the show." Mrs. Anderson laughed and then managed to suck down a container of yogurt in a single slurp. Madison was starting to get mildly nauseous watching the Andersons eat.

"Sorry we left you with the professor there last night. I guess you could say that he's not really our kind of people," said Michael.

"Oh that's fine. We understand," said James. "Dr. Sword isn't most people's kind of people. I've found that the intelligentsia seldom interests the rest of us. Still, he does make some interesting points."

Michael and Judy sat slack jawed, food showing between their parted teeth.

"Uh huh... Well, I think the kids would rather just eat pizza and burgers for dinner anyways, so I don't know how much we'll be seein' ya'll at dinner," said Judy finally.

"Oh, of course. We understand completely," said Madison. "Well, I think I'm ready to get into my swimsuit. How 'bout you, Lawrence?"

"I wouldn't mind getting into your swimsuit, either," James said. Madison turned red with embarrassment while the Andersons erupted in horrifying guffaws. James and Madison excused themselves from the table.

Madison punched James in the shoulder as they walked through the carpeted halls back towards their stateroom. James snickered.

"Intelligentsia? Wow..." said Madison finally admitting that James had handled the Andersons brilliantly. "That was amazing. You might as well have just held up a sign saying 'Do not converse with us'."

"Ah, the power of a single word."

≈⚔≈

Madison and James lay side by side on two chaise lounges one deck above the Lido deck on the Panorama deck. They had chosen a couple of chairs far from the other sunbathers. Contrary to what they had told the Andersons, Madison had not changed into her swim suit and instead lay in the shade under an awning in a thin, white halter top and khaki shorts. The ocean breeze and majestic view of the sea proved restful and inspired her to return to her book on Caligula.

"Poisoned," said Madison.

"I'm sorry?"

"Germanicus. He was poisoned," said Madison putting down her book, "so he never got a chance to become Emperor."

"That's right, but poisoned by who?" asked James, looking up. He also rested in the shade, though instead of reading, he carefully looked around the deck and occasionally scribbled in a leather-bound journal in his lap.

"Well, he was in Antioch at the time. That's in Asia, right? But it doesn't really say who killed him."

"Because we don't know. Some speculate that it was Piso, the governor of Syria, acting on his own. But more likely it was Piso at the order of Tiberius."

"Why would Tiberius order the assassination of his own son?"

"His adopted son," corrected James. "Well, Germanicus had grown in popularity after stunning victories in Germania and Asia. No doubt Tiberius was afraid that Germanicus would come back to Rome and have all the support he needed to usurp Tiberius' power."

"So what does this have to do with Caligula?"

"It has everything to do with Caligula. Once Germanicus, his father, was killed, his mother, Agrippina the Elder brought the family back to Rome. Only one problem…"

"The family was just as much of a threat as Germanicus."

"Exactly. Caligula was almost as well known and well liked as Germanicus. He was with his father in Germania as a young kid. The empire thought of him as their little mascot. Think of JFK Jr. in the '60s. Heir apparent, well mannered."

"So Caligula's mom brings the family back to Rome and," Madison flipped a few pages, "people start dying."

"Yes, mysteriously. Agrippina, first, then most of Caligula's brothers."

"And so Caligula flees to Capri to hide from Tiberius, right?"

"No. First he lives with a bunch of his relatives, but it isn't really his choice. He's essentially a political prisoner. Then, he goes to Capri to be with Tiberius."

There was a long pause.

"Explain that."

"Well, Caligula, instead of running from Tiberius, endears himself to Tiberius, his adopted grandfather. Tiberius nearly kills Caligula's entire family but curiously spares Caligula."

"Caligula had to have known it was Tiberius who was killing his family. How could he live with a man like that?"

"It's a great question. However he did it, he convinced Tiberius that he could be trusted. Tiberius even gave him a quaestorship."

"A whose-er-what-ship?" asked Madison.

"Like trustees in a church. They watch the money and make sure the empire's spending is accounted for."

"So Tiberius dies in 37 AD and Caligula becomes emperor. No wonder Caligula was screwed up. You'd be screwed up too with an upbringing like that."

"Well don't feel too sorry for the guy. Actually, Tiberius named Caligula and his own grandson Gemellus as joint heirs, but as soon as Tiberius died, Caligula had the will nullified on reasons of insanity: a clever political trick. And some claim that Tiberius was murdered in his sleep and that it may have even been Caligula that murdered him."

"Like I said, with an upbringing like that-"

"You two are unbelievable." Brennan approached, carrying a book, and stood over Madison's chaise lounge with a disgusted look on his face. He grabbed the book from her hands, pulled the dust jacket from his own book, placed it around her book and returned it to her. "There may be agents on this boat looking for us, and you're sitting here reading a book on Caligula."

Madison turned the book over and read the dust cover.

"Oh, this is much better. Now I'm reading something much less conspicuous." She held up the book so that James could read the cover.

```
Twelve Secrets for Nailing Any Girl
in the Bar by Brock Johansen.
```

James laughed out loud.

"Yes, much less conspicuous," said James between chuckles.

"Well, maybe she's into other girls," said Brennan.

"I think not. I'm a married woman, after all. I'll get a different dustcover from the gift shop. Why are you reading this?"

"Oh, it's a classic in my library. I brought it along so I could brush up. You get rusty pretty quickly," he said. Then he turned to James, "So, found our agent yet?"

"Not yet. We've run into that family from dinner but that was probably coincidence. Giovanni usually doesn't involve kids. No, I think we're looking for either a couple, man and woman, or two single agents operating independently."

"Recognize anyone up here?" asked Brennan.

"No. There's not a lot of overlap between dinner, breakfast this morning, and here on the deck. Of course, once they make us, they probably will keep themselves pretty scarce."

"They know what we look like, right?" asked Madison.

"Probably. But it's a big ship. First they have to find us, and then they have to track us to find out where our room is," said James. "What would you do if you were them, Bren?"

Brennan ran his hand through his hair and then scratched at his cheek.

"If it was me? I'd lay low for a couple of days, and not force anything. If I find you, then I find you. If not, I've still got 12 more days on the cruise. Then, once I spot you, I'd follow you to your room and note it, and then come back when you weren't there to search it."

"That's what I was thinking. Maybe we need to set a trap."

"What do you mean?" asked Madison.

"I can't stand being a target. Let's bait our pursuer; from mark to marksman."

"What if there aren't any agents on the ship?" asked Madison.

"Then we'll get some practice in before we get to Rome. You don't think things are going to get easier once we hit Italy, do you?"

"What do you have in mind, chief?" asked Brennan.

"People on cruise ships go to their rooms at weird times; sometimes to change clothes, sometimes to nap, sometimes to get a book or whatever; never at a predictable time. But there's one time when you can count on people heading to their room."

"Bedtime," said Madison.

"Exactly," said James. He closed his journal as if the idea was now final. "And if they think they're tracking a married couple, they could look for us in the evening show and then track us right to our room, minimizing their exposure."

"So you two go to the show tonight," said Brennan, "and I'll track anyone who follows you when you leave. Of course you don't go to your room."

"Of course not. We'll just lead him through the hallways long enough to be sure that we're being followed and you can either identify him, or jump him if you get into a confined space."

"Maybe he can go for a swim," said Brennan with excitement on his face.

"Let's not get ahead of ourselves. We'll want to question him first."

"Sounds like a plan," said Brennan. "I'll see you at the late show tonight. Get there early and sit close to the stage so everyone can see you. I need to move on; I've spent too much time in public with you guys already. Oh, you know tonight is formal night, right?"

"Formal night?" asked Madison.

"Yeah, Captain's Welcome Dinner. You can rent some formal clothes at the formalities shop above the grand lobby."

"Ugh, really?" said James. "Maybe we should set our trap for tomorrow night. I don't do formal clothes."

"You don't *do* formal clothes?" asked Madison with a raised eyebrow.

"Yeah I-" James shifted uneasily in his chair, "They're too constricting, I feel cooped up. I'd rather not do this on formal night."

"Don't tell me I brought my little black dress on our anniversary cruise for nothing," said Madison with a teasing tilt of her head.

James hesitated, clearly a conflict raged in his mind. Brennan cast an accusatory glance towards Madison.

"When did you get a little black dress?" James asked, his voice cracking a little.

"The night we left Dallas when I went out shopping."

James cleared his throat, gathering himself as he scrutinized the teak decking.

"Well, perhaps we should... You know, to preserve our cover," he said at last.

"To preserve the cover... right..." said Brennan. "Now if you'll excuse me, there's a delicious looking brunette at the bar just begging for some attention."

"Goodbye, Dr. Sword," said Madison. Brennan straightened his clothes and went off in search of his prey.

"Has he always been like this?" asked Madison.

"Like how? You mean with the girls?"

"Yes."

"Oh, no. He used to be much worse."

"Worse? Goodness." Madison returned to her book shaking her head.

James got up and left the deck. A few minutes later he returned with two lemonades from the bar.

"So what's your story?" he asked, handing her one of the lemonades.

"My story?"

"You interrogated me about my upbringing, but you've been scarce about details of your life. It doesn't seem fair that you should know so much about me and I so little about you."

"What do you want to know?" Madison took a sip of the cool beverage. It was lemonade from a mix, but out on the deck of the ship, in the warm ocean air, it was the perfect accessory for a lazy day of lounging.

"How did you get to where you are? Where did you grow up? Where did you go to school? What did you want to be when you grew up?"

"That's a lot of questions. I'll give you the short story, as uninteresting as it is. I didn't grow up on an island in the Pacific, you know. I grew up in Cleveland."

"Ohio?"

"Yeah, actually a suburb of Cleveland about twenty miles east of downtown. A suburban girl in a suburban family. Mom and Dad were college sweethearts, also from the Cleveland area."

"So what was life like growing up in middle class America?"

"It was… boring, honestly. I mean, there was plenty of drama, but it was mostly manufactured. You know: who's dating who; the occasional catfight in the school cafeteria; so and so got a new car, a convertible, or whatever. Generally immature and superficial kind of stuff."

"You don't seem to think much of your childhood."

"I mean, it was a good childhood. I was blessed to experience it, but it's so... mundane. Not exactly exotic."

"Maybe not to you, but that's all you knew growing up. To the Filipinos, the American life is glamorous and the Filipino life is boring. So, there's Mom and Dad. Any siblings?"

"One younger sister, whom I dearly love."

"How much younger?"

"Eleven years. I know, big difference, right? Her name is Sam."

"Sam?"

"Samantha. I miss her so much. She's still in high school."

"So how did you end up in the Midwest?" Madison folded her arms.

"That's kind of how life goes for me..." Her voice trailed off, unwilling to elaborate. He was entering territory she didn't want to discuss.

"What do you mean?"

"Life just kind of happens to me. I went to college, not really the college I wanted, but it worked-"

"What did you study?"

"Well, I changed majors a few times, but I ended up studying music." She smiled thinking of the classes she took at the small private school in the rural Midwest.

"Music?"

"Instrumental performance, actually."

"What instrument?."

"Piano. I love music. But it turns out that it's easier to get a job as an administrative assistant with no training than it is to get a job in music with a four year degree. Anyway, after college I moved back home. That was fine until-" She stopped.

"Until what?"

"Until... I moved out."

James shot her an expectant look.

"It... was just time. I took a job in a city an hour or so from my college as an admin and I've been there ever since."

"What happened? Did your parents kick you out?"

"No. They would never... I just had to get out, okay?"

Madison stared at the deck and then looked up at James to let him know that he had asked enough questions for one day. He sat patiently in silence. She drained her lemonade and then thoughtlessly rolled the empty glass around in her hands.

"Look, James. Some people plan everything out. They get this grand plan that they're going to go to college, study what they love, get a job in that field that's exciting and rewarding, find the perfect guy, have three perfect children and a perfect house. And then, poof, that's exactly what happens and they live happily ever after."

"Is that not what you want?"

"I've found it doesn't matter what I want," she said. "What I get is seldom that. Perhaps I want too much, I don't know. So I've learned to take life as it comes, disappointments and all. Life is a bobbing, weaving, unsettled ocean with wave after unpredictable wave bringing us havoc and disorder. Some sail across the ocean as fast as they can so they can get to their golden shore, and some of us just float along in the limitless sea."

Madison fell quiet. Her thoughts left the deck of that ship, soared across the ocean and wandered back into her past, into the vast chasm between what she'd wanted and what life had brought her. She felt the well of a lifetime of disappointment starting to flood her mind and she forcibly pushed it back into the deep recesses of her soul. She inhaled deeply, shook her head and focused her mind on the white puffy clouds that dotted the horizon. Settling back into her chair, Madison opened her book and forced herself to ponder the ancient Romans and their tormented ruler.

X

JAPANESE CHERRY BLOSSOM

"Boys will be boys. And even that wouldn't matter if
only we could prevent girls from being girls."
Anne Frank

"I don't know about this," James heard Madison say behind the bathroom door. James sat on the couch in the stateroom in his rented tuxedo. He wondered how anyone could have invented clothing that was as uncomfortable sitting down as it was when standing up. He squirmed a bit and then checked his watch. The newsletter said that the Captain's reception began promptly at 5 o'clock. The hour of 5 o'clock had come and gone and Madison had yet to finish getting ready.

"What do you mean you're not so sure? Come on, we were supposed to be down there ten minutes ago," he said.

"Well, it's just… It's not what I remembered."

"Your dress?"

"It's not as modest as I thought it was… It's a little low cut."

"It can't be that bad. Come out of the bathroom, we need to go," James said.

A few suspenseful seconds of silence passed until the door opened like the deliberate swing of a bank vault door. She stepped out of the bathroom as if she was stepping onto a sheet of ice and stood before him, her shoulders shyly thrown forward. Her little black dress was indeed low-cut, but it also seemed to compliment her figure expertly. Two thin straps ran over her shoulders and plunged to a deep vee in the front, exposing much of her milky skin. The satin black fabric hugged her curves down to her waistline and then the dress billowed gracefully to her ankles. Her black heeled shoes set her stature and called attention to the curves of her calves exposed through a slit that ran halfway up her thigh.

"Wow, um, yeah…" was all the James could muster. Realizing he was staring, he returned his gaze to catch her eyes. She had spent a lot of time on her make-up and hair and the investment showed. Her eyes sparkled, her cheeks were ruddy and warm, and her hair, pulled delicately back, fell to her shoulders in casual curls piled upon each other. Her lips were a statement of their own, shining in bright, alarming red.

"I can't go out in this. It's too immodest," she said, biting the tip of one of her fingernails.

"Look, there's no time to get you another dress. Either we go like this or we don't go at all. Besides, I've already seen you in your underwear, if that's what you're worried about."

Madison cocked her head and narrowed her eyes.

"Okay, first of all, I was unconscious for that so it doesn't count. And second, I'd be okay if you never brought that up again. Anyway, it's not you so much, it's everyone else. If I could get a shawl or something I'd feel better."

James thought for a second.

"Wait a sec, I might have something you can use." He rummaged around in a drawer where Madison had unpacked his things and returned with a white silk scarf complete with white fringe on either end. "Will this work?"

Madison took the scarf and opened it. When unfolded, the scarf was nearly a foot and a half wide: wide enough to work as a shawl. She threw it around her shoulders and was pleased that it made up for where the dress came up short.

"Thank you. But why do you carry a white scarf around with you? Going to be flying a biplane anytime soon?"

"I always carry one with me. It's not only useful as a scarf, but it can be used as a sling, a satchel, a tourniquet, or a make-shift shawl for a girl who has trouble picking out her own clothes. It's handy and silk is rather durable."

Madison shook her head, fixed her hair and stood up straight to present herself.

"Do you like it?" She pursed her lips in a playful pout.

"Much more... um, modest," he said.

"I mean the lipstick. I put it on to match your bowtie. Besides, sometimes a girl needs to wear bright red lipstick just to feel like a woman. And surprisingly, it works."

"Oh, yeah… it's very... red."

"You're not big on compliments, are you?"

"Sorry. I'm guess I'm just more comfortable with sarcasm."

"That's all right." She played with the scarf as she looked in the mirror above the vanity. "I think I'm more comfortable receiving sarcastic comments from you. It would be a little weird if you just kept telling me that I looked beautiful."

"Do you even need to be told? That's like telling the sky that it's blue or the ocean that it's wet."

Madison paused. James was fairly sure he had said something wrong and was relieved when she changed the subject.

"Speaking of that bowtie, where is it? You're the one who wanted to get to this party so badly. Let's go."

"Yeah, about that..." He sheepishly held up the tie in his hand. "Can I just wear the tux without it?"

"Are you kidding? You can't wear the tux without the tie. You'll look ridiculous. Come on, put it on."

James was silent.

Madison asked, "You don't know how to tie it, do you?"

"I thought it was a clip-on."

"The lady offered to show you when we rented it."

"I didn't want to tell her I didn't know how."

"Men." she said, exasperated. "Give me that." Madison took the tie from him and turned up his collar. She draped the tie around the back of his neck.

"Don't tell me you know how to tie one of these things," he said.

"Trust me, when you go to as many proms, weddings, and formal nights as I have, eventually you learn these things." She tied a knot, looped the fabric around her finger and stuffed the first bow through.

"You've been to a lot of those?"

"More than I can remember. Some were wonderfully romantic, but unfortunately most of were hopelessly forgettable." She looped the second bow, stuffed it through and tightened the knot.

She stood close to him as she made some final adjustments. Looking down at her and her golden hair he was suddenly overtaken by a pleasing aroma. She had finished tying his tie but she still stood close to him.

"Are you wearing perfume?"

"No. It's just a lotion I put on. It keeps my skin soft. Is this what you smell?" Madison held her hand up to his nose. He breathed in the intoxicating fragrance.

"Yeah, that's it. What is it?"

"Japanese Cherry Blossom. I'm glad you like it. It's one of my favorites."

She took an awkward half-step back and then needlessly adjusted his coat collar.

"I do like it," he said. "So you've been on a number of dates, huh? I suppose it's only natural that a woman like you would get asked out a lot,"

"A woman like me?" She looked up at him with a half smile.

"You know, beautiful, energetic, out-going-"

Madison held up her hand.

"Just cool it, alright? Look, I appreciate it, but we've got a job to do. You've got to stay focused."

Embarrassed, James buttoned his coat unsure of what to do next.

"I am focused. Don't worry about me. I'm fine."

"I just don't want you to think that this is..." She paused, looking at him with wide, scared eyes.

"That this is what?"

"Real. I mean... it's not a real date. We can't. We're playing parts, right?"

He looked down at her hoping she couldn't see what he was thinking. Even an exhale could be a betrayal. Finally, James picked up Madison's purse and handed it to her.

"Yeah, we're playing a role. I was just trying to be nice. Don't worry about it. It'll be over soon," he said as he escorted her from the room.

He walked her to the elevator wondering how things had gotten so complicated.

❧⊱⊰☙

Madison found the *Captain's Reception* to be somewhat disappointing as the conversation flowed far less readily than the complimentary beverages. It was held in the aft end of the ship on the Promenade deck where all of the nightclubs were located. There was no formal program and some of the passengers interpreted formal night to be a pair of khakis, a ruffled button-down shirt and a sloppy tie with no coat.

After sitting at their table for a few minutes and watching the other passengers on ship meet the captain and crew, James suggested that they go to dinner. As predicted, the Anderson family did not attend.

"Looks like Brennan is doing all right," said James a few minutes after taking their seat. Brennan entered the dining room, again dressed in his three-piece suit, accompanied by the tall brunette he had spotted on the deck earlier that day. The woman wore a small red dress that sparkled and shimmered in the dim lighting. Her impossibly high heels and tight dress— which stopped a full ten inches above her knees— gave her walk a stilted cadence. It wasn't so much the way that she mindlessly played with her hair or her medically-enhanced bosom— prominently on display thanks to the scandalous neckline of her dress— that made Madison immediately dislike this woman. There was something she couldn't quite identify that told Madison this was not someone with whom she'd get along.

"Mr. and Mrs. Vash? May I present, Miss Claire Rennalt?" said Brennan.

"Very nice to meet you. I'm Lawrence, and this is my wife Valerie," said James. Brennan and Claire slid into the booth across from James and Madison. "Are you Dr. Sword's traveling companion?"

Claire giggled. "No, I just met Aaron a few hours ago," she giggled again. "I didn't have a date for formal night, so Aaron offered to be mine." She giggled once more.

Wow, two sentences and three giggles, thought Madison.

"I'm actually here with my two bestest friends. It's fall break."

"You're still in college," said Madison.

"Yep. Three more years." Claire tittered one more time and took a drink of water. It was at this point that Madison noticed that

Claire— whether because she was either nervous or because no one had told her how silly she sounded— had the obnoxious habit of starting and finishing every sentence with a giggle. Madison folded her lips between her teeth, trying not to mock the young naïveté.

"So, did you know that Aaron is an author?" said Claire with an accompanying battery of giggles.

"Yes, I believe he did mention it yesterday at dinner," said James.

"Aaron read me one of his poems at the Captain's reception thingy. Have you read it? It's awesomely beautiful."

"No, I don't believe we've had the pleasure," said Madison. "Dr. Sword, why don't you share it with us?"

Brennan's face snapped from a pleased expression to one of dread as if he'd just realized he'd sat in a puddle of water.

"Oh, I don't know. I don't think it's appropriate for... uh... this moment."

"Go ahead Aaron," said Claire grasping his arm.

"Yes, please. We're dying to hear it," said James through a suppressed smile. "It would be fantastic to hear a published author read his own work."

"No, no. I can't... I just can't," Brennan's face turned an indiscreet crimson.

"Please, Aaron. I want to hear it again. Read it... For me?" Claire lowered her head and looked at him with pleading eyes, giggles replaced by a manipulative pout. It was a look that undoubtedly had compelled her father to do whatever she wanted of him and probably had excused her from a number of speeding tickets.

"Oh, all right. I'll read it," said Brennan. "But it's not my best work. I'm a novelist by training. Poetry is more for my own... enjoyment." He sighed and then fished around in his pocket, finally withdrawing a crumpled piece of paper.

"It's called *Ocean of Dreams and Love*," he said. Claire sighed. Brennan cast a scowling glance at Madison then cleared his throat.

"Sailing across the deep blue sea
Like Ahab and his insatis quest
Pursuing naught but tranquility
And a chance to breathe and rest

102

Across the ocean I do sail
Alone but for the moonlit gleam
Searching the horizon through the hail
For someone to share my dream

For on a ship you leave it behind
Your inhibitions, your fears and the mire
For on a ship you're free from a mind
That denies you what you truly desire

This Ocean of Dreams and Love
Can be had in only one way
But time is short, so embrace the dove
And enjoy what you can today."

"Isn't it beautiful?" said Claire with a soft reverence in her voice.

"You see, the ship is a metaphor, of sorts, and-" said Brennan.

"Yes, a metaphor. MmmHmm. I get it," said Madison. The wine from the reception an hour earlier had started to fade, but she found herself chuckling despite her efforts to keep a straight face.

"It's so freeing, so open. It's about independence and release. It really affected me deeply," said Claire with absolute seriousness. James grunted sympathetically, covering his hand with a loosely closed fist, unable to compose anything to say that wouldn't end in outright laughter.

"Well, I'm going to the ladies room to freshen up, I'll be back in a snap," said Claire. "Aaron, if the waiter-guy comes by, just order me the light salad, no dressing, and a lava flow from the bar, 'kay?"

Claire got up and shuffled towards the public restroom. A pregnant five seconds passed before James and Madison burst into howling laughter.

"You two can just shut up," said Brennan as he hung his head in embarrassment.

"*Sailing across the deep blue sea,*" mocked Madison through spurts of laughter.

"You've got to be kidding? You passed that off as poetry? aha-ha," laughed James, clutching his stomach.

"Well, it rhymed," said Brennan. This brought more laughter. "Look, she asked to hear some of my writing and I had to come up with something. I wrote it in five minutes in the restroom. I never claimed to be a good poet." The laughter continued. "Oh, forget you guys."

"Let's translate the poem, shall we dear?" asked James, snatching the piece of paper from Brennan.

"Oh, yes. Let's." said Madison eagerly.

"Stop it."

"Sailing across the deep blue sea
Like Ahab and his insatis quest
Pursuing naught but tranquility
And a chance to breathe and rest" read James in a pompous voice.

"'We're on a boat and I think we should have sex'," said Madison.

"Very good. I think that sums it up perfectly. Shall I continue?" asked James.

"Please do," said Madison.

"Across the ocean I do sail
Alone but for the moonlit gleam
Searching the horizon through the hail
For someone to share my dream"

Again Madison translated, "Seriously, girl, we're on a boat, I'm here alone... Let's have sex."

James nodded that Madison's translation was accurate.

"For on a ship you leave it behind
Your inhibitions, your fears and the mire
For on a ship you're free from a mind
That denies you what you truly desire"

"Ignore that little voice in your head called your conscience. Let's have sex."

"This Ocean of Dreams and Love
Can be had in only one way
But time is short, so embrace the dove
And enjoy what you can today."

"Yeah, about that sex... Is now good for you?"

"Subtle, but effective. Was this a suggestion in your book you were reading this afternoon?" said James.

"You two are jerks," said Brennan snatching the paper back. "Let's see who's laughing tomorrow morning."

There was something defensive and vulnerable in Brennan's voice; a tone that sobered Madison slightly. She reached across the table and took his hands into hers.

"Brennan, seriously? Do you really want her?" asked Madison, speaking tenderly. "You don't even need to try that hard. That lame poem was probably more work than you needed. Two more lava flows from the bar ought to do it. That's all it takes. She doesn't have a thought in that pretty little head of hers and you know it. She's nineteen years old for Pete's sake. There's no prize in getting a girl like that into bed."

Brennan withdrew his hands, folded the paper and stuffed it back into his pocket.

"I'm just entertaining myself, okay?" he said. "Not everyone has a cover story of traveling with his gorgeous wife."

It was an odd comment that left them in awkward silence until Claire returned.

"I don't get it," she said as she returned to the booth. Claire scooted along the bench, bouncing as she went. Her wiggling drew a hypnotic stare from James and Brennan. Madison kicked them both under the table.

"What's that, Claire?" asked Brennan.

"They have a little plastic table in the restroom labeled 'Baby Changing Station'. But it's not. It's a diaper changing station. If it were a baby changing station you'd pull down the table, there'd be several babies in there, you'd put your baby in and take out a different one."

The three sat in a confused silence.

"It's a joke, people. Geez, lighten up," Claire said at last. James, Brennan, and Madison smiled, exchanging various sighs of understanding and compliments.

Dinner passed quickly with Claire talking excitedly about her creative writing class, her position as treasurer of the homecoming committee, her ex-boyfriend and why she's done with dating for a while, and her desire to solve the Darfur "issue" as she called it, though she admitted she didn't really know where the country of Darfur was. Madison and James ate mostly in silence, occasionally sharing glances and raised eyebrows.

Madison smiled as she realized they were now talking with their eyes. It was something intimate friends do and it had been a long time since she had shared that with anyone.

After dessert, Claire asked them if they would like to join her and her friends at the dance club *Blue Jazz*. James politely declined saying he and the wife were going to take in the evening show. Brennan, of course, had to be in position to follow whoever might be tailing James and Madison so he suggested that he might come by later in the evening. He fumbled through some excuse about having some writing to do, but Claire didn't seem to notice the clumsiness.

James and Madison left the dining room and headed towards the Amber Palace, the grand theatre at the bow of the ship, for the evening show.

❦

What surprised Madison about the show was not the quality of the singing, the power of the music, the lights and sound, or the sets— for those were all rather standard fare for a musical revue. What surprised her was how easy it was to forget that she was on a ship crossing the Atlantic and not in the local professional theatre a few blocks from her now burned-out apartment.

The show was, as it was nearly every night, a musical revue featuring a troupe of eight dancers in various outfits, a live band made up of mostly Indonesian and Japanese musicians, and two American singers, a man and a woman, who took turns filling the spotlight. Each night was a different theme but the format was the same.

Tonight the show was entitled *A Salute to Musicals* and featured songs from musicals throughout the decades. They played various songs from *Grease, South Pacific, Oklahoma, Godspell,* and *Singing in the Rain,* among others. Some of the most famous musical numbers or more recent musicals were noticeably absent. Madison assumed it had more to do with royalties than anything else.

When the curtain call finally arrived, Madison was startled to realize that her hand was curled around the top of James' hand with her fingers tucked into his palm. She jerked her hand back, wondering how long they had been holding hands. Her face must have betrayed some confusion because his eyes narrowed.

"What?" he asked as the crowd applauded.

"Why were you doing that?" she asked.

"Doing what?"

"Holding my hand?"

"I believe you were holding mine."

"No I wasn't."

"Sweetheart, you took my hand about halfway through the show and held it until just now. I was wondering how long you were going to do that."

"I'm sorry, I- I didn't realize..."

"It's fine," he said as the house lights came up and the crowd filed out of the auditorium. "I thought it was more appropriate for a newlywed couple, rather than a couple of five years, but it worked."

"Okay, yeah, it worked," she said.

"Are you ready to do this?" asked James. He looked up into the balcony to his right confirming that Brennan was in position. Brennan was alert and ready. Madison nodded to James and rose, draping the white scarf around her shoulders.

Madison took James' arm and walked with him down the center aisle and out the back of the theatre. They walked slowly, occasionally pausing to remark about the various paintings on the wall. The couple arrived back at the grand lobby. A middle-aged woman sang love songs in a breathy voice while her husband played a keyboard near a circular dance floor. Surrounding the dance floor were couches and chairs and around the outside was a bar.

"Stop doing that," said James as they strode through the lobby.

"Doing what?" Madison asked.

"Looking behind us. That's Brennan's job. Let him do his job. If they suspect that we know they're following us then we'll lose them for sure."

"Sorry."

James brought them to a halt at the bar, ordered a Manhattan, straight-up and another glass of merlot for Madison. While they waited for their drinks, Madison noticed Brennan appear in the doorway from the theatre. James made a quick hand signal to Brennan who casually signaled back.

"What's that mean?" asked Madison sipping her merlot.

"It means we have to dance," said James. He took her drink and set it on the bar. He grabbed her other hand and led her to the dance floor. The musicians were just starting a slow, jazzy version of "Natural Woman".

"I don't understand," said Madison, placing her hands on the back of his shoulders. She held her breath as she felt his wide hands press into the small of her back. His arms drew her into his finely pressed tuxedo and she felt their bodies align as they picked up the rhythm of the music.

"Bren wasn't able to see anyone following us, so we have to make ourselves a little more visible," he said bending his words to her ear.

They danced around in a shuffling circle, making small talk and passing the time. Neither were exquisite dancers but they were able to keep time and avoid trodding on each other's feet.

"We're center stage with the lights on us," Madison said through a halting laugh. "It doesn't get any more visible than that."

The song finished and the two stepped back, holding hands. Madison looked at James and saw something she hadn't seen in his eyes before. It was subtle, it was veiled, but she could see it. She saw in his eyes: mirth. His eyes were bright and a droll smile stood buried beneath his stoic countenance. Eventually he took her hand and led her out of the lobby toward the glass elevator that ran from the lobby up to the top deck of the ship. He called the elevator and stood back while the glass elevator descended to retrieve them.

"You're enjoying this, aren't you?" she said.

"And you're not?" he said as they entered the elevator. He pushed the button for the seventh deck and then turned around. "Look," he said.

Madison turned around to see the grand lobby fall away from her as they ascended through the ship. They hadn't taken the glass elevator before. Of course, they hadn't been trying to be seen before.

"That was cool," she said.

They reached floor seven and he led her by the hand towards the front of the ship. There was something exciting about being with a man who knew where he was going and wanted to take her with him.

Up a hall to the bow, across the ship, back down a hall, up the stairs, zigzag through the halls, down stairs, down elevators, up more stairs; the ersatz couple wound their way around the ship—each hallway a never ending row of identical doors with marginally different numbers on them. Remembering James' admonition, Madison fought the urge to turn around and see if anyone was following them. She didn't hear anyone, but her imagination quickly conjured up dark shadows following behind. She felt a unique kinship to Lot's wife, desperate to turn around and see what lay behind her.

James led them up to the bow and through a door that led onto an outdoor deck where the two sides of the ship came together. They stepped out onto the deck and into the roar of the wind. Madison could see the point of the bow of the ship stretching out before them, the dark ocean below them and the jet black sky above them. A light mounted to an overhead post lit the platform.

The ship was sailing directly into a stiff ocean wind. That wind, combined with the considerable speed of the ship, meant that the wind coming over the bow was formidable and unrelenting. The bow of the ship was no place for the casual passenger and thus they found themselves alone.

The wind pressed into their faces, tossing Madison's hair into disarray as she stepped out onto the decking. Quickly one hand went to her head— to keep her hair out of her face— and the other hand shot to her billowing dress to keep James from seeing the lacy red panties she wore to match her red lipstick.

"Why are we here?" shouted Madison above the thunder of the wind. James led them across the ship to the forward-most point on the deck.

"Just wait," yelled James staring back at the door they'd come through.

The constant rush of wind deafened Madison. James leaned against the rail, his back to the wind. Madison clung to him, hiding in the small pocket of stagnant air by his chest. He put one arm around her to help keep her silk shawl in place and with the other arm firmly held the railing.

"Look," he said at last, pointing to the door. It shuddered first and then slowly swung out against the wind. Someone was coming through.

XI

HER NAME WAS MICHELLE

"Obsession is a young man's game,
and my only excuse is that I never grew old."
Michael Caine

Madison clutched James as fear paralyzed her legs. Soon the figure of a man emerged from the doorway—an indiscernible shadow silhouetted by a light behind him. The dark figure staggered beneath the sheer volume of wind and then stumbled towards them into more direct light.

"Brennan!" shouted Madison with effervescent relief. She ran and hugged him. "You scared the crap out of me."

"I never saw anyone following you," he shouted to James as he returned her hug. "You weren't being tailed. Maybe there aren't any agents on board after all."

"Perhaps. Either that or they were wise to our trap," said James. "We can't stay here. Brennan, head to the club and meet up with Claire. I'll take Madison to the room and then meet up with you later."

"You got it, boss," said Brennan and turned and went inside the ship. A few minutes later, James and Madison followed Brennan through the door.

"We shouldn't go right back to the room," said James as they caught their breath in the stillness of the hallway. "It's possible they saw Brennan and were just waiting for him to leave. How'd you like to take a walk on the Panorama deck? There's a beautiful—and less harrowing—view of the ocean up there."

❧

The music from the Lido deck wafted through the air like the alluring fragrance of fresh bread from a bakery. It rose and mingled with the wind, swirling amidst the turbulent eddies of ocean air that passed over the ship. Madison and James walked along the rail of the Panorama deck. To their left they could see wide stairs leading down to the well-lit Lido deck and the intoxicated revelers undulating to the thumping dance music. To their right, the waves of the ocean crashed against the side of the ship a hundred feet below. The moon, partially obscured by high stratus clouds, reflected dimly off the ocean. Madison and James walked the narrow space between the vibrant party and the desolate Atlantic. The deck, protected from the wind by glass walls, offered quiet and peacefulness without solitude.

Further down the rail a young couple embraced, lips interlocked in the fiery throws of reckless passion. Madison and James dared not continue their walk past the couple.

"In England, they'd say he's giving her quite a snogging," said James.

"It looks more like he's trying to fit her entire face into his mouth, poor girl," said Madison. "I've had a few boyfriends who liked to kiss like that."

"Yeah? How long did you date those guys?"

"Not long. Being a bad kisser is grounds for dismissal, you know. Whether you call it snogging or slobbering."

"And when was the last time you received a proper snogging?"

"Oh, we are not talking about that. Let's just say it's been a while, okay?"

James stopped by the railing and looked out at the ocean, letting the topic drop. Madison followed his lead, looking out at the forbidding sea.

"Looks like we might be in for some weather," he said.

"How can you tell?" She looked into the blackness.

"See the horizon over there?" He pointed to starboard of the ship's heading.

"Yeah?" Madison strained to see something appear.

"The stars are gone. They stop about ten degrees above the horizon. You can't see the storm, but you can see what it's blotting out."

"The presence of an absence," said Madison, "How existential."

Just then, a miniscule flash of lighting illuminated the clouds far in the distance.

"James. I wanted to apologize for the show. You know, holding your hand and all. I didn't mean that," Madison said.

"It's fine, Madison. I admit you're full of paradoxes and mixed signals, but it's okay."

"No, it's not okay. I shouldn't have done that."

James turned around, resting his elbows on the railing, and looked at her.

"So, what did Brennan tell you?" he asked.

"Tell me about what?"

"About me."

"He didn't tell me anything," she lied.

"Yes he did. What did he say?"

Madison knew that the expression on her face was betraying her thoughts.

"Look, Madison," he said, leaning in closer to her. "I know there are a thousand different levels to a woman's heart, so I won't pretend to know what you think of me. I know we get along, at least. But every time something that might be construed as genuine affection happens, you freak out."

"I don't freak out."

"Don't you? I know Brennan said something about me. What did he say? Did he tell you to stay away from me?"

Madison considered maintaining that Brennan hadn't told her anything, but decided that honesty was called for in this situation. Besides, she wanted to know more about James and right now, he seemed willing to talk.

"He told me that you had some problems in the past. And that I shouldn't encourage you."

"Encourage me?" James tossed his head back with an offended laugh. "Encourage me to what?"

"I don't know why he thinks this, but he said you might be-" she stopped. To say it out loud just sounded ridiculous.

"—In love with you?" said James.

"He said there was a girl, and that she hurt you."

"Did he tell you the whole story?"

"No."

James walked further along the railing. The young couple had left, presumably to continue their encounter in a more secluded location. Madison kept beside him.

"Yes, there was a girl." James shook his head. "Her name was Michelle."

"What happened?"

"Just your typical story. Boy meets girl. Boy falls in love with girl. Girl finds power in boy's affection and uses it against him. Girl destroys boy through manipulation, sedition, subversion, and deception."

"You're kidding."

James sat down on an abandoned chaise lounge.

"I wish I were. Michelle was in artifact recovery, just like me. Devin hired her about four years ago to do research, but she quickly worked her way into field work and going on the recoveries with me. She was intelligent, inquisitive and damn, did she know her history."

"So you two fell in love?"

"Sort of. I fell in love with her. Obsession, really, is more like it. I don't know if she ever loved me. She acted like she loved me, but she took my affections and turned them on me. Michelle was driven to wealth and fame and all that crap I could care less about. She used me to get to that. We were on a dig in Syria, looking for the Lost Scepter of Babylon. You ever hear of that?"

"No, I haven't."

"Of course not. No one has. We found the thing and were arranging to have it shipped back to the museum for restoration and then display. It was the museum's biggest find to date. It was going to put the museum on the map in the world of antiquities.

"Late one night, while we were still on-site at the camp, I got to thinking about the significance of finding the scepter—a solid gold stick with ancient Babylonian writing on it, really exquisite—and I figured the money the museum would give us would really set us up well. I decided maybe we could get married. So, that night, I went over to her tent to ask her to marry me. I found an empty sleeping bag. She was gone. So was the scepter."

James set his jaw as bitter resentment crept into his normally stoic eyes.

"That's horrible, James. I'm so sorry. Did you ever hear from her?"

"She'd left a note that basically said, 'Sorry James. Thanks for the laughs.'" James sat quietly looking at his own hands tremble slightly. "It took a long time to get over that."

"Not all women are like that." Madison took his hands into hers, more to steady them than anything else.

"It wasn't just her. There were a lot of problems before she left. I had problems. You know, I hear that there are guys who will get up and go to their nine-to-five and just focus on work. And then, when the whistle blows, they'll hop into their car and start thinking about their girl, and how they want to take her to dinner, and watch the sunset and make love to her. Then, the next morning, they'll get up and think about work for another 8 hours.

"I can't do that. For me, if I want something, it's all I can think about. 'Singular Obsession' I think is how they put it. There's something wrong with me."

"It just means you're passionate." Madison pulled a little closer to him on the chaise.

"It means I'm a sap. Whenever I get close to a woman, I mean, into a real relationship, everything goes sideways. I hate it."

"Is that why you live like you do? Secret lair and fake names? Is it because of her?" It was a question that had been ruminating in her mind for a while.

"Now who's asking questions that are off limits?" said James shaking his head. "No, that's a different story altogether."

He didn't elaborate. Madison knew that this riddle of a man wasn't going to give up all of his secrets in one evening. She returned to the topic he was willing to talk about.

"When was that, when she left with the scepter?"

"About two and a half years ago. After Michelle left, I quit the museum and was generally nomadic for two years. I didn't want anything to do with archaeology, lost artifacts, dead kings, or history."

"So what finally turned you around?" she asked.

"It was Brennan. I was sitting in a café in Prague and he walks in like a ghost out of the past. I still don't know how he found me." James smiled.

"I'll bet you guys had a long talk."

James laughed. "Huh, Not really. It doesn't really work like that with guys. He walked in and said 'So, are you done feeling sorry for yourself yet?' I put down my mulled wine, thought about the question for a few seconds, and said 'yes'. Then he said 'Are you ready to start doing something with your life again?' I got on the next plane back to the States and started working on the Key of Caligula's Bath."

"Brennan seems like a loyal friend."

"He's definitely got his idiosyncrasies, but he'd drop everything in a heartbeat to come help me out. You can't buy that kind of allegiance."

"He loves you," said Madison softly.

"I owe him a lot. So, if he seems a little protective, it's because he's got a lot invested in me."

Madison sensed the deep affection shared between the two men. It was something that seemed to come easily to men, but so difficult for women. She admired them both.

"Bren said that I look like her. Like Michelle. Do I?"

James tilted his head in thought. "Somewhat. Your smile is different."

"How so?"

"You use yours."

Madison smiled involuntarily.

"Look, Madison, the only reason I told you about Michelle is to tell you that you don't have anything to worry about with me. I know my weaknesses and I'm not going to get distracted here, okay? My one and only interest is finding that empire marker and letting you get back to your normal life."

"That's your only interest?" An edge crept into Madison's voice. James missed it.

"Believe me. I have absolutely no interest in starting anything with you. So you have nothing to worry about, see?"

"You have no interest in me, whatsoever."

"None at all. I'm not even attracted to you. Not even a little bit." James grinned as if he was delivering the exact words she needed to hear.

Madison stood up, folded her arms, opened her mouth to speak, closed her mouth, turned, and walked away. James quickly hopped up to follow her.

"What's wrong?" Madison refused to acknowledge him until she reached the stairs leading down to the Lido deck. Finally, she spun on her heels and scowled at him.

"Where do you get off saying that to me?" she asked, hands on hips, daggers out.

"I thought that would be good news to you."

"What right do you have to talk to me like that? You have a lot to learn about women." She spun back around and started down the steps.

"This I know," he said. It was an easy point to concede. "Where are you going?"

"Back to the room. You can change in the morning. You can sleep in your tux for all I care. Enjoy your night alone. Or maybe you'll find a girl you are attracted to." She stormed off down the stairs and towards her stateroom, leaving him standing waist deep in the hole he'd dug for himself.

The book *Caligula: When Power Corrupts* sailed across the room in a tumbling line drive, striking the mirror and clattering onto the vanity. Madison had tried to read the unwitting victim but, after reading the same paragraph four times, decided to translate her emotions into physical action. Her thoughts kept returning to James and his blatant denial of his feelings for her. *How could he say that?*

She thought of one of her favorite lines from *Jane Austen*:

"I could easily forgive his pride, if he had not mortified mine."

The world of *Pride and Prejudice* came alive in her mind. She longed for men that spoke what they meant and felt, and unashamedly declared their intentions. There was no silliness of impossible adventures mucking everything up. Where were the men like that in the world today?

Was she being prideful? Madison sat at the vanity and looked at her reflection. She searched the mirrored face for the tell-tale signs. Pursed lips, eyes on fire, deep breaths drawn in through the nostrils.

They were all there. She slumped her shoulders in disgust. Pride. Her old nemesis.

After a few minute's contemplation, Madison stood with a new resolution. She would march down to the Blue Jazz Lounge and find James. She would apologize for the way she reacted and would play along for the time being. *Of course you don't love me, James. I understand. It's for the good of the mission.*

She left the room, took the elevator to the Promenade deck and walked along the ship on the way to the *Blue Jazz* club where she expected to find James, Brennan, and probably that airhead Claire. As Madison travelled, a fresh and exciting fantasy developed in her mind.

She would appear in the doorway of the club and he would smile. Brennan would see her and escort Claire away silently, leaving James alone at the bar. She would apologize and he would wave his hand demurely to make her feel at ease. She would tell him she understood what he was trying to do, that she appreciated it, but honestly felt that they should just get their true feelings out. He would shyly admit that, yes, he was lying. He did find her attractive. He would probably admit to loving her from the first moment he saw her; in her crashed car just a few weeks ago. They would agree to live this adventure together, and when they'd found Caligula's Bath and everything was set right, they would consider proper dating. He would hug her and they'd spend the rest of the evening sharing drinks and talking about their future dates together.

By the time she got to the *Blue Jazz Club*, the script was written. All she had to do was to make her entrance. She stood in the doorway but froze at what she saw, unable to take the step into the club.

James and Brennan stood at the bar sharing a drink. Brennan had his arm around Claire who leaned into him to contact his body at as many points as possible. But there was a fourth—a new girl in a blue mini-skirt and a white top. She looked to be as old as Claire and was probably the best friend with whom Claire was traveling. James stood next to her with his arm wrapped around her waist. James made some comment and all four laughed, Brennan raising his glass as a salute. James bent his head and whispered something intimate into the new girl's ear who giggled at his comment.

Madison stood mortified in the doorway. She recalled a demonstration in her high school physics class where her teacher had taken a gorgeous red rose and dipped it into a vat of liquid nitrogen. He removed the flower and casually dropped it on the table. The rose shattered into a thousand pieces. Madison stood in the doorway, watching the shards of her heart, dignity, and pride skip along the floor in all directions.

A burning anger welled up inside of her. Her first instinct to flee the scene was quickly replaced by a fury known only to the female gender. Clenching her fists and hissing through her teeth, she stormed into the bar and approached James from behind. Brennan saw her first, and his face betrayed his thoughts. He knew there would be trouble.

"Lawrence. Can I have a word with you?" she asked in a commanding voice. James spun around in shock. He quickly recovered and attempted a quick feint. The girl nearest him tensed up and moved away in a guilty slink.

"Valerie! Hi." said James. "I thought you went to bed. Val, this is Claire's friend Beckie. Beckie, this is-"

Madison interrupted him by taking her thumb and forefinger and pinching him on the meaty part of his hand between his thumb and palm. She led him away keeping sharp pressure on the nerve in his hand with only the curt phrase, "A word."

As she let him out of the club and into the hallway, she heard Claire utter a sophomoric "Uh-ohhhhh," as if someone's mother had shown up to discover her kids were misbehaving.

"What in the hell do you think you're doing, James?" demanded Madison when they were alone outside the club.

"Just being social. I told you I was meeting up with Brennan." he said.

"Who's Beckie?"

"That's Claire's friend. Why are you so upset?"

"Are you out of your freaking mind? Damn it, James, you're supposed to be travelling as a married man, are you not? On your five-year anniversary. What the hell are you doing with her?"

"Well, you told me to find some other girl. It was the last thing you said to me."

Madison nearly smacked him.

"I was being sarcastic. Don't you understand sarcasm?"

"We were just talking, Madison."

"You had your arm around her, James. She was flirting with you."

He was silent. He had no answer for that.

"What did you tell them?" she asked.

"Just that you weren't feeling good and went to bed early. Look, I'll go back in, make my excuses and get out. No more socializing."

"You will not. You're going back to Bren's room right now. You just got pulled out of a bar by your furious wife. You are not returning, are we clear?"

"But what about Bren?" he asked.

"Bren can sleep with both of them, for all I care. As for you, you're stuck with me and this ridiculous cover story. You will not disrespect me like that again, either undercover or in real life, do you understand me? "

"I wasn't trying to disrespect you."

"Good night," said Madison. She marched back to the elevator without looking back.

∾⋙⋘∾

Madison fumbled with the keycard in the door. She was angry, and the fact that every time she put the keycard in, the door flashed a red light and refused to unlock didn't help her mood.

"Open up!" she shouted, louder than she intended. She struggled with the card some more.

"Mrs. Vash? Can I help you with something?" Lupe, the stewardess, stood just down the hall. Genuine concern showed on her face at Madison's outburst.

"Oh, Hi Lupe. I just can't get this stupid door open, that's all. It worked a few minutes ago." Madison sniffed and then realized that she had been crying.

"You have wrong way up. Here, let me." She took the card from Madison, and turned it over, inserted it into the slot. A green light illuminated and she opened the door.

"Oh, stupid me," said Madison flushing. "Just a little distracted, that's all." She wiped her eyes with the palm of her hand.

"No Mr. Vash?" asked Lupe.

"Oh, um. Yeah, he just went to get me an ice cream, the dear. He'll be here in a bit. Thanks for the help," she lied.

120

"Well goodnight, Mrs. Vash. Take care tonight. Crew say storm is coming. Is going to be wet tomorrow."

Madison entered the room and slammed the door behind her. It took her nearly an hour to calm down enough so that she could get ready for bed. Finally, with make-up smeared down both cheeks and her eyes puffy, she pulled her dress off, threw on her silk nightgown, washed her face, and then climbed into bed. Rain soon tapped against the window, first in short bursts then in a continuous rattle, as she sorted through her confusing mess of feelings for that arrogant, infantile, self-centered jerk she inexplicably had begun to love.

XII

THE DARK FIGURE

"Action cures fear, inaction creates terror."
Douglas Horton

Madison slept in disquieting fits most of the night. Her dreams were a jumble of stressful images, drawn together in an incoherent tangle of nonsensical horrors. At some point in the middle of the night, she rolled over and awoke, aware for the first time that it wasn't just her mind that was in turmoil.

Her first sensation that something was wrong was that, despite lying still, she found she was tossed around in her bed. As she fought for consciousness, she became aware that the entire room was moving—first rolling to the window, and then rolling sharply away from the window.

She processed the noise. It was constant but intense, like the rumble of a passing train. She put her brain to work trying to understand what she was hearing. *Rain. Lots of rain. Wind. Rain being driven into her window by a howling wind.*

She opened her eyes. The room was dark, but would occasionally illuminate in stark white light followed by a growling rumble. The window and sliding glass door were covered by a sheer linen curtain that under normal circumstances helped to darken the room and provide privacy. The lightning sparking outside the window projected a white rectangle and dominated the room. As her sleep-blurred eyes strained for definition, her awakening brain told her that she was in the midst of a tempest. It also told her that something else wasn't right.

In time, clarity came to Madison's eyes. She sat up in bed, fully processing the storm that ravaged the ship. Another flash of white light illuminated her window curtains. That's where she saw it.

Every time the lighting flashed, she could see distinct shadows cast on her window. She saw the long horizontal shadow from the railing, and the unique outline of the two chairs on the balcony. However, it struck her as odd that something the size of a narrow Christmas tree was also on her balcony. Then another flash, and the shadow was bent to one side. Flash. A branch extended from the middle of the tree.

Someone was on her balcony.

Her heart leapt in her chest. She stifled a gut reaction to scream. Her alarm was overridden by her desire not to inform the mysterious, slow-moving figure that she was awake. Besides, in the torrent of rain and thunderclaps, no one would hear her cry for help.

She picked up the phone and dialed 1394, solely by feel. Had she been less stressed and more able to assess the situation, she would have been quite impressed with herself that she remembered James and Brennan's phone number and was able to dial it in the dark.

She pressed the phone to her ear, whispering "Please, please, please, please, please" until someone answered.

"Hello?" answered James in a raspy voice after three or four rings.

"There's someone on my balcony. Get up here!" she whispered in a panic.

"What?" It was a confused 'what'; the kind asking for more information and a little time to get his bearings. She couldn't oblige. She repeated what was important, with each word being its own sentence. "Get. Up. Here."

James hung up before she even took the phone from her ear. Flash. The figure on the balcony moved closer to the door handle.

The door! She was so upset last night that she wasn't sure whether she'd locked it before going to bed. Could it be as easy for the intruder as just pulling it open? Again she crawled on the floor, terror striking her numb as she crept towards the door: towards the figure that stood on her balcony. Another flash and she saw the figure grab the railing as the ship rolled again.

Her breathing grew shallow and panicked as she crept closer. The lightning hadn't flashed in a few seconds and she was dying to see where the figure was now. She reached up to the handle, carefully reached around the curtain and felt for the lock. It was up; the door was unlocked. *My god, it's open!* She tried to remain quiet, but she could hear an unintentional whimpering coming from her throat. Madison slid one unsteady finger on to the lock and pushed it down. The lock clicked shut just as a rumble of thunder rolled through the room.

She scampered away. Feeling along the edge of the bed, she worked her way back to the nightstand. Flash. The figure now stood near the door handle.

She wanted to flee, to stand up and run from the room, but her body froze up, the panic taking its hold. Madison was beginning to succumb to shock and her brain stopped processing things logically.

Madison was a spectator.

A new noise caught her attention as she jerked her gaze back to the window. The room was dead black, but now she heard the faint whirring of an electric motor along with a distinct grinding sound on the glass. She listened with her head cocked to one side, trying to identify the bizarre sound. At last, it came to her. The person on the other side of the curtain, standing out in the storm, was drilling a hole through the glass near the door handle.

Instinctively, Madison backed further away from the door, still crouching on the ground. The drill motor whirred louder along with a soft tinkling as glass shards landed on the door track. The drill had come through the glass.

There was no doubt that a small hole had been drilled. However, she couldn't understand what the intruder meant to do with such a little hole. The rain beat against the glass, but no lightning came to show her what the intruder was doing.

Then she heard it. The sound of the sliding of metal on glass until: click. The door was unlocked. It moved a few inches and the howling sound of the wind and rain filled the bedroom.

Madison couldn't keep quiet any longer. She screamed with every vapor in her lungs and scrambled to the door leading to the hallway, her legs finally finding their strength. Dressed as she was, in a nightgown, having to get up from a crawl, and the superior athletic ability of the intruder, all conspired against her. The man dove into the room, timing his lunge with the roll of the ship. Another flash but Madison, turned away from the window, saw his shadow cast on the opposing wall. The man had something in his hands as his arms were raised over his head.

Then, in a whoosh, everything went quiet and dark as a canvas bag was thrust over her head. She screamed again, but it was muffled. A drawstring drew closed around her neck and she crumpled to the floor.

Madison's hands went to her throat to loosen the strangling drawstring. A quick zip and her hands were bound together by a plastic tie. She could neither see nor speak. She could neither scream nor hear. A powerful hand held her head to the carpet. Madison kicked her legs wildly in every direction, bruising her legs as they contacted the vanity, the table and, occasionally the intruder's legs.

There was an electronic beep and the crash of the stateroom door being flung open. Madison could not see them, but she knew that James and Brennan had made it to her room and practically kicked the door open.

The intruder was off of her immediately. Madison ripped the canvas bag from her head with her bound hands. They had turned on the light in the bedroom and James, wearing only pajama bottoms, and Brennan, in a grey shirt and boxers, stood on either side of her. Madison looked towards the window just in time to see a black robed figure disappear out the door, hop up on to the balcony railing and then climb up to the next deck.

James chased after the agile ghost, but only managed to snag the edge of his robe before the intruder slipped away. James looked up to the deck above, before coming back into the room. He was drenched after being outside for only a few seconds.

"Brennan go forward, I'll go aft." shouted James over the roar of the storm. He dashed through the room and out the stateroom door.

"Wait, James. You're not leaving me," yelled Madison as she struggled to her feet. She grabbed her keycard from the nightstand and ran out the door after James.

James bounded up the stairs two at a time to the Panorama deck. There, he sprinted along the corridor until he exited onto the outdoor part of the deck. James threw himself at the railing and peered overboard trying to see any sign of the intruder. Madison, out of breath and hands still bound, was soon beside him along the railing. The rain pummeled her body through the thin silk nightgown.

They looked farther forward, straining to see Brennan appear on the deck above the bridge. The rain was too heavy and kept the visibility to no more than a hundred feet.

"There." said James, looking aft towards the funnel. Madison spun around to see a dark clad figure climbing a railing up to the Sun Deck, the highest deck of the ship. The Sun Deck was little more than a jogging track that went around the ship's funnel.

James dashed across the open deck, past the stairs to the Lido deck; past where Madison had angrily left him just a few hours earlier. He climbed the railing after the dark figure, holding on as the ship continued to roll. Madison, unable to climb with her hands tied together, stood helplessly waiting on the Panorama deck as James dashed off into the darkness.

Lightning and thunder surrounded her as she felt the ship roll again. She grabbed onto a railing as her hair fell into her eyes. The storm, the wind, the unsteady ship, and the sudden realization that she was alone, out of her room, in nothing but a drenched nightgown, overwhelmed her. As she dropped to the deck, she cried.

A few minutes later, James returned with an angry fire in his eyes.

"I lost him. He got to an elevator and I have no way of knowing what floor he went to. I'm sorry."

Madison did not stir. Her brain shut down from sensory overload, unable to process everything at once.

"Hey, stay with me," said James as he pulled her to her feet.

Madison stood and grabbed his bare shoulder, depending on him for stability. She shook her head, clearing her head like dust from an old book. The rain did not relent as it poured down on them.

"Somehow he knew you were in your room, alone," said James as they walked back towards the stateroom.

Madison pushed open a door and they entered the hallway leading to their room. Madison's nightgown dripped on the carpet.

"So they thought no one was there and decided to search my room?" asked Madison.

"No, they knew you were there. They're not after just the ruby arrowhead. They're after you as well."

"What? Why?"

"It's the same reason they put the arrowhead in your car to begin with. At first, I thought they might have just picked you randomly to be a delivery agent for them, but now it's obvious that they need you, specifically. Why? I don't know."

Madison walked numbly to her room. She could hear James talking, but found difficulty in believing what he was saying. She felt an other-worldliness about herself; as if she was watching a movie about someone else.

Madison held up her hands, showing James the zip-tie.

"There's a knife in the dresser drawer in your room," he said. "So who knew you were here by yourself?"

"Lupe, did."

"The lady that cleans our room?"

"Lupe helped me get into the room last night. She knew you weren't with me and probably had guessed that you weren't spending the night here. I think she's part of it," she said as she opened the door to their room.

Madison screamed.

The first thing Madison saw was a figure she could only assume was Brennan's, sitting tied to the chair at the vanity. He had a black canvas bag over his head, while his feet and hands were bound with zip-ties. Blood trickled down his arms and pooled on the floor. A man in black silk robes stood behind him with a silenced semi-automatic pistol pointed at Brennan's sagging head.

"I told you they'd be back," said a voice that Madison recognized.

A woman stepped from the back of the room and into the light with a smirk on her face.

"Claire?" said James in utter astonishment.

"You three have got to be the worst undercover agents I've ever seen. James Kynan. Your new girlfriend, Madison Dawn. And this sorry guy," she said slapping her hand on Brennan's sagging head, "must be Brennan Nash." Brennan let out a dull moan.

"Who are you?" asked James.

"It's not important. What's important is that you give me the ruby arrowhead or your friend, the poet, won't live to see landfall." Claire folded her arms and shifted her weight to one foot, her pride on full display. The man in black robes, stood behind Brennan—an unflinching figure—just waiting for permission to fire.

"I don't know what you're talking about," said James. "Even if we had whatever it is you're looking for, do you think we'd keep it here?"

"No, I expect you to go and get it for me… if you expect him to live. Madison, sweetie, come sit by me," said Claire. She motioned to the couch. "Thankfully, you're still bound so that saves me the trouble of having you tied up again." Madison looked at James for direction. He nodded, so she moved slowly to the couch and sat down.

"What? You don't have a gun to point at her head?" asked James.

"This one? No, no, no. This one is too precious," said Claire running her hand through Madison's wet, tangled hair. Claire bent down and looked Madison in the eye. She ran the back of her hand gently across Madison's cheek. "I can't afford to let anything happen to this little goldmine."

"What does Giovanni want with her?" asked James.

"You're not in a position to ask questions," said Claire with a bite in her voice. "The only thing you're in a position to do is get me the arrowhead. We've got the girl, now we need the arrowhead."

"I don't have it."

"You lie! Giovanni wouldn't have put a bounty out like this if he wasn't sure you had exactly what he wanted. Now hand it over or my associate here will put a bullet in your friend's head."

"I said I don't-"

"James," said Madison, interrupting him. "It's not worth Brennan's life."

"I'm not giving it to her, Madison." James was angry, but Madison could see that his mind was working on a plan. Finally she caught his gaze. He didn't move. He didn't speak. But the way he looked at her said something plain to her. *Are you ready?* Madison nodded her head slightly. James looked at her and then quickly up to Claire and then back to Madison. The message was clear: *She's your responsibility.*

"Give it to her, James. It's in the dresser," said Madison with distress in her voice.

James stood motionless, leering at Claire. Claire couldn't help but laugh.

"Honestly, James. It's your only play here. Give me the arrowhead."

James turned and opened the top dresser drawer, he paused for a second. Madison knew that it was a cue for her. Now was the time.

In a flash, James drew the knife from the drawer, spun and lunged for the man holding the gun. With a violent slap, James knocked the gun towards Claire and the man staggered backwards. Before the man in black robes could recover, James was on him, a four inch switch-blade knife slicing through the air. Another sudden lunge and James plunged the knife into the man's wrist. The gun hit the floor while the man in the black robes fell back onto the bed, screaming in agony.

At the same instant, Madison leapt upon Claire who had only begun to understand why James was moving so suddenly. Madison pushed her onto the bed face first. She looped her hands around Claire's head and choked her with the zip-tie that bound her hands together.

The man in the black robes struggled to get up from the bed, but before he got his footing, James threw him against the sliding glass door. The man fought back, first punching James in the ear, and then kicking the knife out of James' hand. As James staggered from the blow to the head, the man turned and opened the sliding glass door to make his escape, even as blood trickled down his arm.

"Where are you going?" gasped Claire, fighting for air. She watched her last hope of success flee onto the balcony.

Once again, the black robed figure climbed on to the railing to pull himself up to the next deck. This time, James was within striking distance. With a desperate leap, James dove through the open door and threw his body against the man as he balanced on the railing. The impact knocked the wind out of the man and jarred his grip from the railing. In a split second of abject horror, the man cried out, spastically reaching out for anything that would hold him. His hands found no purchase. He tumbled away from the deck, disappearing into the torrential blackness and towards the writhing ocean a hundred feet below.

James turned and reentered the room. He pulled the canvas bag from Brennan's head. Brennan's head slumped against his chest as blood trickled from a gash across his cheek bone. Brennan's face was already getting puffy and purple, no doubt from being pistol whipped. James picked the knife up off the floor and cut Brennan's bonds while gently slapping the non-bruised side of his face.

"Come on, buddy. Wake up. I need you awake my friend."

Brennan's head rolled back and forth until it finally rose out of the mire of unconsciousness. His left eye opened and he looked around.

"My head is killing me."

"You took a pretty good shot to the face. Probably have a concussion, so don't sleep." James stood and laid his hand on Brennan's shoulder.

"Hey James," said Brennan. He spoke with a wandering lilt in his voice. "I don't want to alarm you, but I don't think we can trust Claire."

"Yeah, we got that, Brennan. We're way ahead of you."

"I was making a joke," he said as he winced.

"Easy there, Madison, we need that one to breathe if we're going to get the answers we need." Madison let up on Claire's windpipe. James picked up the gun and waved it at their new captive.

"Alright, Madison, you can let her sit up," James cut the zip-tie that bound Madison's hands. Claire looked at James with a caustic stare.

"Let's find out what she knows," he said.

⋲⊂⟩⊃⟆

Brennan flinched at Madison's mere touch as she dabbed a cold washcloth to his face. His right eye had completely swelled shut.

"The swelling doesn't look like it's subsiding. I wish I had some ice to put on your face," she said. "Here's some Ibuprofen in the meantime." She handed him four of the brown pills and a glass of water.

Across the room, James stood over Claire in absolute control.

"Let's start with first things first," he said in a steely voice. Claire's slumped shoulders demonstrated bitter resignation, though her eyes failed to admit defeat. She didn't struggle against the cord that bound her hands behind her back. "Where is your friend?"

Claire glared at the carpet.

"Your friend at the bar? Beckie. The one that seemed so captivated by everything I said. You're working with her and I need to know where she is."

Claire's gaze shot up to James. "Beckie has nothing to do with this. I used her to get on the boat. I only had a few hours to make arrangements, so I brought her along."

James sat down on the bed and studied Claire's face.

"Who is Beckie? A long time partner of yours? Another agent?"

"Leave her out of this." Claire trembled, but was it from fear or anger?

"Ah, I see." James chuckled. "She means something to you. Only, I'm not sure it has anything to do with your work as a bounty hunter. Perhaps that can be useful to us. Does she even know that you're on this ship to kidnap and steal?"

"She has nothing to do with this."

"It's no matter. We'll find your little girlfriend, and she'll tell us what she knows."

"Please. Leave her alone," pleaded Claire.

"Well, we might. It depends how cooperative you are with us. Are you ready to answer a few questions?"

Claire was silent. James proceeded with the questioning.

"Who was the guy in the robes? Why did Giovanni send you if he already had a freakin' ninja onboard?"

"He wasn't a *ninja*, his name was John. He was a bouncer and a friend of mine. I brought him along as extra muscle. Giovanni said you'd be trouble. Oh John," she said in a soft voice, "I can't believe he's gone…"

"Why were you told to kidnap Madison? Why is she so important to you?"

"I don't know why they needed her. I was just told to get her. The girl and some arrowhead, that's all I was told."

"I don't believe you," said James. His face twisted in frustration and he placed his hand on her neck. Madison thought James was going to hit her; maybe a pistol-whip to make up for what she'd done to Brennan. James was quivering and it scared Madison. She wanted to place her hand on his shoulder to calm him down, but found she was too afraid.

"James," Brennan said, wincing as he spoke. "James, look at me." His voice was weak, but it still had power. James snapped his head. "Be cool, alright? Just be cool."

"She knows something, Bren."

"It doesn't matter. She's not going to talk. This isn't how we do things. We're better than this."

Brennan was right. James released his grasp and paced around the room, visibly frustrated, but regaining his composure.

"Hold on a minute." His eyes lit up with a new idea. He ran his hands up and down Claire's body and then slid his hand into each one of the four pockets in her jeans.

"Is that what you want?" said Claire. She fell silent when James withdrew a plastic keycard from her back pocket.

"Ah. Now which room does this open?" asked James in a calm voice, once again under control.

"I'm not going to tell you. Why would I?" asked Claire. "You'll have to try every door on the ship. You'll never-"

"-Room 7277," said Brennan in a weak voice. "She invited me up there last night?"

"Damn it," said Claire and again her shoulders slumped in resignation.

James handed the gun fitted with the silencer to Madison. "I'm going to go search her room and see if I can find anything useful. In the meantime, hold this. If she does anything other than sit on that bed until I get back, you can shoot her."

The door clicked shut as James left the room. The atmosphere changed with each passing breath. What had been a stable situation with James in charge— barking orders and extracting information— became a quiet fog of tension. The rain began falling harder again, rapping against the sliding glass door.

Madison glared at Claire while holding the pistol. She wanted her to know that she was still a prisoner, even though James had left the room. Keeping the gun pointed loosely in the captive's direction, Madison sat on the edge of the bed near Brennan.

"Brennan, dear?" Claire's voice changed to a sing song- lilt. "Bren, we had something, didn't we? Sure, we were both doing our jobs, but honestly, sweetie, there's something there. Don't you think?"

"I'm trying to remember but the concussion from that pistol-whip is making it a little difficult," said Brennan.

"Oh, sweetheart," she laughed with a calculated giggle. "I'm so sorry about that. John wasn't supposed to do that. He got carried away, that's all. Look, just let me go and I'll promise to make you forget about that little bruise."

"You're not serious," said Brennan.

"Come on. People have come together under far worse circumstances. I like you Brennan, even if I had to call you 'Doctor' for a couple days. Let me go, and I'll show you my appreciation."

"Would you please gag her?"

"You all are monsters," Claire said in disgust. "All these grave robbers are monsters. Don't get too close to that one," she said to Madison. "Your boy James will sell you out the first chance he gets if it'll bring him closer to what he's looking for. They'll kill anyone in their way to get what they're after."

"That's funny. A mercenary lambasting a treasure hunter for his ethics," said Madison. "Here, chew on this a while, Miss Pot. Mr. Kettle should be back soon." Madison took a towel from the bathroom and tied it around Claire's mouth, gagging her.

"Bren," said Madison after a few minutes had passed. "Thanks for coming to rescue me. You have no idea how scared I was when that hood-" her voice choked with emotion. Brennan nodded and patted her knee, but said nothing.

The lock on the door beeped followed by the door swinging open. James moved quickly through with a heavy load wrapped in a sheet slung over his shoulder.

"Now, maybe we'll get somewhere," he said. He dropped the bundle onto the bed, pulled at the sheet, and unwrapped Beckie. Her hands were zip-tied in front of her and her mouth was taped shut with black tape. She looked around the room, her eyes wide with panic.

Madison expected her to be full of hate like Claire, but the way she shook with fear, the way she whimpered, told her that Beckie hadn't the slightest clue what was going on. Madison concluded that Beckie was innocent even before she'd heard the first protest from her taped-shut mouth.

Claire looked at Beckie and a new pain showed in Beckie's eyes. James removed the towel from Claire's mouth.

"I'm sorry, Beckie. I'm sorry I got you into this," said Claire.

"Okay, enough chit-chat," said James. "Now, Claire, you're going to tell me why you needed Madison. Why is she involved in this?"

"I told you, I don't know," said Claire. "I got a call from Green Light. He said you were headed to Italy with a girl and an object—the ruby arrowhead on a cruise ship. I was supposed to be on that ship, find you, get the arrowhead and capture your girlfriend. He didn't say why."

"She's not his girlfriend," said Brennan. "What's Green Light?"

"It's a code name. We don't know many people in the organization. We all have code names. Anyway, Green Light is like my dispatcher and my agent combined. He finds me work."

"You keep saying 'me'" said James, "why don't you include your other two friends in this?"

"Because they don't work for Giovanni. John was a bouncer I knew. I hired him because I knew I couldn't kidnap someone on my own."

"And Beckie?" asked James.

"Beckie… uh, goes to school with me." Her gaze dropped to the floor. "She was part of my cover story for being on the boat."

"You're not telling me anything I can use," said James raising his voice. "You must have heard something. Giovanni told you more. You wouldn't give up all that information if you didn't have something else to hide."

"I'm telling you everything I know."

"It's not good enough." James moved suddenly and his quickness amidst the verbal sparring startled Madison. James had Beckie wrapped up in his arms before Claire could even react.

"What are you doing?" Claire asked.

James opened the sliding glass door. The sound of the rain crashed into the room.

"No! Brennan, please. Stop him!" screamed Claire.

James stepped onto the balcony and sat Beckie on the railing, her back to the raging sea. Within seconds she was soaked through. Beckie tried to scream through the tape over her mouth.

"Stop it." Claire jumped to her feet but Madison waved the gun in her direction. Claire could not stop James. He held Beckie by the front of her shirt. A small shove would send her tumbling into the sea.

"Now tell me everything," said James in a terrifying voice over the roar of the rain.

Madison couldn't believe what she was seeing. She was about to watch an innocent girl be murdered for information. The ship rolled as the storm renewed its vigor. Madison stumbled under the pitching deck. Beckie lost her balance and slid backwards towards the open sea.

James held her tight by the shirt but her hips slid towards the ocean. Beckie's knees and his grasp were the only things keeping her from falling into the churning sea below. It was too much for Beckie. Her eyes rolled into the back of her head and she lost consciousness.

"What do you know, Claire?" asked James again, unfazed by the storm. "This is the last time I'll ask."

Claire was in tears. Her spirit finally broke.

"Okay! I'll tell you. Please don't drop her. Please? Don't kill her. Please don't. Don't kill her," Claire sobbed into the bedspread.

James pulled Beckie into the ship off the balcony and tossed her limp body onto the bed.

"You bought your girlfriend a few more minutes," said James with a firm voice. He slid the door closed. "You'd better start talking."

"She's not my girlfriend, you psychopath. She's my sister." Claire collapsed on top of Beckie and held her soaking-wet and lifeless body.

It was several minutes before Claire could compose herself enough to speak. Beckie regained consciousness, but with her mouth taped shut, she laid there immobile.

"So what do they want with Madison?" James sat on the couch, the gun not needed anymore. He'd won the battle of wills and he was confident that Claire would give him what he wanted.

"Madison has the other half," said Claire in defeated resignation. "The arrowhead is only half of the key. It fits to a second piece. Giovanni believes Madison either has it or can get it."

James and Brennan turned to Madison with raised eyebrows.

"I haven't any idea what she's talking about, James," said Madison.

"What does it look like?" asked Brennan, returning the attention to Claire.

"I don't know." Claire looked fearfully at James, "I swear, I don't know. My instructions were to grab the arrowhead and the girl in the first two days of sailing. I was to receive further instructions if I succeeded. Otherwise, I was supposed to track you into Rome where you could be apprehended."

"Why the first two days of sailing?" asked James.

"We're still in range of one of Giovanni's fishing boats that's been tracking us since we left. I was supposed to get off the ship and activate this homing beacon." She turned the top of her pants out and showed a small electrical device sewn into the waistband. "They'd then pick us up."

"This storm was no match for your fishing boat rescuers. Even if you had gotten the arrowhead and captured Madison you'd have been in the water a few days before your boat found you. Maybe longer."

"I hate this job," said Claire flopping back on the bed. "So what are you going to do with us? Are you going to kill us?" she asked.

"Kill you?" said James through a cough. "Well, contrary to popular belief, I'm not a psychopath. But good question, though. I'm not about to spend the next 12 days with prisoners in my room." James rose and opened the top drawer of the dresser. He withdrew a black nylon case with a zipper around three sides. "I think we need to go for a walk. If you two will come with me? Brennan, are you up to it?"

"I'm with you boss," said Brennan rising with an appearance of strength.

"Madison, are you coming?" asked Brennan.

"I'm not staying here," she said.

❧

The elevator opened onto the Lobby Deck, the deck with the lowest public spaces. Madison and Brennan stepped out with Beckie and Claire close behind them, their bonds temporarily freed. James stood behind them, the gun concealed in his waistband.

A bartender cleaned up a pile of broken glasses and another maintenance man mopped up some standing water. Other than that, the lobby was empty as the storm kept the sick and weary passengers confined to their beds.

"This way, ladies," said James as he opened the door to the lowest external deck on the ship, the same deck where they had taken their life boat training the day before. Fighting against the wind and rain, they staggered their way to the railing.

"Now what?" asked Claire, as the rain poured over her in sheets. A bubbling seas seethed below them.

"It's sleepy time," said James. He pulled two small plastic containers with short protruding needles from his black case and handed one to Brennan. Simultaneously, they each lunged for the two prisoners: James to Claire, and Brennan to Beckie.

"Ow!" said Claire. "You jabbed me." She rubbed her arm. Beckie rubbed her arm as well. "What was that?"

"Something to help you sleep for your journey," said James.

"I'm not going-." She never finished the sentence. Claire fell unconscious into James' arms and he set her down on the wet decking. A second later Beckie lost consciousness.

"Those are more powerful than I remembered," said James.

"I made them extra strong this time," smiled Brennan.

"What was that?" asked Madison, stunned by the immediacy of the drug's effects. "Did you poison them?"

"Just a little ketamine hydrochloride. Knockout juice, just like your doctor uses."

"Only, a bit more concentrated," said Brennan.

"This is insane. Now what are we going to do with two lifeless bodies out here in the open like this?" Her question was answered by a clang and chatter as one of the overhead cranes lowered a lifeboat to the deck. Madison wanted to protest, but found herself choked with sea-mist as the rain swept through the deck.

James opened the covered top to the lifeboat and quickly loaded the two prisoners into the vessel. The two bodies fell into the boat like two sacks of potatoes being dropped into a truck bed. He pulled at Claire's pants and activated the homing device sewn into her waistband. James resealed the top of the boat and let fly the crane. The boat splashed down into the water, nearly capsizing on impact before righting itself. The chains continued downward until they slipped off the hooks that connected them to the boat. Now free of the lifeboat, James retracted the chains to their highest position.

"Hopefully they'll think that the boat was ripped free in the storm," said James into the wind. "If not, at least it will be daylight before they even know that it is gone. Let's get inside."

Brennan stood in the bathroom in Madison's room checking the swollen side of his head.

"That's going to be black and blue for a while," he said. "He hit me right on my cheekbone."

Brennan took four more ibuprofen and stepped back into the stateroom. James sat at the vanity taking apart the pistol.

"Must you field strip every new weapon you get?" asked Brennan flopping down on the couch. "I tell you it's a disease with this guy."

Madison sat on the bed in silence. She was still.

"This storm is a godsend, isn't it?" continued Brennan. "The crew was so busy trying to keep this ship afloat that they didn't even see the lifeboat go out. And the storm kept all those witnesses in their rooms. Beautiful."

He's awfully chatty for a guy who's been hit in the face with a pistol, Madison thought.

James said, "Bren, I think Madison could use a drink. Would you mind heading to the café to get her some lemonade or something?"

"I'm fine," said Madison.

"She says she's fine."

"Bren. A drink for the lady, please." James tone had changed. It was an order.

"Ah," said Brennan, catching on, "I might be a while. It's so hard to find good lemonade on this ship." He turned and left the room.

A quiet settled into the room. Madison's thoughts were a jumble and her emotions difficult to identify, but they all swirled around one question that tormented her conscience. James said nothing, but sat in patient silence as Madison scrutinized the fibers of the carpet. Finally, convinced that James was not going to speak, Madison looked up from the floor asked, "Would you have killed that woman?"

The question did not surprise James. He answered without mirth, "I didn't have to. Claire told me what I needed to know."

"What if she didn't, would you have killed her?"

"I always knew she'd tell me what I needed to know."

"What if you were wrong, James?" Her voice was a plea now.

"It was obvious she cared about Beckie. I thought it was a lesbian thing, but they were sisters. Even better. She wouldn't watch her sister die for the Key of Caligula's Bath or any other artifact."

"But, if you had to? If she called your bluff, would you have killed her? Look James, I appreciate what you did for me tonight. Thank you for coming when I needed you." James nodded. "When you pushed that man off the railing… yes, it was terrifying, but he had tried to kidnap me and would have if he had another chance. This woman, Beckie… she didn't know what was going on. She was innocent, wasn't she?" *Hell, just a few hours ago, you were ready to go to bed with her,* she thought. "Claire and Beckie weren't threatening us," she continued. "You were just trying to get information about the artifact. Would you have killed her for that?"

"I can't answer that. I knew I wouldn't have to. You have to be able to read people pretty well in this job. I'm fairly good at that." James flashed a sheepish smile.

"Is that so?"

"I'd stake my life on it," he said.

"You certainly staked hers." The smile on James' face disappeared. Madison asked, "If you're so good at reading people, what am I thinking?"

"Now?"

"Yes."

James tilted his head in consideration.

"Right now, you're thinking you don't know if you like me. I was fun when I was your tour guide and protector. But, now you've seen something about me you wish you hadn't, something that you're not sure you like."

"And what's that?"

"That I'm dangerous."

And for once, Madison thought, he was right.

XIII

LITTLE BOOTS

"History will be kind to me for I intend to write it."
Winston Churchill

Madison moaned as she awoke reluctantly from a long and detailed dream of fantasy. She didn't open her eyes, so waking was merely the acknowledgement that she was lying in bed, her heart racing, and that she was, unfortunately, *not* on the best date of her life.

The dream included a romantic dinner at a hotel restaurant. The man sitting across the table from her was both familiar and strange. He looked like an old boyfriend with whom she'd long lost contact, but his voice wasn't his own.

She opened her eyes and was reminded that she was in her stateroom still aboard the cruise ship. The room did not sway and the soft hum of the ship's engines told her that they cruised through calm waters in good weather. Moreover, Madison remembered that she was not alone. She rolled over and looked at Brennan sleeping soundly on the couch. He breathed heavily but looked uncomfortable folded up on the short couch.

She peered over the edge of the bed and saw James lying on his side with a pillow crushed into a ball under his head. James also breathed deeply, still asleep this early morning.

It had been over a week since they had sent Claire and her sister adrift in a lifeboat. Since then, James had decided that it was too risky to leave Madison alone again. They communicated with Devin through their email account and he said he couldn't be sure that there weren't other agents onboard. With the newfound knowledge that

Giovanni wanted Madison personally and their cover obviously blown, the decision was made for the three of them to stick together. Someone was always with Madison, day and night, and the three had taken to camping out in Madison's stateroom.

Madison closed her eyes again and recalled the dream. The date played itself out again in her mind; her old boyfriend treating her like a princess. But again, his voice was not his own, nor were his mannerisms.

She stopped the fantasy, trying to identify the owner of the voice that called her name. Then, in a flash of comprehension, she got it. The face was her old boyfriend's, but the voice, mannerisms and physical build was that of James Kynan.

It was puzzling to her. In the past week things had been rather cool between them. Brennan reminding her that James was relationally vulnerable and the realization that James was dangerous, (though, admittedly, on her side), were enough to cool her interest in him. Furthermore, she admitted to herself that something that Claire said made her question her attraction to him.

Would James really sacrifice anything and anyone to get what he wanted? Before that night a week ago, she would have disagreed. Madison would have said that he's an aggressive man and a driven man, but kind, loyal, and virtuous as well. Yet, the way he threatened those women, the anger in his voice and his intensity scared her. So she'd put some distance into the relationship. She was always cordial and friendly, but she'd stopped sharing intimate details about her life and she asked no personal questions.

On the other hand, Madison and Brennan had spent quite a bit of time together in the past week. Brennan seemed to have stopped pursuing easy women at the bar and instead had taken a keen interest in Madison. Brennan was charming, quick witted, and honest despite having the moral chastity of an alley cat on roofies. Moreover, he seemed far less driven and single-minded than James. While James was an adventure at every turn, Brennan was the safe harbor in the storm of this adventure. Brennan was mostly harmless.

Yet, here was James in the middle of her dream in the guise of her old boyfriend. She sighed aloud.

"Is something wrong?" James sat up on his elbows, staring at her with bleary eyes.

"No." She pulled the sheets up to her neck wondering how long he'd been looking at her.

"You sighed. Why?"

"No reason to speak of."

"Sighs don't come without cause," he said.

"This one did, okay?"

"Fine. It was just a sigh." James lay back down, closed his eyes and fell back asleep.

Later that afternoon in the Ivory Room, Madison reclined in a comfortable leather chair reading her book on Caligula. The Ivory Room took residence on the lowest public level of the ship and spanned its full breadth. Its wood-paneled walls, dark red paisley carpet, and plush leather furnishing lent it the air of a British manor house. It was a room where the master of the house might display his hunting collection from a recent safari on the Serengeti. Though lacking stuffed lions and tigers, faux ivory tusks arched over various sitting areas where passengers were welcomed to take afternoon tea or enjoy a fine cigar. It was the only interior public space in the ship where smoking was allowed and several men took their daily dose of tobacco there. Dark canvas curtains blocked out all natural light and the moody sitting areas were illuminated by brass chandeliers fixed rigidly to the ceiling.

In the center of the room, a grand piano held court. Beethoven's "Pathetique" Sonata in C minor undulated through the room, wrapping Madison in a blanket of hypnotic chords. The sweet smell of cigars from other passengers wafted along with the music taking Madison momentarily to the early 19th century.

In the course of the past week, Madison had found ample free time to read up on the Roman ruler and was nearly finished with her book.

"I thought you could use some tea."

Madison looked up to see Brennan holding a tray with two tea cups, a tea pot, a plate of scones, jam, and clotted cream balanced on it.

"Oh. Hi, Brennan. Thank you. That sounds great," said Madison. She took a cup and saucer from him, poured the tea and sampled it. Brennan took up residence in the leather chair next to her.

"Darjeeling?" she asked.

"Yep. Thought you could use something tangy yet smooth. So, what've you learned about our friend Caligula?"

"Well, to say he was an unpopular ruler would be an understatement. I mean, he was popular enough as 'Little Boots", their cute mascot, but when he got into power, he changed."

"How so?"

"He became a tyrant," she said.

"The power went to his head?"

"I don't know what it was," she paused. "He began his rule well, with the small exception of the possibility that he killed his grandfather, Tiberius, to become emperor. But, he increased pay to the military, eliminated treason trials, made some infrastructure improvements to help fight a famine, and generally did some popular things. The first half of his four year reign actually went pretty well. A couple years in, something happened."

"What?"

"We don't really know. The book says he was sick for a while and that might have caused it. Maybe he went insane, who knows. After that, it was chaos: The prompt execution of political prisoners. Lavish, unnecessary expenses. Indiscrete orgies-"

"-Would it have been better had they been discrete?" asked Brennan.

"You know what I mean. He turned his palace into a brothel, quite literally. He built two huge ships on a lake, uh Lake Nemi," she said flipping back a few pages for the reference. "Two of the largest ships of the ancient world and he had them built on this little lake. One was a temple, the other, essentially a party boat. A total waste. He built a bridge over a bay just so he could ride his horse across it. A two-mile floating bridge!"

"Such are the excesses of power," said Brennan.

"I know, but there's more. He was rumored to have affairs with other men's wives and then brag about it. Some say he had incestuous encounters with his three sisters. He executed people without trials and was one of the first to encourage the violent gladiator games. This is more than a little splurging on oneself."

"Shhhh," said a woman thumbing through a gossip magazine on a couch a few feet away. Madison smiled and sent her an apologetic wave.

"So he went psycho. What's the big deal?" asked Brennan, lowering his voice.

"I don't know, Bren. I mean, he obviously hated the tyranny of Tiberius, but after a few years in power he became exactly what he hated. It's just sad to think that you can be one person one day then be the polar opposite the next day."

"It's happened to lesser men than Roman emperors."

The pianist finished the sonata and waved at the ripple of polite applause from around the room. A waifish red-headed girl joined him with a violin and the two launched into a piece by Schubert-Impromptu in G flat.

"Know anyone like that?" asked Madison as she prepared a scone for herself.

"Yeah I do. You know him too."

"James?"

"You should have seen him three or four years ago." Brennan hitched a leg over the arm of the chair and destroyed the class and civility of the room's ambiance.

"You mean before Michelle," Madison said.

"I don't know what that girl did to him, but before her, James was a confident and fun-loving treasure hunter. He owned this world, Madison. Every major collector wanted him on their payroll. Major museums were actively recruiting him and he could have had any woman he wanted." Brennan sighed. "Nothing was out of reach for James. He was invincible. Some people started calling him *Lucky Jim*. A bit of envy at his success, I'm sure."

"Brennan?" said Madison softly as she leaned forward, "The way James threatened that girl, when he hung her over that balcony—"

"Did that scare you?" asked Brennan.

"It did."

"It never would have happened like that in the old days. To be honest, he scared me too. I hadn't seen that kind of anger in him before. I've seen him improvise, fly by the seat of his pants, so to speak, and I've seen him handle some of the toughest guys on the planet, but always with a smile and a wink, you know? We moved quickly and surgically and rarely left any traces behind.

"Now everything is serious and handled heavily with a lot of mess. He's cautious now, but sloppy at the same time. If this were the old days, we would be in Rome by now, regardless of the men Giovanni might have at the airport when we landed. We wouldn't be on this blasted ship like sitting ducks with two Giovanni agents floating helplessly in the open ocean. Don't get me wrong, I'm glad he's not sulking around Europe. At least he's back to work. But he's changed, like your boy Caligula."

"Well, let's hope he's not too much like Caligula."

"Why do you say that?" asked Brennan.

"Because Caligula's best friend— the man that got him into power and took care of him— was Marco."

"Yeah? Are you saying that would make me Marco? And the significance is…?"

"Caligula had Marco executed three years into his reign."

Madison had expected Brennan to laugh at the comparison, but to her surprise he grew quite sober. He stirred his tea slowly and then muttered,

"Yes, well then… let's hope."

The musicians finished their piece, nodded to the crowd and then excused themselves to take a short respite. The room fell silent for a few moments before conversations resumed and the clinking of porcelain tea cups and silver spoons resonated through the room.

"Look, Madison, I know this is a bad time for this," began Brennan. His voice was different, halting and a little unsure. "But I've really enjoyed spending this week with you, and, I was just thinking, after all this is over maybe you and I could—"

"James." Madison's voice betrayed her eagerness at an interruption. Across the room, she saw James crossing to join them, and his timing was perfect. Madison didn't know exactly where Brennan was going, but she'd heard similar speeches and they never seemed to end well.

James filled a third chair around the low table.

"We're getting off the ship," he said with authority. He then caught a glance from Brennan. "I'm sorry. I'm not interrupting anything, am I?"

"Actually-" said Brennan.

"—Not at all. We were just enjoying some tea and scones. You want Bren to get you a cup?" asked Madison.

"No thanks," said James. "Look, you know we put in at Madeira tomorrow, right? Well, we have to assume that Claire was able to confirm that we were on the ship before we sent her adrift. That means that even if Giovanni hasn't heard from her yet, he'll have a posse of his henchmen waiting for us in Rome."

"But he also knows that one of the ship's ports-of-call is Madeira," said Madison. "Won't he be waiting for us there?"

"Probably, but he doesn't have near the presence in Portugal as he does in Italy. And Madeira is hard to get to even for the Portuguese," said James. "No, I think we'll have better luck getting into Madeira and then working our way from Portugal, up through Spain, southern France, and then down into Italy. Giovanni may have a few people waiting for us in Madeira, but I think we stand a better chance of slipping off the ship there than in Rome."

"What does Devin think?" asked Brennan.

"Here's the latest email I got from him," James said handing it to Brennan. Brennan read it, letting out a loud dissatisfied groan at one point, and then handed it to Madison.

"The code is the same, Madison. 4 5 3," said Brennan.

"Oh, I can't read your stupid code. It gives me a headache to sort through the nonsense." Madison threw up her hands. "Can you just tell me what it says?"

"In short, he likes the idea. And he's going to send us some help," said James.

"Oh, this is just fantastic," said Brennan.

"Why? Who is he sending us?" asked Madison.

"Francisco." Brennan slumped in his chair. "I hate that guy."

No matter how gargantuan the ship, how opulent the accommodations, or how pleasant the weather, all passengers, especially the uninitiated landlubbers, will eventually find themselves anxious to disembark their vessel and to set their feet on solid earth once again. The *Glamour* was no exception. After being at sea for nine straight days and surviving the strong gale followed by the regular chop as they crossed the Atlantic, the passengers buzzed with the prospect of revisiting their long-lost land legs.

The ship slid into the narrow bay on Madeira, an exotic and isolated Portuguese island due west of Morocco. Although Madeira's major contribution to western culture is the wine that bears its name, the island's chief modern-day purpose is to serve as a vacation home to many Europeans and a popular port-of-call to a number of cruise lines. Madeira rests tantalizingly in the Atlantic 700 hundred miles from the Straits of Gibraltar. The island, along with its sister island Porto Santo, welcomes transatlantic visitors and offers them their first taste of Europe.

The port of the capital city of Funchal clings to the south side of Madeira Island and offers its residents protection from the strong northerly winds that accompanied many Atlantic storms and cyclones. The land around the port rises dramatically from the water like the rise of an amphitheater centered on the port. It was as if all of Madeira's attention was focused on the arriving cruise ship. Precisely the opposite of what James wanted.

The ship came to an imperceptible stop and lines were cast from the ship to the pier, securing the mighty vessel against impossibly large rubber bumpers fixed to the side of the pier. From the stateroom balcony, James could see dozens of makeshift tents erected on the pier itself, offering the disembarking tourists their first opportunity to purchase overpriced trinkets and mementos from their eight-hour visit to the island.

The pier arched around the bay and led up to the shore where lines of taxis and charter buses waited to whisk the passengers to vineyards, ruins, and shopping areas throughout the island. It was not yet eight o'clock in the morning and the island was alive.

"You'd think the President had just arrived. Look at that mess down there," said Brennan leaning against the railing on the balcony.

Trevor, the cruise director, issued announcement after announcement over the ship-wide loud speakers along with several groan-worthy puns having to do with having *fun* in Funchal. Some announcements offered extra deals on shore excursions while others chastised the passengers to be back aboard by 4:00pm, lest they be left behind. Trevor reminded them that airfare off of Madeira was uncommonly expensive.

"I wish that guy would shut up. He's been squawking for the last half an hour," said Brennan. "So, what do you think boss? Does Giovanni have some guys down there?" He looked at the throng of people and shook his head.

"You can bet on it," said James as he reclined in one of the plastic deck chairs, his fingers interlocked behind his head. "I'm not worried about the crowd. We've handled a crowd before. But, it will make finding Francisco difficult."

"Great. Another game. Find Francisco before Giovanni's men find us," said Brennan.

❧

James walked across the gangplank with his backpack on his back and Madison's pack slung over one shoulder. Brennan followed across the metal bridge that connected the weather-beaten steel ship with the concrete pier. Madison followed behind, running her hands through her hair and donning her sunglasses as she stepped into the bright sunlight.

They strolled past the tents on the pier. This was still a secure area, and undoubtedly these tents belonged to the cruise line. At the head of the pier was a gate patrolled by two armed guards in the uniform of the Portuguese Navy. Beyond that was the true Madeira.

James approached the gate and his mind shifted to another gear as he scrutinized the mayhem beyond the gate. The casual organization of the cruise ship ended at the gate and the flurry of vendors, drivers, salesmen and con-artists fought for position in the street. Boisterous signs hovered on makeshift wooden posts a few feet above the crowd advertising day trips, discount memorabilia, and all forms of alcohol. James set his jaw and pressed through the gate and into the throng of thousands.

"So, what are we looking for?" asked Madison when they'd come to a stop a few hundred feet down the street. Colorful, two-story buildings with orange roofs surrounded the four lane street; traffic moved swiftly in both directions. James held up his hand. This was no time for explanations.

The situation was the one that James hated most. He didn't know what the dangers looked like and he didn't know what success looked like. He felt like a falling leaf at the mercy of the wind.

He thought back to his training long ago: *Observational Awareness.* It had been another life entirely when he was trained, but he clearly remembered the skills.

You can't see everything.

He remembered being told to walk into a grocery store, glace around for ten seconds, and then, with eyes closed, recite what he could remember. Regardless of his effort, there were always far more things he missed than he remembered.

You can't see everything in its place. But you can see what's out of place.

"What's out of place?" James asked aloud.

"What do you mean?" asked Brennan. He spun his head around as if he'd missed something critical.

"What doesn't fit?" James asked with eyes narrowed. A large tour bus moved past them as an arsenal of digital cameras protruded from the windows. Brennan and Madison scanned the area. Tourists pushed past them into the town of Funchal.

"I don't see anything, James. Nothing's out of place," Brennan said.

"Yeah, that's what concerns me. Neither do I."

James assumed he would have the advantage here. After all, he knew when he'd be leaving the ship and he knew where Giovanni would send his men. Moreover, he knew that he had an ally in Francisco somewhere on the island. Standing on this busy street without a clue as to what the situation was, told him that he was the prey and that he'd lost his advantages. The element of surprise was with his enemy and the longer they stood out in the open the more likely it was that the arrowhead and Madison would be taken from him. He pressed his hand to his sternum, squeezing the arrowhead in its velvet pouch against his chest.

"We need to move," James said. He turned to his right and began moving with the flow of pedestrians up the sidewalk away from the gate.

"Why? What do you see? What's the plan?" asked Madison.

Why must she always assume that I know what I'm doing?

"Bren. Tail," James said. Instantly Brennan turned off and entered one of the shops on the street and inspected a handmade rug in the shop. Brennan would wait a few minutes before following them up the street checking to see if they were being followed.

The crowd hummed with frenetic activity and soon the sidewalk was jammed with people. James reached out and grabbed her hand. He wasn't going to lose her in this hoard.

James led her along the street as it rose up the hill further into the city. They passed a small outdoor café and then James pulled her into a side street. The game was the same as it had been on the cruise ship: Find progressively less and less busy streets until Brennan could positively determine if they were being followed.

"I don't understand. What's wrong?" asked Madison.

"Just follow me."

"I am," she said. James felt her grip tighten in his hand.

The crowd on this street was smaller, but not nearly thin enough to observe if they were being followed. James was about to head down an alleyway when he was jarred from the side by what felt like a potato sack thrown at his knees. He staggered and looked up to see a boy, not yet twelve years old, fleeing with Madison's backpack that had just a second earlier been slung around his shoulder.

"Hey!" was all James could muster and he broke into a dead sprint through the street after the boy.

James flew through the crowd, dodging and twisting amongst the myriad of people, never letting the small boy out of his sight. He was vaguely aware of Madison close behind him, but he wasn't worried about her. She could keep up.

Down the alleyway, around a corner, back into the crowd and the busy street, the boy ran as if possessed, though he never looked behind him. A waiting taxi sat with its back door propped open. The boy leapt into the back seat and exited out the other side. James followed the boy through. Madison, a few seconds later, scampered around the vehicle.

The boy dashed down the street and tore through a local shop making no apologies and exited out the back door. Ignoring the shopkeeper's plea, James charged through the store and exited out the back door a few seconds behind the boy.

The little thief sprinted through the vacant alleyway and then entered an open door just beyond some garbage cans at the other end of the alley. The door seemed to be a small service door on the back of a warehouse. James plunged into the dark warehouse followed a few moments later by Madison. James stopped as he realized that he'd thrown himself into a dark room and couldn't see anything beyond what the natural light from the open door illuminated. Madison, breathing heavily, reached out and took his elbow.

This is not good, thought James. *How could I have been so stupid?*

At that instant, the door behind them closed and everything went dark.

Far overhead, a light flickered once. It flickered again, and then a bank of fluorescent lights flooded the room with pale white light. Standing in front of them was a tall, fit man with jet black hair and rich yellow-brown skin. He wore a tight sleeveless t-shirt, black leather pants, and a pair of eel-skin boots. In his hand he held Madison's backpack. His right hand rested on the boy's shoulder.

"Really?" said James in an annoyed voice. "Is this how you had to do this, Francisco?"

"I am sorry, but the way you blundered out of that cruise ship, we had to do something. I could not allow you to be followed here," said the man in a thick Spanish accent. "But first things first, James, I was told you had a woman with you, but I was not informed as to her immense beauty. This is information that should have been passed along."

Francisco approached Madison with a captivating smile.

"My dear, I believe you have lost this," he said offering her the backpack. "Next time you should leave it with someone who will protect it."

"Thank you," said Madison.

"Francisco del Amante, at your service," he said, extending his hand. Madison took his hand and shook it.

"Madison Dawn," she said. Francisco had other plans for her hand. He took it, turned it over, and gently kissed the back.

"Welcome to Madeira, Senorita."

James could see Madison blush and jealousy welled up inside of him. He was about to interject when a violent bang was heard at the door they'd entered. Another thump. Someone was pounding on the door, trying to force it open.

"*Vá vêem quem é*," said Francisco in Portuguese.

The boy quickly ran to the door, looked through a small hole in the wall and then opened the door.

Brennan stumbled into the room out of breath and covered in sweat.

"Senior Nash. It is good to see you again, my friend," said Francisco.

Brennan recoiled in shock at the image of the man in front of him. "Are you serious? You? I thought these two were taken by Giovanni's men." Brennan let out a long pathetic sigh and leaned up against the wall holding his side. "I'm so out of shape."

"A week on a cruise ship will do that to those who are lazy, eh?" said Francisco. "But come, we have much to discuss and I think this is not the place for it." Francisco smiled at Madison with a good-natured expression and extended his arm. Madison took it and the two walked ahead of them leaving James and Brennan behind in stupefied silence.

"He just called me lazy, didn't he?" asked Brennan.

"Yep," said James.

"Did I mention that I hate this guy?"

James and Brennan shared a frustrated grunt and then followed Francisco and Madison out of the room.

XIV

MADEIRA

"Moral indignation is jealousy with a halo"
H. G. *Wells*

"Wow. Francisco. This place is amazing." Madison stood in the middle of Francisco's apartment with a delighted expression on her face. James entered the door with Brennan just behind him. His look conceded that the apartment was incredible.

Francisco's place was a loft apartment on the third floor of a building that housed a bakery and a hardware store on the ground floor. The back of the apartment consisted of four enormous windows that overlooked the sparkling water of Funchal bay. The windows were flung open wide and a cool sea breeze blew a relaxed and therapeutic air through the apartment which mixed with the scent of fresh baked bread. Sheer curtains hung on either side of the windows and flapped tantalizingly in the ocean breeze.

In the distance James could see the cruise ship, their home for almost a week and a half, moored against the pier. Several sailboats scooted into and out of the bay as the distant cry of seagulls hung on the breeze. The wicker furniture was turned so that every seat looked out over the bay. A small wooden table was set near the kitchenette close to the windows.

"*Você seja uma vigia,*" said Francisco to the young boy. He handed him a coin and the little boy disappeared back through the front door. James didn't speak Portuguese, but he understood that the young boy was going to serve sentry duty while they were here.

"Francisco, who's the boy?" asked Madison.

"Gil? He's a boy I found in Lisbon. He is a, he's a… " said Francisco, searching for the right word. "eh, his parents died. I found him throwing rocks at girls one day. I said to myself, 'Francisco, this boy must learn how to treat the girls.' So I give him opportunity to learn and eat and make some Euros."

"You took in an orphan?" Madison asked. "That's so noble." James snickered quietly to himself. James wouldn't have used the word 'noble'. *Advantageous* would be more appropriate.

"You have not breakfast yet, have you?" asked Francisco addressing only Madison.

"No, we didn't get anything before we got off the ship," said Madison.

"Well come, I make you something. Francisco will take care of you. Sit, please. I will make you an omelet you will not forget," he said.

"That sounds wonderful."

"You should be careful with these two. They'd rather starve themselves and their beautiful guest in pursuit of their treasure than take a break to eat," Francisco said with a wink.

"I'll take an omelet too," said James. This was getting ridiculous.

"Make that three," said Brennan.

"There are eggs here, mi amigos. Help yourself," said Francisco as he washed his hands at the sink and pulled some eggs out of the refrigerator. "Senorita, we have not much time on this delightful island, but you must sample their famous Madeira wine. There is a bottle of it on the table there."

"It's not yet 8:30 in the morning, Francisco," said James. "I think it's probably a little early for-"

"-I'd love some," said Madison. "Wine for breakfast. Brilliant." Madison laughed and opened the bottle of wine before James or Brennan could think to open it for her.

"I just can't get over this view, Francisco," said Madison. "It's beautiful. How long have you been on Madeira?"

"This time? I been here only three days, though, I been here many times before. I got message from your Devin asking to take you to Rome. I borrowed this place from mi amigo."

"So, where do you call home?" she asked.

Francisco tossed the ingredients of the omelet into a skillet on the stove and a hissing sizzle filled the room.

"Have you ever heard of Catalonia?"

"It's part of Spain, isn't it?" said Madison sipping her wine from a large wine goblet she'd found in a cabinet.

"Southeastern Spain, right? Near Italy, I believe," offered Brennan attempting to join the conversation. Francisco ignored him and instead continued to add herbs and spices and chopped vegetables to Madison's omelet.

"Think of the most beautiful and restful place you can imagine. Think of the people who live in that paradise. Okay? Are you thinking it? Catalonia is where *those* people go for vacation. It is a place of soft green mountains, playful whitewater rivers, and mysterious medieval castles."

Madison took a sip of her wine and stared out at the bay, obviously lost in the romantic picture Francisco had painted for her. Francisco finished Madison's omelet, slid it onto a plate, and handed it to her.

"So what is the plan, Francisco?" asked James.

"Well, Devin wants me to get you to Rome. I was going to get you there by next week, but now that I see what charming company you keep, James, I think we'll take an exceedingly slow tramp steamer up the Mediterranean. Should get there in a month or so."

"Francisco. I hope you're joking," said James in a rather humorless tone of voice.

"Ay, always with you Americans and rushing around. No time to enjoy life. Alright, okay. I was kidding. Devin says that time is of essence, but we must also move discretely. A small airline that goes to Lisbon and leaves late tonight. From there we take late night trains to Rome. We'll be in Rome in a couple of days. How's the omelet?"

"Oh, wonderful. I've never had food like this," said Madison. She leaned back in her chair and sighed.

Damn, he's good, thought James. "Is there a landline I can use? I should call Devin and check in," he said.

"Is in the corner there, behind the curtain. The master bedroom," said Francisco.

"And I'll make us some breakfast," said Brennan with a sneer towards Francisco.

When were they picked up, Devin?"

"Two days ago. A US destroyer picked up the lifeboat's emergency beacon and recovered them."

"Beckie and Claire?"

"The girls were recovered in good condition. It was all over the national news, though. They told the press a story about being swept overboard with the lifeboat in the storm. The cruise line is under fire for losing passengers in a storm, but other than that I think it'll blow over in a few days."

"Do I need to worry about those two? They know a lot about us."

"Not likely. They're being returned to Miami. I'm sure they'll pass on their information to Giovanni, though. Is Francisco getting you off that rock soon?"

"Well, it's too dangerous to move around the city during the day. I think the plan is to leave tonight, but I haven't worked out the details with him. He's too busy working his Francisco-esque charms on the girl."

"Francisco will be Francisco, even when there's danger in the air."

"Stealth is our only hope of getting to Rome without twenty Giovanni agents on our tail. We'll take it easy, resting during the day, and taking overnight trains. Probably take two or three days to get in to Rome."

"James, there's something you should know. You need to recover the empire marker as soon as you can."

"Last time we spoke, you said it wasn't a race, Devin. Is it Hardbottle? Is he pulling the plug?"

"No. It has to do with the girl."

"Madison?"

"Her mother, actually."

"What are you saying?"

"Giovanni is on to Plan B." There was silence. *"James. They're after her family now. I don't know much else besides that."*

"You have to protect them."

"We're doing what we can. I've got people heading up there now. Just get that empire marker. There's no time to waste. Once you do that, Madison and her family will mean nothing to Giovanni and she can get her life back."

"Damn it, Devin, Why didn't you say this before? We've pissed away a week and a half on that blasted cruise ship."

"I know, I'm sorry. I thought we had time to play coy. It looks like I was wrong. For that, I'm sorry... for Madison's sake."

"I wish she'd never gotten involved."

"Do you, James?"

ᚹ᚜ᚹ

James emerged from the master bedroom with a heavy weight on his shoulders. He rubbed his chin in thought.

"Okay, Francisco, we need to go as soon as possible," he said.

"They left," said Brennan sitting at the table and scooping a bite of omelet into his mouth. "Your omelet is over there."

"What do you mean, they left?"

"Francisco insisted Madison see the 'charming orchard of immense beauty'," he said mocking the Spaniard's accent. "They went down the hill."

"Let me guess. You weren't invited."

"It was like I wasn't even in the room," Brennan said.

"Francisco is like a dirty magician. He waves his wand and the girls crumble at his feet," James said looking out at the bay.

"Seriously, boss, can't we ditch this guy?" asked Brennan

"You know we need him Brennan. He speaks the local languages far more convincingly than you or me, he grew up in this part of Europe and he has contacts that we could never develop. And besides, he can do things that we can't. Giovanni is looking for you, me and Madison. He doesn't know about Francisco... we hope."

"It's just getting a little crowded, is all."

"The only way to get anywhere close to Rome without Giovanni detecting us is with Francisco's help. And besides, as insulting and infuriating as he can be, he's always been there for us. He's a good guy to have in a fight. Remember Cairo?"

Brennan scratched the back of his neck. "Ha. Yeah. But I had things under control."

"Bren, we were half a day away from starving to death in the desert and somehow he found us and brought us back to life. We'd be a couple of skeletons buried under a sand dune if it weren't for him." James looked around the room and folded his arms. "It's just as well that she's not here. We've got problems."

"What did Devin say?"

"Giovanni is looking for Madison's family, specifically her mother. We need to find this empire marker, like, yesterday."

"Hostages?"

"Not sure. Maybe they want them as bargaining chips. It wouldn't be the first time they've held hostages."

"Are you going to tell Madison?"

"I don't know. Will that just make her freak out?"

"Knowing Madison? Probably."

"Technically we don't know anything. Devin is trying to protect them, so as far as we know, everyone is okay." James put a finger over his lips as he contemplated. "No, I don't think I'll tell her yet."

"She's going to be pissed when she finds out you were holding out on her," Brennan said shaking his head, "especially if anything happens to her family."

"Then I'll bear that burden," said James. "The best way for Madison to help her family is to find that empire marker. Once we have that, Giovanni has no need for her or her family. Somewhere buried in the ruins of Rome is the end to this nightmare for her."

Madison and Francisco burst into the room with Francisco's boisterous laugh. James noticed that Francisco escorted her into the room with his hand on the small of her back.

"Enjoy the orchard?" asked James.

"Yes," said Madison, tilting her head.

"What did your Devin say?" Francisco asked.

"We need to get to Rome, now. What's the fastest way?"

"The fastest way? The fastest way is not the safest way, James."

"I don't care. What's the fastest way?" James didn't want to alarm them, but the truth was that this little party needed some focus.

"We can fly out tonight on airline, like I said. I can have a car we can use in Lisbon and we drive to Rome. If we drive straight through we can be there tomorrow night." Francisco leaned in to James and lowered his voice. "Is that soon enough for you, my friend?"

"That'll do," said James, returning his stare.

"Ay. I will get us five airline tickets," said Francisco, returning to his polite servant tone of voice.

"There are four of us," said Madison.

"You are forgetting Gil. We cannot leave him."

⁹ᑕ᙭ᗝᵇ

Madison would not have said that she was afraid of flying. She did not have an irrational fear of it, and to that point in her life, her experiences had not given her reason to fear flight aboard a commercial airliner. Her recent experience of being shot down in a small single engine aircraft was so different and surreal it didn't seem to have any relevance to a scheduled commercial airplane.

Madison had never flown on IberiAir before. That night, Madison learned to fear flying.

IberiAir was a small regional operation that mainly served airports around Portugal and Spain with special service to Madeira, the Azores and the Canary Islands. The airline was a low-budget airline flying out-of-date aircraft with maintenance performed by the lowest bidder.

The twin-propeller regional airliner slammed onto the runway in Lisbon amidst the deafening downpour as Madison clutched the armrest of the chair and flinched, every nerve a tangled mess. The near-derelict airplane miraculously held together and continued its rollout. During the harrowing two-hour flight, the aircraft had bounced violently amidst the updrafts and downdrafts over the open ocean, hundreds of miles from land. Madison had sweat through her clothing, and now on the ground she flipped her hair over the back of the headrest to cool her neck.

Madison and Francisco were seated together in the back of the nearly empty airplane, while James and Brennan sat a few rows ahead of them. Gil sat alone in a row just ahead of Madison and managed to sleep through most of the flight; blissfully unaware of the rainstorm and their ensuing struggle with controlled flight.

If Francisco had planned for a romantic flight over the ocean, thought Madison, he got something completely different. All I want to do right now is throw up.

"You look little uneasy, no? A bit greenish," said Francisco as he kicked the seat in front of him to wake up the sleeping child. Madison could only return an unsteady glance that demanded she be allowed to leave the airplane.

The aircraft lurched and rumbled its way around the airport as the dark skies continued their unrelenting shower. Standing water pooled just off the runway. The little airliner roared onto the tarmac and shut down its engines with a shudder, a loud pop, and a sickly whine.

"You're kidding me," said Madison, looking out the window.

"Sorry?"

"No jet bridge?" she asked.

Gill was turned around in his seat. "You get wet," he laughed.

"We'll make dash for it, you and me," said Francisco. He removed his light jacket and handed it to her. "You can cover that beautiful hair with this."

The handful of passengers retrieved their belongings from the overhead bins and departed the airplane, creeping to the airplane door, and then making wild sprints into the terminal.

Madison walked up the aisle to find James and Brennan waiting for her at the door.

"Are you a good witch or a bad witch?" asked Brennan.

Madison glared at him.

"You're looking a little green there, ha ha," but Brennan's voice trailed off, his joke falling flat.

"Smooth," said James. "Help her with her backpack and let's get inside."

The sprint across the tarmac took ten seconds at the most. But once they arrived inside the terminal, all five of them were soaked through, regardless of what meager protection they'd brought against the elements.

The airport in Lisbon was a major international airport with many runways and large terminals. However, IberiAir had gates in the diminutive commuter terminal across the airport. Those passengers with connections could take a bus to the main terminal, but as it was shortly after midnight, the bus was not running. The handful of other passengers from the flight quickly matriculated through the terminal and out to waiting taxis or cars of friends, and Madison, James, Brennan, Francisco and Gil found themselves standing alone in the empty terminal.

"Where is everyone?" asked Madison.

"We were hour late getting in," said Francisco.

"So, what do we do for transportation?" asked James. Madison had spent enough time with James to sense the irritation in his voice. James was used to being in charge and setting the pace, but Francisco had made the arrangements and was acting as their guide through this part of their journey. James was forced to follow him almost blindly; and Madison could see that he hated it.

"I tell you, we have a car. Is outside." said Francisco.

"Wait a second. " James walked over to a nearby garbage can. He pulled out the plastic liner and found several other garbage bags in the bottom of the can. "We've got a day's drive and we're all soaking wet. Everyone should have a change of clothes with them that should have stayed relatively dry. Let's change and then we can go. Put your wet clothes in these plastic bags."

"Fantastic idea. Thank you." Madison was a little surprised at James' thoughtfulness at their comfort, and it couldn't hurt to encourage this sort of thing. She gave James a quick kiss on the cheek, took her bag and backpack and marched towards the ladies restroom, or *banheiro,* as it was labeled.

❦

"Wha-?" asked Brennan.

After changing into their dry clothes, Madison and the boys stood under a thin tin awning as the last few sprinkles from the rainstorm plinked off the roof. The five of them stood on the curb looking at the only car in the car park: a bright yellow MINI Cooper.

"Francisco, please tell me you have other transportation," pleaded James.

Madison alternated between looking at the five of them and the littlest car she'd ever seen. Five people. Tiny car. Four adults, one boy. Shoebox.

"Is a good car." said Francisco with the enthusiasm of a car salesman. "Get in. Is fun. Supercharged."

"Francisco, there're five of us. There're only four seats, and the back two are for children. How is this supposed to work?" asked James.

"You drive, amigo," said Francisco tossing the keys to Brennan. "I'll navigate. Gil will ride with me in the front. Okay? Hurry, we must be on our way."

Madison did the math in her head. It'd be her and James in the back for a twenty-hour drive.

"Aren't you glad I had everyone change?" asked James.

"I wish you would have made everyone *shower*," said Madison. She stepped into the little sports car and slid into the black leather of the cramped back seat.

XV

CASA DEL AMANTE

*"The home to everyone is to him his castle and fortress,
as well for his defense against injury and violence, as for his repose."*
Edward Coke

It was a weird dream; one that had less to do with figuring her life
out and more to do with a sleeping brain desperately trying to
make sense of its surroundings. Madison was in a wooden crate
aboard a tramp steamer, deep in the ship's hold. A clap of thunder
told her that the ship was fighting through a storm and the loose
cargo slid around the ship as the ship rocked back and forth, forward
and aft in a sickening swirl. In addition to being in a confined wooden
crate she was also wearing extremely tight jeans and a stifling corset.
She couldn't breathe. She couldn't move. She was at the mercy of the
roll and pitch of the ship.

Madison awoke to find herself still crammed into the back seat of
the MINI Cooper. The whine of the supercharger droned on as
Brennan threw the car around the curves of the road through the
heart of rural Spain. It was still dark out and Madison's only reference
to the outside world was whatever happened to flash past the
headlights of the MINI. No other lights penetrated the dark
countryside.

Madison became aware that she had fallen asleep on James'
shoulder and her cheekbone rested comfortably on his clavicle. Her
first thought was to hope she hadn't drooled on him.

"Sorry, I didn't mean to fall on you," she said in a dazed voice.

"It's okay," said James, and he gave her a reassuring squeeze. It
was then that she realized his arm was around her. She sat up.

"Sorry. It was just more comfortable that way... for me," said James

"Yeah, no. It's fine."

"Did you know that you talk in your sleep?"

"I've been told that. What did I say?" asked Madison.

"You just kept apologizing."

"For what?"

"Dunno. Then you said you had to call your mother."

"Huh....I really should call my mother. I wish I could – oh, OW!" she said as the stiffness in her legs and back flared into shooting pains as she tried to shift around. She hadn't moved her legs in hours, and her back was twisted the entire time she slept. Madison was not claustrophobic, but was starting to understand the fear.

"Where are we?" she asked.

"About an hour away from Madrid," said Francisco. "And good morning, *Princesa Hermosa*. It's good to see you awake."

The eastern sky was just beginning to brighten with the first rays of dawn. Madison yawned involuntarily.

"We're in Spain already? I slept through the border crossing?" she asked through her yawn.

"Heh, you are in the European Union, beautiful one. This is the best part. No immigration. No customs. You entered the EU when you got off the cruise ship in Madeira. It's all EU from here to Rome. We don't stop unless the authorities pull us over," said Francisco.

"We haven't stopped since we left Lisbon?" she asked.

"No. We'll get fuel in Madrid. I know a good place," Francisco said. "Five hours and fifteen minutes without a stop. We're making good time, no?"

"You're such men," Madison said. "A road trip isn't all about making good time."

"Today, it is." said James peering out the window. "We've got to get to Rome."

Brennan focused on the road and shifted from sixth to fourth as he slowed to take the next turn in the road.

"James? Is something going on?" she asked. "Something I don't know about?"

"We just need to get to Rome. We've wasted too much time," said James.

Madison knew when men were hiding something, but she didn't know what precisely James was concealing. Was it a secret resentment at having to tote her around wherever he went? Did he have information he wasn't sharing about Caligula's empire marker? Were he and Francisco having a bona fide pissing contest?

Madison tried to stretch in the back seat, "I think I could use a— Oh, dang it. Ow!" Madison screamed.

"What is it?" asked Brennan, alarmed.

"Pull over!"

A startled yelp came from Gil on Francisco's lap as he was jolted awake by Madison's screaming.

"What? Why? What is it?" asked James.

"Just pull over. I have to get out."

Brennan yanked the car to the side of the road and needed no further instructions. He hopped out, pulled the front seat forward, and physically pulled Madison out of the back seat. Madison leapt up and tried to start walking but her knees gave out. She grabbed on to the car to steady herself as she worked her leg up and down.

"Charley horse," she said at last. The look of mild irritation appeared on Brennan's face. Francisco, Gil, and James climbed out of the passenger side of the car and stood.

"Charley horse? Seriously?" asked James.

"It hurts like hell." Madison rubbed her quadriceps. "People die on airliners from being cooped up so long, you know. And we have less space than that in the backseat of that matchbox car."

"Well, that's why they call it a Mini *Coop*-er," said Brennan. He grinned, quite pleased at his pun.

"Guys, I know we want to make good time, but if the five of us are going to travel like this, we've got to...." Her voice trailed off. She noticed that James was looking back up the road and seemed gravely concerned. "What is it, James?"

"That's strange. Brennan, how many other cars have been on the road tonight?"

"Hardly anyone. I see another car maybe once an hour, if that. Why?"

"That car behind us pulled over at the same time we did."

"What car?" asked Francisco.

"The one two miles back. See the parking lights?" The land was relatively flat, but in the near darkness of the coming dawn, the parking lights gleamed with a curious glow. "Unless we passed him on the side of the road before we pulled over, we're being followed."

"Is not possible," said Francisco. "They didn't track us to apartment in Madeira, or to the airport, or once we got off the airplane. How would they know to follow this car?"

"I don't know, and I don't intend on asking them to find out," said James. "Everyone back in the car."

There was no discussion. James was back in control and his men obeyed. They climbed back into the car and Brennan eased the MINI back on to the road. James watched out the back window. Turning around, he inadvertently placed his hand on Madison's hip. She didn't mind it. She was frightened at the prospect of being followed, and James' warm and steady hand made her feel safe.

"Yep. They're back on the road," said James after a while. "They waited to turn on their headlights, but I can still see them."

"So what do we do?" asked Madison. She found herself leaning into him and speaking in an unsteady and breathy voice.

"What does the car's computer say our range is?" asked James.

Brennan pushed a button on the console. "90 kilometers of fuel left. About an hour at these speeds."

"We'll have to lose them in Madrid. It's our only choice. Right now, it would be nice to not be driving a bright yellow car that is low on fuel." James reached behind the seat and into his backpack and pulled out his handheld GPS. Two vertical creases appeared between his eyebrows as he set his mind to work.

⋐⋙⋑

"Now!" said James. The MINI lurched forward as Brennan opened up the throttle as he exited a corner. The two-lane divided highway had come to a sharp turn followed by a long straight downhill section. Brennan took the roaring car up to red line in fourth, then fifth, and finally a long steady acceleration in sixth gear. Madison reached back and fastened her seatbelt.

"Let's get as much distance as we can on these guys before they know we're on to them," James said.

The sun had yet to crest the tops of the mountains to their east, but daylight was fast approaching. Just twenty minutes outside of Madrid, the overloaded MINI thundered into the slumbering city on a nearly empty gas tank.

"If this doesn't work, we're going to be pushing this thing to Rome," said Brennan as the needle on the speedometer crept past 140 km/hr. Madison had never been in a car going so fast and the extra weight in the MINI was taking its toll. Every bump in the road, every rise and every dip, was accompanied by a sickening mush as the outmatched suspension struggled with the weight. Madison was glad the road was straight, because it didn't appear that Bren had any authority over the steering of the lumbering vehicle.

"Are you sure Bren can handle this thing?" asked Madison. James didn't respond as he scrolled through the maps of his GPS.

"Alright, Bren, if we do manage to lose them they're going to expect us to take the first exit," barked James over the scream of the road noise. "Go past it and to the second exit, we'll get off there and duck into a side street."

"Is a bad idea," said Francisco. "At this hour, you'll be into traffic after the first exit. Better get off first exit."

"Are you sure? A rush-hour in Spain?" asked James.

"Hey, it's my capitol. I would know. Everyone will be up going to work this morning. What do you think we are? Portuguese?" said Francisco.

"Hey!" said Gil, interjecting in defense of his homeland.

"Sorry, Gil. Not you," said Francisco.

"We're in Spain, James," said Madison. "Listen to the Spaniard."

"Thank you, my sweet," said Francisco with a wink.

"The first exit is coming up. What do you want me to do, boss?" asked Bren.

"Take it. Let's head north into the city. There are some warehouses through there that we can hide in. Hopefully we can find a gas station too."

Traffic on the A-5 was starting to become a problem, and Brennan had to negotiate around a large truck before quickly floating over two lanes to catch the exit. Brennan heel-toe downshifted as the right hand curve of the exit ramp tightened up, keeping the car perfectly balanced around the bend. He downshifted again, brought the car back in balance and then, switching directions to the left, drifted the MINI smoothly around the round-about as the tires squealed like whimpering dogs. They never dropped below 60 km/hr.

Wow, thought Madison.

"Bren can handle this thing," said James with a smile, answering her earlier question. "He's the best wheelman I've ever known."

"I had no idea," said Madison as she tugged on the seatbelt which had locked up during that last maneuver.

The yellow MINI tore down the side street towards the warehouses. James and Madison twisted around to watch the exit ramp. Before they reached the warehouse, Madison saw a silver sedan come off the exit and enter the round-about.

"Hide us, Bren. Now!" said James.

Bren jerked the wheel and pulled up on the handbrake and the MINI went into a violent spin. The world blurred sideways for Madison as the g-forces threw her into James. The MINI slid off the road, spun three quarters of the way around, and came to rest behind a bush, next to a warehouse, facing the road they'd just come from.

For a moment, everything was silent. Then-

"*Idiota!*" yelled Gil and punched Brennan's shoulder in a flurry of tiny 10-year-old haymakers.

"Shhhh," said Francisco as he restrained the boy. "I think you frighten him."

Brennan killed the engine.

"Did we get off before they got around that round-about?" asked Brennan.

"I don't know. It was hard to see once everything became a blur. But I think so," said James.

"If we didn't, we're sitting ducks."

Silence prevailed in the MINI as they waited for the silver sedan to pass by. The interminable waiting bothered Madison and she found herself holding her breath.

"Maybe they turned around."

"There they are," said Brennan. A silver Mercedes rolled by slowly at a speed far less than the speed limit. Two men in dark sunglasses in the front seat scanned the sides of the road.

"They know we've turned off," said James. The men in the Mercedes continued past and were soon out of sight as they disappeared behind the next row of warehouses down the road.

"Recognize them, Francisco?" asked Brennan.

"I do not. It is difficult to tell looking through this bush," said Francisco. "Then again, I do not know everyone working for Giovanni in Spain. He may have new thugs."

"How could they not see us?" asked Madison. "They had to have seen us. They looked right at us."

"I don't think they did," said Brennan. "They would have reacted. Besides, we're behind this landscaping."

"But we're a bright yellow car," said Madison. She couldn't understand why the rest of them weren't as freaked out as she was. Everything in her body was telling her to run.

"In front of a warehouse," said James calmly.

"Yeah?" Madison failed to see how that made everything better.

"And what color is the warehouse?" James asked.

Madison twisted around in her seat and for the first time considered the color of the warehouse. It was a pastel yellow, faded by sunlight; not an exact match of the MINI's color, but good enough to hide them.

"Oh," she said.

"You didn't know our yellow color could be our camouflage, did you? We're actually hidden quite well here," said James. He leaned in to Madison and said, sotto voice, "Be aware of your surroundings. It might save your life."

Madison smiled. "Well, that's why I have you." She gave him a gentle pat on the cheek.

Brennan started the MINI and they backed away from the road, drove around the warehouse, and returned to the highway from which they'd come.

Half an hour later, after fighting rush hour traffic and finding an open gas station, James replaced the fuel cap, returned the nozzle to its cradle, and took the receipt from the fuel pump. Madison emerged from the convenience store with a mocha and an open bag of animal crackers. She systematically bit the heads off of the animals before devouring their bodies.

"Do you get some sort of pleasure out of that?" asked James.

"I like my food to know who's boss," she said with a devious grin. Brennan, Francisco, and Gil emerged from the store a few minutes later with their assortment of road-trip fare.

"Gets me every time I come to Europe. They've got naked chicks in their everyday newspapers," remarked Brennan. "I mean, they're not in paper bags or anything. Just right there for everyone to see."

"Yes, you will find that Europe has a much more liberal view of sex than the frigid Americans," said Francisco. Madison decided she rather liked not having naked women in her newspaper and would gladly be called frigid if that's what it took.

Everyone stood around the MINI, not really wanting to climb back inside until it was absolutely necessary. James folded his hands atop the MINI and rested on the car, looking stern.

"We need a new car, Francisco," he said. "Giovanni knows what we're driving, we have to switch."

"I can't get you another car. Not on such short notice. What, do you think I'm made of cars? It would take a couple days at least."

"You can't borrow a friend's car?" asked Brennan.

"Not to cross borders," said Francisco, throwing his arms up in comical animation. "Every country has cameras that record your license plate. They will pull you over if they think the car is stolen. It took nearly a month to get this car in the system and linked to a fake driver's license."

"Francisco, we've got two choices," James said. "We can't drive all day in this car towards Rome. We have to assume Giovanni has us marked. He knows where we're headed. So either, we can stash this car somewhere all day and drive only by night or we can take a detour and approach Rome from a different direction."

"If we wait until tonight, we lose 12 hours of driving, easy," said Brennan.

"What would we do for 12 hours?" asked Madison.

"We go home," said Francisco.

"Home?" asked Madison.

"Catalonia! My home. We go there for the day and leave at dark. Is only 2 hours from here. And is a safe place, too. Come, come."

Francisco waved them to get into the car. "Is a pity we're not staying overnight."

"Why's that, Francisco?" Madison asked as she climbed into the back of the MINI.

"Every princess should get to spend a night in a castle at least once," he said.

"Castle?"

Now, Madison was interested.

❦

Francisco leaned out the window of the idling MINI and spoke animatedly in Catalan with the man who had emerged from the stone building. Madison couldn't understand what they were saying, but there was obviously a disagreement. She peered out the car window at the old stonework, iron gates, and gothic arched windows of the large structure.

"This castle is beautiful," said Madison.

"This isn't the castle, sweetheart," said James. "This is the guardhouse. The castle is up there on the hill." Madison thrust her head between the front seats and gazed in the direction James was pointing. Up on the hill, a towering castle of limestone and granite loomed above her. Several turrets and spires dotted the corners of the structure.

By castle standards, Casa del Amante was quaint and square. It was a classic medieval castle built in the 11th century on three floors arranged around a narrow inner courtyard. Built on a low mountain in the middle of the valley, the castle had a commanding view of the surrounding countryside. This fortification once protected thousands of square miles of Catalan farmland and villages.

The discussion grew more animated until the impassioned guard stormed back to his guardhouse and slammed the door. A few minutes later the guard emerged with what Madison assumed to be a supervisor. This man spoke in a British accent.

"I am sorry, Mister del Amante, but the castle is not ready for visitors. Your father assured us there would be no need to keep it prepared this month."

"My father did not know I was coming," said Francisco. "It doesn't matter if it is ready or not, let me in. This is my house."

"It is your father's estate, sir. You have not lived here these last seven years. I'm sorry. The castle is not fit for occupation." The short British man was snide and disdainful.

"We are not even staying the night. Let me in."

"I can't be held responsible for the condition of the property. I do not have the staff to make it acceptable for you, sir. We cannot run Casa del Amante like a common summer chateau." The irritated man motioned to the other guard who then opened the gate.

"Your father shall hear of this!" he shouted as Brennan revved the engine and dropped the clutch, shooting the MINI up the driveway and toward the looming rock-hewn structure.

✥

A few minutes later, Madison and the boys entered through stalwart oak doors reinforced with massive black iron hinges. They passed through the antechamber and then into the great hall of the castle, dwarfed by its towering ceiling.

The great hall was morgue-like in its stillness, for there were no lanterns, lights, or torches, and every window was shuttered. The echo of their hesitant footsteps rebounded off the limestone walls and granite floor drawing further attention to the eerie quiet. Every piece of furniture in the room, including two chairs nearest the door, was covered by dusty white sheets. Madison inhaled the musty air of idleness as Francisco, Brennan and Gil began opening the shuttered windows and restoring power to the chandeliers.

"So what's the plan, James?" asked Madison privately.

"Well, we have to hide out here for a while. Hopefully Giovanni's men lost us back there and are currently out looking for a yellow MINI. Tonight, at sunset, we head for Rome. Assuming we don't have many more interruptions, I think we can reach Rome before sunrise tomorrow."

"So what do we do in the meantime?" she asked.

"Well, there's some ground work to do for Rome; equipment planning and site scouting for finding Caligula's Bath once we get to

Rome. Other than that, we can rest here. We'll have a long night, so get some sleep."

"I'd rather we were on our way," said Madison.

"You and me both," he said with a sigh.

As light poured into the castle as each window opened, details became clearer and the atmosphere more welcoming. The great hall greeted them with enormous electrified chandeliers and soaring tapestries now vibrating with color. Suits of armor, moments ago ghastly shadows, gleamed in the light as noble watchmen of bygone centuries. The light brought warmth to the castle and Madison breathed easier and relaxed in the rapid transformation.

"Light is the lifeblood of a castle," said Francisco, sauntering over to Madison. "Come, sit on the divan. The sheets have not been here long. Let this be your home for the afternoon." He guided Madison to the couch and sat with her. Madison's eyes sparkled more as she took in the interior appointments of the great hall.

"The closest I've ever been to a castle is Cinderella's Castle at Disneyworld," she said with naïve joy. "I had no idea the real thing was so beautiful."

"Francisco's family spent a small fortune restoring this beauty," said James. "Thank you for bringing us here, Francisco. We can wait until the sun sets and start out for Rome then. In the meantime, I recommend everyone try to get some sleep."

"It's the middle of the day, James," said Madison. "I'd like to see the rest."

"Of course, Seniorita," said Francisco. "Careful, you two. Those are sharp."

Brennan and Gil had pulled a couple of swords off the wall and bowed to each other to initiate a duel. As Brennan bowed, Gil hit him in the arm with the flat of his weapon; more dagger than a sword. Brennan mocked injury and then bopped the boy on the head with his rapier.

"Let the children play," said Francisco. "Take my arm, and I shall give you the grand tour."

"James, are you coming?" asked Madison.

"I think I'll stay here," he said. "Someone needs to keep these two from destroying the place. You two have fun." Madison looked at James quizzically.

Is he really going to let me go off with Francisco, alone? He returned her gaze with a quiet assurance then cast his attention to the friendly swordfight. Madison and Francisco turned and walked into the east corridor off the great hall.

Apparently, he is.

Francisco walked Madison around the castle, showing her the first of the three floors. He told fascinating stories of the various purposes of each room throughout the centuries; the places where nobles were murdered, traitors were tried and found guilty, and secret love affairs were consummated. Each room held many secrets and Francisco was a captivating storyteller. To Madison, it was like stepping into an adult fairytale, where good and evil often wore each others' clothes and time did not heal all wounds.

He led her up a winding staircase to the second floor and dazzled her with the rooms on the floor. The ballroom, the billiard room, the library and servants quarters amazed and intrigued her. Up the spiral staircase they went to the third floor. She began to understand that this was a well-rehearsed tour and that it was leading to a certain destination.

They meandered through the rooms of the third floor and then up a narrow winding staircase inside the largest turret on the castle, reaching a wooden door. Francisco del Amante turned the handle and pushed it open.

"The highest room in the castle," he said. "This used to be the chief lookout post for the castle's defense but my family thought the view was too exquisite to be left to the security firm. So we converted it to the penthouse suite."

Madison followed him into the room and discovered that, unlike the rest of the rooms in the castle, this room was not shuttered and preserved. The circular room had been modernized with hardwood floors, new, hand-carved furniture, central heating, air condition and expansive glass windows that brought breathtaking views of the lush green countryside from all directions. An oversized four-post bed was placed in the center of the room, while the rest of the amenities were arranged against the curving walls. The shades on the windows were open and the warm early-afternoon sun flooded the room from every angle.

The bedroom had obviously been prepared for their arrival. Fresh flowers had been placed on the dresser, the bed was made up with clean sheets and turned down, and in the far end of the room a bubbling Jacuzzi murmured to her in an incoherent babble. Soft classical music drifted on the air from a small .mp3 player on the nightstand.

"This room is absolutely stunning," she said. She found every nerve in her skin was tingling with excitement. "You had them set this up, didn't you?" asked Madison.

"For you, my princess."

"But, I thought they didn't know we were coming. That guy at the gate seemed furious that we'd shown up unannounced." Madison noticed that Francisco had moved closer to her and looked at her with a half smile. He smelled of olive oil and fresh cut grass.

"He didn't. No, no. He would never allow this. But I have a close friend on the staff. I give him a call, and he gets things ready. Would you like to slip into hot tub?" he asked.

"Oh, I don't know," she said, "All of my stuff is still in the car. I don't have a bathing suit with me, anyway."

"Who needs bathing suits?" Francisco asked, and he began unbuttoning his shirt. Madison turned from him and inspected the fresh flowers.

"James is downstairs. He'll be wondering what happened to us."

Approaching her from behind, Francisco wrapped one arm around her waist and with the other arm he moved her hair to one side. He breathed lightly on her neck.

"They will not mind," he said. "We have all day to spend here, Madison. Why not spend the afternoon pleasurably?" He ran his lips over her neck.

Shivers ran through Madison's body and she felt her knees weaken. She grabbed on to the dresser for stability as he pressed his body into hers.

"What do you think is happening here, Francisco?" She turned around to face him.

"You know what is happening. You've wanted this to happen from the moment we met."

His arrogance, while charming at first, was becoming a turn-off.

"Francisco, look." She pushed him away to arm's length. "While making love to an exotic Spaniard in a beautiful room in a castle is high on my list of fantasies— actually, it might be my number one fantasy. But in any case, for some reason, it just doesn't feel right."

"What could be more right?" he asked.

"I just met you yesterday. I don't even know you."

"And why is this a problem?" Francisco placed his hands on her shoulders.

"You give this tour a lot?"

"Only to the exceptional women I meet," he said placing his hand gently on the side of her face.

"Consider me the exception to the exceptional women." She pushed his hand away and walked over to one of the windows.

"It is a beautiful view though," she said doubting her stance, suddenly. The prospect of taking advantage of a unique opportunity to have a little harmless fun crept into her mind. She'd long had a fantasy that involved being surrounded by such a view high up in a stone tower, though her fantasy was outdoors in the warm sunlight.

"There is a roof, you know. We could go up there if you'd prefer," said Francisco.

Oh my. "Yes, let's see the roof," she said in an unsteady voice.

They climbed the stairs as Madison's inner will fought with itself. On one hand, she wasn't the type of woman to give herself away to just anyone, especially someone she hardly knew. On the other hand, she was in an extraordinary setting and he was a practiced Spanish lover that could probably show her things she'd never experienced before. The battle between pleasure and self-respect was fought and won as she climbed the stairs to the roof.

The roof of the turret was small with dizzying views of the surrounding countryside and the castle far below. The circular platform was ringed with jagged parapets and two chaise lounges which faced the sun. A steady wind blew through Madison's hair.

Madison had made up her mind and was willing to live with the consequences.

"Francisco, I…."

"Yes, princess?" he answered as he placed his hands on her waist. Madison paused.

"What is that?" she asked as she looked to the countryside below.

"Sorry?"

In two quick steps, Madison stood at the low stone wall and peered out on the road that approached the castle. A large dust cloud moved quickly up the road, clearly headed to the castle.

"That," she said. Her question was answered a few seconds later as the dust cloud was swept away by the wind and revealed a sedan roaring up the road; a silver Mercedes. It would be at the castle in minutes.

"How did they find us?" she asked.

"Is impossible."

"We've got to go!" She fled down the spiral stairs inside the turret. James and Brennan didn't know yet. They didn't know that they were out of time.

Sprinting down a spiral staircase is one of the more difficult things a person can do, requiring dexterity and athletic ability. Madison did not have these abilities and several times caught her heel on a stair only to throw herself into the wall of the turret.

What she lacked in athletic prowess she made up in determination and adrenaline. She and Francisco clamored down through the tower and then down the three stories of the castle staircase shouting in a naïve hope that their voices could penetrate three stories of cut stone.

"They're coming! They're here!"

"Go! Go!"

Finally, they reached the ground floor in the corner of the castle and tore through the hallway towards the grand hall.

"What? What is it?" asked James. Madison was too winded to speak. Francisco pointed to the front door and James understood.

In a flash, the five of them sprinted through the great hall and into the antechamber towards the car. They opened the door and then stopped.

They were too late.

The silver Mercedes roared up the drive and skidded to a stop between them and the MINI; their only hope of escape.

"So much for our guardhouse. I don't think he even slowed them down. Perhaps I can send them away. Stay here." Francisco walked out the front door, leaving James, Bren, Gil, and Madison to watch from the antechamber through the ajar front door.

Francisco walked up to the sedan in full Spanish anger, shouting and gesturing with both arms. Three men emerged from the sedan, each with a dark pair of sunglasses. The first of the three men wore an overcoat, the other two matching beige jackets.

"What do you mean by this? This is private property. You are to leave at once!" screamed Francisco in English.

The men slowly walked to the front of the car and formed a menacing triangle in front of the car. At last, the man in the overcoat spoke.

"Madison Dawn," he said. His voice was quiet but his Italian accent was unmistakable.

"I don't know who or what that is. This is Casa del Amante and I am Francisco del Amante. Now you must leave at once. My security detail is already on their way."

"We know who you are, Francisco," The three men reached into their coats and each drew a semi-automatic pistol. They held it at their sides and glared at Francisco.

"You must leave at once," said Francisco. He tried to speak with authority, but a wavering crept into his voice.

"We'll ask you one more time. Where is Madison Dawn? Is she inside?"

"I don't know who you're talking about," said Francisco again.

The man in the front sighed deeply, then raised his pistol and shot Francisco in the chest.

Francisco crumbled to the ground and the man stood above him and fired twice more. Following the explosive bark of each gunshot, Madison screamed. She didn't mean to scream and she knew not to scream, but, against her will, she let out three terrified shrieks of grief.

Madison had seen people killed in movies, on TV, and in video games tens of thousands of times. Contrary to the warnings of parental advocacy groups, it did nothing to desensitize Madison to seeing someone killed in real life. Witnessing a murder, especially someone she knew and had just minutes earlier been debating the intimacy of their relationship, shocked Madison into complete catatonic inaction. She remained a motionless statue, watching the men look up from Francisco's body at the door and then start running at her.

James did not suffer from this paralysis. He slammed the door shut and bolted it, grabbed Madison by the hand and took her with him. Mechanically, without thinking, she ran with him. She did not see the blur of the castle halls or the turns they took to get through the courtyard. She did not see Brennan running through the castle looking for weapons to mount some sort of defense, cursing the fact that they'd left the pistol in a backpack in the MINI. She did not see Brennan pick up Gil and carry him along. She only saw Francisco's body falling limply to the ground. She saw it in vivid detail; in slow motion, again and again, yet all the while she ran wherever James' stalwart grip led her.

James stopped at a nearby window on the backside of the castle and looked out. "Okay, it looks like this lawn runs downhill a few hundred yards to a tree line," he said between gasps of breath. "We've got to get to the woods without them knowing. If we can do that, we can hide out until they've gone. Okay?"

Madison stared vacantly at him.

"Madison? We're going to have to run, sweetie," he said.

Madison nodded vaguely. James looked out to the left and right and then pushed open the window.

"Just stay with me, hon," he said. "Ready? One, two, three!"

James leapt out the window and then pulled her through. He turned to run and was immediately cracked in face by the butt of a pistol wielded by a man in sunglasses. The unexpected blow caught James squarely on the jaw and he crumpled to the ground in an unconscious heap.

Madison screamed and raised her arms, expecting a similar blow to the face. Instead, the man reached into his coat and pulled out a black canvas bag and a white handkerchief inside of a plastic bag.

She took a step away from him, but he grabbed her arm. He towered over her and his grip cut off all blood flow to her hand.

Now in full fight-or-flight mode and unable to flee, she attempted to fight. She lashed out at him with an adrenaline-fueled violence, throwing punch after punch with her free arm towards his face.

The effort was in vain. No punches landed and soon she found herself on the ground with the man holding the white handkerchief over her mouth. She smelled a pungent odor and the world darkened.

Through a gray haze, Madison saw the man open the black bag with his free hand. Just before the man placed the bag over Madison's head, everything went black.

XVI

IMPRISONED

*"We are all sentenced to solitary confinement
inside our own skins, for life."*
Tennessee Williams

Madison was no stranger to mind-splitting, spirit-crushing headaches. There were the headaches she suffered when her job stress overtook her. Then there were the self-inflicted headaches after a night of partying with friends and one too many complementary adult beverages. Worse yet were the migraines to which she was prone that snuck up on her unannounced and disabled her for most of the day.

None of these headaches could compare with what Madison felt when she awoke from her ether-induced slumber. A searing blaze of pain sprung from just behind her right eye and extended to the base of her skull as if a scalding iron had been jammed into her brain. A terrifying ring in her head sounded like a jet engine two feet from her head.

Madison took stock of her surroundings. She was lying on her side but unable to move her arms or legs. The tug on her skin told her that her hands were bound together with some sort of tape and she assumed that her ankles were likewise bound. Despite her attempt to open her eyes she detected no light. Her brain entertained the various possible causes of this: Perhaps it was nighttime. Perhaps she was in an interior room with no lights on. Perhaps she'd been struck blind.

She rubbed her face against the floor and felt fabric against her skin. The black bag was still on her head. Consciousness came to her as the specter of a man emerging from a fog and the interminable whine resolved itself. It wasn't a jet engine after all. It was road noise, but why was it so loud?

Attempting to sit up, she hit her head on sheet metal just inches above her head. Her memories returned to her: the silver sedan, the men in sunglasses, the castle. She put it together: Madison was in the trunk of the Mercedes speeding down an unknown road.

More images came back to her, in reverse order: Being grabbed by that hateful man. James getting sucker-punched and the strange way he had flopped to the ground. She remembered running through the castle, being led by James, hearing only the drum of her heartbeat and the quickness of her breathing. She saw the men arrive, and Francisco-

Oh, God. Francisco!

The murder came to her like ice water poured into her heart. Every muscle in her body contracted as the reality of Francisco's violent end struck her. He'd been shot dead without even a second's thought, and now she was in the car with those same murderers.

She let out a panicked scream that at first seemed to do nothing more than to double the pain of her headache. Yet, a few seconds later, the car pulled to the side of the road as the road noise subsided.

Footsteps. Footsteps approaching the trunk. The click of the lock. She heard the trunk pop, but she still could see no light.

"You are awake, no?" said a man's voice in a thick Italian accent. Madison instantly recognized the voice as belonging to the same man who had killed Francisco. "Perhaps you would wish to ride in the cab like a person, rather than back here like cargo."

Madison attempted to compose a searing retort that made liberal use of references to pigs, whoremongers, and child molesters, but the pain in her head slowed her speech. Before she formed the first syllable, several strong hands pulled her out of the trunk. She was carried around the car and tossed into the back seat. Her captors did not remove the bindings from her hands and legs or the black bag from her head.

"Who are you?" she asked.

The car doors slammed, the engine fired, and the sedan returned to the road.

"You know who we are, Miss Dawn," said the man. "You've been running from us for weeks. It will soon be time to give us what we want."

"I don't know what you want," Madison said. "I'm here on vacation-"

"-Save your charades," said the man. "You know what we want, and you'll give it to us." Madison knew they wanted the ruby arrowhead, but James had kept it from the beginning. *Why hadn't they taken him, instead?*

"What if I don't have it?" she asked.

"Oh, you'd better have it. For your sake," said the man. Madison felt another man in the back seat lean into her, though she still could see nothing. He smelled of cilantro and tomato paste. Suddenly, she heard the ring of a knife being unsheathed and she flinched automatically. With meaty hands, the man pushed her face down, grabbed her arm, and cut the tape that was holding her hands together.

"*Quello dovrebbe stare più bene,*" said the man dismissively as he put his knife away. Madison didn't understand Italian, but the way he said it invited her to relax. Perhaps freeing her hands was his only intention with the knife.

Madison sat back, pulled the tape from her hands, and reached for the black bag covering her head. The same man quickly pinned both of her wrists together with one meaty hand.

"It is okay, Renzo," said the man in the front seat. "We are almost there."

"Almost where?" she asked.

The painful clamp released and Madison removed the bag.

At first the light was blinding and she couldn't see anything. As her eyes adjusted, she saw a large sprawling city with blocks of tan, orange, and beige buildings. The car moved quickly through traffic on the highway. Then she saw it. She'd never seen it in person before, but she recognized it right away: The Coliseum.

Madison was in Rome.

Madison sat back, stunned by the realization. *How did I get here?* Of course she knew that these men had driven her from Francisco's castle, across the southern border of France and into Italy, following the north shore of the Mediterranean. But, how did she get *here*, in this hopeless situation, when three weeks ago her biggest stress was sending out reports, filing time cards, and making sure everyone in the office knew that Friday was wacky tie day.

But there was that cell phone; that stupid cell phone stuck in the visor of her car, the crash and the men who'd come to grab her. James had shown up and pulled her out of the car and taken her to his sparse apartment. They'd burned her apartment to the ground looking for the jewel that James now wore around his neck. The past few weeks flashed through her mind like slides on a silver screen: The museum and Devin. Meeting Brennan who'd seemed so cocky and obnoxious. The flight to Dallas and the plane crash. That bastard at the Army base. The flight to Miami and the cruise. *The cruise;* Possibly the most enjoyable part of this adventure. Then there were those two women who just threw themselves at James and Brennan. *Of course, the boys didn't exactly fight back,* she thought. The storm, the man in black robes who was pushed into the ocean. Sending those two women on their way. Beautiful Madeira. Francisco and Gil. The flight to the mainland at night in the storm. The yellow MINI Cooper and Casa del Amante.

She'd endured all that for the secret treasure of a marginal ruler who'd served less than four years as emperor of a long dead civilization. Yet, through all that trouble, James had been there for her. Sure, he'd made his mistakes and at times he'd been nothing but infuriating. But when things got tough, he was there for her with Brennan not far behind. But where was he now? Did he even know where she was?

"You know, my friends will come looking for me," she said in a stern voice. She wanted them to have a little fear of their own for a change. "They will hunt you down and make you pay for what you did to Francisco."

"Oh you mean, James Kynan?" laughed the man in the front passenger seat. Madison could see him clearly now. He was the leader of the pack of dirty hit men, and the man who'd shot Francisco. He wore dark sunglasses and had jet black hair. He had a pock-marked face, and a sour expression even while laughing. Madison privately named him *Moonface*.

"No, Miss Dawn. I doubt James will come looking for you."
Moonface laughed again and then the other two men in the car
laughed with him. It was sickening to Madison.

"What have you done to him? Did you kill him like you killed
Francisco?" Madison's temper flared into a boiling rage.

"Let us say that your former boyfriend won't be any trouble to us
anymore."

It wasn't possible, was it? She'd seen James knocked cold by that
pistol-whip, but that's all she remembered. Was it possible that they'd
gassed her and then killed James? But Brennan was still somewhere in
the castle with Gil. He wouldn't have let that happen, would he?
Unless he too was dead....

The questions swirled in Madison's mind in a tumultuous mess
until one horrifying realization descended from it. *Maybe James and
Brennan really are gone. Maybe I'm out here alone without anyone to help me.*

That thought crushed Madison's spirit in ways that no amount of
torture or hardship could. She had been frustrated and despondent in
her life before, but never to this level. Never before had she been
without hope, without some chance of bettering her situation.

What would become of her? And what would they do to her
when they found out she didn't have the ruby arrowhead and didn't
know where to get it?

ᒉᑗᔿᓑ

The silver sedan turned off of the main road and entered a long
driveway made up of brilliant white paver stones. The sun flashed
through tall arching vines that crawled along hemispherical trestles
bent over the driveway. The sedan pulled up in front of a stately
three-story villa fronted by four marble columns.

A man in a black suit rushed to the car and opened the doors for
the occupants. Moonface spoke softly in Italian to the attendant. Slug,
Madison's name for the sleepy, do-nothing, say-nothing driver, slowly
handed the keys of the car to the valet. The third man, whose name
Madison actually knew, Renzo, walked Madison towards the
gargantuan villa with one meaty hand on her shoulder. She wasn't
bound, but it didn't matter. There was no escaping Renzo's grip.

Moonface, Slug, Renzo, and Madison walked up the marble steps and into the front foyer of the sprawling mansion. The gaping entryway sported a soaring cathedral ceiling from which a sparkling crystal chandelier was suspended. Moonface gestured to Slug and Renzo and continued into the rest of the home alone. They were to wait in the foyer.

Renzo guided Madison to an ancient looking wooden high-back chair that rested against one wall. She sat and marveled at the exquisite taste of whomever had decorated the home. African rugs, Aboriginal idols, a Mayan calendar, the horn of a Viking, and many other priceless treasures decorated the entryway. In fact, no two pieces of decoration seemed to come from the same culture or time period. It was a United Nations of home décor; a museum where the curator simply couldn't decide and so put a taste of everything in one room. Madison felt lost in the splendid disjointedness of the palace.

After several minutes of waiting quietly, Madison heard the low rumbling of a tense conversation in Italian. She recognized the voice of Moonface, but not the person to whom he was speaking. It was a woman's voice. The muddled tones of the conversation echoed through the foyer and made it nearly impossible for Madison to understand, even if she spoke Italian.

The tense conversation erupted into contentious shouting. However it was not Moonface who was shouting, but the woman.

The shouting came to a crescendo and then ceased as abruptly as it had begun. The snap of footsteps echoed through the villa as high-heels clacked rhythmically on the marble floor. Through a door on the side of foyer, a woman emerged followed by Moonface.

The woman was dressed as if she were a lawyer or investment banker. If her matching dark blue blazer and knee length skirt attempted to hide her feminine features, they failed as the tall black heels, hip-hugging skirt and sheer white blouse with the top three buttons unfastened revealed her shapely curves. She wore a stern expression on a countenance creased with anger, bitterness, and selfishness. Her long wavy blonde hair had been pulled back, twisted around and pinned to her head as if to mute its siren-esque qualities.

As the woman entered the foyer, Madison stood. The woman stopped, looked Madison over from head to toe and then let out a single, condescending puff of laughter.

"Of course," she said and then laughed again. If the blonde hair didn't convince Madison, the traditional mid-west accent succeeded. This woman was American, not Italian. Madison decided the woman needed a name as well, and called her Kitty because she walked like a sauntering lioness.

"Come with me," said Kitty.

She turned with Moonface closely behind her. Renzo grabbed Madison's arm.

"I'm going. You don't have to push me everywhere," she said, jerking her arm away from Renzo.

The woman led them into a large study replete with mahogany bookcases, randomly scattered artifacts, and a wide oak desk in the middle of the room. The study reminded Madison of Devin's study back in Kansas, yet bigger, and less charming. The woman sat behind the desk in a red leather chair and Madison was asked to sit in a smaller leather chair facing the desk. Moonface took a chair against the wall, and Renzo stood at the doorway.

"I can see why he liked you. I didn't know why he should go to so much trouble, but now it's clear." Kitty shook her head as if she'd just found the last clue to a difficult puzzle.

"I don't know what you're talking about," said Madison. "Who are you?"

"Please, sweetie. Who I am is not important. Don't waste any more of our time than you already have. You know who we are and we know who you are. You're Madison Dawn. You're a secretary, are you not?"

"Administrative Assistant. Well, I was. I'm sure I don't have a job anymore."

"You've stolen from us, Madison Dawn. Why would you steal from us?" The woman's voice was cold and bitter. "Why didn't you just answer the goddamn phone instead of wrecking your car like a complete ass? Why? Tell me why?"

"You put that phone there?"

"Of course we did."

"Why?"

"All you had to do was answer the phone, drive to our buyer's house and give him the briefcase. Was that so hard?"

"I didn't even know I had a briefcase in the car. I don't work for you. None of this makes any sense."

The woman rose and walked around the desk. She stood behind Madison's chair so that Madison couldn't see her.

"Of course it doesn't. Stop being such a simpleton." Kitty's voice then softened. "If we told you that you were carrying a 520 carat ruby, don't you think you might have asked questions?"

"But why did you need me to deliver it? You've got people everywhere. Have them deliver it." Madison stared at the empty desk.

"Because the ruby arrowhead is a key, sweetie," the woman placed her hand on Madison's head and ran her fingers through Madison's hair. "But it's only half of a key. By itself it doesn't do anyone any good unless they want a particularly gaudy piece of jewelry."

"You think I have the other half?" Shivers ran down Madison's spine as Kitty continued to play with her hair.

"Oh, don't tell me you don't know." Madison sat forward in her chair. Kitty came around to the front and sat on the desk.

Madison was tired of this line of questioning. Her total lack of understanding of the situation, the constant insults, and the weird sexual tension she was getting from the woman was unnerving. It was time to change the discussion.

"I know who you are… Giovanni," Madison said.

Kitty laughed again in that same puff of condescension.

"You're dumber than you look. Do you think I look like a 68 year old Italian man? Look at me." She ran her hands over her hips. "You're telling me you see a greasy, lazy, three-hundred pound Italian godfather? No, I'm not Giovanni." She sat back down behind the desk.

"But I might as well be," she said. "I run his operation. And I've seen his losses; losses inflicted by you and your friends. Do you have any clue how expensive it is to hire a sheriff's helicopter to intercept an airplane on one day's notice? Do you? Or to mobilize agents to track you all over the damn U.S. and onto a cruise ship of all things?" Kitty's face flushed red before she took a breath to compose herself.

"And so, Miss Dawn, we've come to the reason that I brought you here." The woman opened a folder on her desk and her tone returned to that of business. "You, Madison Dawn, have our ruby arrowhead and we want it back. Moreover, you've cost this organization hundreds of thousands of Euros trying to locate you. You will reimburse us by providing us with the ruby as well as the second half of the key to our buyer. Once that transaction is complete, you may return to what's left of your life and I would advise you not to return to artifact hunting ever again."

"I don't have the ruby and I don't know what the second half looks like," said Madison.

"My terribly stupid associate," Kitty said, motioning to Moonface, "did not have the presence of mind or the simple common sense to bring the three bodies of your friends back from Case del Amante, so I have to go on his report that they searched the bodies and did not find the ruby. Therefore, I assume you either have it or know where you stashed it."

Three bodies? James. Brennan. Francisco. Gil. There were four people she'd left behind at that castle. Did someone survive? She knew that James still wore the arrowhead around his neck in that velvet pouch. If they killed him and searched his body, why didn't they find it? Things weren't adding up.

"And if I refuse to cooperate?" she asked.

Kitty stood and walked to Madison's chair. She motioned that Madison should stand and Madison tentatively obliged. The woman was probably Madison's height, but with her heels, she stood three inches taller. The woman brushed aside Madison's hair, exposing her ear and neck.

"I warn you, Madison Dawn," she said in a soft whisper. "You will stay here at this villa until we have the ruby. You can spend your time in degrading, painful torture, or you can spend your time in pleasurable comfort. The choice is yours. You understand?"

Madison nodded, though she felt the blood drain from her face at the thought of being tortured for information she didn't have.

"Vincent, show her to her room. See to it she gets a proper bath and then is chained to her bed." Moonface responded and escorted Madison through the door held open by Renzo.

"Vincent, huh?" she asked as he walked her up a flight of stairs, fighting to regain her composure. She looked at her escort and grinned. "I like Moonface better."

Moonface said nothing.

When Madison heard the order to be bathed and then chained to her bed, she envisioned being tossed into a cement block building, hosed down with frigid water, given a tattered potato sack to wear, and then being strapped to a couple of rough cut boards covered in a wool blanket that passed as a cot. At least, that's what the American cinema told her to expect.

Her expectations were pleasantly unrealized. The bath resembled more of an oblong hot tub than a bath tub. The round marble basin rested inside a quaint courtyard surrounded by a garden. To bathe in full view of the many windows that looked into the courtyard disturbed her at first, but once she was in the hot bubbling water, she relaxed and attempted to enjoy the luxurious bath.

Indeed, the rest of the accommodations were equally posh as, instead of a filthy potato sack, she was given a white silk nightgown. The nightgown covered her, but also made her uniquely apprehensive to escape. Its length made it impossible for her to run, and the lack of any clothing beneath the nightgown inhibited her from removing it to escape. It was a clever addition to her confinement.

After she had bathed and dressed, Moonface showed Madison to her room. The half-smirk Moonface wore told Madison that he had been watching her bathe. The discomfort of the thought was disregarded with a shrug. *If he's going to watch, then fine. It's the closest he'll ever get to being with a woman like me.*

Moonface led Madison to a resplendent room at the end of the villa. A wooden four-poster bed was pushed up against one wall, while bookcases lined the other three walls. A comfortable ottoman was set against an open window that looked on to the courtyard in which she had just bathed. The room had its own private toilet and vanity, though it contained no shower or bath.

The disagreeable Italian motioned to Madison to sit on the bed, which she did. He then locked a steel shackle around her ankle. A heavy chain attached her shackle to the bed which, she discovered, was bolted to the floor. Without a word of instruction Moonface left Madison to herself. In the quiet, the silence of being absolutely alone and powerless in a foreign place soon overwhelmed her.

Madison threw herself flat on the bed at the onset of despair. The silk amenities, no matter how luxurious, could not erase from her mind the general hopelessness of the situation. These people would stop at nothing to get what they desired and she had no way of giving them what they wanted. If James and Brennan were truly gone, then the only other person who knew she was in Europe was Devin. Her sole hope rested in a grumpy man that was just as likely to write her off as a lost investment as he was to send help into the Giovanni fortress.

Madison wept until the silk sheets were soaked through with her salty tears.

After an hour of emotional venting, she lifted her head up and resolved to explore her surroundings. She discovered that the chain allowed her to reach all the way to the bathroom and every corner of the room. It would not let her reach beyond the window, nor could she get but a step or two out the door. The chain was the perfect length to keep her in the room, but yet allow her to utilize the various amenities.

Madison explored the bookcases that lined the walls and found a section that contained many books written in English. These books included several works by Italian authors such as Rafael Sabatini, Niccolo Machiavelli, and Dante. There were also British books by Jane Austen and Charles Dickens. In short, she had novels she knew and loved at her disposal. There was no television or radio. The silence would need to be endured somehow. She reached to the bookcase and withdrew a time-worn tome almost at random: *The Shame of Motley* by Sabatini.

It was one of Madison's favorite stories and she was eager to read it again. She flung the book on the bed and crawled onto it ready to hear about the exploits of Boccodoro the Jester.

Madison spent the day in that room, prone on the bed, reading her leather-bound book. At six o'clock in the evening a man she hadn't seen before brought a tray of food. He entered without knocking, set the tray on a dresser at the end of the room, and left without speaking a word. She waited for the unknown man to leave and then she devoured the bowl of pasta like a ravenous piranha. She went to bed early with *The Shame of Motley* open at her side.

The next morning, she awoke to find that her room had been cleaned while she slept. The tray of food was removed and her book was put back on the bookshelf. Again, breakfast was brought to her by a silent man who placed the food on the same dresser across the room. Madison's creativity failed her as she referred to this man as Food Guy. Madison retrieved her book, and continued reading over breakfast.

At midday, her isolation was broken by the arrival of Moonface. He entered as she sat upon her bed, her legs tucked under her in a defensive position.

"Am I to be bathed?" she asked. It had been fully twenty-four hours and she was ready to freshen up. Moonface stood next to the bed and spoke in a dry monotone.

"Tell us where the ruby is," he said.

"I will not," she replied.

Moonface nodded, opened the door and a small man with a toolbox entered the room. Moonface turned towards Madison and put his meaty hands on her shoulders, pinning her to the bed. The dwarfish man, no more than four feet tall, took the chain from her foot and began working on it with a few small metal tools. Madison could not see what he was doing but spent her energy managing her fear at being held down by the murdering Italian.

As abruptly as they had entered, Moonface and the dwarf left a few minutes later and Madison was once again by herself.

"What was that about?" Then she saw three metal rings sitting on one of the bookcases.

They had taken out three links from the chain that bound her to the bed.

ᘐᓏᕁ

"What do you mean, he's not an orphan?" James gripped the phone a little tighter. He stared across the hotel room at Gil half-heartedly playing tic-tac-toe with Brennan.

"He's not an orphan, James. He's a runaway. His parents have been looking for him for over a year." There was weariness in Devin's voice. He hadn't been sleeping much since Francisco was killed and the whole operation had come unglued three days ago. "His parents have bulletins out. I'm surprised Francisco didn't know."

Didn't know or didn't care, thought James. "Look Devin, we've got to move and this kid is going to slow us down." Perhaps it was a heartless thing to say, but they'd already lost three days to Giovanni. And while Madison was no doubt somewhere in Italy by now, James, Brennan, and the not-an-orphan Gil were still stuck in Spain.

"Certainly you must get Gil to his parents. Take him to the police station two miles north of your hotel. Make sure they don't ask too many questions."

"Alright." James ran a hand through his hair. "But once he's turned over, we're headed to Rome. They no doubt have Madison back at the villa by now doing God knows what to her."

"Madison will be fine for a while, James. You overestimate Giovanni's malevolence."

"Overestimate?" Fire leapt from James' lips. "Don't you tell me about their malevolence. I saw Francisco die in cold blood. Don't you tell me about their-"

"-Francisco was not useful to them, James. Madison has a lot to offer. They went to a lot of trouble to get her. In the meantime, what are you going to do? Walk into Giovanni's villa and rescue the princess like you're Errol Flynn?"

"Who?"

"Never mind. The point is that you have nothing to bargain with. You need some leverage."

"What do you suggest?"

"You have the key, you know where to take it, and Giovanni thinks they have what they need. Use this time to find the empire marker."

"And then use it to bargain for Madison?"

"Once you have the empire marker they won't have any need for her."

"You would let me trade the empire marker for Madison's life?"

"At the very least it's what we should do for her. The fact that you haven't considered it should tell you something."

"Spare me the therapy, Devin. I'll check in when we've reached Italy." James hung up the phone, picked up his bag and walked over to Gil and Brennan. "Come on, Gil. Let's go find your parents."

"Find his what-now?" asked Brennan, eyebrows bent in hemispheres.

Madison endured her imprisonment, day in and day out, with the same repetition of activity. She spoke to no one save her conversation with Moonface at midday. He would ask her for the ruby and she would decline. Then the dwarf would enter and remove another few links from the chain that bound her. Every morning her room was arranged exactly as it had been the morning before, with every book returned to its bookshelf, and her meals were placed at the opposite end of the room.

"So this is my torture," Madison said aloud to herself one day after they'd left. "The chain gets shorter and shorter with each refusal. Until... what?"

After a week, Madison's chain would not let her comfortably reach the toilet. The next day, a ceramic pot appeared next to her bed to handle the sanitary aspects of her confinement. One morning she could not reach the novel that she was reading at the end of the last day. The chain was too short. The novel went unfinished. Once every three days she was taken to the round basin in the middle of the courtyard for a bath.

She passed the time in a number of ways. She sang, as there was no music of any kind to fill the air. At first her songs were upbeat and encouraging; an attempt to cheer herself up. But as time wore on, her songs became more melancholy, reflecting her breaking heart and the incredible loneliness that was enveloping her soul.

She also began reciting her favorite movies as a form of entertainment, but soon, her thoughts drifted to her own life; her own adventure. Madison thought of her mother, of friends, past lovers, her old life in the States which seemed so far away at that moment. She also thought often of James. When she thought of him she usually cried.

Ten days after being first confined to her bed, she was unable to stretch to reach her food. She pulled and stretched but could not bring her fingers to tug on the tray. She pulled the sheets off of her bed, twisted them together and tossed the sheets onto the tray. With a slight tug the tray slid off the dresser and fell to the floor with a crash. She scrambled to the floor to retrieve the scraps, broken bread and noodles, pulling her dinner from the carpet.

One day, as the next link was being extricated, she asked Moonface, not really expecting him to respond, "What happens when I run out of links?"

He turned to her and shrugged. "This, I do not know. No one has ever gotten that far." He turned and left.

What does that mean? That everyone cracks, or you kill them before they have a chance?

❦

The Tiber River cut its way through the center of Rome, shifting left and right like a snaking train approaching a station. The river moved methodically, bringing water to a city two and a half millennia in the making.

Each bank of the river bore a stifling assortment of stone and brick buildings set at odd angles to one another. The city was not the result of the singular vision of a master planner, or even the ordered necessity of natural geography, but rather the chaotic shifting of time, political power, and the economic rise and fall of the Roman Empire and the rise of the Italian state.

Brennan peered out the window of the second floor hotel room which overlooked the Tiber. Across the river and through the haze of the morning, Brennan could just make out the long oval-shaped depression in the earth, known as Circus Maximus.

"So Caligula lived over there, you say?" Brennan held a finger to the window.

"Just to the left." James joined Brennan at the window. "That hill is Palatine Hill. That's where they built Imperial Palace."

"They built a palace on Palatine. Convenient."

"It's where we get the word "palace." Every palace in the world can trace its origin back to Caesar Augustus and his home on Palatine Hill. Let's go." James tossed a backpack to Brennan, picked up one for himself, and exited the hotel.

Brennan fell in love with Rome every time he visited. Its streets were reminiscent of many European cities with narrow passageways and small buildings that came right to the curb. Yet Rome functioned like a modern world capitol. Public transportation ran efficiently (when the public workers weren't striking), streets had been improved with storm sewers and the walk near the Tiber River had been modernized for aesthetics and cleanliness.

James and Brennan navigated the streets of Rome finding their way to the Biblioteca Nazionale Centrale di Roma, the city's public library.

"Good morning," said a shy woman in a white button-down blouse. She was clearly middle aged, but her long, dark hair gave a hint of youthfulness.

"English?" said James. "Is it that obvious that we're not from around here?"

"You seem a little lost. And you just entered through the exit doors."

"Ah. I guess we are a bit lost. Can you help us?" said James with a sheepish smile.

"I'd be glad to. What are you looking for?"

"Old maps of Rome. Or rather maps of Old Rome. We're interested in seeing the layout of the city two-thousand years ago, if you have something like that." Brennan noticed that James didn't attempt an elaborate story for why they were looking for this information. He smiled understanding the beauty of only telling someone the minimum that they need to know. There's no point in inventing an elaborate rouse when it's not needed.

"Of course," said the librarian. "We have an extensive map collection. This way." James and Brennan followed the woman up a flight of stairs and into a small room on the second floor of the library. Thousands of rolls of paper and large format books crowded the room. A video projector was mounted to the ceiling. The woman pulled a screen down from a retractable reel and turned on the projector.

"We are in process of digitizing our maps. Not all of them have been scanned but many of them can now be accessed digitally." She moved to a small desk with a keyboard and mouse. "Now, you asked about Rome itself? At the time of Caesar Agustus?"

"Actually, a little later. Maybe 40AD," said James.

"Ah, Caligula." The woman moved a mouse around clicking a few times. Eventually a birds-eye view of ancient Rome shone on the screen. "This is from our Claudius collection. This should be Rome just after Caligula's death."

James and Brennan searched the map. The structures still had Latin labels, but they were still able to work out most of the names.

"It's weird," said Brennan. "A map of Rome without the Coliseum on it."

"There," said James, pointing to a few rectangular buildings. "Palatine hill."

"Are you two with the excavation?" The woman asked.

"Excavation?" asked Brennan.

"Yes, on Palatine. They're working on the imperial palace itself."

"That must be the same palace Caligula lived in. He built lots of houses, but there was only one palace." James stepped closer to the screen. "Now where would he have put the bath?"

"Bath?" asked the woman.

"Yes. I understand that there was an expansion to the palace built by Caligula. Where was the bath?"

"Oh, I don't know of any bath, although, that's a question more for an expert. I find the history interesting, but I'm not as studied as you seem to be. But according to this map, there doesn't seem to be a bath attached to the palace."

The woman was right, no matter what James had been led to believe, there was no getting around the fact that Caligula did not build a bath complex at his palace. James and Brennan slumped against a table confused by what they saw.

"They did find a grotto a few years back. That has water in it," the woman offered.

"A grotto?" James stood.

"Yes, that's what the excavation is working on. It's 15 or 20 meters just below Augustus' palace."

"Thank you very much for your help." Urgency leapt into James' voice. Brennan knew that the next step had been cast and James was already on his way there.

"Fortune has smiled upon us," said James as they walked out of the library and onto the street. "The archeologists at the excavation have opened the door to Caligula's empire marker and they don't even know it."

❡

Two weeks into her confinement Madison lay on her bed with her legs dangling over the edge, her chain too short to allow her to fully recline. The door opened for the next interrogation and, to Madison's surprise, it was not Moonface who had come to ask her the repetitive question.

Kitty entered the room. She sat on the bed next to Madison, took Madison's face into her hands and spoke.

"Maybe you don't understand what's going to happen here, Madison," said Kitty. "You have twelve links left. That's four days worth, okay? When those are gone, we start taking pieces of your flesh out. Do you understand me? You will lose your pretty little arms and legs until you bleed to death. Why make us go through that? Just tell us where the ruby arrowhead is."

The prospect of mutilation horrified Madison. At that moment, had she known where the ruby arrowhead was, she certainly would have said so.

"I don't know where it is, I swear." Madison knew she must look like a crazed hermit, her hair matted with neglect and four weeks of speaking to herself. "I would tell you, but I don't know. Please!"

"So where was the last place you saw it, Madison?" Kitty spoke with a quiet rage through clenched teeth.

Madison clutched at Kitty in a desperate plea. "James had it. They should have found it when they searched his body. I don't know why he didn't have it on him."

"Is this right?" asked Kitty. She rose, went to the door and opened it. Moonface entered.

"This girl says James had it. Why didn't you find it?"

"I don't know, Madam. We searched his body," said Moonface. His eyes widened in fear.

"Can you go back and check the body? Where did you leave him?"

"At the castle, Madam. It's been a few weeks, but it's possible that no one yet has entered the castle. Not likely, but possible, Madam. But I tell you, he didn't have it on him."

"Vincent says you're lying to me, Madison," said Kitty turning back to Madison. "You have four days left until we start taking flesh." The little person removed another three links and they left the room, slamming the door behind them.

Brennan picked the blue ball cap off the ground and fit it to his head. The matching blue coat was a little tight, but in the darkness, no one would question it. James, also wearing a blue jacket and cap, stepped out of the guard shack and shone his flashlight in a sweep around the excavation site. Two guards slept in a pile in the back of the shack, sans coats and hats. Brennan had put them to sleep with the same drugs he'd used on Claire and Beckie aboard the cruise ship.

A cool breeze brought moist Mediterranean air to the Roman night. Brennan glanced at the remaining arches of the Basillical Nova and the Capitoline Museums, shining under dramatic lighting. For tourism purposes, many of the monuments around Rome are lit at night. However, active excavation sights are not. These sights are staffed with low paid guards armed with flashlights and radios to scare off any wayward tourists. They were not equipped to deal with experienced artifact recovery experts like James and Brennan.

James led Brennan through the palace ruins, dropping down into the lowest level of the structure. It was here that the excavation had unearthed a small hole that led into a grotto beneath the palace. According to a few English language journals Brennan found at the library, all excavation work had been halted over fears that the ruins would collapse if they were destabilized by more digging. The excavation was awaiting the arrival of a remote camera. James had no such concerns.

This lower level stank of the thousand year ooze of subterranean mud. The tile floor remained remarkably well preserved and the surrounding columns and walls were still square to each other. In the back of one of the rooms, orange cones surrounded a 6 inch square opening in the floor.

"What do you want to bet that this is our entrance?" asked James. "Too bad they haven't opened this hole up yet."

"Look out." James stomped on the corner of the hole and kicked a few tiles down into the abyss. The pieces tumbled away and a half second later splashed in the darkness. James shone his light down the hole and it reflected off the surface of the water.

"How deep do you think that is?" asked Brennan.

"Only one way to find out." James removed a coiled up rope from his backpack and tied it to one of the columns in the room.

"Seriously? That column predates Christ and you're going to trust it to hold you up?"

"It's held up this long, hasn't it?" James swirled the rope around his leg and disappeared down the hole. A few seconds later the rope went limp. "It's only a couple feet deep here." James' voice echoed with profound reverb. "I can wade through it."

"What do you see?"

"Well, this room was more than just a storage room. The ceiling has… oh wow. Holy cow. You should see this."

"What?"

"The ceiling is covered in seashells and mosaics. It's remarkably well preserved. Whoa. Look at that."

"WHAT?" Brennan was getting frustrated.

"The white wolf. In the center of the ceiling is an image of a white wolf."

"The symbol of Rome."

"Exactly. Bren, you know what I think this is? I think this is the Lupercal."

The Lupercal. The very origin of Rome. Brennan was familiar with the story of Romulus and Remus who were found suckling on a wolf near the cave that would later be known as the Lupercal.

"That's a legendary story James. No one thinks it was a real place."

"Someone thought this was the real place Bren. There were priests of Lupercal all the way to the end of the fifth century. I think this is where they performed their ceremonies."

"Are you kidding me? We found the Lupercal?" Brennan tried to get his head into the hole for a better look but found he couldn't see much more than James standing 20 feet below him.

"The archeologists found it. We just went down the hole first."

"So would Caligula have hidden his empire marker here?"

"I don't know. The legend specifically mentions a bath, but that could have been one of those words that got translated too many times. A grotto beneath the palace, the Lupercal no less. I can see him hiding it here." James removed the ruby arrowhead from the pouch around his neck hoping it would give him a clue as to where in the grotto the empire marker was hidden.

A wave of nostalgia washed over Brennan as he watched James scour the chamber for clues. "Hey boss?"

"Yeah, Bren."

"I like this. You and me on a recovery. Just like old times."

"Yeah. Just like old times." James waded his way out of Brennan's sight. Finding himself staring into a dark hole, he decided to make a sweep of the perimeter to make sure no one had wandered onto the excavation site.

A quick hike around the excavation site later, Brennan returned to the lower floor of the palace. He found James crouched on the floor, dripping wet, hovering over a small object.

"It was just sitting on a recess in the wall. Like a little alter or a shelf for candles," said James. He looked down at a bronze box, roughly eight inches in length and three inches square. Faint lettering could be seen on the cover of the box, but in this light they couldn't read it.

"It's smaller than any empire marker I've seen," said Brennan.

"Shall we see what Caligula left for us?" James pounded on the latch with a small hammer and chisel. The crusted latch broke and James opened the lid.

"I don't get it," he said.

Madison passed the days in a fitful cycle of terror, panic, depression, and apathy. She lay upon the once luxurious silk sheets unable to rise from her bed. She tried to do push-ups and sit-ups on the bed, but even with that exercise, she could feel her muscles atrophying.

She was withering away, surrounded by books she would love to be reading, in a country she would have loved to be exploring, looking at food she had no way of reaching.

With nothing else to do, she often dozed into slumber during the day, such that she could no longer sleep at night. She slept an hour or so, only to awaken from another nightmare, a night terror, where her limbs were torn from her body or she was run down by rabid dogs. She blamed the violence of the dreams on the hunger pangs that stabbed in the abdomen without mercy.

It was understandable that she should doubt her senses when, lying on the bed in the middle of the night, she heard a unique noise outside her window. She looked at the window quizzically, but still assumed that the noise had been a fabrication of her overwrought mind.

Her senses deceived her yet again when she saw a shadow pass over the window, cast by the brilliance of the full moon. *So this is it?* She thought. *It's the moment where my I lose my mind. They've broken me. They've broken me for good.* She looked at her ankle where just three links were attached to her prison bed.

She looked back at the window and gasped. Every muscle in her body tensed up in fear. A shadowy figure loomed at the window. The apparition wore a dark cloak and a hood that concealed the intruder's face. The window creaked opened and the shadow, a silently moving specter, perhaps the approach of death himself, climbed through the window.

Madison's voice was paralyzed. She could not speak. She could not scream. She lay in abject terror as it approached the side of her bed.

"Madison? Wake up," it whispered.

Madison responded with a shudder and near hyperventilation. The figure straightened a bit.

"Relax, sweetie. It's me," and the figure pulled the hood back revealing his face.

"James?" she managed to squeak out. Was this a ghost that had come to her in the middle of the night?

"Let's get you out of here."

The emotions that flooded Madison's mind at that moment were like a lifetime of grieving, joy, and relief all rushing her at once. It was the rush of a mighty waterfall in the midst of a placid stream. Madison broke into tears and spoke incoherently. She sat up and James embraced her.

"I'm sorry I've been so long," he said.

She melted into his arms, devouring the first kind human contact in almost three weeks. A hug, when properly given, can be a wonderful thing, restoring hope, strength, and assurance that words could never muster.

"Moonface told me you were dead," she said, still in a guarded whisper.

"Who?"

"Sorry. I think his name is Vincent. I've given everyone nicknames since I don't know their real names. There's Moonface, and Slugo, and Food Guy, oh, and Kitty who runs the place.

"So Vincent Giovanni told you that I was dead? They'd like to believe that," he ran his hand down her leg and examined the shackle that bound her to the bed. "Brennan can tell you how we survived. I was out of it for a while if you remember."

"Brennan is alive too?" she almost shouted.

"Of course. He's waiting for us outside."

"And Gil? Please tell me that they didn't hurt the little boy."

"Heh. Yeah, he's fine. Funny story about Gil. He wasn't an orphan."

"What?"

"No. He was a run-away. His parents had posted him missing almost a year ago. Devin found the posted information once we told him what happened. Bren and I got him to the authorities and he's on his way back to his family."

"So Francisco knew…"

"I don't know. If he knew Gil was a run-away, he didn't care."

Madison lowered her head as she thought of the Spaniard.

"Is he really dead?"

"Yes, Madison." James spoke with a solemn gravity. "Francisco is dead."

"I don't understand how you three survived. When they took me you were unconscious, and they had guns and everything."

"Mads, it's a great story, but for another time. I promise you I'll tell it to you, but for now, we've got to get you out of here."

James pulled a small tool kit from his robe and began sawing and prying at the last link of the chain. Madison's mind was sharpening and a new realization came to her.

"So you two have been alive all this time while I rotted here in this prison? What took you so long? Where've you been?" She surprised herself at the biting ferocity of her own tone of voice.

James stopped work and turned to her in sincerity.

"Madison, you have a right to be upset. Look, with you taken by Giovanni, Devin thought that the best way to get you back was to find Caligula's empire marker. Then we'd have something to bargain with."

"They just want that stupid ruby," said Madison. "You could have bargained with that."

"They want more than just the ruby. They would have let you go if they didn't need you. We thought that with you imprisoned, that it might buy us a break from Giovanni chasing us. If we could get the empire marker we could trade it once they no longer needed you. So Bren and I went to Rome to find Caligula's bath under the city. That's what we've been doing." James returned to trying to pry the links apart.

Madison could see a certain wisdom in what he was saying. However, it didn't erase the weeks of grieving she'd been through, thinking he was dead.

"So, you found the bath? Did you find the empire marker?" she asked.

"That's just the thing. It's not there."

"What? You're kidding." Madison was astounded. This whole trip, the flight to Miami, the cruise ship, the drive across Europe, was all to get to Rome and find Caligula's bath. And now even that goal turned into a fool's errand.

"Nope. The empire marker is somewhere else. Apparently, Giovanni is right. We need both you and the ruby. We're missing something."

"What?"

"I don't know yet, but I knew that we were out of time. Devin said it was foolish to try to break you out of here, but I had to try. Can you walk?"

"I don't know, it's been a while," she said.

James pried the last link of the chain away and helped her to her feet. The heavy shackle weighed on her ankle like an anvil.

"James," she said softly. He paused and looked at her as he held her around her waist. "Thank you for coming for me," she said.

James was about to respond when the door flew open and the light in the room illuminated. The overhead lamps blinded Madison for a few seconds as Kitty with Moonface and another unknown henchman stood in the doorway. All three of them carried pistols.

"Well, I certainly didn't expect this. Back from the dead," she said. "Somehow I knew that these simpletons hadn't killed you. Hello, James Kynan."

James stuttered for a second before replying.

"Hello, Michelle," he said, his voice like a razor.

And then it all started to make sense.

XVII

CRAZY MAKES A GOOD AGENT

"Temptation is the fire that brings up the scum of the heart. "
William Shakespeare

The next day, Madison's treatment changed dramatically. She was no longer a prisoner but a guest, and was treated as such. The chain and shackle were removed, the clothing she was wearing when she was captured was returned to her, cleaned and pressed, and she was welcome at the dinner table with Michelle, Moonface, Slugo, Renzo, James, and a few other Giovanni employees Madison didn't know. It was an inexplicable change in attitude towards her that she could only guess was related to James' history with Michelle.

Dinner was the first time she'd seen James since the attempted rescue the night before. James and Madison had been discovered in her room and James was led away without explanation and apparently without immediate consequence. The next morning, the shackle was removed from her ankle and she was given leave to wander the villa and examine the artifacts which ornamented every wall, column, and sconce. She was referred to as Miss Dawn by the housekeepers and wait staff and breakfast was served out on the terrace in the fresh morning breeze. It was clear that Giovanni's organization did not believe that she would try to escape while James was in the villa. They were right. If Madison had devised any escape plans, she certainly wouldn't go through with them without first consulting James. He had risked everything to rescue her. How could she desert him?

At that first dinner with James, she longed to speak with him. She yearned to find out his plan of escape, to learn when Brennan would come storming in to save them, and just to hear his voice and hear that everything would be all right.

They were seated at a long dinner table, ornately decorated with china place settings for twelve, sterling silver utensils, crystal goblets, and fanciful floral centerpieces. Michelle sat at the head of the table with James seated to her immediate right; the place of honor at any dinner table. Madison, on the other hand, was seated at the far end of the left side of the table; far enough away that she had trouble hearing the conversation at James' end of the table.

To Madison's disappointment, James said just two things to her at dinner.

"Are they treating you well?" he'd asked when they first sat down and she'd caught his eye.

"Yes, now that you're here," she'd answered, thinking it was the beginning of a conversation. However, he did not speak to her again until the end of the meal.

As the dessert dishes were cleared, the only other thing James said was, "Not bad hospitality for a bunch of Italian thugs, huh?"

It was directed at her but it was not intended for Madison. The rest of the table laughed at his jab as if it had come from a good friend. Michelle touched his arm as she chuckled, her laughter carrying on a little longer than the rest of her table companions. Madison left the table confused and upset. She was being tortured yet again.

≈☙⚔☙≈

James took off his shirt and slumped into a plush chair in the corner of his spacious and elegantly appointed room. He tossed his shirt onto the nearby gold vanity and rubbed his chin. It was well past midnight yet his mind would not let him sleep. He counted his failures the way others counted sheep. Keep the ruby arrowhead safe? Failure. Avoid messy situations? Failure. Keep Madison safe? Failure. Find Caligula's empire marker? Epic Failure. Evade Giovanni's agents— a knock came at the door.

James rose from the chair and opened the door a crack. Michelle stood in the doorway.

"Hi, James." She gave him a sheepish smile and tugged at a long lock of her hair.

"It's late."

"Can I come in?" she asked.

James hesitated and then opened the door fully. "It's your castle."

Michelle glided into the room. She was wearing a blue night gown and a dark blue satin robe.

"Do you like your room?" she asked.

"It's a bit ostentatious for me. Giovanni seems to be doing well." He picked up an auburn vase from a round table. "Is this Persian?"

"Fifteenth century. We found it in Istanbul. It's flawless. It's the only complete vessel like it in the world."

"It would make a decent vase," said James, setting it back down.

"James," said Michelle with a newfound directness. "I wanted to apologize for Francisco. I know you and he were close."

"You knew him too, Michelle. You met him at the Museum's New Year's ball three years ago. Or have you repressed that from your mind too."

"No, I remember. James, I never ordered them to kill. You have to believe me."

"I have to believe you? Why should I?"

"I didn't want Francisco to die."

"Didn't you? You sent your henchmen to his castle armed with Glocks."

"It was Vincent. He's a little crazy." She ran her hands through her curly hair.

"So, why don't you fire him?"

"Fire Vincent Giovanni? The heir-apparent to the whole organization? I could never. Besides, crazy makes a good agent."

James went to the vanity and pulled on his shirt.

Michelle asked, "You're still angry with me, aren't you? For leaving the way I did?"

"I let that anger go."

"No you haven't. I see the venom in your stare," she said. She drew close to him and put her hands on his shoulders. "Am I that evil in your eyes?"

James couldn't stand to look at her pleading face. He turned away and looked to the window. "The night you left." James paused and swallowed. "I was coming to your tent to propose to you."

Michelle emitted an uncensored laugh, before covering her mouth with her hand.

"Oh, honey. Marriage? We'd only been together for a few months."

"Yeah. I get that. I made a bad choice. Your empty tent was my first clue."

"It's not that," Michelle sobered. "I had no idea you were so…"

"Attached?"

"James, listen to me. I left because I had an opportunity with this organization. I could move from assistant researcher working with you to lead artifact recovery expert for the entire Mediterranean with Giovanni. It was four times the salary. Honey, it was a career move, nothing more."

"You took the scepter."

"Of course I did. It was part of the deal. Giovanni wanted the scepter and was offering me the position if I brought the scepter to him."

James sat on the bed. "You could have told me you were leaving."

"Let me ask you this. If I had asked, would you have left the museum with me to go work for Giovanni?"

"Never."

"See? I had to leave without telling you. What would the museum have done had they found out that you knew I was leaving? I did it to protect you. For your own good."

James was silent. Her story, the way she looked at him, the sing-song in her voice, none of it concurred with the demonic image in his head that he'd grown to loathe over the last two and a half years.

Michelle sat on the bed next to him and took his hand into hers.

"James. I swear I didn't know you were so enamored with me. I had no clue you were even thinking about anything permanent with us. For all I knew, I was just one of your many adventures. Just another girl."

Just another girl. James shook his head at the irony.

"What do you want from me, Michelle?"

"This empire marker, this Key of Caligula's Bath is bigger than anything you or I have ever found, James. I could forcibly take the arrowhead from you. You know I have the muscle here to do it. But I'd prefer if you helped me."

"Helped you?" asked James.

"Yes. We need to work together on this, James. Think of what we could accomplish. You and me. Just think of it."

Madison's only respite was physical exercise. The next afternoon Renzo showed her to a gym in another part of the villa. She was encouraged to rehabilitate her body after it had atrophied during the three weeks of confinement. Her body felt like an aged rubber band which had lost its elastic and now was brittle and frail. Madison was never one to hit the gym and exercise, but it offered a welcome relief from worrying and wondering just what exactly James was doing.

She was given some shorts and a tank top in which to exercise. She stood before the mirrored wall in the exercise room, mouth agape at her appearance. She was skinny, but in an unhealthy way. Her legs were thin and her bony hips had lost their shapeliness. Her face was sallow and her eye sockets deep from worry and stress. She wore no make-up and the pasty white skin, having been confined indoors for almost a month, glared in the harsh fluorescent light of the gym. In a few weeks they'd taken from her the one thing she'd always used to her advantage; They'd taken her beauty.

Madison's spirits spiraled downward and her insecurity turned to anger. She tackled the various machines in the gym with a ferocity she seldom displayed.

Madison spent the next days in turmoil; a constant tempest of physical activity to ward off the emotional pain, the hurt, the worry, the unknown. She'd never really exercised at a gym before, and some of the more convoluted machines confused her. Yet twice a day, once in the morning, and again in the evening, she worked until every fiber of every muscle cried out in pain and exhaustion. After a few days of being ignored and humiliated at the dinner table, she started intentionally working out through dinner. She couldn't bear to see him fraternizing with those evil people. She would take her meal in her room, still dripping with sweat from her work out. In the evening, she bathed, climbed into bed with a good book, and went to sleep as early as she could to avoid the lonely late night hours.

⚜

Two weeks after James attempted his rescue, Madison lay in bed as the darkness of the moonless night permeated every corner of the villa. She knew it was late, probably well after midnight, yet sleep would not come to her. She could hear the quiet hum of a handful of hover flies holding station in the room. Hover flies looked more like yellow jackets to Madison, but instead of a sting, they simply annoyed their victim to death by keeping them awake with their incessant buzzing.

Every night it was a battle to fall asleep; her unending worry gnawing at her conscious and keeping it from resting.

A click. A squeak. Her bedroom door slowly swung open and the unmistakable silhouette of James Kynan stepped inside the room escorting a flood of light from the illuminated hallway. He closed the door behind him and walked softly to the edge of her bed.

"Madison?" he whispered.

"I'm awake, James." Madison answered in a normal conversational voice that conveyed her disapproval of him.

"Oh." He sat down on her bed. Two weeks ago he had come to her as a rescuer and she had embraced him with the passion of the destitute finding hope. This night, she lay there quietly and did not even sit up.

"Where the hell have you been, James?" she asked.

"I've been waiting for you to recover your strength. I've been told that you've been faithful in the gym. That's good to hear."

"Where's Brennan? Why hasn't he come to get us yet?"

"Oh, Bren?" A lilt crept into James' voice. "I sent him away. I told him he was no longer needed here. He's on his way back to the States."

"What? Are you kidding me, James?" Madison exhaled in exasperation.

"We're leaving tomorrow morning."

"Wouldn't it be better to escape now? We can go under cover of darkness-"

"No. You, Michelle, and I are leaving in the morning. We're going to find Caligula's empire marker." Madison could not see his face in the darkness but could feel his nervousness as he shifted uneasily on the side of the bed.

"Why is she coming? James, what is happening here?"

"Michelle and I are going to work together on this. We want the same thing, and I think we can help each other."

"Are you crazy, James? Have you lost your freaking mind? You're going to work with her? James, she imprisoned me for over a month. She killed Francisco in cold blood-"

"-Something she never wanted to happen. And have they tortured you too badly? Look at this room. It's a far cry from a prison cell."

Madison was speechless. Was he actually apologizing for these thugs?

"James, you can't trust Michelle. She abandoned you when you thought you were going to marry her. Don't you remember this?"

"Michelle and I have had some good talks. She's sorry for what happened in the past."

"She's sorry?"

"She was caught up with ambition. Who wouldn't have their judgment clouded by ambition in a business like this? I might have done the same thing."

"No you wouldn't. You're not like that. At least, you weren't…"

"She's got a good gig here now. She runs all of Giovanni's artifact recovery operations. It's worked out for her, and she says her only regret was leaving me like she did."

Madison felt a sickening churning of her stomach. Live before her eyes she was witnessing the spine of man torn out by his own Achilles heel. All of the warnings that Brennan had issued about James and his attachments, all of the caution that she had exercised to avoid any romantic interaction, all of it made perfect sense now. She could see a man broken from within, desperately clinging to a fantasy of happiness, a fantasy that could never exist.

James stood with some semblance of strength. "We're leaving at 0600 tomorrow morning. Be dressed and ready to go."

"James, wait."

"And get some sleep." James left, closing the door behind him.

Madison ran her hands through her hair and pulled until her scalp burned.

≈⊱⊰≈

Two minutes before six in the morning Madison stepped into the same foyer that had greeted her when she'd first been brought to the villa. She tossed her backpack onto one of the wooden high back chairs and, since she was the first one there, checked the clock to reassure herself that it was in fact the appointed time to meet. The sun was not yet up and Madison's body informed her that she should return to bed with all due haste. She rubbed her eyes and yawned. She was up and dressed, but to say that she was awake was an overstatement.

Footsteps approached. James and Michelle entered the foyer together from another hallway.

Did they come out of the same room? Madison forced herself not to think about it. Moonface entered just behind them. Apparently he was part of this little adventure as well.

"Good morning," said James. "I see you got the backpack we left for you. It should have everything you might need in it. Are you ready to go?" He put his hand on Michelle's back and rubbed it lightly.

Madison glared at Michelle and could feel her cheeks flushing with anger. Michelle stared back at Madison with a condescending smirk. The animosity between Michelle and Madison was so great that it was the mere promise of lethal force by Moonface or any one of her cold-blooded thugs that kept Madison from gouging out Michelle's eyes.

"Yes, I've got my backpack. But where are we going? You said that there was nothing under Caligula's Bath," Madison said as she folded her arms. "The legend about his empire marker was a bust."

"Not exactly," said James. He turned to Michelle, "May I show her?"

Michelle nodded.

Did he just ask for her permission? The thought of digging her thumbnail into Michelle's eye was starting to sound more appealing as each minute passed.

"We did find something, just not the empire marker," James opened up his backpack and withdrew an object the size of a railroad spike covered in burgundy felt. "We found this in a small bronze box." He handed it to Madison.

The object was heavy; clearly made of stone or metal. She unwrapped it until she was looking at a pointed stone maybe eight inches long. It was square in cross-section, but tapered from one end to the other with a small pyramid shape at the tip.

"How phallic," said Madison as she held it erect.

"Do you recognize it?" asked James.

"Yeah, I do," said Madison. "It's an obelisk, like they made in Egypt."

"And?" asked James. Madison shifted uneasily. Why was she being quizzed like this?

"Yeah, I remember it from that book I read on the cruise. Caligula brought an obelisk back from Egypt."

"So you know where we have to go," led James.

"Vatican City. St. Peter's Square. The obelisk in St. Peter's square is the obelisk Caligula brought back from Egypt," said Madison.

"Hmm," said Michelle finally. "She's smarter than I thought. We're guessing that there's something on that obelisk that points us to the true location of the empire marker. Okay, get your backpack, Dawn. We're going as tourists so don't do anything stupid to blow our cover. Vincent will make sure that you do as you're told."

"You don't have to talk to her like that," said James.

"Quiet. I don't want this little whore ruining this recovery."

That was all it took.

Madison lunged at Michelle with blood in her eyes, intent on doing as much damage as she could to that smug face of hers. She never reached her nemesis as James stepped in front of her. He held her back, holding her wrists as she fought him with passionate zeal.

"Tell your girlfriend that if she wants my help she can start treating me with some respect," Madison shouted.

"I give respect to those who deserve it," said Michelle.

"Stop it, both of you." James' voice thundered through the villa in a deep resonating echo. He stood between them, arms outstretched, as a mediator and peacekeeper. "Michelle, Madison and I have been through a lot for this artifact. She's been nothing but honest and true with me. You won't disrespect her like that."

He turned to Madison, "And you. I know that you don't like Michelle, but she's with us now."

"You mean you're with her now," said Madison.

"Promise me you won't attack her again."

"I can't promise that," Madison said, under control once again.

"Promise me, Madison," said James. "I'm not doing this, wondering when you're going to take a swing at her. We all need to get through this together."

Madison slowly shook her head. Was this the same man that heroically pulled her from her wrecked car when Michelle's thugs were moments from taking her? Was this the same man that on the cruise ship so bravely fought the assassin Michelle had ordered? Is this the same man that had snuck into the fortified Giovanni Villa at great risk to himself just two weeks ago to set her free?

"You don't even see what she's doing to you. You don't even know what you've become," said Madison. She picked up her backpack and without another word went out the front door towards the waiting car.

This battle was over. The war was not.

༄ུ

The early morning air was cold as winter had finally arrived in Italy. Madison zipped her fleece up to her neck and plunged her hands deep into her pockets.

The line to enter the Vatican Museum had already formed by the time they arrived. Hundreds of tourists from all over the world stretched along the Vitale Vaticano, the road nearest to the Vatican Museum. The line, a virtual United Nations of tourism, stretched along the towering stone wall that surrounded the ancient city-state. Nearly every nationality was represented in line, with the singular exception of Roman citizens. Locals seldom visit their own attractions and Rome was no exception. James, Madison, Michelle and Moonface bypassed the line on their way to the Piazza Pio XII and St. Peter's Square.

The foursome rounded a corner and before them stood St. Peter's Basilica, a behemoth of granite and marble on the other side of the oblong St. Peter's Square. The ellipse of tall columns surrounding the square formed welcoming arms that beckoned all to worship at the gilt-domed basilica. Dramatically lit by the rising sun behind them, a giant obelisk made of red granite stood in the center of the ellipse: the Vatican Obelisk, Caligula's signpost to his empire marker.

They crossed the street and entered through a gate in the wrought iron fence that kept street traffic out of the square.

The imposing, needle-like structure soared nearly nine stories and was topped with a bronze cross. Madison could see what appeared to be gargoyles or stone lions at the base of the obelisk. The obelisk stood on a square stone pedestal which added to the height of the monument. They reached the base where a circle of chains prevented them from getting any closer.

"Vincent, get some pictures and make sure you cover the whole monument," said Michelle. Moonface pulled a sophisticated DSLR camera from his bag and affixed a long lens to it. He began systematically taking pictures of the entire obelisk in high detail.

"He does photography too?" asked James.

"Oh yes, he's quite good," said Michelle. "You should see what he can do with landscapes."

"So Caligula brought this all the way from Egypt, huh?" said Madison. "What's that say?"

Madison was referring to the Latin inscription on the pedestal of the monument.

"My Latin is a bit rusty," said James. "Um. Behold the cross of the Lord. Enemies, flee. The Lion of Judah has conquered."

James walked around to the next side of the obelisk where the inscription continued.

"Pope Sixtus V, with great effort, moved the Vatican obelisk, um, something about pagans… to the something of the Apostles, in the second year of his pontificate, 1586."

"Fifteen eighty six?" said Madison. "I thought you said Caligula brought it here?"

"He did," said Michelle. "He brought it to Rome and installed it as part of a circus he built in the gardens of his mother Agrippina. It wasn't until 1586 when it was moved here in the center of the square."

"So where was it before?" asked Madison

"About 800 feet away," said James. "The important point here is that this base, and yes, the bronze cross atop the obelisk, were built much later than Caligula. What we're looking for will be on the obelisk itself."

The three of them stood staring at the obelisk stupidly as Moonface continued his photographic coverage. They didn't know what they were looking for and they didn't know how to tell when they'd found it.

"James?" asked Madison.

He grunted after a few seconds delay.

"Don't these things usually have writing on them? Hieroglyphics?"

"I was just thinking that. This one is smooth. Nothing at all inscribed on it." James was puzzled, as was Michelle. Madison stepped back from the obelisk and found a bench that faced the obelisk. Soon James and Michelle joined her on the bench. The three of them sat staring at the monolith, saying nothing to each other, wracking their brains for the answer.

"What about those lions?" asked Madison, breaking the silence.

"The bronze lions at the base?" asked Michelle. "Those were added much later, just like the cross."

Madison was not going to sit there and be insulted so she got up and took a thoughtful stroll around the obelisk.

Around the other side of the obelisk, a third lion guarded the corner at the base of the obelisk. *So these are the Lions of Judah?* But on the fourth corner, she saw something different. Instead of a lion, she saw a woman. Something about this inconsistency made her skin tingle, like the electricity in the air before a thunderstorm. She ran back to James and Michelle on the bench.

She pointed and asked, "What about her?" James and Michelle stood and followed her to the other side of the obelisk.

"The bronze statue?" asked James. "I told you those came much later. Probably 16th century."

"But why a woman? Why not four lions guarding each corner?" asked Madison. "Let's see that stone you found under Caligula's bath," said Madison.

James delved into his backpack and pulled out the stone obelisk and looked at it.

"See no cross, no pedestal. It's just the obelisk," he said.

"Oh," said Madison dejectedly. "There's nothing else?"

"Wait a second," said James.

"What is it?" asked Michelle.

"Look. Look at the corners of the base of this stone. I thought they were just broken corners worn down from 2000 years. But look, this isn't broken at all. It's carved."

Madison looked closer. The image leapt out at her. It was the face of a lion carved into the stone. It was time worn and difficult to make out, but now that she knew what she was looking for, the carved image was clear.

James turned the obelisk over in his hand, examining each corner of the stone.

"Lion. Lion. Lion... Woman. Those bronze statues are original. Or at least, replicas of what used to be there. The statues are from Caligula."

James dug in his backpack and retrieved a pair of binoculars. Though the statues were at the base of the obelisk, they still stood atop the granite pedestal above their heads. He trained them on the figure of the woman.

"I can't believe it," said James.

"What?" asked Michelle.

"It's the arrowhead. Look."

Madison pulled her own set of binoculars from her backpack. The woman was seated on a rock, holding a spear, with a spiked shield propped beside her. The woman was wrapped in a flowing cloth and her right breast was exposed.

Something on the spear caught Madison's gaze and she focused more closely on it. At the end of the spear was a stone cut into the shape of an arrowhead, the same shape as the ruby she knew as the Key of Caligula's Bath.

"I see it," said Madison. "But wait, I-" Madison felt her heart drop into her stomach. Her heart restarted and then raced beyond control.

"Yes?" asked James.

"That spear. I've... I've seen it before."

"The spear the woman is holding. The spear with the arrowhead mounted in it?" asked Michelle.

"Yes."

"Tell us," demanded Michelle. Madison's brain sifted through all the stored memories of her life. The shape of the spear was unique, with a forked section near the top and a spiral chine running continuously from top to bottom. *Where have I seen that before?*

"Come on, Mads. Where have you seen it?" said James.

Madison closed her eyes and images of her childhood flashed passed, like a hyperactive slideshow of memories. The details shifted and merged together. It was sitting on a bookshelf. No. A buffet. A china cabinet. It was an heirloom; something of her mother's. She remembered the snow globe and the story of the princess and her lost kingdom, her mother returning the snow globe to the shelf next to-

"The candlestick!" she shouted. Several tourists near her glared at her for having the audacity to disturb their peaceful morning.

"What candlestick?" asked James.

"My mother has this candlestick. We always asked her why she kept it, but she said it was an antique, passed down through the family. It was just one candlestick, not even a pair. Candles didn't even fit all that well so it sat unused in her china cabinet. James, that spear looks just like that candlestick."

"Are you sure?" asked Michelle.

"Yes, positive."

"Fair enough. I'll have your mother and the candlestick brought to us," said Michelle.

Madison had to replay what Michelle had said in her mind several times before she actually heard it.

"You'll do what, now?" Madison asked.

"Oh, hasn't he told you?" asked Michelle with a sickening smirk. "Your mother is in our care now. We'll get the candlestick from her."

"You have my mother? What the hell? Leave her out of this! She has nothing to do with this." yelled Madison. The sudden thought of her family being in danger from these thugs sent Madison into a rage.

"Apparently she has everything to do with this, Dawn. Don't worry. As long as we get what we want, no harm will come to her."

Madison's anger turned to James.

"You knew? You knew my mother had been kidnapped and you didn't tell me? How could you betray me like that?"

"Madison, it's not—. The only way to get you out of this is to find this empire marker. Worrying about your mother would have just distracted you."

Madison felt her cheeks flush with anger and her eyes narrowed, boring deep, penetrating holes into James' soul. Venom welled up inside of her and, for the first time, she saw fear in James' eyes. She saw doubt on his face.

"I'm sorry, Madison," he said. "I thought we would recover this empire marker before she ever entered the picture. I- I'm sorry." James turned around as if merely looking at the hurt on her face was more than he could bear. He stared at the obelisk for a second before turning his head to one side.

"Now what?" asked Madison.

"That woman holding the spear," said James. "That's the Roman god Britannia."

"Britannia?" asked Madison.

"Yes, Caligula didn't bury his empire marker at the heart of his empire. He buried it in the most remote reaches of his empire, just like any other empire marker. Of course..."

"What are you saying?" asked Michelle.

"He buried it somewhere on the island of Britain."

XVIII

THE OLD CANDLESTICK

"Remember, upon the conduct of each depends the fate of all."
Alexander the Great

"It's time to go, Madison."

"Why?"

"It's just time. Oh… You look radiant today. My beautiful daughter."

"Mom, where are you going?"

"I'm going away. This is goodbye."

"I don't want to say goodbye. I want to go with you."

"Remember to brush your hair. You know how it gets when you neglect it."

"Mom?"

"I left some money in the dresser drawer."

"I don't understand."

"I'm sorry I didn't tell you."

Madison awoke with a start; the images from the dream fresh in her mind. Her jaw ached and she realized she'd been clenching her teeth while she slept. She looked up as the flight attendants were asking the rest of the passengers to put their trays in the upright and locked position and to ensure their seatbelts were fastened securely. They were on approach into London Heathrow airport.

The flight had been one of isolation for Madison. She sat by herself near the back of the airplane. Moonface was seated across the aisle, her ever-vigilant guard, while a few rows ahead of her sat James and Michelle. It was just as well. Madison had no intention of talking to either of them.

James' blatant obsequiousness to Michelle was killing him and he didn't realize it. Each moment spent with that manipulative charlatan withered James a little more. Michelle would request something; he'd hop up to get it. She'd say something and demand his undivided attention; he'd give it absolutely, every time. Madison could see his shoulders slump into the seat like a once proud dog broken and humiliated by its owner. James wasn't happy, but he was deluding himself that he was.

This man, this *hero* of hers, was self-destructing.

Madison would almost pity him if it weren't for the fact that her mother was involved. Nothing came between Madison and her family. Madison's mother was probably also on an airplane crossing the Atlantic right now. She was no doubt afraid, not sure why she'd been kidnapped. James had known about this and had done nothing. *Nothing.*

He would get no sympathy from her.

The flight landed and they made their way through customs and into the sprawling and chaotic London Heathrow terminal. It was strange to Madison to hear dozens of different languages all conversing at the same volume. Half the people in the terminal loitered, and seemed to have been waiting for hours, while the other half moved quickly through the terminal to the next chore in their journey. No one wanted to be here, yet the place was more crowded than a shopping mall before Christmas. There was a metaphor there that Madison couldn't quite articulate. Something about spending more time in our lives enroute than at the places we want to be; a life of waiting and moving but never really *being*.

The philosophy would have to wait. Madison turned to the others as they exited the secure area and were dumped into a waiting area in the heart of the terminal.

"Okay, geniuses. We're in England. Now what? It's a big island. Do we just start digging?" Madison asked.

"Your pessimism is noted," said Michelle. They were the first words she'd spoken to Madison since they'd left St. Peter's Square. "We have a room reserved for us at a hotel downtown. We'll go there and await the arrival of your mother. Once she arrives, we should know exactly how to proceed."

"My mother isn't going to be able to help you. I'm telling you, leave her out of this."

James grabbed her shoulders from behind.

"Relax, Madison," he said. "We're just going to ask her some questions about the candlestick. When she's given Michelle the information we need, she'll let your Mom go."

"Is that right?" asked Madison. *No way is it that simple.*

"Of course, Madison. I promise," said Michelle.

⁘⳥⳥⳥

The noise from the streets below wafted up into the air and penetrated the tall windows of the hotel room. A dull murmur could be heard from the center of the financial universe; downtown London. Madison sat on the edge of a chair, turned to face the window, and stared in awe at the bustling city twenty-three stories below.

The Victorian architecture of some of the smaller buildings reminded Madison of many *Christmas Carol* plays she'd seen with brick row houses, dotted with flower boxes on the window sills and wrought iron guarding the windows. A few miles away she could see the sprawling Waterloo train station on the other side of the Thames. Around the bend of the esteemed estuary she could see the Houses of Parliament, glittering in the morning sun with Big Ben towering over all. To her left the London Eye, a gargantuan wheel with a dozen passengers seated in each of forty glass orbs, churned like a gigantic chicken rotisserie. She had heard that the wheel was so ostentatious they called the rides "flights".

James and Michelle occupied the room behind her, though, at this moment, she cared little for what they were saying or doing. Two thugs of Michelle's, who'd met them at the hotel, waited outside in the hall until needed. Madison hadn't seen them long enough to give them insulting nicknames, but she assumed she soon would. It seemed this organization had agents everywhere, available on a moment's notice. Moonface had been sent to the lobby on the ground floor to await the arrival of the prisoner.

The prisoner. That's what that vixen had called Madison's mother. Madison caught James' eye twice that morning to plead with him. The first time he looked away, ashamed at what was transpiring. The second time… was different. She couldn't quite tell what it was, but she saw something of resolution in his eyes. Was it a weakness? A change of heart? Or was it a hardening of his soul, the way people are hardened when they're determined to follow through on their own self-destructive plans?

Madison turned from the window and the spectacle that is downtown London just in time to see James approach Michelle from behind and put his hands on her shoulders. It was an innocuous show of affection, yet Michelle spun around, knocking his hands from her body, and glared at him. She mouthed the words "not here", and James retreated with an apologetic recoil like an overeager puppy who thought it was playtime when its master wasn't in the mood.

Staring at the door, Madison wondered when her mother would enter. How would they have treated her? Would she walk in bloodied and bruised, unable to stand without help? Would she have a bag over her head, those same canvas bags they'd put on Madison when they captured her at the castle?

Then, as if by the mere power of her gaze, the lock on the door beeped, the handle turned, the door swung open and her mother walked into the room.

Tara Dawn entered the room carrying a grocery bag-sized purse and wore an obnoxious straw hat and oversized plum sunglasses. Behind her, Moonface entered carrying two extremely heavy leather suitcases. His eyes bulged under their weight.

"Oh, what a gorgeous room. Thank you, Vincent, you can put them down anywhere." She rustled through her bag before withdrawing a five dollar bill. "And here's for your trouble. Sorry I haven't had time to get English currency," she said handing the bill to Moonface. He awkwardly took the tip and exited the room after Michelle excused him.

"Mom!" is about the only thing Madison could stammer out after a dozen painful seconds of choked silence. Madison ran to her mother and embraced her in a violent bear hug.

"Madison! Oh, it's so good to see you. But sweetie, you're choking me a bit." Madison released her grasp.

"Sorry, oh, I'm so glad to see you. How are you? You're here. Have they hurt you? I can't believe you're here. I'm so sorry to drag you into this. I'm sorry. I'm sorry." Madison spoke like a torrential mudslide wiping out a village.

"Hurt me?" said Tara. "Heaven's, Madison. The way you talk. I couldn't be having a more wonderful time. Sure I was a little miffed you didn't tell me yourself, but it's so exciting that I can join you on this trip."

Madison was speechless.

"Don't look so surprised, my daughter." Tara put her bag down and sat in one of the chairs near the windows. "Did you think I was going to let you win a prize like this and not share it with you?"

"Prize?" Madison asked.

"This vacation. A tour of Europe. Honey, whatever is the matter? You're looking at me like I have two heads."

Michelle intervened. "Mrs. Dawn, welcome to London. I hope you've had a good flight over."

"Oh yes. First class. Quite impressive."

"And I trust you brought the item needed to complete your tour," said Michelle.

"Absolutely, of course," said Tara. "Why I had to bring this thing across the Atlantic, I'll never know. It's a family heirloom. I'd hate to lose it."

"We just need to verify its authenticity and then we'll return it as quickly as we can," said Michelle. Michelle had altered her voice and now sounded like an over-eager real estate agent; bossy, yet kind.

"Alrighty, then," Tara removed an object from her bag. Madison immediately recognized the old candlestick that used to sit in her mother's china cabinet.

"Mom, don't," protested Madison as Tara handed it to Michelle.

"Honey, if I don't give it to them, then they won't let me go on the trip with you."

"Mom, no. Give that to them and then you're going right back home," said Madison, her eyes starting to well up with tears.

"Madison. I just got here. Don't you want me to go on this vacation with you? Is that why you didn't tell me you were going?"

"Mom, Mom…" Madison took her mother by the hand she leaned into her mother and spoke in a hurried whisper. "Mom, there is no trip. These people are dangerous. You must get out of here."

"Dangerous? These are the nicest people you'd ever meet," said Tara.

"Madison," said Michelle, stepping into the conversation. "You'll find us to be a reasonable organization. We usually find it best to lead with a carrot rather than drive with a stick."

"Lead with a carrot?" yelled Madison. "You kidnapped me and put me in the trunk of a car. You killed Francisco. You call that leading with a carrot?" Madison stood face to face with Michelle. Tara emitted a gasp at the sudden show of anger from her daughter. Madison's yelling drew Moonface in from the hallway. He was there to protect his employer.

"No! No, that's not how it happened," said Michelle in a controlled spat of anger. "We placed a priceless ruby in your car and then called you on a cell phone. It was then that you decided to botch the whole operation and *steal* it from us. You brought your treatment on yourself."

"Treatment?" said Tara softly. "Have you been hurt, Madison?"

"More than you know, Mother," said Madison. "I've had enough of this. They promised you'd be allowed to go. But I'm guessing you're going to stay with us." She turned to Michelle. "Isn't she?"

"For the time being? Yes, of course," said Michelle.

So there it was; another lie. Madison's mother would not be released and Madison now doubted that she ever would be freed.

"And now that we're all here, we come to it," said Michelle. "Please, sit down." She motioned to the chairs and the bed.

"You've got both halves of the key, Michelle," James said. "Let them go. We can figure this out from here."

"James, so help me. We talked about this. I need information from them." James took a seat on the bed. The two burly men across the room straightened up but did not otherwise move.

"So here we are," said Michelle. "Madison, Mrs. Dawn, James Kynan, and the key to Caligula's Bath. Furthermore, we are in the country where the empire marker was buried. But it is here that our quest is stalled. It is clear that we are still missing a piece of the puzzle. One of you is holding out on me. I intend to get that missing piece."

James, Madison, and Tara looked at each other in silence as the noise of the in-window air conditioner dominated the room.

"James and I have a bond that goes far deeper than any interrogation or coercion," continued Michelle, "so I don't believe that he is the one withholding the information. So that leaves the ladies Dawn."

"I must say that I feel a bit out of the loop on this one," said Tara Dawn.

"I'm just supposed to believe that you've had the spear, the second half of the key to Caligula's Bath sitting in your china cabinet for years, and you have no idea what it was for? You so quaintly thought it was a candlestick?" The sarcasm dripped from Michelle's mouth like lava from a volcano.

"Good heavens," said Tara. "It was my mother's. We didn't know where she got it. We almost sold it in a garage sale."

"You almost sold it?"

"I was asking fifty cents for it. No one wanted it. Look at it. It's an ugly candlestick."

"MmmHmm." Michelle eyed Tara suspiciously, though did not vocalize her thoughts. She turned to Madison and took her face in her hand. "What about this pretty little one here. What aren't you telling me, Madison?"

"If I knew, I wouldn't tell a monster like you." How could a woman like that demand anything from her?

"Oh, I think you're wrong, Madison. You will tell me. James?" James arose from his perch on the bed. "Get her to talk," she ordered.

James approached Madison and stood before her.

"So James, is this how it's going to be? She's got you doing her dirty work?" asked Madison.

"Just tell us what you know about the candlestick," he said.

"What are you going to do to me, James? If I don't tell you are you going to torture me? Are you going to kill me like you did that man on the cruise ship?"

James looked at her, pain in his eyes, his hands were shaking. Doubt clouded his face and he looked to Michelle. She raised her eyebrows and folded her arms but said nothing. James looked back at Madison. She flinched when James stooped over her. He put his mouth to her ear and whispered.

"Get your mother and run." He said it only once, but Madison had to replay it in her mind several times before she understood it. It wasn't what she'd expected him to say.

James stood up again and walked to Moonface who stood near the door. The two thugs stood on the other side of the room with a glazed look of indifference. Michelle leaned against the vanity just outside the bathroom.

And then, without a statement of any kind, James erupted into an explosion of action so furious Madison could not follow it. In a single motion, James struck Moonface with a vicious elbow, breaking his nose, while pulling the gun Moonface carried from the under-arm holster inside his jacket. Moonface went down with a yelp, blood covering his hands. James now leapt at Michelle, grabbed her by the hair and held the pistol to her head. The two guards in the back of the room, slow to react, reached for their guns.

"A-ah. Nope. Drop it or she's dead," shouted James.

"James! You ass," yelled Michelle.

"Guns on the floor, boys," said James. The two agents dropped their guns in front of them after seeing the look of fear on Michelle's face.

"What the hell are you doing?" asked Michelle.

"Madison, go!" said James.

Madison was frozen in place, overwhelmed by the flurry of activity. She looked at her mother; her eyes were two portholes opened wide in amazement. Madison remembered his instruction and leapt up from her chair and grabbed Tara's hand.

"Let's go mother."

"But Madison, my things."

"Leave them."

James ripped the candlestick and ruby from Michelle's hands and tossed them to Madison. "You might want these."

Madison and Tara opened the door and fled out of the room. They ran down the hall and to the elevator. Twenty-three floors of stairs was too far to run down. Besides, Madison didn't think her mother could keep up.

The elevator doors opened and they entered the car. A clamor of running footsteps startled them as James sprinted down the hallway. He leapt into the elevator just before the doors closed.

"James. What was that?" It was all Madison could say as the elevator descended to the ground floor.

"Ah- well," he said, still out of breath from his moment of exertion, "I had to make a choice."

"And?" asked Madison.

"I made the choice I should have made years ago. To stop thinking that Michelle and I would ever be together again."

"You had me worried, James," said Madison. It was a lie. She was still worried.

"I know. I have problems. Can we talk about this later?"

"So what's the plan?"

"We need to get out of here," he said. "They won't be far behind us."

The doors swung open and they ran out onto the sidewalk just in front of the hotel. There were no taxis and no immediate form of transportation.

James motioned Madison and Tara to follow him around the building to the left. He sped down a side street towards the loading docks on the back of the hotel. They ran, but Tara did not move quickly. She was rather portly and had not run for any reason in decades.

They fled down the alley and turned to find themselves in a dead end populated by garbage cans and dumpsters.

"Damn. We have to hide," said James, "just until they are convinced we went a different direction." An empty garbage can was perfect for Tara since it required no climbing. She stepped in to the can without a word of complaint.

"It's just for a few minutes," he said, "but you must be quiet." James put the lid on when she had worked her way inside.

"What about us?" asked Madison.

A large dumpster with an open top stood to her right. It was half filled with garbage and smelled of rotting fish.

"In you go," James said.

"I am not getting in there."

"Don't argue." He gave her a boost and she hopped into the dumpster. James followed closely behind and flopped on to the pile of garbage next to her.

"Oh, what is that smell?" asked Madison holding her hand over her nose and mouth.

"Shhh" James and Madison held their breath. The sound of men running echoed off the surrounding building façades.

A half a minute passed before they heard a few words of Italian and then the sound of men running away. Madison exhaled deeply, relieved they were not discovered.

She turned to James to tell him how much of an idiot he was for thinking he could be with Michelle and how it was going to take a long time for her to ever trust him again. However, when she turned to look at him she found his face surprisingly close to hers. James looked into her eyes and a mischievous half-smile illuminated his face. Her admonishments got lost somewhere between her brain and her mouth. He rolled up onto his side, took her face into his hand, and kissed her.

Caught completely off guard, Madison stiffened at first. But soon, as the warmth of his lips loosened hers, her body relaxed and she melted into him. It was not a kiss of extreme passion or shameful lust. It was a kiss of apology; a kiss of reassurance. A moment later, she opened her eyes and withdrew from him. She couldn't help but smile.

"James Kynan. We have been in hotels, on luxurious cruise ships, dressed up and dancing, in exquisite places from Miami to Madeira, a castle in Spain to a villa in Italy. And after all of that, you decide to kiss me here… on a pile of smelly garbage."

"I wanted it to be special."

"You're infuriating, you know."

"I know. One kiss doesn't make up for it all. I-" but he stopped. The rumble of an engine told them that a car was driving down the alley towards them. The car roared into the alley and screeched to a stop. Madison and James lay perfectly still. Had Michelle's goons come back?

They could hear the sound of the transmission click into park and then a door opened.

"Well, are you coming?" asked a brash and obnoxious voice in a distinctly American accent.

Madison sat up and peered over the front of the dumpster and saw a black taxicab parked in front of their dumpster. Standing next to it, holding on to the door was the first person she could have hoped to see and the last person she expected to see.

"Brennan," she cried.

James climbed out of the dumpster and then helped Madison out and down to the ground. She ran to Brennan and threw her arms around him in an enthusiastic hug.

"Hey, doll face." said Brennan, "Good to see- oh, good Lord, you stink."

"Yeah, sorry. That was James' idea." James leapt down from the dumpster. Madison continued, "James said you went back to the States."

"Well, that's what he told me to do, but I know better. Do you know how hard it is to trail someone when they fly to another country?"

"How did you find us?"

"I followed you to the hotel, but decided to camp out here until I saw your next move. I was at the café when you three came running out the front door." Brennan pointed at the umbrella covered tables across the street. "I figured it was time to get my cab and give you a lift."

"Nice wheels," said James.

"Once we get into traffic, Giovanni won't be able to track us. There are ten thousand taxis that look just like this in London."

"Thanks, Bren. Thanks for not doing what I asked you to do," said James.

"Hey, someone's got to save you from yourself," said Brennan.

A muffled voice rang out from a nearby garbage can, "Can I come out now?"

"Oh, Mother!" Madison pulled the lid off the garbage can and helped her mother out.

"This is the strangest trip I've ever been on," said Tara after she'd smoothed out her dress and fixed her hair. "And who might you be?" she asked of Brennan.

"I'm just a driver, ma'am. Brennan Nash, at your service. So where to, James?" He pounded the bonnet of the taxicab.

"It'd be nice to find that empire marker," said James.

"We don't know where it is," said Madison. Honestly, she was getting a little weary of the search, and now that her mother was safe, she truly just wanted to go home.

"Sure we do," said Tara. "You have all the pieces you need."

"Mom, you don't even know what we're talking about."

"Madison, honey. There're many things I know that you don't think I know."

"So, then where do we go from here?" asked Brennan.

"You want to find what's buried in Caligula's Bath, right?" asked Tara.

"We've been there. We found an obelisk," said James.

"Well, unless I miss my guess, there's something special about this candlestick and your ruby," said Tara. "Here, let me have them."

Tara took the candlestick as James removed the arrowhead from his pocket and handed it to the matronly woman. She slid the point of the ruby into the base of the candlestick. The ruby nested perfectly into the bronze scepter.

Tara looked at it with a discerning eye, viewing it from all sides. Finally, she held it down at her waist and looked into the ruby.

"Ah. There it is. Does this mean anything to you, Madison?" she handed it to her daughter. Madison took the scepter and attempted to view the ruby in the same way as her mother.

At first, she saw nothing. Then, she flinched as a flash of words glimmered in the ruby. Again she carefully rotated the scepter around until the letters revealed themselves. At just the right angle, the words appeared; faint but indisputable.

AQUAE SVLIS

"Ah-kway-soo-lis?" Madison read aloud. "What does that mean, James?"

"What did you say?" asked James as his eyes opened wide.

232

"Here, look," said Madison. "The ruby acts like a magnifying glass for something written in the scepter. It was so small you'd never see it with the naked eye. *Aquae Sulis*. What's that?"

"Of course. How could I be so stupid?" shouted James. "Aquae Sulis!"

"You mean-" started Brennan.

"Bath, England. The old Roman town of Aquae Sulis is now known as Bath. Caligula's Bath is... Bath!"

"Let's go." Brennan hopped in the taxi.

"Ha ha." Tara clapped her hands. "That was one of our guesses. Never saw the writing on that candlestick, though,"

"But mother, how do you know about all this?" Madison's head swam with impossibilities and inconsistencies.

"I'll explain in due time, Madison. This candlestick has been in the family for a long time. What do you say we finally get to use it?"

Madison slid into the taxi in silent bewilderment. She seemed to be the only one who didn't know what was going on and she didn't like the feeling at all.

XIX

CALIGULA'S BATH

"The ancient Romans built their greatest masterpieces of architecture,
their amphitheaters, for wild beasts to fight in."
Voltaire

In the small town of Maidenhead on the outskirts of London, Brennan parked the taxi and they transferred to a rented blue Opel sedan as arranged by Devin. Outside of London the taxi would be far out of place. Furthermore, Brennan had borrowed the taxi from an acquaintance that expected the taxi to be returned that evening.

"Get it back in one piece or else I'll break your bloody legs." Brennan quoted his friend in a thick cockney accent.

Once past the town of Reading, Brennan eschewed the M4 motorway for ancient country roads. Brennan feared that the M4 was too predictable of a route into Bath, should the Giovanni organization figure out where they were headed.

Tara Dawn was prone to motion sickness and so she asked to ride in the front of the car allowing her to better see the bends and twists in the road. Once again, James and Madison sat together in the backseat. It was an all too familiar situation for Madison. She thought back to the yellow MINI and Francisco and little Gil.

The adventure seemed so pure then, so straight forward. The danger was real, but somehow it seemed like it couldn't touch her. Then, James was a man she could trust, Francisco was full of life, and Brennan… well, Brennan hadn't changed. Now her mother rode in the front seat instead of the quirky Spaniard, the countryside was now hedgerows and thatched roofs, and the man sitting next to her was undeniably flawed.

"James?" she asked quietly. The road noise provided a bit of privacy allowing them to talk in the backseat without Brennan or her mother overhearing.

"Yes?"

"Help me understand."

"Understand what?" James, though occasionally insightful and understanding, was still a man and needed some guidance in these kinds of conversations.

"Michelle. You know she's wrong for you, right?"

"Yes."

"Could you see what you were becoming with her? Could you see that she was destroying you?"

"I could."

"Then why?"

James was quiet. He was searching for an answer that was long in coming. Madison interrupted his search with her own fear.

"And what if-" she stopped to compose herself. "What if she comes back? What if she gives you everything you hope for?"

"Madison, why are you asking this?"

"James, I'm scared. You kissed me. Now there's an *us*. And that terrifies me."

"There doesn't have to be an us, Madison. Sometimes a kiss is just a kiss."

"I know that song."

"Look, I'm sorry about Michelle. I'm sorry for the way I've acted. I have no excuse. But, haven't you ever wanted something so badly that you'd do absolutely anything to get it?"

"Anything? Including destroying yourself?"

He looked out the window and picked at the seal at the top of the window. "Yes, including that."

"You're delusional."

"Some call that love, Madison."

"I call it addiction."

"And yet, the line between the two can seem so fine," he said with a smile.

He reached over and gave her knee a friendly squeeze. The contact created a buzz in Madison's leg that shot right up into her chest. Regardless of whether he was broken or not, there was definitely an electric connection between her and James that she couldn't deny. She patted the top of his hand and then returned his hand to his own lap.

"You have a lot to learn about women, James Kynan," she said.

"I completely agree."

The English countryside rushed passed the window in a blur of dark greens and earthy browns. Madison rolled down the window and let the turbulent breeze play with her hair.

ᴄ◡ᴊᴖ

"One thing I just can't figure out," said James as the blue Opel cruised down the main street entering Bath, "is how Caligula even knew about Bath."

The pale yellow limestone buildings swept past outside the window. Madison marveled at how the architecture of the buildings aged as they approached the center of the city, like layers of the Grand Canyon showing the eras of the past.

"What do you mean?" she asked.

"I mean that Caligula's empire didn't extend into Britain. It was Claudius, Caligula's successor that conquered Britain in 43 AD."

"Two years after Caligula's death," said Madison.

"Exactly."

"So how did he bury his empire marker in Bath?" Madison wrinkled her nose attempting to reconcile the discrepancy. "Well, there was trade beforehand. According to the book, Julius Caesar was there almost a century earlier. Maybe Caligula had someone take it there for him."

"But in 40 AD Caligula was planning an invasion of the island," said James. "He marshaled troops on the other side of the channel but he never crossed. Why would he plant an empire marker in a land he had yet to conquer?"

"Overambitious?" suggested Madison. "Perhaps his eyes were a bit bigger than his stomach?"

Brennan pulled the car to a stop in the center of town and shut off the engine.

"The Roman Baths. Who wants to find what our friend Caligula buried for us here?" he asked in an excited, if not overly cheerful, tone of voice.

The four intrepid explorers got out of the car and walked past a gothic building she recognized as a house of worship.

"That's Bath Abbey," said James. Madison looked up at the soaring pinnacles and countless pieces of stained glass in the towering arched windows. She longed to go inside.

"It's too bad we can't visit," said Madison. "It's a magnificent building."

"You can be a tourist on your own time. Let's get in and get out," said James. Madison wondered if James ever appreciated the exotic and intriguing locations his career allowed him to visit.

They rounded the corner and discovered a four-columned limestone structure lining the left side of the street. An inconspicuous sign labeled Roman Baths hung above the doors.

James led them through the entrance and into the lobby of the Victorian building that surrounded the Roman Baths. Inside, the rotunda of the lobby differed little from other museum lobbies. A round desk in the middle sold tickets while an ornately carved dome floated above their heads. James approached the ticket counter.

"Hello. Four please," he said to the distracted girl in a blue blazer sitting behind the desk. She flipped through a stack of papers on her counter before looking up.

"I'm sorry, love. We close at 5:30," she said as she oscillated on her swivel chair. "Can't sell any more tickets after 4:30. You can come back tomorrow, if you like,"

James looked at his watch; it read 5:02pm.

"Um, Chloe, is it? Wow, that is a pretty name," said James reading the girl's nametag. The young woman smiled. "We have to catch a flight tomorrow morning so we can't come back. My mother just wanted to see the baths before she left." He pointed to Tara who did her best to give a pathetic smile. "Is there any way we can get in just for a half hour? We promise to be out by five-thirty."

"I'm terribly sorry, but the computer won't let me sell tickets after 4:30."

"Isn't there anything you can do? We've come all this way. To miss the baths would just be heartbreaking."

Chloe looked at James like a bank teller trying to determine if a check was forged or not.

"Oh, who cares," she said throwing up her hands. "I'm quitting in two weeks anyway. What's the big deal if I get sacked? I've got to walk through in a few minutes to make sure everyone is on their way out. You're welcome to walk with me, if you'd like." She led them to the velvet ropes and pulled one aside allowing them to pass.

"Yes, that'd be lovely," said James slipping into British parlance. "That's very kind of you."

"The audio guides are all put up for the night, though. I'm afraid all you've got is me."

"Well I can certainly think of worse ways to spend my time. You're the best, Chloe. Come along, Mother," said James taking Tara by the arm and following behind Chloe.

They made their way through the hallway that led from the entrance to the terrace above the Grand Bath. Just off James' shoulder, Madison asked in a whisper, "Do you flirt with every girl you meet?"

"Not every girl. Just when I think it'll help. Are you jealous?" said James.

Chloe led them outside to the terrace that surrounded the Great Bath. The bath was a full story below street level so, though they entered at ground floor, Madison found herself looking over a stone railing and down into the large rectangular pool of water.

"Below us you can see the magnificent centerpiece of the Roman baths. This pool is lined with 45 sheets of lead and filled with hot spa water," said Chloe, becoming their personal tour guide.

"Lead. Is that safe?" asked Madison.

"Absolutely not. You'll see signs warning visitors that there's no swimming here. The lead-lined pool and the lead-lined irrigation pipes are just one of the reasons why we don't allow anyone in the water." Chloe led them down a flight of stairs and soon they were at water level.

"So you're telling me that you can't bathe in the baths, is that right?" asked James raising an eyebrow.

"Look at the water. Would you want to swim in that?" asked Chloe.

The great bath was a rectangular pool surrounded by columns on all four sides. The columns supported the balcony from which they had just descended as well as a number of Roman statues. What struck Madison was the opaque swamp-green water. It was clearly crawling with algae and who knows what other creatures.

"The pools were closed in 1979 after a young girl died of amoebic meningitis. She had picked up the killer amoeba in this very pool. A bit ironic, don't you think?" said Chloe. "A place known for its healing waters is now unhealthy for swimming."

"So the Romans built this?" asked Brennan. He searched the walls looking for any clues as to the whereabouts of Caligula's empire marker.

"Oh, goodness no. No, what the Romans built was destroyed centuries ago; sometime around the 5th century after the Romans left. The only thing we have left is the pool and the irrigation system. Since the 12th century some kind of structure has always stood here, but what you see was actually built in the 18th century and then used primarily by the Victorians a century later when the legend of the healing waters began to spread.

She led them down a flight of stairs and into a serpentine series of displays and presentations. "Just down this way," she said pointing to a hallway off to the side, "is where we've assembled what we discovered of the ancient temple. The other direction leads to changing rooms once used in the 18th century." Eventually they walked through the temple remains and hot rooms until finding themselves standing at the edge of the Grand Bath.

"So where does the water come from?" asked Tara.

Chloe pointed to a dark corner of the pool where water flowed from a stone chute. "Over there you can follow those steps to see the Sacred Spring. It's off limits to visitors, but you can see it through the openings in the wall. The hot spring feeds the Great Bath…. If you'll excuse me just a tick," she said.

Chloe moved to a couple who were attempting to stick a bare foot in the water. In a polite voice, she chastised them about the health risk and then encouraged them to move along as the museum would soon be closing.

"What do you think, boss?" asked Brennan quietly while Chloe was away.

"I think we're screwed," said James.

"Why do you say that?" asked Madison as she and Tara joined the huddle.

"This place has been one giant excavation after another for the last two thousand years. Each new culture builds a new structure here. What the Romans built has fallen into ruin or been dug out. Everything here is less than 400 years old, and we're looking for what was stashed in the building that was here 2000 years ago. The odds that anything here has survived long enough for us to find are slim at best. I'm afraid we're about 1500 years too late."

The group wandered around the complex. Madison walked with her mother but was alone in her thoughts.

So that's it, then? They'd come all this way, these weeks and months, for something that doesn't exist? Michelle and the Giovanni organization were willing to kill, burn her apartment, and destroy her life, for what? A myth? For something that couldn't possibly be found? Is this how these people operated? Madison exhaled sharply through her nose and felt her ears grow warm with anger. To Madison, the profession of artifact recovery seemed like a quixotic and desperate quest for the futile.

"It's time to go," said Chloe. "I'll show you out through the gift shop."

Brennan returned from the therapy rooms at the other end of the complex, while James emerged from the room known as the cold bath. Chloe led them out through the gift shop and said goodbye. They thanked her for her kindness and they exited the shop where the door was closed and locked behind them.

"I didn't even get a postcard," said Madison looking back through the glass doors at the gift shop. "So, now what?"

"We have to get back in there," said Brennan.

"Yeah, I saw it too," said James. He spoke with urgency, like a child on Christmas Eve.

"What? You saw what?" asked Madison.

"We'll wait for nightfall and come back. We can talk about it at the pub. Who's hungry?" said James.

The Bear and Kettle pub was a classic Charles Wells pub nestled amidst the other two-story buildings crowded around the city center. A small plaque on the outside of the squatty structure informed visitors that the current building had been proudly serving patrons since 1759. However, a dozen pubs had resided in this exact location dating back to the 12th century, and nearly all of them were destroyed by fire.

The ancient wooden beams running across the low-slung ceiling forced James and Brennan to duck as they found their way to the bar. Madison and Tara followed and surveyed the selection of wooden cask ales. Madison ordered an Eagle since she liked the look of the label, and then ordered a gammon steak with pineapple slices. Tara ordered a Guinness, while James and Brennan each ordered a Stella Artois. The congenial barkeep began the task of drawing the ales up from the cellar with the manual pump. Madison and her mother took a seat with their backs to an outside window and waited for Brennan and James to retrieve the beers once they were poured and settled. Smoking in pubs in England had been made illegal years before, yet the establishment still smelled of stale tobacco.

"So is someone going to tell me what you saw, or are you just going to keep me in the dark forever?" asked Madison once the four of them had settled around the stout oak table. She sipped her beer and winced at the bitterness.

"Did you not see the marking?" asked James.

Madison looked between Brennan and James with a frustrated impatience. If she had seen it, do they think she'd be asking?

"You said that everything was destroyed by the rebuilding of the pools over the centuries," she said. "You said it was hopeless to think that anything from Roman times survived."

"Well, I was wrong," said James sitting back in his chair. He was admitting to being wrong, but his eyes sparkled at her with amusement. He did not offer any explanation.

"Brennan. Please? Put me out of my misery."

"Did you happen to look at the stonework in the northeast part of the pool? The corner of the Great Bath?" Brennan asked in a hushed tone.

"Where?" asked Madison.

"In the corner of the Great Bath. Through the water you could see a marking. Faint, but perceptible," he said.

"Well, aren't you a couple of detail-oriented kids," said Tara. "I could have been there for a week and never found it."

Madison popped to her feet. The fact that her mother was involved drove Madison crazy.

"Mother, I have to use the ladies room, come with me?" she said.

"Um, of course, dear," said Tara. "If you'll excuse me..."

Madison led her mother by the hand to the small water closet at the back of the establishment. The restroom was only designed for one occupant, but Madison and Tara wedged their way in and closed the door.

"Mom, what do you know about all this? Why did we have half of the key to Caligula's bath in our house all these years? Why are you not as surprised as I am that we're involved here? It's time I got some answers and I'm tired of riddles."

Tara looked her elder daughter in the eyes with compassion, but she shook her head.

"Just tell me. Are we thieves?" Madison asked. "Have we done things that are illegal? Is that why you can't tell me?"

"Oh honey, no. No, there's nothing illegal about this. That key is rightfully ours."

"Mom, it's just been so scary not knowing what was going on." Madison reached her breaking point, and in the bathroom of the Bear and Kettle pub, Madison wept into her mother's arms. Mother and daughter held each other until Madison's tears soaked through her mother's shirt.

"Madison, if you think we can trust those boys, I will tell you the story," said Tara softly.

"Really?"

"Yes. I'd always imagined telling it to you some evening in our living room, but this pub will have to do."

"Thank you, Mom," said Madison. "James and Brennan aren't perfect, but they've certainly taken care of me. You can trust them."

A knock came at the bathroom door.

"Un momento, por favor," said Tara.

"Mom? We're in England. What's with the Spanish?"

"I'm sorry, I panicked. It just slipped out. You're the one with the gift for acting, honey." The two looked at each other and, as what often follows a good cry, they laughed.

XX

AN UNSUSPECTING PRINCESS

"Archaeologists are underpaid publicity agents for deceased royalty."
John Agar

Madison and Tara returned to the table to find that their dinner had arrived.

"So what does this mark look like? How did you recognize it?" asked Madison as she took her seat.

"Faint in the stone is an impression of the spear from the statue on the Obelisk in Vatican City, which, of course, is the same shape as your 'candlestick'," said James with a mouthful of overcooked sirloin steak. "It's right next to the old sluice they used to drain the pool."

"But, how is that still there? Wouldn't the erosion of two thousand years of water running over it have erased it?" asked Madison.

"For one, it's granite, so it withstands erosion," explained James. "Also, remember that the baths didn't run between the 4th century and the 12th century. My guess is that the granite from that little shoot between the sacred spring and the great bath was covered in mud for centuries and wasn't cleaned up until recently. The marking was effectively protected."

"So, we got lucky," said Madison.

"Hey, fifty percent of this job is ninety percent luck," said Brennan.

"Thanks Yogi," said Madison acknowledging his paraphrase. "So after we get out of here, what's the plan? Break back in and see where that marking leads us?" James nodded. "And then after that, maybe we can find some place to get a decent beer," she said.

James laughed. "Not a fan of English beer?"

"In the States, if a beer is warm and flat and bitter, we throw it out. Here, they sell it at a premium."

The noise in the pub had quieted as most of the patrons left for the evening. As they finished their meal, Tara leaned forward and got the attention of the table solely with her anticipatory expression.

"Madison has asked me to explain why my family has had this candlestick and how it is that I'm familiar with some of your exploits," said Tara.

"I think it's time I know the truth, Mother."

"Yeah, I wouldn't mind hearing the explanation myself," said James.

Tara looked around the pub to confirm that they were effectively free to speak. Even in the dim light of a single lamp in the corner of the room, Madison could see an intense seriousness set into her mother's face. This was going to be no garage-sale-find story of happenstance.

"What I'm about to tell you has been a secret of my family for two millennia. The only reason I tell you two," she said looking at Brennan and James, "is that I believe you can help us. Obviously other people seem to know about this and it has brought much danger to the ones I love." Tara reached over and gave a squeeze to Madison's hand.

"Mrs. Dawn, you can trust us with this information," said Brennan.

Tara sat back in her chair and began her narrative.

"As you know, Caligula is just one of many Roman Emperors; Nero, Claudia, Caesar Augustus, and so forth. This is the story of their lineage.

The Roman Empire thrived as the greatest kingdom in the world for hundreds of years. No country could attempt to conquer Rome, such was its power. But over time, people became lax, undisciplined, and petty. The empire crumbled from within. The Roman Empire split in two in 395 AD, creating the Western Roman Empire and the Eastern Roman Empire. The Western Roman Empire crumbled a hundred years later.

"I'm sure these studied anthropologists know all about this. What you don't know is that Julius Caesar, when he created the empire, also commissioned a box to be made. This box contained the secrets of the empire and was handed from ruler to ruler for safe keeping. It was in this box that Caligula placed the spear, the candlestick as we know it, along with the ruby arrowhead. Reign after reign, Caesar after Caesar, the box of valuables was handed down, entrusted to the next ruler to protect it. In times of civil war or strife, powerful members of the Senate held the box until a fit ruler could receive the Julian Ark, as it came to be called. In 395, the Julian Ark traveled with Constantine to the city Byzantium, which Constantine then named after himself. Constantinople became the new capitol of the Eastern Roman Empire.

"It's here that most historians start to lose the thread. They refer to this empire as the Byzantines and many people forget that this empire is an extension of the Roman Empire. In fact, the Byzantines called themselves Romans, for they were still the Roman Empire. They called the new capitol "New Rome". Therefore, the box, the Julian Ark, was passed down through the Emperors of the Eastern Roman Empire for another thousand years.

"Now with the move to Constantinople and the upheaval the Empire had seen over the years, the rulers stopped putting valuable things in the box some time after the 10th century. Instead of placing things of great value in the box, they only placed the starting point, the key, the map, or what have you. "

James said, "So they took the idea of an empire marker and turned the Julian Ark into a hide-a-key."

"Yes, they felt that mystery and a good hiding spot were a better way to store the empire's secrets than a simple box.

It was also about this time that the box was replaced. Julius Caesar had commissioned an ornate box of finely carved figures and gold covering. This box had deteriorated and was replaced by a plain looking, bronze box, to better conceal its importance.

In 1453, the Eastern Roman Empire came crashing down as the Ottomans took Constantinople. It's here that historians have let us down in their description. They refer to this as the end of the Roman Empire, or Byzantines, but that does a disservice to the ingenuity and resiliency of the mightiest empire in the history of the world. For the empire did not fall. Rather, it moved yet again.

"To understand this, you must understand a woman named Zoe Palaiologina. Zoe was the niece of Emperor Constantine XI; the last Byzantine Emperor. In early April, 1453, with the Turks marching towards the capitol city, Constantine XI sent for Zoe who lived in nearby Morea. Constantine had no children and was reaching out to his next of kin, his only successor. He gave the Julian Ark to Zoe who then fled the city on April 4. The Ottoman army arrived and launched their siege the next day. Constantine XI would die a month later in a last suicidal charge to defend the city.

"Constantine's last wish was that Zoe would carry on the traditions of the Roman Empire and instructed her to travel to the next great Rome. You see, Constantine knew that any male successor would be in jeopardy of losing his life as he would soon be a ruler with no power. Therefore, he relied on the foibles of the patriarchal system to pass on his legacy. By passing the legacy of the empire through a female successor, the Empire was able to survive.

"Zoe and her family were captured by the Ottomans the next year, yet Zoe kept her secret as we women are wont to do. She was taken to Rome where she changed her name to Sophia, as she is now historically known. She lobbied the Pope to help her escape to the north. Finally, nine years later, a marriage was proposed by Pope Paul II with Ivan III of Muscovy, or Moscow as we know it today. The Pope said that it would unite the Orthodox and Catholic churches, but secretly he knew that he was giving life to a dormant empire, the great Roman Empire that had brought Christianity to the world through its vast road system, universal language, and official adoption of the Christian faith in the 300's.

"The widowed Ivan III took Sophia to be his second bride and, remarkably, the Muscovites adopted the ways of the Roman Empire. Sophia was clearly at work, teaching those men in the Kremlin the ways of the empire. Vasili, her son, became Grand Prince of Moscow, and Vasili's son Ivan IV, became The Tsar of All Russia. Tsar means Caesar. They even adopted the title of the emperors of old Rome. Moscow became the Third Rome and the Roman Empire lived on. The Julian Ark passed from Constantine XI to Sophia to Vasili to Ivan the Terrible and on through the Tsars of All Russia. Eventually, the box passed to the Romanov family and through to Nicholas II, the last Tsar of Russia."

"You're kidding. The box survived until last century?" Brennan struggled to suppress his amazement. Tara continued:

"It is here, 1917, where the legacy of the Roman Empire faced its greatest threat yet. The Bolsheviks had taken control of Russia, and the time of the Tsars was coming to an end. Taken prisoner in his own country, Nicholas II and his family lived under house arrest as prisoners of the Communists. He knew that his reign was over, that the Russian Empire had come to a close, and that time was running short on the two millennia of Roman lineage. As he contemplated the future of the Empire, he reflected on the past. He remembered Sophia and her ability to evade the Ottomans five hundred years earlier just by being a woman. Nicholas II, in a fit of inspiration, turned to the same strategy.

"Nicholas II met with his mother, Maria Feodorovna, in Mogilev, ostensibly to discuss the revolution. During that meeting, something critically important happened. Nicholas gave the Julian Ark to his mother and charged her with the survival of the Roman Empire. Nicholas foresaw the death of the Russian Tsardom and the threat to all male heirs. He asked his mother to protect the family secret, and to pass that inheritance on through the female line until a new male heir could wield enough power to build a fourth Rome.

"A year later, Nicholas II and his entire family including all of his children were slaughtered in Western Russia by the Bolsheviks. Empress Consort Maria Feodorovna, mother to the slaughtered Tsar and Tsaritsa, eventually fled to London and entrusted the Julian Ark and the two millennium legacy to her daughter Grand Duchess Olga Alexandrovna, sister to Nicholas II. This began a tradition of passing the Julian Ark down through the women of the family while the empire was powerless. The Grand Duchess fled from London to Denmark and lived there until the Second World War.

"In 1940 Grand Duchess Olga, concerned for the charge of the continuation of the empire, decided to send her two sons and her only daughter to North America with the Julian Ark. Guri and Tikhon, her sons, were entrusted to deliver their sister, Elena, to the west and to ensure her safety. Elena, who was only 18 at the time, immigrated to the United States. In order to preserve her secrecy, Elena Kulikovsky changed her name to Helen Kuwisky and settled in a small farming town in Ohio. There she met and married a local farmer and spent the rest of her life as a doting wife, running a humble farmhouse on the edge of Lake Erie.

"Helen named her first daughter Tara."

"Grandma Helen was niece to Nicholas II?" A deep furrow appeared between Madison's eyes as she struggled to believe this astounding tale.

"Yes, Madison. Do you remember the snow globe I used to tell you stories about? Do you remember the bedtime stories of lost kingdoms and the princess who must save them? Grandma Helen was the heiress to the Russian Empire, the protector of the legacy of the Ancient Romans, Byzantines and Russians. I, as her first born daughter, am heiress to that same tradition. As are you, Madison."

It was too fanciful for Madison to believe. Her mother was the direct descendant of the Tsars of Russia; of Ivan the Terrible; of the Byzantines; of Constantine; of Caligula. They were all connected, not by blood but by tradition, by the right of rule, by the bond of leadership. The thread had continued uninterrupted for two thousand years. Then, another profound idea struck her.

"Holy crap, I'm a freakin' princess!" she exclaimed louder than she intended. A few patrons of the pub looked in her direction.

"We'll have to work on your decorum, but yes, you're a Tsarina. Our family is royalty," said Tara smiling at her daughter's jovial reaction.

"Madison, I guess you could say you were born under a lucky tsar," said James.

"You really have a tsar-studded ancestry," added Brennan.

"Don't get all tsarry-eyed on us," said James through a goofy laugh.

"Okay, stop. My first order as Princess is that you stop making bad puns about my heritage." Madison said. "Mom, this is so strange. I'm a Princess," she said, once again feeling the weight of her mother's story.

"To be fair, though, these titles pass through the male line. This is the beauty behind our secret. Grand Duchess, Princess, Countess; these titles mean nothing other than to whom you are married. But to own the Julian Ark, to be able to trace your lineage through the most powerful empires in history… Now, that is true authority, true power."

Madison sat back in her chair as the dull hum of sudden awareness buzzed in her mind. Somehow… she'd known. She'd always known that she was meant for something more than being a receptionist at a tech firm. It was more than just the oft repeated bedtime story her mother used to tell her. There was a feeling that she was meant for more than the nine-to-five, partying on the weekend, marrying rich, homemaking lifestyle so many of her friends had found so comfortable. She was heiress to an empire; a princess. Madison was keeper of the legacy of the greatest empire the world had ever known.

"Madison, this power and knowledge comes with a price," said Tara. "You are charged as I was charged, and my mother before me, to act in the footsteps of Sophia so many years ago. When the time comes, and this experimentation with democratic republics and parliamentary procedures draws to a close, and the world is ready for benevolent monarchies once again, you are to marry into the next great Empire. You will help to establish the Empire in the fashion of the Romans, civil, ordered, just, and strong, as Sophia did with the Russians.

"If the time is not right," she continued, "and we must wait another generation, then you may marry whom you wish and your daughter will be charged when she comes of age as I have charged you now. The fate of the Roman Empire, the Byzantines and the Russian Empire lies in you, Madison."

The table drew silent for a few minutes as each pondered the implications of Tara's story. Finally, James stood, went to the bar to pay their tab, and returned.

"What do you say we find out what Caligula has stored for you, your highness?" he said with a smile.

"Yes," said Madison, taking his hand as he helped her to her feet. "Let's."

ᶜᴄ✈ᴅᵇ

Madison, James, Brennan, and Tara peered through the windows of the Opel at the narrow street which led to the Roman Baths. The street was lit with sparse security lighting for passersby, but otherwise, each building looked buttoned up for the night.

"So, how do we get in?" asked Madison.

James scowled. "There's no way we're getting in through the front door. Not tonight anyway. Bren, let's take a look around back."

Brennan moved the car down the street a few hundred feet until they were looking at the concrete handrail that marked the end of the terrace of the Baths.

"See any security?" asked Brennan.

"Are you kidding? These Brits are in love with cameras. Yeah, there it is. Up high on the next building."

"The black thing that looks like a little trash can?" asked Madison.

"Yep. Okay, here's the plan. Bren cuts the wires going up to the camera. Then the Princess and I climb the wall and up over the handrail. I'll secure the rope to the handrail and we can descend to the pool together. Tara, here's a radio." James handed her a walkie-talkie. "If you see anyone suspicious, or anyone taking an inordinate interest in this museum, you let us know. We'll get out of there to try another day."

"Yes, sir," said Tara. "I didn't see myself getting over that handrail anyway."

"Alright. Let's go," said James. The tsarina and her escort emerged from the car. Brennan popped the trunk and tossed James a duffle bag. James removed a multi-tool, tossed the plier/knife combo to Brennan, and slung the duffle over his shoulder. Brennan grabbed one of the backpacks with the radio and the two halves of the key to Caligula's Bath. A quick look around and then James moved along the street opposite the museum while Brennan and Madison followed closely behind. Brennan walked past the camera, crossed the street, snuck up behind the camera and cut the wire leading to the camera with the multi-tool. James and Madison dashed across the street.

"We're getting over that?" asked Madison in a hushed tone staring up at the ominous barricade.

"Piece of cake," whispered James. With two quick movements he was up over the four foot wall and then atop the concrete handrail. He leaned down and reached for Madison's hand.

Madison put a foot in between two bricks and leapt for James' hand. They connected and he pulled her up and over the handrail. They crouched low so as not to be seen by anyone in the street. A faint grunt and the sound of shoe leather against limestone and Brennan was also over the wall a few dozen yards away.

James fixed one end of the rope around the handrail bollard, gave it a firm tug to be sure it would hold, and then tossed it over the other handrail nearest the pool. The water, green and stagnant during the day, loomed uninviting at night as a black abyss that soaked up all of the light.

"Are we climbing up this rope to get out?" asked Madison.

"Yeah. Just like gym class." James threw his legs over the handrail, grabbed the rope and shimmied his way down before stopping just above the water. He pushed off a stone step lining the pool, briefly swinging out over the pool before he swung back towards the walkway like a human pendulum. He let go of the rope, quietly landing on dry ground.

"Alright, highness. You're up." Brennan handed Madison the rope.

"I don't know about this, Bren. I don't know that I have the strength to pull myself up. Why don't I keep watch up here, while you two do your thing." Madison had visions of being trapped around the pool unable to get out.

"Suit yourself. We won't be long." Brennan grabbed the rope, hopped over the edge and was soon standing beside the pool. "We're in," said Brennan into the radio. He heard back a click in response, as Tara wisely said as little as possible.

A door swung open on the terrace and James emerged with a quick wave to Madison. She scampered along the terrace and arrived at the door.

"Brennan followed you down the rope."

"That's fine. The locks on the museum doors on this side are pretty weak. Follow me."

"Should I untie the rope?" asked Madison.

"No. Leave it," was all James said. They bounded down the stairs, through the various exhibits and then finally found themselves at pool level.

"Okay, so where did you see this marking?" asked Madison noticing that her heart was pounding. These artifact recovery experts probably were quite comfortable breaking and entering, but it was a new thing for her.

"Just this way," said James. He retrieved a flashlight from the backpack and shone it at the water. "You can see it in the daylight… " He ran his flashlight up and down the stones under the water, methodically searching for what he'd seen earlier. "There!"

The light beam fell on a wide, rounded stone in the corner of the pool. Through the four inches of water that shimmered over the stone Madison could see a faint etching. It was only about four inches long and looked like a miniature version of the candlestick that was now in Brennan's backpack.

"I see it. What does it mean?" asked Madison. Then, like the break of a wave that crashes upon a surfer, the gravitas of the moment hit her. They were about to uncover the personal treasures of a tyrannical dictator that ruled the Roman Empire two millennia ago; a dictator with whom she now shared a common fate. Madison staggered backwards. She could see the flowing robes, the laurel leaves, the chariots, and the carved granite of Rome. She could see the journey that this emperor would have made, covering thousands of miles over weeks and months. The little mark in the corner of a pool of water made this all tangible to Madison. It was real.

"Here," said James, "Give me the spear." Brennan handed him the candlestick.

James wiped his hand across three spots that looked like dirt or blemishes on the rock. A dirty cloud kicked up.

"Holes?" asked Madison.

"Just full of dirt," said James. "If I had to guess…" James never finished his sentence. Instead, he took the spear, and aligned the center spike with the center hole and pressed it down, perpendicular to the floor. At first, nothing happened, but then slowly, the spear settled into the hole. James put more weight on it and it struck Madison as looking a little like the reverse of King Arthur and Excalibur. James pushed the spear into the stone with his entire weight. A few inches into the stone, the other two spires of the candlestick lined up with their respective holes. The candlestick submerged further into the rock and then the top of the sluice gate lifted.

The sluice gate was used to divert extra water from the pool to the drains and then down to the river below the town of Bath. Once used to drain and clean the pool, the gate until now had appeared rusted and rotted. Now, this spear, candlestick as Madison knew it, returned purpose to the old Roman valve.

The undeniable sound of rushing water filled the stone walled room. The water fell away from the top of the stone walk around the pool, and a torrent of water emptied into the drain behind them.

"I don't believe it," said James. "We're emptying the Roman Baths." James pointed to the Grand Bath. Already the water level had dropped a foot.

"So the empire marker is in the bath," said Madison as they walked along the bath to get a better view. Moonlight danced off the metallic surfaces tinted green from centuries of algae with steep stairs leading down to the bottom of the pool. In ten minutes the entire pool was empty.

No one said a word. The next step was obvious. At the bottom of the pool was a square stone tile that was smaller than the rest of the lead sheets that lined the pool. In the center of the stone tile was a depression in the shape of an arrowhead, precisely the size of the ruby that they'd been carrying.

"It's time to use that key," said James. Brennan handed him the ruby from the backpack and James dropped down into the empty pool. He slipped on the slick mat of algae and debris, landing on his elbows and knees with a painful crack. James cursed under his breath before regaining his feet and moving to the stone tile.

"I'll help you," said Madison moving to the edge of the pool.

"Better stay up there, Madison," said James. "I'm going to need both of you to help lift me out of here. These stairs are steep and covered in slime."

"Right."

The radio crackled with a bit of static.

"Police car," was all Tara said. James, Brennan, and Madison froze.

"Come on, let's get out of here," said Brennan stooping down and extending his hand to James.

"We're not going to get a second shot at this," said James. "We have to do this now."

"How many cops?" asked Brennan through the radio.

"One. He's walking around the building right now with a flashlight. I'll let you know if he enters," said Tara.

Mom is a pretty good lookout, Madison thought.

With a frenetic wiping of his hand, James cleaned the scum and debris from the arrowhead shaped depression in the stone and then set the ruby arrowhead into the depression. He pressed down and they heard an authoritative click.

Madison didn't know what to expect, but she'd envisioned the grand opening of some sort of door, or a chime, or the singing of angels. For some reason, this moment lacked the production qualities she'd anticipated.

"I need a crowbar or a screwdriver or something," said James. Brennan dug in his backpack and fished out a straight screwdriver and the multi-tool he'd used to cut the wires on the security camera.

"Maybe one of these will work," said Brennan tossing him the tools. James dug at the corners of the stone until he could get the screwdriver underneath.

"He's coming in the front entrance," said Tara over the radio. A cold shiver ran up Madison's spine. They were caught.

"You'll have to stall him," said James. "He can't see me in here."

"How?" asked Brennan.

"I have an idea," said Madison.

She scampered up the stairs and to the terrace. Quickly, she untied the rope and tossed it down to Brennan. She heard faint whispers of protest below her as Brennan told her to wait.

Sorry, Brennan, there's no time. Madison laid on the handrail on the terrace and waited.

She looked up at the clouds for a brief moment. Her heart pounded with adrenaline. The street and freedom below her to her right, James and Brennan and their quest across the terrace and below her to her left, and through the glass windows of the museum the unmistakable bounce of the policeman's flashlight approached. The light worked its way down the hall and then forced open the doors to the terrace. Madison rolled to her side, fluffed her hair and put her right hand on her hip in an attempt to appear as curvy as possible.

"Well if it isn't one of London's finest," she said in an unsteady, sing-songy voice. For some reason, she switched to a southern belle accent. The man carrying the light trained it immediately upon her face. She squinted, but tried to maintain a blissful and relaxed countenance. "Come to have a drink with me?"

"You're trespassing," said the policeman. "What are you doing here?" The policeman, with his ruddy cheeks and smooth skin, was probably no older than Madison. She knew this kind of man and if he had any heterosexual desires in his body she would use that to her advantage.

"Well, the pub woont leh me stay, and it was such a booful night. I thought I'd climb up here and take a lil look," she said running her hand through her hair. "You gonna arrest me on such a booful night azis?"

"You're American," said the cop.

"Yup." She giggled. "You're a quick one, officer…?"

"Flaherty. Officer Flaherty. Look, mum, you can't be in here. The museum will open in the morning. Why don't you go home and sober up."

"Can you show me the way out? The world is kinda spinning right now." She pretended to almost roll off the ledge. He quickly came to her side and steadied her.

"Certainly. Let's get you home. Why are you here alone- Ugh". The officer was interrupted by a crash and a violent jerk of his head. His eyes rolled up into the back of his head and he slumped to the ground. The flashlight clattered on the limestone floor. In the dim reflected light of the flashlight, Madison could see Brennan holding the remains of a ceramic pot with which he'd just knocked the police officer unconscious.

"Brennan! What are you doing?"

"Saving your butt," he said. "What were you going to do? Have drinks with him?"

"I wasn't going to kill him. He was about to show me out. That would have left you and James to get the empire marker." Madison knelt beside the fallen officer and felt for the policeman's pulse. "Well, thankfully you didn't kill him."

"Too bad he got a good look at you," said Brennan.

"Now we're out of time. Once the police notice him missing, it'll be a manhunt for the idiot who attacked him," said Madison exasperated.

"Well, let's go, then."

"You're the idiot I was referring to, by the way."

"Yeah, I got that," said Brennan. He grabbed her hand and they ran for the stairs that led down to the Great Bath. When they returned to the empty pool, James was still working on the stone lid that he had unlocked with the ruby arrowhead.

"Is he gone?" asked James, continuing to jab the tool into the crevices.

"No. Knucklehead here administered some blunt force trauma."

"So, he's not a problem?" asked James.

"No. But we'd better get out of here fast," said Madison. *Not a problem?* She had a plan that would have worked much better and without injury to the defenseless man. Madison's irritation subsided as James began lifting the lid.

"Whatever they used to make this water-tight also made it almost impossible to open. I had to chisel it all the way around," said James. He lifted the heavy stone and let it fall upside down next to the hole.

It was too dark for Madison to see anything in the open cavity in the bottom of the pool. James hovered over it, momentarily paralyzed by what he saw.

"Well? Is it there?" she asked.

James reached into it and carefully extracted a bundle wrapped in dirty fabric. He set the bundle down beside him on the bottom of the pool and pulled at the fabric. It dissolved as he pulled on it, revealing a fragile ceramic vessel. *Caligula's empire marker.*

The pot was no bigger than a beach ball and had a short neck with a sealed ceramic lid fused to the top. A handle had been cast into the pot.

"Let's get out of here," said James. He handed the ceramic pot up to Brennan and then held up his hands so they could pull him up.

"Don't you want to open it?" asked Madison as she struggled to lift her share of his mass up the slippery steps of the pool.

"Not here. We'll get it somewhere safe and open it," he said as he reached the walkway. "Okay, let's get back. Brennan, pull that candlestick out of the stone. Hopefully it refills."

As they moved along the walkway to re-enter the museum and retrace their path out, Madison grabbed the walkie-talkie.

"Mom, we're coming out," she said.

Brennan pulled the candlestick out of the stone and the sluice dropped back into place and the pool began filling.

"Make sure the street is still empty," said James.

"Mom, is the coast clear?" asked Madison through the walkie-talkie. No response. "Mom, are you there?" she asked again. The radio showed its contempt with an insubordinate silence. A sense of dread fell over Madison. Something was wrong.

"She's not there," said Brennan.

"What happened to her?" asked Madison, almost afraid to hear the answer.

"Not good," said James. They climbed the stairs to the terrace, exited the museum and were stopped in mid-step. The way was blocked.

"Next time you leave a guard dog to keep watch, you'd better make sure it has some teeth." Standing between them and the handrail that lead to the street was the threatening visage of a fuming Michelle. Michelle leaned against the balcony and seethed contempt. To her left, Moonface held a pistol against the head of the frightened Tara Dawn.

"I'm sorry," said Tara in an unsteady whisper. She gripped the railing with white knuckled terror. "I never saw them coming." Two more of Michelle's agents appeared from the dark museum behind them, blocking any hope of retreat.

"It's okay, Mom. It'll be alright," said Madison. Even as she spoke words of encouragement, her voice cracked.

"Michelle, leave her out of this," said James. "Let's not do anything stupid."

"Stupid?" said Michelle with a contemptuous laugh. "Stupid is turning your back on me, running out of my hotel room with everything I've worked so hard to get. Stupid is walking away from me when I've offered you everything you've ever wanted."

"Let Mrs. Dawn go, Michelle," said James.

"Mrs. Dawn? Don't you mean her highness the Tsarina?" asked Michelle. There was a palpable silence that followed. Michelle continued, "Or has he not told you yet, princess?" she asked Madison.

"I know who I am. I know who we are," said Madison with a pride until then unknown to her.

"Let her go, Michelle. You have nothing to gain with that hostage," said James. "She is no longer useful to you."

"You want her? Bring me that ceramic pot that Brennan is so cautiously holding. Oh yes. You thought I was stupid? I figured it out. I know why you're here. This bastard remnant of a dead empire led you right to Caligula's empire marker. Come on, come here."

Madison, James and Brennan approached Michelle and her henchmen. They looked at each other across the terrace walkway. Madison with her back to the bath and Michelle with her back to the street.

"That's close enough," said Michelle.

"Prisoner exchange?"

"Hardly. You're outnumbered and we have guns. You're in no position to bargain. You have no power."

"Perhaps you're right," said James. "Really, all we have is this fragile old piece of pottery. It probably doesn't have anything but a bunch of dried out pieces of parchment, which are no doubt disintegrating just by the jostling of getting carried around. You're right. We don't have much to bargain with."

"So hand it over."

"Unless…" he said with a devious lilt.

"Unless?" Michelle asked.

"Unless I'm willing to destroy it."

Michelle was, for once, speechless.

"What are you talking about?" she eventually squeaked out between gasps and grunts of condemnation.

"What you really want is this pot and the fragile artifacts contained inside. You don't care about Tara or us. If I were to throw it over this balcony and on to the granite below, it would destroy it. Wouldn't it?"

"You wouldn't. You know the priceless value of that artifact as well as I do." Michelle's eyes grew wide, betraying her fear.

"I also know the value of human life. I have to destroy this pot. You said it yourself; I have nothing else to bargain with."

"If you destroy it, I'll kill all four of you," Michelle shouted uncharacteristically out of control.

"And if you so much as harm Mrs. Dawn, I'll smash this pot. So now we have a stand-off," said James. "So let's start by your men putting their guns down. I don't want anyone getting accidentally shot."

"This is starting to remind me of Cairo, boss," said Brennan.

"Yes, Bren. Exactly."

What just happened? thought Madison. Why did Brennan say that?

"We will not put our guns down," said Moonface in English.

"Michelle, tell them to put their guns on the floor or Caligula's empire marker is dashed to dust." James held it at arm's length over the railing.

"Put your weapons down, boys," said Michelle. "There will be plenty of time to pick them up and shoot him if he starts to run." Moonface and the other two agents laid their pistols on the floor.

"Alright, Michelle. We'll give you the pottery, and you give us Mrs. Dawn," said James.

"Does she really mean that much to you?" asked Michelle.

James looked at Madison. She could see a reassurance in his eyes, yet the whole process of seeing her own mother used as a bargaining chip was nauseating.

"It's not enough," said Michelle. "I know you James. As soon as we make the exchange you'll try something ridiculous. I don't trust you."

James looked at the ground, thinking. After a few seconds, he raised his head.

"Fine. Let Tara start walking towards me. I'll start walking towards you with the pot. As long as Tara, Madison, and Brennan get away, you'll have your artifact and me as insurance that they won't do something stupid."

"James. What are you saying? She'll kill you," Madison said. "It's suicide."

"I don't think so," said James. "Like she said, we have a connection. But we'll leave it up to her, won't we?"

"A-ha. And so the truth comes out," laughed Michelle. "You do still feel something for me. It's so cute how you can't bear to be without me. Okay, fine. But understand you're not leaving here anytime soon. Start walking."

James turned to Madison, held her by the shoulders, and kissed her gently on the temple. He turned to Brennan who gave him the pottery and took a step towards Michelle.

"Brennan. Stop him! There has to be another way," said Madison.

"There's no other way, Mads," said Brennan. "Trust him on this."

Tara, free of Moonface's grasp, slowly took a step towards Madison while wringing her hands. Another step. Another step. At the halfway point, James and Tara passed each other and then Tara ran into Madison's arms and the two embraced.

James stood before Madison, head bowed.

"Your artifact, my dearest," said James. He laid it on the floor at her feet.

Michelle smiled.

"James Kynan. I knew you'd come around. You know you'll be my prisoner. You'll do what I say, when I say it, exactly how I want it."

"Just like when we were dating," said James.

"I knew you'd come back to me." Michelle laid a hand on James' cheek. "You tough guys always like it when a strong woman comes into your lives. You missed it didn't you? Is this your little way to get back with me?"

"Michelle, your insight is commendable," James said. Then Madison saw him tap his left elbow with his right hand. Michelle couldn't see it, but she and Brennan could.

"Ah James. I feel like we're starting over. I'm pleased with you. There's hope for us yet," said Michelle. James moved to just a few intimate inches from her face, pressing his body into hers as she leaned against the balcony railing.

"Michelle. Do you remember when I said I was done with you and wasn't coming back?"

"It's alright, dear. We all say things we later regret." Michelle shifted her weight and smiled.

"I meant every word."

In a blink, James crouched, drove his hands up under her arms and, with an explosive thrust of his legs and arms, dragged her across the terrace. With one last thrust, he threw her over the railing. Michelle screamed at the sudden assault until she smacked into the water of the slowly filling pool.

The shock at seeing their boss thrown from the balcony was all the time that James needed to grab Moonface's pistol laying just at his feet. Brennan had leapt at the first explosive motion. He rolled along the ground, picking up the pistols of the two thugs in mid roll and, coming to rest, trained a pistol on each of the agents.

"Just like Cairo, huh, boss?" said Brennan.

Moonface lunged at James, but James danced, flipped the pistol around, and whipped the pock-marked Italian. Moonface went down in a heap and did not move.

"Let's get out of here," said James. James, Brennan, Tara, and Madison threw themselves over the railing and on to the roof of parked cars just over the railing. They slid down the cars and fled down the street. As they ran they heard the cries of Michelle and her screams to Moonface to retrieve her from the hazardous water. Madison carried the pottery as James and Brennan led the way around the corner and to their waiting sedan.

Brennan started the motor, dropped the car into gear and sped down the darkened streets of Bath. The secrets of Caligula, the ruthless tyrant with whom Madison now felt a powerful kinship, rested   on   her   lap.

XXI

A New Future

"Life is either a great adventure or nothing."
Helen Keller

Madison, her mom, and the boys reclined around a small table in one of the two hotel rooms they'd rented near London Heathrow Airport. It was well past three in the morning and they had an early morning flight in just a few hours, but the excitement of the day and the long drive from Bath kept anyone from turning in for the night. The pottery they'd recovered from the Great Bath held court in the middle of the table, yet to divulge its secrets.

"So, when do we open it?" asked Madison.

"Devin has a lab at the museum that's perfect for this sort of thing." James rubbed his stubble-ridden face.

"You're kidding. We have to wait until we get back home?"

Madison could feel the sleep drag on her like a heavy blanket, but the more she stared at this ancient vessel, the more she wanted to know what was inside. What had Caligula concealed nearly two thousand years ago? What would a ruthless and hedonistic ruler want the world to know about him and his dynasty? What riches lay just inches from her inquisitive fingers?

"It's too dangerous to the artifact, love," said James. "I'm sorry."

This was horrible. It reminded her of Christmas Eve and sitting around the Christmas tree with her younger sister. All the presents were laid out, yet she couldn't open them. It was a unique form of torture saved for impetuous kids who didn't understand the concept of delayed gratification.

"You're entrusted with our legacy," said Tara in a motherly tone. "What do you think is best for the artifact and for the once and future empire?"

Madison sighed and contemplated the frustration. She'd waited years for her career to materialize, months for certain men in her life to decide on whether they would commit to her, and hours in line for the midnight showing of a favorite movie. Her entire life had been a lesson in patience in the face of exuberance and anticipation. This piece of Roman pottery had rested unmolested for 2000 years. She supposed she could wait another day or two to find out what was inside.

"It can wait," said Madison through a yawn. "I just hope it makes it to the States okay."

"I'll hand-carry it on the airplane. It'll be alright," said James.

"I was relieved that Michelle didn't seem to care about our heritage," said Madison. "Somehow, she knew we were descendants of the Russian monarchs, but it's like that didn't even matter to her. Surely if she knew that we had the Julian Ark she wouldn't have let Mom walk away so easily. Perhaps our secret is safe, Mom."

"Truthfully, I wouldn't be so sure," said James. "Michelle said that she had a buyer for the key, right?" he asked. "The buyer clearly asked for Madison to deliver the ruby arrowhead herself. I think the buyer knows about your heritage and more importantly the story of the Julian Ark. He knew that you'd have access to the candlestick; the other half of the Key to Caligula's Bath. That buyer, whoever he is, knows your family secret."

"Good heavens, you're right," said Tara. "We must be careful."

"Mom, if we've had this box, this Ark, all these years," said Madison through narrowed eyes still formulating her question, "then why didn't we have the ruby arrowhead? Why didn't we have the complete key in the box?"

Tara looked at the table and wrung her hands.

"That, my daughter, is our family's greatest scandal and embarrassment." She took a few pacing breaths and then continued. "There's something else you need to know. When I was seventeen, my mother told me about our secret and the mystery of this box she had in the attic; the Julian Ark.

"One evening, when no one else was home, I went up to the attic and opened the box. Inside I did not find priceless jewels and crowns and things. I found broken pottery, jewel-less scepters, and undecorated figures, amongst other things. To my eye, there was nothing of value in this box. When my mother came home, I asked her about the lack of valuables in the box. It was then that she told me that some time in our family's past, since we left Russia, someone raided the box for its valuables. My mother believed that her father, Nikolai Kulikovsky, had taken any riches from the box and sold them to pay for expenses related to their escape from Russia.

"Nikolai was not royalty like the rest of our ancestors. He was a commoner and therefore did not have the vast wealth of the aristocrats. Your grandmother believed that the valuables from the Julian Ark were sold and are now scattered around the world in private collections and museums such that our family will never get them back."

"That's how we found the ruby arrowhead," said James. "Devin saw the ruby come up for auction and it was advertised as an ancient Byzantine ruby. However, Devin recognized that it was not simply some ancient bauble but rather the famed Key of Caligula's bath. He sent Brennan to pull me out of Europe so I could attend the auction with him as he bid on the ruby. Before the auction went to bid, the ruby was stolen by Giovanni. I was able to track one of Giovanni's agents but wasn't able to recover the ruby.

"I spent six months following the ruby and seeing what Giovanni's organization did with it. One day they drove it out to a neighborhood and placed it in the backseat of a green sedan."

"So, that's why you were there so quickly after I wrecked my car," said Madison. "You'd been following me."

"Yes, I had been tracking the Key, but I also thought you were working for Giovanni and I had no idea that it was only half of the key."

"If any of my friends ever ask us how we met, that's going to be one hell of a story," said Madison through a laugh.

"Sorry to interrupt this fascinating recap," said Brennan, "but did we just gloss over some important information here? Tara, did you say that you had a box full of keys, legends, and maps that are now missing their jewels?" he asked.

"I did."

"So all we need to do is track down where these jewels went and we'll have complete maps to dozens of artifacts from the Roman Empire?"

"It appears that the contents of this pot are just the surface of what our empire has hidden throughout the world," said Tara. "Do you know anyone interested in recovering them?"

"Yes, ma'am," said Brennan with a wink. "I know just the guys."

⁌⊶⊷⊶⊷⊷⊷⊶⊷⊷⊷⊶⊷

Two days later, Madison sat on the edge of a hotel bed in the Old Town District of Wichita, Kansas.

"You should have told me, mother," said Madison, irritated at the sudden turn of events. "At least I would have known what I was coming home to."

Madison's absence had become a major news story in her hometown. The story of a local girl kidnapped from her car after an accident took the city by storm, capturing their imaginations and leading to a city-wide manhunt. Local news stations kept a running tally of the number of days since Madison Dawn was last seen.

The story was picked up by national news outlets for several days until a congressman's illicit behavior moved Madison's story to the back pages and then out of the news altogether. But in her hometown, she had become a cause celeb. She was a young, attractive single woman with a made-for-TV face and she'd been taken in broad daylight on her way to work.

Tara accompanied her daughter back to her hometown, but they travelled under assumed names since the Giovanni organization was still active and dangerous. When they arrived back at the city's airport, a local sheriff's deputy recognized Madison and brought the two to the police station.

Fortunately, Devin was able to intervene. Before Madison and Tara were put in the position of having to admit to travelling under a false passport, Devin used his considerable influence to get them released. A story of Madison losing her memory in the accident, and Tara finding her in a town several hundred miles away was released to the media. It turned out that the local media didn't care what the truth was, just that there was resolution to their exhaustive coverage.

The Museum put Madison and Tara up at a local hotel to recover from the journey and to adjust to the new time zone.

"I'm sorry dear. I didn't think it would do you any good to be worrying the entire time. What were you going to do about it? You still had to travel under the assumed name."

"I know. I just don't like not being told things."

Their conversation was interrupted as an envelope was slid under their door. Tara got up and retrieved the envelope, opened it and read the note.

"What's it say, Mother?"

"It looks like you have a date," said Tara.

ᏣᏓ

A black Chrysler 300 rolled to a stop in front of one of the most exclusive Italian restaurants in Madison's hometown. The place was called Bepe's, but everyone at the museum just called it *Gordon's Place*. It was one of Gordon Hardbottle's restaurants, and the site of many museum parties and receptions. A doorman opened the passenger door and Madison stepped out of the car.

Madison adjusted her red shimmery dress, made certain she still had her clutch, and waited for James to give the car keys to the valet. James was dressed in a striking black suit with a satin black vest and a white tie. Usually a person needed a reservation several weeks out to get a table at Bepe's. However, when James and Madison entered, the maitre d' recognized and greeted them, and escorted them to a private room in the back of the building.

"Devin!" said Madison as the door to the private room swung open. Devin sat at a long oval table and rose to greet Madison with a kindly embrace. Madison thought it odd that she greeted him like a long lost friend when the one and only time she'd seen him she'd decided that she didn't like his gruff manner or his condescending tone. But that was before. Before she'd survived a plane crash, been assaulted by an Army colonel, attacked in her stateroom, kidnapped and held prisoner. It was before the death of Francisco, before she was convinced that James had rejoined his old addiction, Michelle. It was before she grew up; before she knew that she protected a dynasty; before she knew the real Madison Dawn.

Seated to Devin's left, at the head of the table was an older gentleman whom Madison did not recognize. Across from Devin sat Brennan, already with suit jacket flung over the back of his chair, chewing on a breadstick and halfway through his first glass of red wine. Next to Brennan was Madison's mother, Tara, in a cream dress that smartly matched the occasion.

"Madison, I'd like to introduce Gordon Hardbottle," said Devin indicating the man to his left. "Gordon is the benefactor of our museum. The great philanthropist."

"Please, Devin. Enough," said Gordon with grizzled yet disarming charm. The barrel-chested elderly man rose with a spritely spirit and crossed to Madison and James.

"Madison it's so nice to finally meet you," he said as he took her hand. He bowed slightly and kissed her hand. "Tsarina."

Madison smiled, blushed, found herself swimming in a sea of not knowing what to do, laughed awkwardly and finally sat down, nearly missing the front of the chair as she did so. She made a mental note to compose a clever response for future occasions.

"James, welcome back," said Hardbottle as he shook James' hand.

"Gordon," said James. "I'm sorry for all the mess."

"Ah, this one was different, James. What you found was worth the headaches and hassle, even if it wasn't in your usual discrete style."

"Finding Caligula's empire marker will do wonderful things for the museum," said James turning the discussion to the topic of the museum's welfare.

"That old pot? No, James, I'm referring to finding this charming young lady; a living descendent of the Russian Tsars, with lineage to the great Roman emperors. Never forget that the significance of human history is in the humanity. It's the people that are important, James."

"Yes, Mr. Hardbottle." James took his seat. "Of course."

A waiter brought James and Madison both a glass of red wine and another plate of oil for the bread.

"Brennan was just starting to tell us about the accident," said Devin.

"The accident?" asked Madison.

"Yes, the unfortunate occurrence where you managed to crash your car with the Key of Caligula's Bath in the backseat due to some cell phone use. Distracted driving, tsk tsk," smiled Gordon.

"It wasn't even my cell phone, and it was in my visor," protested Madison.

Dinner was served automatically in many courses, properly paced, while the story unfolded. Each person added what they knew to the long yarn of the adventure. Several parts of the story were retold from different perspectives until all details were understood. The wine flowed freely and the laughter, suspense, and tears poured out in equal measure.

The main course came; a fettuccine alfredo with lobster and shrimp that made Madison's mouth tingle in pleasure. They took turns eating and telling the story while Devin and Gordon lived vicariously through the lives of the young adventurers.

"One thing you never told me, James," said Madison as she swirled her third glass of wine around the glass.

"There're lots of things I haven't told you, love," said James to uproarious laughter.

"One thing you've never told me is how you got away at the castle, after Francisco… Well, when they drugged and kidnapped me-"

"-Ether, I think it was," said Brennan.

"Yeah, why did they just leave you there? You said it was a funny story," said Madison.

"It is hilarious, for real," said Brennan. "I picked up Gil and ran through the corridors trying to separate from you and James. It's just easier to take out three guys if you split them up. Anyway, so we make our way to this library that is loaded with armor, you know, as decoration. As I looked for weapons or at least a place to make an ambush, Gil decides he's going to wear a bunch of armor. I turn around and he's sitting in an armchair wearing a helmet, a breastplate, and thigh and shin protectors; none of which fit him, of course, 'cause he's three foot nothin'. The two goons that followed us burst through the door so I hid out on the other side of it. They looked at the room and didn't see him sitting there. I think they thought he was a statue or work of art or something.

"Suddenly, Gil jumps up, makes this awful screeching sound and starts ambling toward them. The armor is way too big for him so it's just bobbling around his head. He looks like a four foot tall zombie. The two goons have guns. I mean, it's just medieval armor, after all. The bullets would go right through. But this sudden onrushing collection of clunky armor and that high pitched screech completely spooks them.

"They turn around and run as Gil stumbles after them. I followed them to the main hall where they found their third friend and you. By that time, you were unconscious. In the distance they could hear Gil clomping down the hallway, still making that sound. The three picked you up, hopped into their car and sped off. I swear, if I wasn't so worried about you and James, I would have laughed out loud. It was the funniest thing I'd ever seen. That Gil is one ballsy kid."

The laughter at the table was raucous as each person, goaded on by a few glasses of wine, imagined a small child in awkward armor chasing away two hired gunmen.

The conversation turned somber when Madison was finally able to relate what happened to her at the villa when she was held prisoner. The table listened to her story in respectful sympathy as they had not appreciated the torture to which she'd been subjected.

She spoke of James' arrival in the middle of the night. James' decision to join with Michelle was described as an intentional decision to infiltrate the operation undercover. Madison allowed this revisionist history as James, in the end, had in fact seen the real Michelle. Men were allowed to fight their battles and lose on occasion, just as long as they won the war.

Midnight came and went as the table of six finished the story of the key of Caligula's bath. The sweetness of the sherbet tickled Madison's tongue as she listened to Brennan describe that singular moment when James chose the high road and threw Michelle into that algae infested bath. Michelle, his object of infatuation, the woman that held his heart in a prison, had no more power over him. A tear trickled down Madison's cheek as she realized how significant a moment that was for him. She was proud of him.

"And now, I suppose all you need is a nice little bow on your story," said Devin. "What was all this for? What was in the pottery?"

"Oh, thank God. I thought we'd never get to that," said Madison. "Yes, what did Caligula leave for us?"

Devin made a small gesture to a waiting attendant and a few moments later, a silver cart was rolled in. Atop the silver cart was a Roman pot with a handle; Caligula's empire marker. The seal was broken and the top was open.

"First and least importantly, our technicians found several dozen non-descript jewels of various sizes and value." Devin poured the jewels out on to a velvet piece of cloth and poked at them with a short wooden rod. "These appear to have no archeological or anthropological significance and they are already being prepared for sale. Our experts expect them to fetch three to four million dollars. This should fund the museum operations for a while."

"What it does is pay your exorbitant salaries," laughed Gordon.

Devin patiently waited for the laughter at the table to die down before continuing in his matter-of-fact, professorial tone.

"Caligula, as you know, was a vicious tyrant, a sexual predator, and a heartless egomaniac," said Devin.

James interrupted, "Remind me not to ask Devin to give my eulogy,"

"And inside we found this," continued Devin. He withdrew a muslin doll. It was fragile, but intact. It was clearly a horse.

"A stuffed animal?" said Madison.

"Apparently this was Caligula's, from when he was a child. We also found this." Devin withdrew a pendant on a lanyard. He passed it around the table in a white cloth napkin. The pendant had an image of a woman etched into it.

"The woman is Caligula's first wife. Junia Claudilla. She died whilst giving birth to Caligula's first child. Sadly, the child also died during the birth. Written on the bottom of the pendant is the Latin phrase *diligo usquequaque* which means "loved always".

"Additionally we found this scroll." Devin held up a clear tube that housed a roll of parchment rolled up inside. "The parchment is extremely fragile, so I will spare passing it around. Our lab has only just begun to discern its contents. My lead researcher believes that we have a diary from Caligula himself; Caligula's history in his own words. Truly this is a find of epic proportions."

There were gasps, laughs and grunts from the intoxicated table of revelers. Gordon burst into spontaneous applause with a giant smile on his beet-red face.

"And last but certainly not least, we found this." Devin held up a golden cross about four inches long with what looked to Madison like an X with a P over it carved into the center. "It is not the most ornate cross we've ever seen, but the implications of a chi-rho symbol of Jesus Christ, carved on to a cross is staggering. Both the cross and the chi-rho symbol are early marks of Christianity, but to have them this early, so close to the crucifixion is most perplexing."

"Are you saying that Caligula was a convert?" asked Madison. "He wanted to put up a statue of himself in the temple in Jerusalem. He practically thought he was a god. There's no way he became a Christian."

"I'm saying no such thing, Madison," said Devin. "The death of Christ came roughly eight years before the death of Caligula. In many ways, they were contemporaries. In fact, at the time Christianity was considered a sect of Judaism. To say that the gospel of Christ had reached Caligula's ears before he died is quite a stretch."

"Indeed," said James. "It's preposterous."

"But yet we have the cross," said Devin.

Madison asked, "So what are you saying?"

"What I'm saying," said Devin in a soft but stern voice, "is that there is another side to Caligula, a side that history has completely ignored. Once this scroll is read and translated, perhaps this will make more sense. The only things we know about Caligula today are from the histories his enemies wrote. How would you be viewed if the tales of your bitterest antagonists were the only way you'd be remembered? In viewing these objects, it occurs to me that Caligula may not have been the tyrant we think he was.

"What you have found, James, Brennan, and Madison, will change the history of this Roman ruler forever."

It was a weighty statement, and it quieted the room with a sobering thought. Was it possible that for two millennia this man has been slandered and vilified without cause? Was it possible that his bizarre behavior came from depression at the loss of his wife and child? Could it be that he had found redemption in a new religion, and that history had missed that redemption?

James stood up and mumbled something about getting some air before he exited the room. A minute later, Madison followed him out the back door, through the kitchen and into the parking lot behind the restaurant. The night air was chilly but the sky was clear and the stars were numerous.

"Some night, huh?" said Madison through chattering teeth. James looked at her and put his coat around her shoulders.

"You should go back inside. Your lips will turn blue," he said.

"You seem upset, James."

James stood and stared into the blackness of the night. Madison was no stranger to men who wouldn't talk, but she considered James an extraordinarily difficult case. He seemed to have every meaningful thought, every insecurity and emotion buried deep within a wall of practicality, necessity, and survival. Madison was determined to bring down a few of those bricks in the wall.

"Is it Caligula?" she asked.

"How could that be?" he asked almost rhetorically. Madison gave him the space he needed to formulate his thoughts. After a few moments of head shaking, he continued. "How can a man live his life and be remembered as a tyrant and sexual predator? How can those less than him, his enemies, get away with destroying his reputation for two thousand years? Why did it take us this long to get it right?"

"This isn't about Caligula, is it?" said Madison.

James clenched his teeth but did not speak.

Madison asked, "Are you afraid that this will happen to you?" She put her hand gently on his shoulder.

"It has happened, Madison," he said. "Why do you think I travel under assumed names and live in an unregistered apartment? I used to work for some important and powerful people doing some significant work and then things went all pear-shaped. Those people, those jackasses in the government, will see to it that I'll be demonized for the rest of my life."

"Honey, I don't know what you're talking about. And I don't need to know. I know the real you, James. I know your heart. I know the man you are, not whatever happened in the past."

James turned towards Madison and she saw a glimmer of tears in his eyes. He enveloped her in his arms and squeezed her in a desperate embrace. She pressed her head to his chest and could hear his heart racing. For the moment, James seemed to be a young boy, insecure and unsure of himself, just wanting to know that he had what it took to be a man. Madison briefly saw a passing window of transparency into a man's heart.

As quickly as the window opened, it closed. James stepped back and looked at her. He smiled and breathed deeply. The public James was back, the hidden James concealed once again.

"So what are you going to do, love?"

"What do you mean?"

"Are you going to go back to work?"

"Work? You mean my secretary job?" Madison laughed. "I don't think they kept the position open while I was away, if you know what I mean. No, I don't know what I'm going to do. I don't even have a place to live. I'm living in a hotel at the moment."

"Why don't you come and work for the museum?" asked James.

"As your secretary? You sir are brave to ask me to file papers for you and get you your coffee."

James flashed his crooked smile. It was good to see that confident swagger return. This was the James she'd come to know and love.

"No, darling. I mean to help us with artifact recovery," he said. "According to your mother, there is a whole chest of jewels from the Roman empire to find. We could use an agent like you."

Madison looked at the ground. "You're patronizing me, aren't you? It's not nice to tease a Tsarina."

"I'm not kidding, Madison. We need people with your kind of talent working for us," he said.

"What do I have to offer to the dark world of treasure hunting?"

"You're a natural actress. Think about the way you carried yourself on the cruise ship as my wife; or when that cop was about to discover us at the Roman baths."

"Brennan knocked him out before I got anywhere with him," said Madison.

"Doesn't matter. What matters is that in a period of extreme stress, when you could have just frozen up, you dreamt up a scheme and adopted a false persona in a matter of seconds. And according to Brennan, the cop was buying it. Do you know how rare it is to find an actress of your abilities who can operate in a real world environment? Trust me. You're a rare find indeed."

"You're serious?" Madison looked at James with wonder and confusion.

"I'm dead serious, Mads. Join our team. Devin wants you onboard as soon as possible. Brennan wants you on the team desperately."

Madison pulled his jacket around her shoulders tighter and looked at him with her sparkling eyes.

"And what about you, James. What do you think?" she asked.

"I want you too, Madison."

"Desperately?" she asked in a breathy whisper as she leaned into him.

"Desperately," he said.

James wrapped his arms around her and kissed her with a fiery passion. The energy from the kiss warmed Madison's face and sent electricity down to her toes as their tongues interplayed. After a few passionate moments, they separated, exchanging goofy smiles.

"This is going to be complicated."

"I like complicated. It keeps things from getting boring."

"You'll never be boring, will you James?"

They kissed again and a cold breeze blew through the night air.

"What do you say we rejoin the party?" James held the door open to return to the restaurant.

"Sounds like a fine idea."

"After you, Princess."

Afterword

So what is real? What is truth? If we're talking about a philosophy class, we can argue this for days. However, after finishing a book like this, the reader is often left with the persisting question "How much of this is history, and how much is the disturbed dream of the Cartesian demon residing in the author's head?"

It will surprise no one to learn that there is an actual place called Wichita, Kansas, though they do not have a museum called the Museum of Lost Antiquities. There are many fine museums in Wichita, though none of them to my knowledge commission artifact recovery agents to search for lost treasure.

The idea of an empire marker, a concept wholly critical to this tale, is a fabrication of the author. Unfortunately as romantic as the notion of finding buried treasure is, it doesn't appear there is much historicity to support the idea. Outside of burials of heads of state in Egypt, a few cases of accidental burials, and the occasional pirate booty, searching for buried treasure in the real world is often a fruitless endeavor.

The Julian Ark, central to this story, is also a fabrication. However, you'll find the history of Caligula as explained by Madison from the fictitious book Devin sends her, is entirely true, or at least sourced from historical texts. Caligula was known for some rather hedonistic things, he did seem to lose his way after the death of his wife, and the story of Germanicus and Tiberius are all true.

There is an obelisk in St. Peter's Square in Vatican City which was brought to Rome by Caligula. It is bare though it contains four lions at its base (not three) and makes no mention of Britannia. In 2007, archaeologists discovered the Lupercal, the legendary place of origin of Rome, though there was no mention of a miniature obelisk hidden there by Caligula.

Caligula did come near to Britain, though it was his successor that took the island, a fact with which our protagonists struggle in this story. There is a fantastic Roman bath in Bath, England, though it only takes a lifting of the sluice gate to empty it. It requires no candlestick and sadly there is no chamber storing valuables at the bottom.

Yet, the history in this story goes beyond Caligula. Historians will tell you that the Roman Empire moved to Constantinople and thrived as the Byzantines. For more than 1000 years, the people living in Constantinople considered themselves Romans. The fall of Constantinople in 1453, and the death of Constantine XI Palaiologos as alluded to in the prologue, truly happened and marked the end of the Byzantines, and thus the Roman, Empire. However, it is here that we run into history in a most peculiar way.

The story about Zoe Palaiologina, Constantine XI's niece, going to Moscow and taking with her the essence of the empire so that the Roman Empire could live on is true. She was taken to Rome and then Pope Paul II married her to Ivan III in an attempt to unite the Orthodox and Catholic churches. The Russian aristocracy adopted many of the Roman ways and Tsar, meaning Caesar, came in to vogue shortly thereafter. The scene in the prologue between Constantine and Zoe as a young girl is a fabrication as Zoe was in truth only a year old when Constantinople fell.

Furthermore, Nicolas II in Russia was assassinated in 1917, but not before he could meet with his Mother, Maria Feodorovna in Mogilev. After the revolution she fled to Denmark. Her daughter, Olga fled to Canada with her two sons Guri and Tikhon. It is here that the author has fabricated a daughter for her to carry the Julian Ark through to Tara and on to Madison. With a little imagination, it is possible to see that an object of significance like the ark could tie Julius Caesar to Madison, as it was passed down from Roman Caesar to Roman Caesar, Byzantine Emperor to Byzantine Emperor, Russian Tsar to Russian Tsar, then down through the women to Madison Dawn to be kept until the Fourth Rome rises.

~DJS

ABOUT THE AUTHOR

David J. Swanson is an aerospace engineer who lives in Wichita, Kansas with his lovely wife and son. In his free time, he is an author, pilot, playwright, and musician. He is the author of *Theater for Church: Vol* 1, a collection of scripts, and *The Julian Ark: A Madison Dawn Adventure.* In addition to writing for several websites, he is currently working on his first full-length play and planning the next Madison Dawn adventure.

Please visit his website at www.davidjswanson.com.

www.ingramcontent.com/pod-product-compliance
Lightning Source LLC
Chambersburg PA
CBHW031256170626
46807CB00001B/177